Riding Out

Sally-Anne Robinson was born in Hampshire, but now lives with her thirteen-year-old son in Devon. Her studies of English literature as a mature student inspired her to write and *Riding Out* follows the successful publication of her first novel, *Seduction*.

SALLY-ANNE ROBINSON

RIDING OUT

HarperCollins*Publishers*

For Jo and Robby

HarperCollins*Publishers*
77–85 Fulham Palace Road,
Hammersmith, London W6 8JB

A paperback original 1995
9 8 7 6 5 4 3 2 1

A catalogue record for this book is
available from the British Library

ISBN 0 00 647320 2

Set in Linotron Meridien

Printed in Great Britain by
Clays Ltd, St Ives plc

Prologue

Sultry; the man was restless and had only slept fitfully that hot August night. Now the dawn was creeping into the room through a gap in the curtains. He decided to get up and make himself a cup of tea.

Tiredly, he rubbed his eyes. There was a sheen of sweat along his forehead and his back was uncomfortably sticky against the sheet.

He sighed, and then turned to look at his wife. She slept peacefully on. Beautiful, he thought as he smiled to himself. She was unaffected by the clinging heat and her white skin glowed almost translucently. Her thick chestnut hair fell in lustrous waves against the pillow. He picked up a glossy lock and ran it through his fingers. It was like the sheerest silk and he loved her for it. That and the fact that her face in quiet repose, with smooth forehead, straight nose and ever-kissable lips, was more beautiful than he thought he deserved.

And then, his mind becoming distracted by the most delicious of sensations, he forgot about tea. He ran his eyes hungrily over the rest of her body, sheathed in a gossamer nightie. He could see, if only in his imagination, the curve of her belly, the fullness of her ivory breasts, the length of her legs and the dark inviting places that he knew so well and yet could never have enough of.

'Morning,' he whispered, pressing himself against her hot back and delicately stroking her upper arm.

She stirred. He kissed her shoulder. She stirred again. He nuzzled his face against her hair and then kissed the nape of her neck. She sighed, her lips slightly parted.

His interest fully aroused, he cupped a hand around a

breast and caressed her nipple. She was awake now. There was no mistaking the small animal-like moans; the slowly rotating hips; the way she reached behind for him, her hands exploring; the soft feel of her touch against him.

'Emma.'

They kissed. Lying in each other's arms, the sun's first rays breaking through the curtains and lighting up motes of dust hanging in the still, hot air, they came together.

'Morning.'

She smiled, looking at him, her gaze at once amused yet desiring. 'And what have you got for me this morning?'

'I thought,' he murmured, 'that first I would kiss your lips . . . and then I would kiss your neck . . . and then, sliding this garment of yours off your shoulder . . .'

He stopped, his breath caught in his throat. She never failed to do this to him. The sight of her perfect nakedness left him speechless.

'And then what?' she asked, her voice low. She took one of his hands and lay it against her full breast. 'What would you do then?'

He heard her but the noise of his own heartbeat was more insistent. He wanted her so much.

'I . . . will . . . do . . . this,' he whispered and their lips hungrily sought each other out.

A shrill cry brought them back to earth. He wanted to ignore it, pretend the demanding yell would go away, hold on to their moment of physical oneness that was building and building but . . . It was gone.

'Move, darling.'

His wife's voice was no-nonsense and determined. As the mother to their ten-month-old daughter, she took her duties seriously, but that didn't stop him from trying.

'Do you have to?' He took hold of her hand as she went to get out of bed.

'Yes,' and she turned away wrapping a bath robe around her.

6

He sank back into the pillows, desire thwarted.

The crying ceased and was replaced by a gentle cooing. Initially angry at the baby's untimely interruption, he could feel his frustration evaporating. His daughter, Victoria, the miniature of her mother, could wrap him around her pudgy fingers with no more than a dimpled smile and gurgle. Thinking himself immune to such things in his pre-parental days, it had come as a huge but delightful surprise to him to realize just how much he loved this daily disruption in his life. She cried, she sometimes irritated him, she frequently made a mess and she cost a fortune but he loved her desperately.

He closed his eyes, smiling to himself, relaxed and content. Maybe now he could get some more sleep.

Two days off; a whole two days. It was practically unheard of in his profession, especially at this time of the year when the racing season was in full spate, but with both cars off the road after recent accidents, there was little for him to do until the next meeting. He frowned. He'd been reckless, but in his sport you had to take risks. He relaxed again and started to snooze. But not for long. Unseen and unheard, a firm little hand hit him on the nose.

'Ow!'

'Mmm, mmm, mmm,' Victoria smiled, her pink cheeks dimpled and her round guileless eyes, ringed with amber lashes, laughing at him.

'And what do you want, miss?'

She grinned, saliva dribbling down her chin, and then giggled.

'Come to see your daddy, have you?'

'Mmm, mmm, mmm,' and stout arms grabbed at him before she sat back with a heavy thump on the carpet. She started to cry.

'Oh dear, up we get.' He picked her up on to the bed where the tears vanished as quickly as they had started. He noticed with minor alarm that she had no nappy on.

'Emma!' he called.

His wife popped her head around the door. 'Just look after her for a minute while I have my shower, will you?' she asked and then disappeared again.

'But she hasn't got a nappy on!'

'Then do something about it.' But he didn't. All that fiddling around with plastic sticky bits . . . He could never get them to stay put. It wouldn't matter, not this once. He smiled at his daughter as she sat on the bed studying him, her blonde-red hair standing up in a comical quiff. She sucked her thumb, her face serious with intent.

'Mmm, mmm, mmm,' she gurgled.

'Not Mmm mmm mmm, poppet, but Da da da.'

She looked at him, her head tilted on one side. 'Mmm, mmm, mmm.'

He swooped her up into the air holding her at arm's length. She screeched with delight.

'Say Da da da, you little monkey.'

She was giggling so much she couldn't have said anything. Arms and legs flailing, her chubby face wreathed in smiles, she held out her hands for him while he threw her up into the air.

'Up we go! Up we go!'

Then she stopped giggling and wet herself. He scrabbled out of the bed holding her away from him, urine running down his chest.

'You little so-and-so!'

He tried to sound cross but it was hopeless, especially when it was his fault for not getting a nappy for her. He loved these all-too-infrequent moments they had together. He saw so little of her that he would forgive her anything.

'Silly thing,' he scolded gently. She pouted and lay her head against his shoulder.

'Mmm, mmm, mmm.'

'Come on you. Let's go and get cleaned up.'

He carried her into the bathroom where Emma had

just finished showering. She saw his wry expression.

'Should have put a nappy on her,' she said.

'I know, but why didn't you?'

'Because, darling,' she answered, playfully tapping him on the nose, 'if I can change the spark plugs, oil filter and the wheel on the car, then it's high time you learnt to put a nappy on your daughter.'

'I've tried but . . . well, it's those sticky tab things. They never stay done up when I do it.'

'Rubbish!' She took their daughter off him. 'You just want an excuse not to do it, that's all. Honestly, all this talk about the so-called new man. I'm beginning to think that it's a bit like the yettie: often talked about but never seen.' She handed him a towel. 'Here, get washed. Eau de urine doesn't suit you.'

At breakfast, he tried to help Victoria eat her food.

'Open wide, darling. Come on. Here comes the train. Choo, choo, choo,' but she turned away.

'Why won't she eat?' he asked Emma.

'Because,' she said, taking the spoon off him and handing it to the child, 'she likes to do things for herself nowadays. Of course, if you were at home a bit more often, you would know this.'

He looked away, chastened, and drank some coffee. 'I try,' he said.

'Oh yes, you try,' she countered, a small irritation entering her voice, but then she smiled and relenting said, 'So, what shall we do on this rare day off of yours? Go visiting, go shopping or go to the beach?'

'The beach,' he answered. 'All this sunshine won't last so let's make the most of it. We'll go to that quiet one which the tourists never find. That way I won't get besieged with autograph hunters and spotty youths who like to boast about their driving exploits.'

'Er, darling, not everyone recognizes you, you know. Famous though you may be in saloon car racing circles, beyond the confines of Brands Hatch or Silverstone, you're quite anonymous without a crash helmet with your name on it.'

His smile faded.

'Thank you, dear wife. That's just the support one needs from an ever-loving spouse.'

She laughed. 'Don't sulk. It doesn't suit you,' and the baby dribbled some cereal down her chin as she laughed too.

'Right,' said Emma, standing up, 'if we're to make the most of the day, we'd better get a move on. Could you go down to the shop for me and get some bread and some more ham?' and she pecked him on the lips, restoring his good humour.

When the picnic was made, and the beach and baby things packed, they trooped out to the garage.

'Yours or mine?' he asked.

'Mine, and I'll drive. You drive that thing of yours far too fast.'

'You used to like that once.'

'Yes, well, that was before we had Vicky, wasn't it? I'm not taking any chances nowadays.'

They got into the estate car and Emma turned on the ignition. There was an ominous silence. She tried again. Still nothing. And again. It still didn't work.

'Damn!'

'Starter motor,' he said, getting out of the car and lifting up the bonnet. 'I told you to get it seen to last week.'

'I forgot.'

He closed the bonnet. 'Well, it's not going to work, so whether you like it or not, we'll have to use my car.'

She shrugged.

'Promise me,' she said as they drove off, the powerful engine throbbing, 'no racing.'

He smiled reassuringly. 'Of course not. What on earth do you take me for?'

They reached a junction. He indicated to go left when she stopped him.

'Actually, it's straight on.'

His face hardened. His mother-in-law lived in that direction.

'Don't tell me,' he said slowly, 'she invited herself along again, did she?'

'No. I rang her up while you were out getting the bread.'

'Why? God, I can't understand this. It's supposed to be a family day out, one of the few we ever have, where just you and me and Vicky can be alone – you know, one of those days where I get to play Daddy and we spend some time together. God, you go on about them enough.'

'I've asked her along because I thought she needs a day out. She's not been feeling well lately and it would do her good.'

'Yes, but what about us? What about me? It's certainly not going to do me any good if that bloody woman comes along!'

'Don't shout!'

'I'm not shouting!'

'Yes you are!'

An icy silence fell between them.

'Honestly,' she said folding her arms across her chest, 'you're so selfish sometimes.'

'Me? Selfish? How the hell do you work that one out?'

'My mother has done so much for me and you begrudge her this one little trip.'

'Oh God. Here we go again.'

'And why not? Where were you when I needed you most? How about the time we got burgled? You were in Germany testing a new engine and you couldn't be disturbed. And how about,' she said fiercely, her voice rising with indignation, 'the even better time when I went into labour? Who was it who took me to the hospital? Not you, that's for sure. Too busy at the racetrack. So let's not forget how much we're indebted to Mother, shall we?'

'But I've told you before! It's my job. It's what I'm paid to do. It's why we live in a really nice house, entertain lavishly and go on very expensive holidays. My money pays for all that and no job would mean an end to it all and precious little future to look forward to. Is that what you want for our children?'

'But you're never home!' she cried. 'I rarely see you. Look at this morning at breakfast. You didn't even realize because you don't see us that often, that Vicky can manage to feed herself. Is this how we're going to spend the rest of our lives? With you only turning up now and again?'

'But you knew when you married me that I wouldn't be around often because of the demands of driving. Your brother's a bloody mechanic with me, so don't say you didn't know what it was like, because you did!' he yelled.

The baby started crying, frightened by the shouting. Emma turned to comfort her.

'There, there, sweetie. Here, have your dummy. See,' she said angrily, 'you've upset her.'

He ignored her. They were being held up behind a camper van that was crawling along the road.

'Bloody grandads!' he swore, pulling out to see if he could overtake. 'They should pension these oldies off the roads. They're such a damn nuisance!'

'Oh, for goodness' sake, have patience, will you? Maybe he's a tourist and doesn't know where he's going.'

The car horn blared but the camper van driver took no notice.

'Don't!'

'Shut up, will you? I can't stand it when you start fussing. There's nothing worse than a back-seat driver.'

He pulled out again to overtake but a lorry was coming the other way.

'Blast!'

'Please, don't. Just slow down. We'll soon be at Mother's anyway, so what does it matter?'

He glared at her. 'Wonderful! That's just what I want on my day off!'

'You should hear yourself sometimes, you know. Me, me, me. That's all you ever think about.'

The car swerved out as he crashed down through the gears, the powerful engine roaring as he put his foot to the floor.

'Don't!' she yelled.

'Be quiet. You're getting hysterical.' And then a tractor appeared coming out of a gateway.

'Look out!' she screamed, and it was the last thing he heard.

One

'Sian!'

'Hello, Helen.'

'Come in, come in! What a lovely surprise!'

The two women embraced, Helen shorter and quite plump, Sian tall and elegant.

'My dear, what on earth are you doing here?'

Sian picked up her suitcase and walked into the small hallway. She looked at her friend with tired resigned eyes, her face pinched.

'It's a long, long story,' she said wearily. Helen put her arm round her and squeezed her shoulders affectionately. With that Sian began to cry.

'Oh, come on now, you're safe here. I'll take care of you. Sit down and I'll make us a cup of tea and you can tell me all about it.'

Helen steered her sobbing friend into the flowery sitting room, sat her in one of the over-stuffed chairs and handed her the box of tissues that was sitting on the coffee table. Sian took one and blew her nose.

'Thanks, Helen,' she sniffed, tears still falling down her pale cheeks.

Helen ruffled Sian's red hair as she might a small child's.

'Come on, nothing's that bad.'

Sian looked at her. Something in her expression told Helen that perhaps this time it was. Her large green eyes were puffy and bloodshot, her full mouth turned down at the corners and her finely chiselled nose uncommonly red.

'Oh dear,' said Helen, kneeling down and taking her friend's cold hands in her own. 'That bad, eh?'

Sian nodded, a lock of thick wavy hair escaping from behind her shoulder and hanging over her downcast face. Helen patted Sian's hands.

'You sit there and I'll make the tea or perhaps,' she added standing up and readjusting her jodhpurs, 'you want something a bit stronger?'

Sian gave a weak smile. 'No thanks, I feel sick enough as it is.'

'Oh?' Helen raised her thick eyebrows quizzically. 'Why?'

Sian looked at the floor and twisted her tissue. 'I'm pregnant,' she announced dully.

Helen's face exploded with delight. 'Wow! That's fantastic! Brilliant! When's it due? What do you want? Boy or girl?'

Sian took another tissue from the box and wiped her cheeks dry. She felt absolutely wretched but at the same time relieved. She couldn't join in Helen's joy. Not now. Not after what she had seen.

'A long time yet,' she sniffed and wiped her nose, 'but it's why I can't drink.' She rubbed her aching neck muscles. She was exhausted.

Helen bounced down onto the sofa, beaming. She was delighted for her friend. 'And Eddy?' she asked. 'What did he say when you told him?'

Sian looked at her and then started crying again.

'Oh dear,' said Helen, 'I'd better get that tea.' She handed Sian another tissue and then walked out to the kitchen. A few minutes later she returned and handed Sian a steaming mug.

'Here you are, get that inside you. It will make you feel much better.'

Thank goodness for Helen, thought Sian, sipping her drink. A school friend from their days in Exeter, she could always be relied upon to be there when the going got tough, although they hadn't seen too much of each other since Sian's marriage. She wasn't entirely sure why, but she guessed it had something to do with Eddy but even so, when either of them had a problem, it was to the other they turned. So here she was, looking and feeling dreadful.

'Here,' said Helen, opening a packet of biscuits, 'have one. Have lots. You look far too slim to me and if you're pregnant, we'll have to look after you, won't we?'

Sian smiled and took one.

'Now,' said Helen, 'tell me what's happened. You and the old bastard had a row, did you? I can't think why. Surely he would be over the moon about the baby?'

'It's more than that, Helen, much more.' And out it all came.

In the bathroom mirror, a typical ballet dancer's face stared back at Sian. At least that's what her mother had said to her when she was small and taking ballet classes. Almond-shaped green eyes, smooth white forehead, straight nose and a pair of perfect lips. Sian thought herself pleasingly attractive, but not much else. She had never been one to flaunt her beauty. She was far too modest. Other women might have made more of their looks if they had been in her shoes, but although she was pleased with what she saw in the mirror when she looked, and did her best to keep herself in good shape, beyond that she had no time for vanity.

She twisted from side to side running her hands over her hips. She might have been a professional dancer if she hadn't grown so tall and too top-heavy – tall, slender with a enviable bust, all together the wrong shape for a dancer. She didn't mind, her childhood ambitions were behind her. Now it seemed she would have other far more important things to think about.

She had just been sick again. That was three mornings on the trot. If she wasn't mistaken, a visit to the chemist's was in order. She could hardly contain herself and her excited anticipation made her feel even more nauseous. She couldn't wait to tell Eddy. After last year's miscarriage, it would be wonderful if she were pregnant.

She bent down and washed her face in the sink, hair falling over her shoulders. She stood up and flicked it back out of the way. That would have to go. With its thick red waves and determination to stick out at all angles, her long hair would be much too much to look after when she had a baby.

She pulled herself up short. She must not think like that. She didn't know for sure and until she did, there was no point making plans. First a test, and then she could crow about it. She gave her hair a quick brush, teased out the curls around her heart-shaped face and stepped back into the bedroom. Her husband was still asleep, snoring gently.

There was a quiet tap at the door: one of the chambermaids with their tea.

'Okay, I'm coming.'

Taking the tray from the young girl, Sian thanked her and shut the door. She poured out the tea and went over to the bed.

'Eddy.'

The man, half asleep, grunted a reply to his wife's quick kiss before pulling the duvet closer around him. He had no intention of getting up yet.

'Your tea, Eddy.'

No response.

Sian looked down fondly at the snoring body with his tousled brown hair, slightly darker moustache and heavy handsome features. He was still attractive despite the obvious need for a bit of a diet. As a hotel manager, all the access he had to good food and drink was far too much of a temptation for him. She was the opposite. Where he gorged, she ignored it; where he drank too much, she stayed sober. She sighed. Good thing too, she thought.

She put her hand on his shoulder and shook him. 'Come on, Eddy. Time to get up.'

A bleary, red-rimmed eye momentarily opened.

'Wha . . . what's the time?'

'Seven thirty. You're late. Remember who's visiting next week. We've got to get organized.'

Both eyes shot open. 'Christ!' He quickly sat up, instantly regretting it. His face crumpled as his hand held his head like an over-ripe melon. 'Ah, my head,' he groaned.

'Got a hangover, have you?' Sian asked, a smirk on her face.

'Shut up, darling. I don't need you nagging at me before I've even got out of bed.'

'Oh dear,' she laughed. 'We are in a foul mood this morning, aren't we?'

'Yes, we are,' he growled, fixing her with a bad-tempered glare, bloodshot eyes peering out from under his thick brows, 'and it doesn't help having you making such a song and dance about it.'

Sian smiled to herself. Four and a half years of marriage and she knew exactly what to expect of him. He grumbled and he snapped, especially first thing in the morning, but basically he was a good man and she loved him very much. They had had their problems and she would be the first to admit to it. Last year it had got very bad but they had come through it and she thought they were stronger for it. Together they would make good their future.

She stood up and walked over to the window where she drew back the curtains. Instantly bright sunshine of the sort you only get at the coast where it sparkles across the sea, flooded into the room.

Eddy winced and groaned. 'Yuck. Summer. I hate it. For Christ's sake, shut them!'

She chuckled. 'Now, now, Eddy. That's no way to talk. Remember, our business depends on this good weather,' but he wasn't listening, his eyes closed again. She looked out of the window. 'It's going to be a beautiful day,' she said as some seagulls swooped and swirled around the hotel windows, their white bodies like miniature missiles in the clean air, 'a beautiful, beautiful day.' Across the bay she could see and hear the trawlers as they came in and out of the harbour, their engines chugging, and small boats with white triangular sails setting out for a morning's fun bouncing across the swell. She smiled to herself. Brigham was so beautiful at this time of the year.

Eddy slurped his tea. 'Any toast?' he asked hopefully.

'No.'

'Well, darling, you know I can't get out of bed until I've had something to eat.' He paused and then seeing she wasn't responding to his hopeful hints said, 'Be a poppet and go and get me some from the kitchen, will you?'

She turned to face him and he blew her a kiss. He could be very charming when he wanted to be.

'Please, baby. I feel rotten this morning and I'm sure I'll feel better if someone were to get me something to eat.'

'In that case,' she answered smiling, 'I shan't get you anything. You could do with losing a few pounds.'

He pulled a face, his bottom lip thick and sulky. 'Oh go on, Sian. I don't need to lose any weight. It's relaxed muscle, not fat.'

'Really?' But she went anyway, taking the private stairs so she would not meet any early guests.

The hotel kitchen was hot and busy as the breakfast chef and two waitresses saw to the guests. As Sian walked through, exchanging hellos, the smell of cooking began to make her feel unwell again. She hurriedly got Eddy's toast and left. All the way back to their bedroom, she was fighting down the waves of nausea.

Eddy was snoring again.

'Toast, Eddy.'

'Eh?'

She left him to it and went into the bathroom. She stood poised over the sink, sweating. If this was what it was going to be like for the next couple of months, she didn't know if she wanted to be pregnant. She took several deep breaths.

'What's it like downstairs?' he called.

She closed her eyes. She hated being sick. 'Busy,' she managed to say.

'Good. Can't have Killington coming down if we're half empty. We'd never hear the end of it.'

She turned on the tap to disguise the noise of her vomiting.

'I suppose,' Eddy continued, 'we'll have to put him in the Cliff Top Suite. Apparently, he's bringing someone with him this time. God knows who. 'Course, if I'd managed to get to that bloody meeting of his . . .'

'What's that you said?' Sian asked, standing in the bathroom doorway with a towel to her face. She felt better now.

'Oh, nothing.'

She dropped the towel on the end of the bed and undid her robe. Her silk nightdress clung to every curve and he was well awake now.

'Sian?'

'Mmm?'

'Do you have to get dressed yet?' and he patted the bed next to him. He glanced at the bedside clock. 'We don't have to go downstairs just now.'

She pulled a resolute face. She had things to do.

'Forget it. There's too much on. Remember, it is the middle of the tourist season and our boss is coming and we must get things organized.'

'To hell with him. We've got plenty of time.'

She pulled off her nightdress. Eddy stared and ran his tongue around his top lip. His eyes were fixated on her perfectly sculptured body, every line and contour just waiting for him to get his hands on it, inviting him, pulling him, enticing him. Everything else had been forgotten except the throbbing in his groin.

'Come on, Sian. That bastard can wait.' His voice was thick with desire as his eyes ran over her. She ignored him and walked over to a chest of drawers, each rounded breast with its pert nipple being closely watched.

'No, Eddy. Of course, if you hadn't got quite so drunk last night and come to bed a bit earlier, we might have had a bit of fun then.' She pulled on her bra. 'As it is,' she added with irritation, 'you rolled up here at three, woke me up, fell into bed stinking of cigars and booze and then fell asleep after a few minutes of manhandling me. Very romantic. Quite frankly, I didn't find you remotely attractive then and I'm not sure I do now, given you still smell and look like a toilet brush.'

'Well, thank you!' he snorted, his desire withering. 'And tell me, dear wife, do I have to make an appointment for sex these days because it seems to me that most of the time you're too damned busy or too bloody tired!'

'Don't start that again!' She angrily pulled up the zip of her skirt, momentarily wondering just how much longer she would be able to wear it. Their arguments were getting more and more frequent again, especially the ones about sex. She was getting tired of it. Didn't he realize how much work she had to do? And now with a baby on the way . . .

'Look, Eddy,' she explained, the exasperation heavy in her voice, 'I'm not feeling well at the moment. All this hard work and now Killington coming next week – it's just what we don't need, so do us both a favour and get out of bed and dressed, and above all stop hassling me, okay?' She turned to her dressing-table mirror and started to brush her hair. He scowled, his arms folded across his hairy chest like a petulant schoolboy.

'Perhaps you'd like three days' notice in future? Will that do?' he sneered.

'Oh, for goodness' sake!' she snapped. 'Do you have to be so damned childish?'

She threw down her hairbrush and marched into the bathroom, slamming the door behind her. She really couldn't stand him sometimes, with his selfish petulance and ever-demanding libido, regardless of how she felt.

Eddy sat and brooded, glaring at the door. It wasn't fair, he decided. He had his needs and they were being ignored. He was a man with appetites and if he didn't get what he wanted, well ... then he'd just have to do something about it, wouldn't he? No one could accuse him of being unfair to her. He had done his best by her; had been patient, kept his promises, but he was being sorely tried at the moment and if she wasn't going to be understanding she couldn't blame him if he took the opportunities that were presented to him.

He picked up his cup and took a mouthful. Yuck! The tea was cold. Couldn't she ever get anything right?

The bathroom door opened and Sian stood looking at him, her arms folded and her lips pressed tightly together. At first he thought she was going to have another go at him but then the expression melted and she smiled. She walked over to the bed, hands held out for him.

'I'm sorry, darling,' and she kissed him on the top of his head. Then she sat down next to him. 'I didn't mean to snap but ...' and she shrugged before breaking out into a grin, her green eyes twinkling mischievously. Quietly she said, 'Know what day it is the last Friday of the month?'

He looked blank. 'No.'

'Our anniversary, silly, and I might have a wonderful surprise for you.'

'You will? What?'

She nodded. 'I'm not going to tell you about it now. You'll just have to wait and see.'

She was longing to tell him about the baby. He had been upset about the miscarriage although, unlike her, he had got over it quickly.

'What surprise?' he asked again, trying to undo her blouse.

She moved his hand away. 'Wait and see, will you? It won't be a surprise if I tell you now, will it?'

He put a hand on her breast and started to fondle it,

23

squeezing it gently. 'Will it be to both our satisfaction?' he asked.

She moved his hand again. 'Yes, Eddy, only if you carry on doing that, I might forget about it altogether. So come on, get up and when we've got all this business over with Killington, then we'll relax properly. And who knows?' she said suggestively, giving him a sly smile, 'it might be a surprise you won't forget.'

He grinned and rested his head back in his hands. This was what he wanted to hear. No one could be more inviting than she when she wanted to be and he couldn't wait. He watched her finish dressing and spray on some perfume. He was one lucky man and he knew it. Plenty of his friends lusted after her and were openly envious of him. Really, she ought to be enough for any man . . .

She left in a breath of fragrance while he smiled after her. He was hoping the surprise would be a down payment on a new boat. He had been after a decent one for some time and she knew it. The clapped out thing he had tied up in the marina was well past its best. He was positively embarrassed by it. Or perhaps it was a new car. His Mercedes was a couple of years old now and he rather fancied one of the latest models, top-of-the-range, with all the latest gadgets. He knew she could afford it because she had recently been left some money by one of her great-aunts.

He got out of bed feeling much better, his sexual frustration forgotten. Yes, that was bound to be it: a brand-new car or boat. There wasn't anything else he wanted.

Breakfast was over by the time Eddy finally got downstairs. He hated being rushed in the morning, especially when he had a hangover. He ambled into the kitchen, shared a smutty joke with the chef, stuck his fingers into several of the sauces and a large creamy gateau before pouring out the first of his many cups of strong coffee and lighting up a cigarette. He then walked over the back courtyard to the office.

Sian was already stuck into the paperwork. She didn't look up as he came in so she failed to see him wink at their assistant, Rowena Gibson, a buxom blonde with oversized everything encased in a too-tight dress. She fluttered at him.

'Morning, Rowena.'

'Morning.'

Their eyes held for just a fraction too long before Sian's voice interrupted them.

'I've got to go out, Eddy. Mum wants some shopping done and I've got several other things to do.' She continued scribbling while she talked. 'Rowena can carry on here with this stuff if you will have a word with the meat supplier when he arrives. Bloody man is overcharging us again and I won't have it. The details are here.' She looked up suddenly. Eddy's eyes were innocent. 'Okay?'

'Right,' he answered. 'Anything else?'

Sian stood up and came around the desk. 'Wages. Make sure all the time slips are in by Wednesday. Have a word with the staff.' She stopped, looked around the mountains of paperwork and sighed. All this and Killington too. She didn't have time for it now. She had more pressing matters to see to. She picked up the car keys.

'I'll be back soon,' and pecking Eddy on the cheek, she almost skipped out of the office. She was half an hour from finding out if she was going to be a mum.

Eddy and Rowena waited until Sian had disappeared into the back of the kitchen and could no longer see them. There was an air of expectancy between them. Without turning to face her, he put his arms around her waist and drew her to him, all thoughts of his wife dismissed.

'Now,' he said huskily, 'where did we get to last night?'

'Not here, Eddy. Someone might come in.'

'Meet you upstairs then.' He took a key off a hook on the wall. 'The spare linen cupboard, coffee break time. No one will go in there,' and he kissed her on the lips.

* * *

25

Sian flew into town. It was still reasonably early and yet the traffic was already building up. In a coastal resort like Brigham it happened every summer. The visitors packed the small winding streets of narrow, painted houses, and the esplanade and harbour, which bobbed with trawlers, and the marina packed with pleasure boats.

'Stoneygates', the hotel Sian and Eddy managed, sat at the highest point of the town overlooking all of this. Big, grey and squat, it was the only four star for miles with its luxuriously appointed rooms, numerous indoor and outdoor attractions and acres of cliff-side land. For the best part of sixty years it had withstood the most ferocious of winter gales which lashed this part of the southwest coast, and in the summer, with manicured lawns and an abundance of flowerbeds, it welcomed the wealthy and discerning visitor.

Sian loved it even if she wasn't too keen on the owner, Marcus Killington. His visits invariably meant trouble. Whenever he came down there arrived with him an air of menace and anxiety. The staff were all in awed terror of him, and for a few days life would be unpleasantly nerve-wracking. She tutted to herself as she slowed down to let some tourists pass, and resolved to put Killington out of her mind for now.

After her visit to the chemist's, and picking up her mother's shopping, Sian drove to her parents' house, which was on the other side of the harbour with an unspoilt view of the sea. Her father was standing in the garden with a pair of binoculars.

'Any interesting ships?' she called as she got out of the car.

Richard Edwards put his binoculars down and smiled at his younger daughter. Trim, fit and tanned, he was enjoying his early retirement. His light blue eyes shone out from a face of good-natured wrinkles.

'Hello, dearest, and no, it's just the usual trawlers and things, although the harbour master did say the Fisheries

26

Protection Vessel was really busy nowadays. He also hinted at some drug-running going on, but I can't believe that. Too many tourists, for one thing.'

'Oh, but you never know, Dad. All this tie-up regulation stuff has meant a difficult time for many of the fishermen. I would have thought that a bit of extra money from the odd illegal load would be a mighty tempting proposition for some of them.' She kissed him on the cheek. 'Anyway, where's Mum?'

'In bed. She's got a bad back again,' and he looked heavenwards with a meaningful glance.

Sian left Richard to his binoculars and found her mother propped against a pile of pillows, sipping tea and reading the paper with a large magnifying glass. A bad back meant an excuse to lie in bed all day and watch the world pass by from her panoramic windows.

'Sorry your back's not good again, and why don't you get your eyes seen to, Mum?'

'I did and I still can't see.' Megan turned back to her paper. 'That bloody optician is useless.'

'Then go back again.'

'And see who?'

'There must be another one.'

'Maybe.' She smiled and proffered a cheek for a kiss. 'How are you?'

Sian sat on the bed, beaming. 'I think I might be pregnant.'

There was only the slightest change in Megan's attitude. 'Well, my dear, isn't that wonderful? Let's just hope it takes after you, that's all.'

'Mother!'

'You know what I mean. He's hardly the one I would have chosen for you but there you are, you would be bloody-minded about it.'

'Honestly, can't you like him just a little bit?'

Megan put down her paper and looked at her. 'I'll think about it.'

'Great.'

'I'm sorry, darling, but you know how I feel. The news of the baby is wonderful, especially after last year, but . . .' she frowned, her eyebrows puckering, 'Eddy isn't exactly the best you could have done, is he? Not what you call . . . acceptable, especially when he behaves like he does sometimes.'

'As he so rarely comes up here, I think it's a bit harsh of you to judge him on just one or two . . . unfortunate incidents. Anyway,' she added defensively, 'I told you at the time that he was under a lot of pressure.'

'That doesn't excuse him, you know. He's just an oik. Always will be and there's no getting away from it.' Megan sipped her tea and grimaced. It was cold. Sian's face had lost its warm glow too. 'Please, let's not argue. We should be happy, elated, joyful. Another member of the clan is on the way even if it will have the misfortune of being fathered by him, but nonetheless,' she held up her hand to stop her daughter's protests, 'nonetheless, I'm very happy for you, so be a sweetie and ask your father to make me a fresh pot of tea. I did ask him but I suppose he's forgotten again.'

'Okay, and your shopping is in the kitchen.'

'You're not going, are you?'

'I have to. Work, you know.'

Her mother smiled. 'I *am* happy for you, darling, believe me. And please don't pull that face. You used to do that as a child and one of these days, you'll stay like it.'

'Bye, Mum.'

In the hot dimness of the small windowless room, smelling of detergent and mothballs, hands reached out to explore.

'Eddy,' Rowena whispered, her voice full of promise.

'Rowena,' and their mouths latched on to one another, tongues probing fast and deep.

For weeks now, ever since he had first employed her,

Eddy had watched and waited, eyeing Rowena up, waiting for that moment when he knew she wanted him as much as he wanted her.

He grabbed both her breasts in his hands, large luscious orbs with rigid nipples straining against his touch. He unzipped the top of her dress and eased it from her shoulders. 'Where's the catch to this bra?'

'At the back.'

He fumbled. Damned silly thing wouldn't give. At last . . .

'God, I've wanted you!' he breathed into her neck, kissing and licking as he went, nibbling her fragrant flesh, inhaling the very essence of her.

She held his head against her, pressing him down. She was melting for him.

Eddy was breathing hard now, and sweating like a pig. His fingers found their way up her dress, venturing closer to their ultimate destination.

Rowena kissed him hard, their lips hungry and teeth clashing.

'Baby . . . baby,' she whispered wetly, smothering his face and neck, pushing him into her hair.

Closer and closer went his fingers, brushing against her hot, moist skin. He was nearly there, to the place he ached to be. His heart was pounding, his chest heaving. And then he found her, velvety soft, warm and wet.

She groaned.

He stroked softly and she groaned some more.

'So good . . . so good . . .'

He was desperate to have her. He undid his flies, and taking her hand, placed it on his bursting organ. A shudder ran through him as she slid up and down, edging him on, bringing him closer and closer.

Sian rushed back to the hotel from her parents', went straight upstairs to her and Eddy's suite of rooms and did her pregnancy test. She watched it intently, urging it on, hoping more than anything that it would be positive. Then the time was up, and she looked closely.

'Yes! Yes! Yes!'

She whooped for joy and threw her arms into the air. She was pregnant! At long last and after all the heartache of last year, she and Eddy had finally done it!

She burst into tears and slumped onto the bed. It was all too much for her. Her relief was overwhelming.

Eddy. She had to find Eddy and tell him. Never mind about the surprise for their wedding anniversary. She couldn't wait.

She ran out of the room and down to the reception area. No one had seen him. She went out to the office. He wasn't there either. She tried the greenhouse but neither of the gardeners had seen him so she went back inside. He had to be here somewhere.

Up in the linen cupboard, consummation was close. With Rowena on the floor, spare blankets underneath her, Eddy was gorging himself on her breasts, taking each one at a time and filling his mouth with it, teasing and sucking as she moaned beneath him. His hand was stuck between her legs, stroking and probing as he worked on her, building her excitement into a frenzy. She would be coming soon. He could tell. He was a man of experience. Unlike Sian, Rowena was all woman and responded so well to him. She was getting more and more excited, pushing his hand against her, rubbing herself harder and harder.

'Yes . . . Eddy . . . yes. Quickly now. Come on. I can't wait.'

He climbed on top of her and slid into that wonderful hot darkness that he had only previously dreamt of. It was all that he wanted. He melted into her, sighing.

'Rowena, Rowena.'

'Yes, baby. Push, push. I want you!' And together, her hands wrapped around his sticky back, her nails digging into his flesh and he pressing down on her, breast against breast, his trousers around his ankles, they started on that timeless roller coaster.

Sian would recognize Eddy's buttocks anywhere. He had a birthmark on one side that looked roughly like the outline of Italy, and when she opened the linen cupboard door, having heard strange sounds, that was the first thing she saw when she turned on the light. That and the two astonished faces.

She stood frozen with horror and then slammed the door shut. She felt sick, and after a stunned pause she turned and ran. On and on she went out of the hotel, across the lawns, out of the gate and up through the wood that covered the nearby hillside. It was a public footway and there were plenty of holiday-makers out, but that didn't deter her. She didn't care if they saw her tears; she couldn't care about anything. She ran past the kiosk at the top of the cliff where they sold ice creams, and out through the Napoleonic fort with its empty gun turrets and lookout posts, and still she continued. It was only when the path finished at the very edge of the cliff, where there was nothing between her and the sea except a drop of over one hundred feet, that she finally stopped.

She gasped for breath, sweating and panting in the unbearable sunshine, tourists all around her staring at this strange female, but she didn't care.

'God damn you, Eddy! God damn you!' she whispered hoarsely, tears falling anew. With clenched fists, she wrapped her arms around herself and stared at the distant blurred horizon. How could he do it, to hurt her like this after all the promises he had made? Hadn't he meant any of them? Had they all been lies? He had promised after the last time that it wouldn't happen again and now it had, the one thing she had dreaded more than anything else.

Sian sat down on the short grass and sobbed quietly to herself. All her happiness, all her life, everything she held dear had splintered apart in one vile second. The scars had

31

only just healed after Eddy's most recent affair, and yet he had done it to her again.

She closed her eyes at the stinging memory of it. She could never forget what she had seen. Their bodies so ugly and naked, so rudely entwined, his flesh on hers, a place where she had been, should be. A place she had loved and thought he did too. It was a memory she wanted to expunge from her mind, to eradicate for ever. Yet it was her mistake in believing his empty promises that shamed her more.

A warm, fragrant breeze caressed her face as if nature, so clean and pure on that bright summer's day, was comforting her. Around and around her face went the gentle breeze, blowing stray hairs into her waterlogged eyes and tremulous lips, but she was too distraught to be soothed by it. She edged closer to the cliff and looked over. There was something in her that she had to destroy. All she had to do was find the courage to end her pain, to get it all over and done with for good so he could never, ever do that to her again. It wouldn't take much. She moved closer and then closed her eyes and . . .

She brought herself up sharp. Of course she couldn't do that. She had another life to think of now, a small precious tiny flicker of a life and there was no way he was going to destroy that as well.

With her heart pounding at her reckless foolishness, she sat back and breathed in the clean salt air, quiet now.

She would survive. She would be strong because she had to be, and because she couldn't let down her child. Eddy might have crushed her faith and destroyed her trust but he wasn't going to destroy her future. She had that to look forward to even if she was on her own. Somewhere, out there, she would find her place in the sun and even if it meant she had to be alone, then she would do it. Being single could only protect her from further agony.

She glanced at her watch. It was after lunch. She had

been here hours and not realized it. She yawned and rubbed her neck. It was time to go, but not back to the hotel. That was over and done with.

'So there you are,' Sian said tearfully, wiping her nose. 'That's how it all happened.' If anyone would understand, Helen would.

Helen sat back in the sofa, lit a cigarette and stared thoughtfully into the distance.

'What a bastard,' she said at last, 'an absolute bloody swine.' She shook her head, her brown curls bouncing. 'Unbelievable!'

'I know,' agreed Sian quietly. 'Could hardly believe it myself.'

'Here, have another biscuit. You've had a terrible shock.'

Sian took one obediently. She wasn't hungry but it was something to do.

'To tell the truth,' said Helen, 'I only gave you two a couple of years. I'm surprised it's lasted this long.'

Sian took another sip of her tea. It tasted foul – Helen always liked her tea strong – but she didn't object this time. She just let the tannin-rich brew scald its way down to her stomach. 'Can I have a cigarette?'

Helen passed her the packet. 'You shouldn't, you know. It's very bad for the baby. Anyway, I thought you didn't smoke. You know, all part of your vegetarian, non-drinking, exercise-mad lifestyle, the sort of crap I can't stand.'

Sian shrugged. 'Desperate situations call for desperate measures. Anyway, I'll only have this one.'

She lit up and inhaled the acrid smoke. It tasted horrible but she resisted the temptation to cough. Her eyes watered. She hadn't done this for years but walking in on Eddy had shaken her up so badly, her whole world had changed.

'So,' asked Helen, 'what next?'

Sian looked at her. She didn't know what to say or do. She had come here because she needed some peace and she couldn't get that at her parents'. They would ask too many questions. Beyond that, she hadn't a clue.

'Dunno,' she said with a sigh. 'It's all such a god-awful balls-up.'

'It may be now,' said Helen, 'but it happens all the time, you know, and although you feel like death at the moment, it will get easier. You can bet on that. Anyway, look at it this way, at least you won't have to count the cracks in the bedroom ceiling any more,' and she smiled.

Sian grinned. 'You're right, of course. He never was the world's best lover,' and she chuckled tiredly.

'Look,' said Helen, 'surely you must have had some idea about Eddy and his . . . well, his extracurricular activities?'

'How do you mean?'

'Well . . . you didn't honestly expect someone like him to be faithful, did you? I mean, he's handsome, charming – far too so if you ask me – and he's a ladies' man. He was bound to go looking for a bit of fun sometime.'

Sian sat upright. 'I can't believe this, Helen,' she said stiffly.

Helen helped herself to another biscuit. 'Why not?'

'Helen! How could you!' cried Sian. 'How can you say such a thing? It's devastated me. It was awful . . . I was so upset!' and then she crumpled. Who was she kidding? Helen was right and she knew it.

'Sian.'

No reply, just sobbing. Then Sian turned round.

'How could he?' she cried, holding out her hands. 'After everything he said, everything he promised. He's humiliated me . . . embarrassed me . . . degraded me! The whole bloody staff knows about it! He's made an absolute fool out of me . . . and he said . . . he promised . . . he wouldn't do it again!'

Helen stood up and went to comfort her friend, rocking her backwards and forwards as she would a child.

'Shh, shh, it's all right now, it's all right. Shh,' and for a while they didn't move.

Then Sian slumped back in her chair, not looking at her friend. They were both silent.

'Sian, I'm sorry, okay? Perhaps I didn't say what you wanted me to say and I'm . . . well, maybe I should have thought a bit first, but honestly, dear, it's just that I'm not surprised.'

Sian was grim-faced, mouth tightly shut with suppressed emotion. 'No, I'm the one who should apologize. I shouldn't have shouted like that.'

'Forget it. It had to come out sometime.'

Sian blew her nose and wiped her face.

'Eddy was a real bastard, you know, only you wouldn't see it.' Helen's voice was gentle.

Sian bit her lip. Her outburst had made some colour return to her face and her cheekbones were even more prominent. She bit her knuckles, trying to stop the fresh tears.

'Oh Helen, I've been such an idiot, so stupid! Why couldn't I see what he was like?'

'Because you loved him and we all behave like morons when we're in love.'

'Do we?'

'Yes, it's just a temporary form of insanity, you know,' and she put her arms around Sian's shoulders again, gently rocking her. 'There, there, have another tissue. Look, dear, we all make mistakes. It doesn't matter. Just put it down to experience.'

'Yes, but what about the baby?'

'Does he know about it yet?'

Sian shook her head. 'No, I didn't tell him. I was so bloody angry, I just packed my things and left.'

'Well, in that case . . .'

The implication of what Helen had started to say hung in the air.

'No,' said Sian, her small chin sticking out firmly, 'absolutely no way. I couldn't do that. Not now, not after everything I went through last year. I just couldn't.'

'All right,' comforted Helen, 'all right. We'll say no more about it then. If you want this baby, then you'll have this baby and if that two-timing git of a husband of yours comes round here, I'll geld him!' She smiled broadly, two dimples showing in either plump cheek. She sat back on the sofa.

Sian took a sip of her now cold tea. 'Oh Helen, what am I going to do?'

Helen waited patiently until Sian had got herself under control and then she said gently, 'Whatever you like. Stay here, move somewhere else, go to your parents —'

'No, not my parents,' said Sian. 'I couldn't possibly face them. I'd never hear the end of it especially from Mum.' She paused. She was so tired. 'Do you mind if I stay here?'

'Not at all.' Helen sighed deeply. 'I could do with the company. The way my nonexistent love-life is going at the moment, I don't think I'll ever get engaged, married, pregnant or divorced.' She smiled wryly. 'So until the man of my dreams comes along, you're more than welcome to stay.'

'Thanks.'

They sat quietly for a while.

'You know what really gets up my nose, Helen?'

'What?'

'It's that I'm the one who does all the work in the hotel. It's me, not Eddy, who spends hours with the paperwork, organizing the staff, making sure the menu is okay, ordering from the suppliers and all the rest of it. All me. But of course,' and she chuckled ironically, 'I don't get any praise for it. That creature Killington, who owns the place, a real nasty case if ever there was one, has never once said how good a job I was doing or anything like that. Whenever he comes down, it's always Eddy he speaks to. It's as though I didn't exist!' Her voice rose with indignation.

'Well, you know what men are like,' said Helen. 'Brains in their balls. They're all the same.'

'You're telling me!'

'Good,' smiled Helen, 'this is what I like to see, anger. I take it then, you'll be telling Eddy to go forth and multiply?'

Sian glanced at her. 'Are you sure that's what you meant to say?'

'Ooops!' laughed Helen. 'Perhaps not. Still, you know what I mean. Talking of which, when are you going to tell him about his prospective fatherhood?'

'I don't know. Not yet. I need time to think.'

'Okay, so what about money? Do you need any? I've got a bit to spare if that's any help.'

'No, no, Helen. Thank you, but a great-aunt of mine left me some in her will and it will be more than enough to get me through this crisis.' She suddenly stopped. 'You know, I was going to spend some of that buying that pig an anniversary present.' She looked at Helen with horror. 'Thank goodness I didn't!' and they both smiled.

'It's a good thing I didn't put it in our joint account either. Eddy's hopeless with money, likes the horses too much. I wouldn't have anything left at all by now if he had got his hands on it.'

'What about a job?' asked Helen. 'I mean, you can still work, can't you?'

'Yes, but what?'

'Horses.'

'Horses? Where?'

'The stables, of course, where I work.'

'But it's been ages since I've done anything like that. Bracken has been loaned out for months now.'

'Never mind about that, you'll soon pick it up again. Anyway, Andrew said he was only looking for someone to help Eck with the mucking out and grooming. You don't need experience for that.'

'Okay,' smiled Sian, her mood lifting.

'And Eddy? What are you going to do if he comes sniffing round?'

'What about him? He can get lost for all I care, him and Rowena.'

'So you're not thinking of going back to him, then?'

Sian snorted with derision. 'Are you kidding? He can just go to hell. I've had all I can take from him and more, and I don't give a damn what he says or what promises he makes. He's a totally worthless man and I don't want anything more to do with him. That ... that ... woman he's with can keep him for all I care.'

'Fighting words, Sian.'

'Yes, and I mean every damned one of them. He's humiliated and degraded me, not to mention committing adultery, so as far as I'm concerned, that's it.' Then in a more subdued voice she added, 'Who am I kidding? I'm a failure, Helen, a complete and utter failure. It's all gone so horribly wrong and I just feel terrible. If I'd listened to you or my parents, I wouldn't be in this mess.'

Helen tutted. 'Come on, Sian, you know that's not true. Eddy's a sod. Always has been and always will be. Anyway, when you met him, you were young and impetuous, and he was damned good-looking even if it does make me sick having to admit it. Mind you,' she added with a grin, 'he's a bit of a debauched wreck now, so he's not so much of a loss as far as I can see.'

'No, perhaps you're right.'

'I am. You wait, ten years from now, when all his hair has dropped out and he's got even more of a pot belly, he'll look bloody terrible so just you remember that when you're feeling sorry for yourself.'

Sian smiled. It was difficult to remain depressed when Helen was around.

'You know, I think I'll have to become allergic to men. I just don't see how I'll ever trust any of them again.'

'Why bother?' asked Helen. 'They're all a waste of time. Right then, let's unpack your stuff and head off down to the pub for a bar meal and a pint, or in your case, an orange juice.'

'Fine, sounds wonderful to me.'

'This Andrew chap, are you sure he'll give me a job?'

They were walking down the narrow main street of the village, squashed cob cottages squeezed together in long multicoloured terraces on either side of them. When a car came towards them, they had to stop and pull in on the narrow pavement for it to pass.

'Yes,' said Helen over her shoulder. 'We've been looking for another part-timer for a few weeks now. Eck's good but he's a bit slow, and when the last girl left Andrew said immediately that we had to get someone else.'

'Eck? That's a strange name. Where does he come from?'

'Who knows? Apparently when Andrew took over the stables, Eck came with him. He worships Andrew. Follows him around like a dog. Got about as many brains as one as well.' She stopped herself. 'No, that's not fair to dogs. Put it this way, if Eck has any intelligence, it's more of a concept than a reality.'

Sian laughed. 'You're kidding me?'

'Honestly, it's true. I've never met anyone who was quite as dumb as he is, well, except one or two of the holiday-makers. No, he really has stupidity off to a fine art.'

They stopped outside a pub.

'Well, here it is, the King's Arms. Reasonable beer and the grub's lovely. Saves me from having to cook and that can only be a bonus.'

'Helen!' The voice came from an approaching car.

'Oh no,' she groaned, pulling a face, 'Billy.' She turned to Sian. 'Fancies himself as the local Lothario. Just think, all those sperm and that got through. What do you want, Billy?'

A spotty young man drove up to them, the tyres of his pink souped-up Ford Capri screeching on the tarmac. He grinned out of the open window. He had cropped, greased hair, a large gold hoop hanging from one ear and a tattoo on his forearm that said 'Liverpool', underneath an emblem.

'Who's your friend, Helen?'

'Sian, and she prefers men who have managed to crawl out of the primordial slime.'

'Eh?'

Sian suppressed a giggle. 'Don't, Helen. You're being mean.'

'Never mind, Billy. Another time perhaps, when your brain's in gear.'

Billy scowled and roared off.

'That should keep him quiet for a while,' said Helen with satisfaction as they stepped in through the darkened porchway into the cool wood-panelled interior. There was a plethora of horse brasses hanging on the beams and old paintings of animals and moorland scenes around the walls.

Helen bought drinks and ordered food, and clutching their glasses, they made their way through the crowded tables packed with tourists and out into the garden. They found some empty chairs under the shade of a large willow.

Sian sighed. 'It's lovely here.'

'Yes, it is. There's something about a pub garden in the summer when you don't even mind the insects.'

When the plates arrived piled high with fresh warm bread and salad, Sian ate with relish.

'Amazing what the moorland air can do to a person's appetite,' commented Helen, watching her friend tuck into the food, 'or is that your hormones?'

'A bit of both, I think.'

When their food was finished, Helen stood up and gathered together the plates.

'Another drink?'

'No, thanks. Too tired.'

'Well, I will if you don't mind.'

While Helen was gone, Sian took the time to examine her surroundings. The large garden was dotted with tables, each with its own sun umbrella under which families with children sat and ate their meals. The pub itself was what was known as a long house. Thatched, with three-foot-thick cob walls, it had been built about four hundred years ago and had all the appearance of lasting as long again. Above the thatch, swifts and swallows were weaving in a fast aerial ballet as they chased after insects, and in the distance came the lowing of cattle from somewhere on the moor.

With all the stress of the day beginning to seep out of her body, she leant back in the white iron chair and closed her eyes in the evening warmth. Devon in summer; nothing could match it.

'Hello.'

Sian started.

'Nodded off, eh?'

''Fraid so. I didn't realize how tired I am until I closed my eyes.'

Helen sat down and took a deep draught of her beer.

'Well, I've got news for you. I've just spoken with his lordship about you and he says that if you want the job and if I'm recommending you, then it's all yours.'

Sian's face broke into a grin. 'My goodness, that was quick!'

'Well, there you are then; a roof over your head for as long as you like and some extra money in your pocket.'

'Oh Helen! You're so good to me!' She flung her arms around her friend's shoulder and hugged her.

'Hang on, hang on, you'll spill the beer if you're not careful!'

They watched some children chasing around the garden.

'Just think,' said Helen, 'yours might be doing that in a few years' time.'

'Mmm, I know and I can't wait. The more I think about it, the more I'm looking forward to it. To hell with Eddy and his bloody hotel. I'm hurt, very hurt, but it's what's inside me that counts,' and her eyes filled with yet more tears. She wiped them away briskly. 'Mustn't get maudlin, eh?' she said, seeing Helen's look of sympathy. 'Tell me, what's he like, then?'

'Andrew? Well . . . I don't suppose I ought to tell you this, given your delicate physical and emotional state, but according to the best informed female opinions I can gather, he's the most delectable thing in trousers that's ever descended on this village. When he first came, there was practically a riot to see who was going to go out with him.'

'You included?'

'Well,' and she smiled, her eyes shining, 'actually, no, I don't like blonds, you know that. I like my men dark, devious and dangerous and Andrew's none of those. At least, not that I know of. He's about six foot two, lovely physique on him – you know, long muscular legs, broad shoulders – blond hair, deep blue eyes and a very Aryan face.'

'And you still don't find him attractive?'

'I didn't say that exactly, but stay away from him. You're in no fit state to tamper with the old heart strings, least of all with someone like him. As far as I can tell, he treats them mean and leaves them keen. Hearts have been breaking all over the place since he arrived and he's had more women than I've had hot dinners.'

'And what makes you think I'll be interested? Haven't I been through enough?'

'Just wait till you see him,' and she smiled at Sian. 'And if I know Andrew, he'll take one look at you and will be after you like his stallion goes after the mares in season.'

'Rubbish!'

'Well, just in case, you make sure you take care.'

'Yes, miss,' replied Sian giving a mock salute. 'Where does he come from?'

'To be perfectly honest, no one knows that much about

him. He's a very private individual, self-contained and a bit mysterious. Maybe that's why so many women chase him; they see him as a bit of a challenge. He turned up a while back, took over The Grange and the riding stables, which are a couple of miles away. He's been quietly building up the business ever since. He never says much except to bark out orders and you'll never get anything out of him about his private life. God only knows what he says to all his women after he's made love to them,' she mused. 'Must be very boring going to bed with someone who doesn't have any interesting postcoital conversation.'

Sian smiled. 'And how about your love-life then? It can't be as dead as you say, not you. I don't believe that for one minute.'

Helen pulled a face. 'A topic best not discussed in polite company. Well, you've seen the thing from the black lagoon . . .'

'Billy?'

'Apart from him . . .' and she smiled mysteriously.

'Oh? What's been going on?'

Helen shrugged. 'The usual stuff. You know, I must have an arrow on my head with a sign attached to it saying, "Married men please go out with me." ' She gave Sian a sidelong glance. 'I met this really nice chap – or what I thought was a really nice chap – about six weeks ago. Took him back to my place, had some wine, you know, the usual, and then nothing happened. Not a whisper. So I rang him up at home after hunting him down through the telephone book, only for his bloody wife to answer!'

'How do you know it was his wife?'

'Because, my dear, I could hear the dear little kiddy-winkles playing in the background. Needless to say, I quickly hung up.' She sighed. 'I don't know, when am I going to have a proper boyfriend? I've never had one, you know, just one-night stands. Pisses me off no end.'

'Come on, Helen, it's not that bad. You could be in my situation with a cheating bastard of a husband and a baby on the way. At least you're free without any responsibilities. You can come and go as you like, do as you like, eat what you like. You don't have to answer to anyone whereas I've spent the last four years putting Eddy first and in seven and a half months' time, will begin eighteen years of worry.' She paused when she realized that her words were only making Helen even more depressed.

'I know all that, Sian, and I want it. I want to be normal like all my friends. I want to be boring with a mortgage. There comes a point, you know, when being single isn't all it's cracked up to be. I want someone to row with, even.'

'What? And end up like me and Eddy?'

'Well, maybe not, but you know what I mean.'

Sian's heart went out to her. 'Cheer up, Helen. Would another drink help restore your good humour?'

Helen took her glass without much enthusiasm and managed to down what was left in one.

'Something a bit stronger I think,' she said, wiping the back of her hand across her mouth.

It was well after closing time when they left the garden. Helen was drunk and Sian had to help her to her feet, Helen protesting against the barman who told her that as much as he liked her rendition of 'Widdecombe Fair', it was a bit late at night for her to be singing, and would she please consider the neighbours as he had to live round here and face them in the morning. Sian apologized.

They weaved across the village square, with its ornate Victorian conveniences and defunct water pump, and up the narrow lane towards Helen's cottage. Halfway along, an expensive saloon car pulled up behind them and honked loudly when they didn't immediately get out of the way.

Helen turned and made a rude gesture.

'Bloody grockles!' she yelled. 'Come down here once a year and think they own the place!'

The car stopped and the passenger side electric window rolled silently down. A blond head looked out.

'Really, Helen, I should have known it was you. I hope you've sobered up by tomorrow morning. I expect to see you at eight sharp and no later.'

Helen grinned inanely but said nothing.

The window rolled up again and the car purred away to the sound of giggling from the driver's seat. The man's female companion obviously found them amusing. Sian stepped out of the shadows. The man hadn't seen her at all.

'See!' said Helen, gesturing after the car, 'yet another example of the cream of British manhood,' and she turned to Sian, her face serious. 'Leave him alone,' she warned. 'He's nothing but trouble.'

Two

Sian slowly opened her eyes. For a moment she had no idea where she was. The flowery walls, the white ceiling, the pink drawn-back curtains. Everything was unfamiliar. She nearly panicked but then she heard Helen's voice.

'Come on, you! Time to get up!'

She looked at her travelling clock: 7.15 a.m. Brilliant white sunshine was pouring in through the small leaded window and a multitude of birds were singing in the garden. She relaxed, relieved but feeling queasy. There was no Eddy to contend with but she still had her morning sickness. It would have to be a quick dash to the bathroom.

Helen knocked at the door and poked her head around just as Sian flung back the duvet and fled past with her hand to her mouth.

'Morning sickness?' she asked.

There was no reply from behind the bathroom door.

'You okay?'

There was a groan.

'Well, I've some fresh orange juice and coffee downstairs if you want some, but I don't suppose you do. Have a shower first. That will make you feel better.'

Sian grunted.

After her shower, Sian did feel much better. She got dressed in a pair of ski pants and an old T-shirt, and ambled down to breakfast, a towel still around her wet hair. Helen looked up from her newspaper.

'Mmm,' she said returning to the sports pages, 'you think this pregnancy lark is worth all this heaving?'

'Of course.'

'Oh well, if you say so. I'll just have to take your word

for it.' She laid the newspaper down and looked gravely at Sian. 'So, what are you going to do today, about Eddy and things, I mean? You've got to tell him sometime.'

Sian sat down heavily. She felt depressed. Helen was right.

'I don't know. In the cold light of day, it's all one hell of a mess, isn't it?'

'Not necessarily. You've got money, you've got friends, you've got somewhere to live.' She paused. 'Think he'll come after you?'

Sian grimaced. 'No way, not him. He's too damn lazy for a start. No, he'll just carry on as though nothing has happened.'

'First-class missing link is that man,' announced Helen firmly, 'and you're much better off without him.'

'I know, but despite everything – all that he's done, Rowena, the lot – I must still care for him because I hurt so much.'

Helen passed her a piece of kitchen roll. 'Here, wipe your eyes. Believe me, you'll get over him. It's not your heart that's aching, it's your pride. No man's worth it. I speak from very bitter experience, I can tell you. Anyway, will you be wanting to come into work today? You don't have to if you're not feeling up to it. I can always tell Genghis Khan that you're sick or something.'

'No,' sniffed Sian, forcing a smile, 'I'll come in. I can't sit here and mope all day.'

'That's my girl,' smiled Helen, patting Sian's arm. 'Don't let the bugger get you down.'

They were walking along the narrow unkempt lane, grass growing up the middle, heading towards the village. The sun was already beating down on their heads, making them sweat. The fecund hedges, overhung with luxuriant greenery, were buzzing with insects that swarmed in the still, shimmering air. It sounded so quiet to Sian after the noise and bustle of Brigham. She had forgotten her

47

sunglasses so when she looked up, she had to squint but she didn't mind. The place was so restful.

'On Saturdays,' said Helen, 'the tourists leave and the next lot come down. They're billeted all over the place with the locals who need the extra money because most are pretty poor round here, as you know. It's only the rich incomers who have any dosh. We take them for five full-day treks and one half-day trek. They're all pretty good riders. We tell them beforehand that they must have some riding experience before they come here. Of course,' she smiled, 'sometimes we get a real wally who doesn't know one end of a horse from the other but thinks because they've seen a few cowboy films, they'll know how to ride. Stupid prats! I had someone once turned up in a skirt! Can you believe it?'

'Yes, I remember the stables where I kept Bracken. We used to get all kinds of people coming for riding lessons and half the time they weren't dressed properly. How many do you take?'

'About fifteen. Certainly no more.'

They turned a corner and were now in the village proper. Cars were parked all along the kerbside, making it look even smaller than it was. The smell of newly baked bread filled the air, and some young children raced around the square.

'Nice place, this,' commented Sian.

'Yes, Leighford is. Full of second homes now. There's not many original families left. They're all wealthy outsiders.'

'Well, what are you? You're from Exeter!'

Helen ignored her.

'Fancy a doughnut?' and before Sian could answer, Helen had disappeared into the bakery. She reappeared holding out a paper bag. Sian took it. She hadn't managed breakfast and was starving now.

'Mmm, yummy,' said Helen, red jam running down her chin.

They sat down on a bench.

'Shouldn't we be moving on?' asked Sian, wondering how they would ever get to work as Helen seemed in no rush. Helen rubbed her hands together to shake off the sugar.

'Nope. Andrew will pick us up in a moment. He has to come down every morning to get a newspaper and to pick up Eck from Mrs Tucker's where he boards. He'll get us at the same time,' and she sighed, stretching out her stout jodhpur-clad legs in the morning sun. 'Day like this I should be sunning myself in the garden and not sitting on the back of some bloody great barrel of an animal who's in no mood to go anywhere but back to its stable. Ah well, perhaps it'll have some compensation.'

'What's that?'

A knowing smile spread across Helen's face. 'Alan Watkins, one of the trekkers. He has a lovely little bum,' and her hands drew an imaginary outline in the air, 'and he's not married.'

They both laughed.

'Ah,' Helen turned to Sian, 'time for you to meet your new boss and,' she whispered hurriedly, 'remember what I said about him last night. Oh, and I forgot to mention, he has a large Alsatian called Blaize. Takes him everywhere, so I hope you like dogs.'

A Land Rover pulled up at the kerb and the door opened. A large black and gold dog jumped out.

'Put him in the back, Helen,' said a deep voice. 'I can't have him slobbering all over my new employee.'

With the dog safely ensconced among some bales of straw, the two women climbed into the cab.

'Hello, you must be Sian.'

In the brief second that their eyes met, somewhere deep inside Sian's soul a fissure opened, and total silence overtook them. Everything stood still and then Andrew held out his hand. She shook it, numb with surprise, and smiled briefly. She sat down. Perhaps it was her pregnancy, perhaps it was Eddy, but for all Helen's warnings about

Andrew, she saw everything and nothing to worry about. He was devastatingly handsome with his blue eyes and blond hair, but he was only a man, she told herself sternly, and right now she had to be oblivious to men, if only for her own wellbeing. He said hello to Helen and they drove off.

Squashed up together, the three of them across the front seat, Sian stared doggedly ahead. She wasn't in the mood for small talk. Her stomach was churning and she felt sick again. Being shoulder to shoulder and leg to leg with him hugely unsettled her and she couldn't understand why.

'Where are you from, Sian?'

His voice was without accent.

'Hampshire, although I've spent most of my life living in Devon.' She was relieved her voice wasn't shaking.

'Sian and I went to the same comprehensive,' interjected Helen. 'We've known each other for years.'

It seemed to satisfy him. He didn't ask anything else.

Sian found herself, quite unexpectedly, looking at his legs, long and powerful, encased in thick beige breeches and mud-splattered black leather riding boots. He changed gear and her eyes followed every move. His fingers were strong and capable. He was obviously someone who had never worked in an office. His bare arm, dotted with freckles but also tanned and covered with a layer of fine sun-bleached hair, pressed against hers. He made her look so feminine, the strength and hardness of his muscles straining under the skin. She looked back at his legs. Upward and upward went her gaze and then she suddenly stopped. What the hell was she doing? Didn't she have enough problems already? Don't be so ridiculous she told herself.

The Land Rover slowed to a stop. A huge ungainly man, seemingly cut from a massive oak tree, stood at the side of the road, smiling inanely. He wore dark blue overalls and boat-sized wellingtons.

'Eck,' said Helen, looking at Sian. 'As large as life and

twice as ugly. Hello, Eck,' she called, opening the window. 'Climb in the back, will you, and look after Blaize? We've got a passenger today.'

The man grinned, a few teeth missing from his mouth, and blinked very, very slowly over round baby-blue eyes. The Land Rover dipped to one side as he climbed aboard.

'Helen says you know a bit about horses,' said Andrew unexpectedly.

Sian glanced quickly at Helen. What had she been saying? Helen looked out of the passenger window. There was no way she was going to bail her out.

'Some,' she answered tightly.

'Well, that's all I need you for, mucking out, grooming, cleaning the yard. I've got one member of staff who thinks she knows it all already. I certainly don't need another. But then perhaps you have better manners,' and he smiled.

He's laughing at me, she thought, and she glanced at Helen, whose look said, 'Charming bastard, isn't he?'

Nothing was said the rest of the way, which suited Sian. She wasn't sure she could trust herself to say or do anything at the moment. She was so unnerved. They drove along yet another tight-cornered narrow lane, high hedges looming up above them on either side, until they hit the moor. The hedges petered out to be replaced by scrubby yellow-flowered gorse, and the grass was thin and close-cropped. A brown-stained stream cut its narrow gorge to one side of the road and standing along its edge was a small group of enormously pregnant and shaggy ponies whisking their tails at the pernicious flies.

'Dartmoor,' announced Helen. 'Beautiful, isn't it?'

Sian nodded slowly.

'I could live up here for ever,' sighed Helen, breathing in the hot clean air.

It had been a long time since Sian had been here. Even though she only lived on the coast, she rarely visited Dartmoor. Eddy always preferred watching the television to walking. Exercise wasn't his forte.

'Not too far now,' said Helen. 'The stables are just before the reservoir. We go swimming there sometimes. There's some good rides around there as well, places that the tourists don't know about,' she smiled.

Bumping down a rutted track, the Land Rover pulled into a wide open yard with loose boxes down three sides and a small grey house standing at the end.

'I brought them in for their feeds earlier on,' said Andrew. 'They'll need grooming and tacking up.' He pulled up the handbrake and switched off the engine. 'Okay?'

Sian noticed how apt Helen's description of him had been the previous evening. When he wasn't smiling, there was nothing soft about his face. Each feature was defined with rigid inflexibility. His eyes were deep-set and guarded, not missing anything. His nose was just a bit too large and very Roman in its arrogance, and his mouth – his mouth, wide but hard, could have been so sensuous. But his was not a face that encouraged intimacy, and Sian was instinctively wary of him. He had seemed quite approachable earlier but he wasn't now. It was time for work.

'Right, out you get, you two. Show Sian around the yard, Helen, then get her to work.'

He spoke as if Sian wasn't there. He climbed out as did Eck, with the dog following his master.

'Yes, sir, no sir,' mocked Helen under her breath. 'He's so delightful, isn't he? Come on then, we'd better do as ordered or no doubt I'll never hear the end of it. This way,' and they walked across the yard.

'His lordship feeds the horses first thing. The feed is kept over there.' Helen pointed to a whitewashed shed at the end of the line of stables. 'Fed and watered, they're turned out again, which is where you come in so let's get on and do some mucking out.' They went into another shed. Helen picked up a wheelbarrow and pushed it out into the sunshine while Sian carried two pitchforks.

'Don't ask Eck any questions,' said Helen over her shoulder, 'ask me. He has a heart of gold but, like I said,' and she tapped her head, 'his brain is missing, presumed dead. Mind you, he does have his uses. He's as strong as an ox and brilliant with anything on four legs. I saw him once poleaxe a horse that wouldn't behave itself when the vet came.' She clenched her fist. 'Cuffed it one between the ears like that,' and one hand punched the other palm. 'It damned well behaved itself after that.'

They went into a stable and immediately Sian was hit by the pungent smell of horse and damp straw. She wrinkled her nose.

'Only a few of the horses are kept in. Most of them are common-bred, thick-skinned animals, good doers who live out all of the time, but we do have a couple of better ones who need a bit of cosseting.' Helen took one of the pitchforks. 'You do in here and I'll do next door. I don't suppose you'll need reminding how?'

Andrew had walked straight into the cottage after the drive from the village. He went to his small study, sat down in the captain's chair behind the paper-strewn desk and forced himself to breathe deeply and relax.

Sian.

Even when he closed his eyes, her face kept swimming into view, its dazzling beauty reaching out to him, taking over his whole consciousness. Wherever she had come from and for whatever purpose, it couldn't do him any good, he decided.

He opened his eyes and looked at his hands. The tremor had ceased. It had been so difficult in the Land Rover. She had sat so close to him, the warmth from her body radiating across to his, picking at his soul, tunnelling down to the secret places he had kept from everybody, even himself. Had there been no one else in there but the two of them, it would have been far too uncomfortable. Thank God for Helen and Eck. Only they had saved him from making a fool of himself. And then he smiled, coming back to reality. She was a real beauty, the like of which he hadn't seen for a very long time.

He stared unseeing at the desk top: bills, bills and more bills, some of them with dire warnings written in large red letters across them; some just straightforward declarations of no more credit. On top of them all sat an unopened bank statement. He knew what it would say. His overdraft was running out and there was little sign of any improvement.

Sian.

Even faced with all his problems Andrew couldn't stop thinking about her. He couldn't let her get to him though, not now; not when he had just about succeeded in burying the past. He decided he would have to ignore her, keep his distance, pretend she didn't exist. There were plenty of other women to distract him; relationships born out of lust.

He sighed and turned towards the window. Outside in the paddock was one of his real loves, his horse, Sebi. The other one was laid out on the floor.

'Women, eh dog? Who needs them?'

Blaize wagged his tail, thumping it against the floor, his large head on one side as he listened keenly. His master's secrets were safe with him.

'My goodness, what a beautiful horse!' Sian put the full wheelbarrow to one side and walked over to the gate. Helen joined her. 'Reminds me of Bracken. She used to carry her head like that.'

'Yes, he does a bit. He's the only really valuable animal we've got here. Must be worth quite a few thousand.'

Sian rested her arms on the top rail and squinted into the sun. She smiled.

'What is he? Hanoverian?'

'Yes, he's from a really good German line. His full name is Sebastian Prince but we all call him Sebi.'

'Who owns him?'

'Andrew.'

'He's very big.'

'Yes, 16.3 hands with nine and a half inches of bone, and this season he's covered quite a few mares. Very popular is our Sebi — just like his owner.'

The horse ambled over like a large black JCB, his glassy coat shining in the sun. Ears forward and enquiring, he looked at them both with intelligent brown eyes. Sian held out her hand in encouragement. He put his massive head over the top rung and stretched out towards them. Helen patted his well-muscled neck.

'Good boy, Sebi. Good boy.'

The horse ignored her. It seemed Sian was more interesting. He snorted at her and then blew through his black velvety nostrils into her face.

'You're honoured,' remarked Helen. 'He's very fussy who he likes and dislikes. Mostly he just ignores strangers, but with you . . .'

Sian stroked his forehead. 'I suppose only Andrew rides him?'

'Pretty much. He's a bit of a handful and very strong, as you can imagine. It takes someone of Andrew's size to control him when he's out hacking. I've been on him a couple of times and he really is something else. Makes the rest of the horses feel like donkeys.'

'Well, I don't suppose I'll ever get to ride him.'

'Why not? You're an experienced rider. I don't see why you couldn't. Haven't you been riding at all lately? What about Bracken?'

'I just haven't had the time.'

'But you still own her, don't you?'

Sian nodded.

'Well, why don't you bring her here? I'm sure Andrew wouldn't mind, and if you're going to stay here, it makes sense, doesn't it?'

'You know,' said Sian smiling, 'I think I will.'

Andrew watched them from the window. They couldn't

see him because of the angle of the gate to the house but he could see Sian perfectly, and it was only her he wanted to see.

Memories – powerful, unwanted, unheeded – began to flood back. This is stupid, he told himself. Sian's nothing like her. It's just the hair, that's all; the same thick red hair.

He shut his eyes and rested his head against the cool of the windowpane. The ghosts never seemed to leave him for long. Now she had arrived, it would start all over again, just when he thought he had got over it.

'Enough!' he told himself sternly, and he turned his back to the window. He wouldn't allow this. He couldn't afford to. He sat down and idly shuffled some papers. Keep a lid on it, he thought, don't think about it. Bury it, forget about it. That's what he had to do. It was the only thing he could do. Perhaps he should ring one of the many new people he had met over the last few years and arrange an evening out. It would certainly be a way of forgetting everything. But he knew he couldn't. One glance at the telephone and the dead weight of certainty told him he was wasting his time. Then he heard a high-pitched laugh and standing up again, he looked back out of the window.

He watched Sian as she stood in the sunshine, red-gold hair, thick and luxurious, blown about her delicate head like an auburn halo. As she laughed, the gentle moorland breeze carried the musical sound across to him, soothing him, calming him.

He abruptly turned away. Business.

'What's that building up there? That large grey one on the side of the hill with all those trees around it?'

Sian and Helen were sweeping the yard, brushes in hand and a pile of sodden straw and dung in front of them.

Helen looked up and shaded her eyes. 'That's The Grange, Andrew's place. Rather romantic, don't you think?'

'He owns that? Good heavens! He doesn't look like someone who owns a castle. I never would have believed it unless you told me.'

'Yes, well, he's a man of mystery is our Andrew. God knows how he ever managed to afford that place. It must have cost a bomb. He moved there last year. Before that it had been empty for years. Damned near derelict by all accounts. These stables,' she said, waving an arm around, 'and most of the land that isn't moorland, from here up to The Grange, belongs to Andrew. Quite something, eh?'

'You're telling me.'

Andrew came out of the cottage.

'Speaking of the devil,' muttered Helen, 'here he comes. Look lively.'

He walked up to them in long strides. 'Have you shown Sian around, Helen?'

He stood with his hands on his hips, the top buttons of his black polo shirt undone.

'Yes,' replied Helen indignantly.

'Then stop gossiping and go and help Eck get the horses in. The trekkers will be here soon,' and he marched back off to the cottage, his dog at his heels.

Helen watched him go.

'He's just so . . . delightful, isn't he, dear?'

Sian didn't answer. She didn't dare to. She felt like an open book: one false move and Helen would know everything.

'Come on then,' urged Helen, 'let's go and see where that other genetic misfit has got to.'

They met Eck down at one of the paddocks, leading out five horses.

'Plods,' said Helen. 'Slow, stupid and totally bomb proof. Just like Eck here.'

Eck grinned sheepishly. He wasn't at all upset by Helen's remarks. He disappeared up the yard, the five horses following obediently.

'We pick them up from auctions, private sales and

occasionally breeders,' explained Helen, shutting the gate behind them and handing Sian some head collars. 'They've got to be really safe otherwise we'd end up with some grockle breaking his neck and suing us.'

She walked over to a large sleepy animal resting with a back hoof off the ground. She slipped the collar over its head.

'Couldn't gallop at all unless you stuck a stick of dynamite up their backsides,' she added, smiling.

Sian tried to get a chestnut's head up to put the collar on. It was determined she wouldn't.

'Stubborn bugger, that one,' called Helen. 'Just hold out your hand as if you had a mint. It will do anything for food,' and the horse duly obliged.

They led their charges up into the yard where they got to work grooming. Helen handed Sian a dandy brush.

'You take that grey Charlie and I'll take this black bastard Mohawk. Don't worry if they're not perfectly clean. They get done every morning.'

In no time at all Sian was sweating, perspiration gathering along her hairline and running down her back. She stopped for a minute and leant against Charlie who dozed on regardless.

'Hot work, isn't it?' said Helen.

'Sure is. I shall have aches and pains in muscles I had forgotten existed. It's been so long since I did this.'

When the animals were done, Helen inspected Sian's work.

'Mmm,' she said, picking a small piece of grass off one of the horses. She turned to Sian. 'It's like cycling, really. You never forget how to do it once you've learnt.' She looked at her watch. 'The grockles will be here soon and they don't like to be kept waiting.'

Eck appeared carrying four saddles. He gave two to Helen. They were just fixing the animals' girths when Andrew appeared, looking serious, frown lines across his forehead. He came straight to Sian.

'We will have to leave soon so you'd better come in and hear about your hours and pay.'

Sian passed a backward glance to Helen as she followed him across the yard. He went into the cottage first and held the door open for her.

The interior was cool and dark after the sunlit yard and it took Sian a while to adjust to the dimness. There was a faint aroma of leather and coffee. Some green waxed jackets hung in the narrow hallway and a pile of dirty wellingtons littered the floor. There were a few framed photographs of horses on the walls, along with rosettes. He led her into the study at the end of the short corridor. Blaize immediately came over and sniffed her. She stroked his large head.

'Very nice dog,' Sian remarked. 'You're a handsome animal, Blaize, aren't you?'

The dog grinned and licked her hand.

'Right,' interrupted Andrew gruffly, 'perhaps we can get on?'

She stopped stroking the dog, suddenly aware that she was being told off. His gaze swept over her, compounding her discomfort. She looked straight at him. He wasn't going to intimidate her.

He turned and faced the window, the sun silhouetting him against the light. One hand held the other behind his back. Sian looked around the room: a paper-strewn desk, his large chair, a filing cabinet, some books and more pictures of horses. There was all kinds of office equipment but nothing personal, no photographs or anything like that, and she wondered why. Maybe he kept such things only at The Grange.

'Right,' Andrew said briskly, turning round, 'you'll work eight to twelve, six days a week with Sunday off. The rate of pay is £3.25 an hour and I expect my staff to be conscientious and diligent. Any questions?' and he fixed her with a penetrating gaze.

'No.'

She didn't understand why he was being so abrupt with her, but she was determined to match his attitude with one of her own. She didn't have to take this. Just a short time ago, she had been handing out the orders. Strange how it had all turned round.

'Good. Then we'll leave it at that.' He nodded towards the door. She was being summarily dismissed. 'Go back out to the yard and after Helen and I have left, Eck will show you what needs to be done, okay?'

'Yes.'

'And I expect I'll see you later.'

Not if she had anything to do with it he wouldn't. She wasn't at all sure she liked him now and it would make much more sense to stay out of his way. She left his office, conscious of his eyes watching her as she went down the short hallway. To hell with him she thought and all the rest of his sex. She slammed the door when she left.

Only after she had gone, did Andrew dare to relax. If he breathed deeply, he could still smell her lingering scent. It tantalized him. He knew he had been rude, but he must not soften in case the floodgates of still raw emotions opened.

'So? What did the almighty and insufferable pain in the butt have to say this time?' asked Helen.

Sian smiled ruefully. 'Hours and rate of pay, that's all.'

'Well, if they're anything like my conditions of employment, you won't exactly be rolling in it. Perhaps now you'll heed my advice and stay away from him?'

'Don't worry about that. As you might say, I wouldn't touch him even if I was wearing surgical gloves and carrying a ten-foot electrified cattle prod!'

Helen burst out laughing.

A noisy red Peugeot 205 pulled into the yard.

'Oh dear, here they are,' said Helen, turning round from the girth she was tightening. 'The Levi sisters, otherwise known as the more-money-than-sense brigade.'

60

Two young women, one dark, the other hairdresser blonde, wearing the tightest of tight jodhpurs over their vast thighs, and gold jewellery dangling from their necks, wrists and ears, giggled and bounced their way across the yard to Andrew's cottage. Sian and Helen watched them wiggle away with amusement.

Helen turned back to her horse. 'They've been chasing Andrew since they got here on Saturday,' and with a squeaky voice she did an imitation of them. ' "Hello, Mr Mann. Can we ride next to you, Mr Mann? You're such a good rider and we'll feel so much safer with you next to us." Yuck!' she spat. 'Makes you want to throw up!'

Sian watched them disappear into the cottage. She could hear the faint shrill of their laughter. Such empty, silly women, such meaningless flirtations. She smiled and laid a hand on her belly. She had other things to think of, things that were much more important.

She turned back to help Helen when she suddenly remembered that she hadn't asked whether she was being paid a week in hand or not.

'Helen, I'm just going to ask him something about my pay.'

'Okay, but don't be long. He doesn't like it if the horses aren't ready on time,' and she raised her eyes to heaven.

Sian went back to the cottage. The giggling was louder now. She hesitated in the hallway, not wanting to interrupt, but then thought better of it. After all, she did work here and she had to ask him, so without further preamble, she opened the door.

It was the linen cupboard all over again only not quite as bad. Andrew and one of the sisters were standing by the window entwined in each other's arms. They both turned and looked at her, dropping their hold.

'Yes?'

It was Andrew but Sian didn't hear him.

'Sorry. Doesn't matter. Another time,' and she quickly withdrew, memories, humiliation and embarrassment all crowding in on her. She ran out into the yard, her face burning hot, and scooted over to the tack room where she hid in the musty darkness, taking deep breaths to try to control herself. Her eyes stung with tears and then unable to hold back, she started to cry.

'Stupid woman!' she ranted quietly, angrily wiping away her tears. 'You stupid bloody woman. Don't you ever learn?' but the question remained unanswered.

Three

Trainer and owner stood side by side, intent on watching the three Thoroughbred horses through their binoculars.

'What do you think, Mr Killington?'

'Mmm, looking better. Especially that one on the outside. He's really striding out well.'

'Phantom,' said the trainer. 'By far and away the best of your two-year-olds.'

The horses thundered past in the early morning mist, nostrils flaring, legs a blur, their jockeys crouched above their backs holding the reins firmly. The trainer put down his binoculars.

'I'd say he was in the best possible condition for the Dewhurst at Newmarket in October or possibly something before that. As you can see, he pulls hard and invariably fights for his head, but as long as he's held up behind the others and comes off the pace in the last furlong, there's no reason why he shouldn't win.'

'What's the competition like?'

'Good. The best. They're all group one winners.'

'And the money?'

'Excellent. Ninety-seven thousand.'

'Even better. Almost makes the sport of kings worthwhile, don't you think?'

The trainer remained professionally nonchalant. A number of owners at his yard had given up keeping horses because of the poor returns on their investments, but not Killington. His string had grown and grown, and now, apart from some Middle Eastern owners, he was one of the largest. Phantom, among the best of his colts, a coal-black

63

animal with an uncertain temperament, was almost an equine version of his owner.

The trainer glanced at Marcus Killington as the other man stared through his binoculars. Tall, dark and powerful, with hard brown eyes, black hair and an overwhelming physical presence, he was handsome in a brooding and dangerous way, at least that's what some of the girls at the stable said. The trainer thought he wouldn't want any of his daughters getting involved with such an individual, even if Killington was reputed to be one of the richest, if most secretive, men in the country.

'Right,' said Marcus suddenly, giving the trainer one of his infrequent half-smiles, 'I think we'll go for it but we'll discuss it again. I'm going to be in Deauville next month looking at a new crop of yearlings so maybe I'll have a few more to my string. I'll let you know.'

'Okay.'

Marcus looked out across the gallops and smiled to himself. He breathed in a lungful of the crisp bright air. It pleased him to be here at Newmarket. It was such a long way from his miserable childhood with its half-remembered secrets. Even now, he hated going into pubs with their stale smell of beer and cigarettes. It was too much of a reminder of his stepfather. Being out in the fresh air; that's what he liked. That, and all the trappings of wealth.

'So, Mr Killington, you'll ring me in a few weeks and we'll discuss Phantom's first race.'

'What? Oh yes, Phantom.'

The trainer looked quizzically at him. 'Are you all right, Mr Killington?'

'Fine,' he said coldly, aware that he had been caught off guard. 'Goodbye,' and he walked briskly back to his Rolls-Royce where his driver was waiting for him. The door was opened and he got in, immediately setting to work on some papers he had to sign.

The driver started the engine.

'Any calls, Bains?'

'No, sir.'

Marcus looked unseeing out of the window. Camilla; why hadn't she called? Where was she? Maybe Patrick hadn't yet found her. Suddenly he was angry. Why did she taunt him? Why couldn't she see that it was only her best interests he was concerned about? His stepsister she may be, but that didn't give her the right to humiliate him publicly with other men, to parade and flaunt herself. She was a very wealthy woman in her own right and she had to be protected from fortune-hunters. She was beautiful though. Tall, slim, with an elfin face and the brightest of aquamarine eyes, she had spent two years working as a model but he had had to put a stop to that. Stories of her wild behaviour, the drugs, the drink, the parties; Marcus had heard it all. He might spend most of his time at his base in Oxford but he had his contacts and everyone had their price, even so-called 'boyfriends'. They all gave her away in the end. And now there was this latest one, a penniless French count. She had disappeared on one of her midnight flits which she so enjoyed for the sheer drama of it all, and the next thing he knew, she was in France and planning to get married. There was no way Marcus was going to have that. A large part of the family fortune was at stake and she wasn't going to throw it all away just because she thought she was in love. It was preposterous. But there was still no news and it worried him.

'Home, Bains, and be quick about it. I have a meeting to attend.'

'Yes, sir.'

Marcus looked back down at the document in his hands. He was worried. Someone, somewhere was betraying him, someone who knew his business secrets, and it was his intention to find out who it was.

The drive to Oxford was pleasant enough until they reached the tall wrought-iron gates of his mansion. There, parked around the entrance with their cameras and portable telephones, were the bane of Marcus's life: the paparazzi. As soon as they saw his car, they ran towards him, their cameras flashing.

'Damn.'

'Mr Killington! Mr Killington!' Bright lights flashed around the car as lenses were pointed at him. He squinted and hid his face. 'This way, Mr Killington! This way! Is it true about your sister? Mr Killington! Mr Killington!'

'Get out of here, Bains!'

'Sir.'

It could only mean one thing: Camilla was home.

The gates glided open and the car rushed through, a swarm of reporters with it. Marcus looked back through the window. He would get the dogs down here. They would soon sort things out.

Camilla was home. He smiled.

He was in a much better mood now – appreciative. Such a beautiful house, he thought, as his home slowly revealed itself through the avenue of trees. At first all he could see were the Doric columns of the porchway but then, in the early summer sunshine, its tall, rectangular many-paned windows sparkled, adding to the majesty of the large residence. In front were formal flowerbeds and neatly trimmed box hedges. Behind were baize-green lawns which sloped down to grey stone steps that finally reached the ornamental lake with its cascades of fountains and trails of weeping willows. There was even a flotilla of ducks. And all of it was surrounded by an estate of acres and acres of rolling Oxfordshire countryside. He even had tenant farmers to till and plough his soil. His castle, his private haven and he loved it. It was so far removed from all that he had known as a child and he had no intention of ever relinquishing it. The virus that had penetrated his organization had to be stopped.

The car pulled to a halt. Bains opened the door and Marcus got out. He glanced to one side and saw that all those he had summoned had arrived. Their helicopters were sitting on the lawns like a gathering of mechanical locusts. Then he turned and looked up at the huge house. Somewhere up there in one of those rooms was Camilla.

Camilla sat in her bedroom staring at her reflection in the mirror. She had been asleep, but only the sleep of chemicals, and it was difficult to come to. But she had to take them. It was the only way she could bear to face her stepbrother.

She yawned, too tired even to cover her mouth. Such a shame she thought, slowly blinking her drug-filled eyes. So beautiful, at least that's what Henri had said. She was the most beautiful woman in the world and all that he wanted and yet ... and yet, he went. Just like all the others. They all went and she knew why. That horrible nasty possessive stepbrother of hers. He was the one behind it all, clinging on to her as though he owned her.

She lit a cigarette, taking her time to make sure she did it properly. It was hard to concentrate when she had taken downers. Things didn't go the way they should. Fingers wouldn't go where she wanted them. Cigarettes wouldn't light. She burnt herself on the match, not realizing that she was still holding it.

'Ouch!' and she giggled at the silliness of it all. 'Clumsy!' she told herself. 'Always clumsy! Silly Camilla,' but her eyes didn't laugh.

She studied her face again. Twenty-five – or was that the number of men she had slept with? She frowned. No. It had to be more than that by now. But she couldn't remember and shook her head slowly, her thick glossy bob swinging around her fragile face. Thirty-five? Fifty-five? Who cared? She didn't. She had long gone past the stage of caring. Marcus had seen to that. And then she asked herself the same old question, the one she always asked when, yet again, he got her back where he wanted her. Why did she let him? What was it about her that let him control her so effectively?

'You're weak,' she told her reflection. 'Bloody weak, and you hate yourself, don't you? Fucking hate yourself.' She took an untidy swig of her vodka and tonic, spilling some of it down her silk kimono. 'Bloody Marcus. Bloody you. Too fucking stupid!' she yelled at herself. Then she burst into peals of childish laughter which stopped abruptly when she saw herself. She should be happy; she should be someone's wife by now with maybe even a baby. She should be doing all the things that ordinary women did but she didn't, couldn't. Always there was Marcus, the dam to her river, only letting her go when he approved of it.

She poured out another drink and held up her glass to her reflection.

'Here's to misery,' and she downed the lot in one.

The huge front door opened and Marcus handed his brief-case to Hildegard, his housekeeper, a German woman even taller and stronger than he was. She didn't smile when she saw him, her blue eyes guarded and her severe blonde chignon giving her already strong face an even more arid look.

'Good day, Herr Killington.'

'Hildegard. How is my mother?'

'As well as can be expected under the circumstances.'

'Good. And have all my associates arrived?' but he wasn't looking at her. He was looking up the wide sweeping staircase.

'Yes, Herr Killington. They are in the Green Room.'

'And Miss Camilla has returned?'

'Yes, sir. I think you will find her in her bedroom. She was most . . . exhausted after her trip from France, but Patrick will be able to tell you more.'

'Thank you. Coffee in the library, I think, and then tell my secretary to get things organized for the meeting. I will be about half an hour.'

'Yes, sir.'

Marcus strode purposefully across the marble-floored

68

hallway, with its vast ornate fireplace, its collection of armour standing against the wall, and swords displayed between the huge paintings of dogs, horses and landscapes. The biggest picture of all, however, was the one of the mansion's owner: proud and erect, his handsome face betraying a streak of cruelty, he looked down from on high, owner of all he surveyed.

He opened the library door. Patrick was standing by the window, his hands behind his back.

'Where did you find her, then?'

No hello. Just straight to the point. Patrick, six foot two, ex-Parachute Regiment and a face that bore all the scars of his tough life, answered just as matter-of-factly.

'Cap Ferrat. She was holed up in some apartment block that she had rented with her chap.'

Marcus sat at his massive walnut desk and began to look through some correspondence.

'Any difficulties?' he asked idly, scribbling down some notes for his secretary.

'The usual,' shrugged Patrick. He was tired after the journey from France and Camilla, with her scenes, never made things any easier.

'Meaning what?' Marcus stopped writing and looked at Patrick but the other man's face was impenetrable. He knew from experience to keep his opinions to himself.

There was a knock at the door.

'Come in.'

Hildegard appeared bearing a silver tray, coffee jug and cup and saucer. There was nothing for Patrick but then she always did ignore him. She placed the tray on the table and clicked back out of the room. Marcus poured himself a cup.

'You were saying, Patrick?'

Patrick looked at the tray. He could really do with a drink.

'She gets a bit upset, as you know, sir, but she calmed down after a while.'

69

'I can imagine. How did you get rid of the Count?'

Patrick reached for his inside pocket and threw some photographs down on the desk. They spread out across the polished wood, the obscene on the sublime.

Marcus raised an eyebrow. It was nothing he wasn't used to. Camilla was capable of anything when she put her mind to it.

'Just showed him these, sir. He didn't like it too much. Got all agitated, like, seeing Miss Camilla with another man. Started ranting and raving. God knows what he was saying.'

'So you didn't have to persuade him too hard?'

'Well, I did mention that if he came anywhere near her again, there might be a small accident. He seemed to understand that, sir.'

'Good.' Marcus gathered up the photographs and put them in a drawer. 'Any bother with the press this time?'

'No, sir. One of them did manage to get a snap of her but . . .' he grinned, showing a broken front tooth, 'but I think he'll have to be buying a new camera, sir. His ended up coming into contact with a wall.' Patrick's blue eyes shone.

Marcus allowed himself a small smile.

'Right then, you can go, but before you finish for the day, take the dogs up to the front gate and get rid of that scum that's hanging around.'

'Sir.' He marched away to do his master's bidding.

Marcus entered the double doors of the Green Room and viewed the assembled occupants with a cold yet satisfied eye. His employees didn't feel the same about him and one by one, as his eyes fell on them, they shifted uncomfortably in their gilt chairs. None liked to return his steady gaze.

Marcus went to the head of the long mahogany table and sat down. His secretary hurriedly placed a folder of papers in front of him and then sat to one side. Marcus didn't thank her but slowly arched his perfectly manicured fingers together before giving the audience a chilling smile.

'Gentlemen, I'm so glad you could all make it, although I see yet again that one of your number has not arrived.' He spoke to his secretary. 'I want to know what's happened to Eddy.'

'Yes, sir.'

There were mumbled greetings from the dozen who sat either side of the table.

'It pleases me to announce that once more, gentlemen, we are seeing an increase in our profits.' He smiled to them all. 'If you would care to look at the figures, you will see exactly how profitable we are.'

There was a shuffling of paper.

'As you can observe, with a kilo of cannabis resin costing between five hundred and one thousand pounds and selling for between eighty and one hundred per twenty-five grams here, that is roughly a mark up of two and a half to three thousand pounds for us. Ditto cocaine. We buy at ten to fifteen thousand per kilo and sell, depending on the purity – and I'm pleased to say that recently we seem to be getting much better stuff – at between forty and fifty per gram. A profit, gentlemen, of thirty to thirty-five thousand.' He paused and looked around the assembled gathering. They had come from all corners of the country for the meeting and it gave Marcus a tremendous sense of power to see how much authority he had over them. 'We are, of course, experiencing a small decline in the number of couriers who are willing to carry for us since all trading blocks were lifted in the EU but I don't see that this will be much of a problem.' He gave a relaxed laugh. 'Since when did a do-it-yourself dealer with a van load of beer to sell ever have the profits that we have? I don't see that we will have any problems recruiting replacements. After all, there are very many people who want to get into the UK. So, are we satisfied?'

'I have something to say,' piped up one of the relative youngsters, resplendent in pink striped shirt and hand-

71

made silk suit and looking for all the world like a respect-
able banker.

'Yes?'

'What about this new stuff, GBH?'

Marcus shrugged. 'Leave this designer stuff for the ama-
teurs. GBH, or gamma hydroxy-butyrate for those of you
who are unfamiliar with the name, is still not a proscribed
substance over here although in the States, it is.' He shook
his head. 'No, the profits are too small and it's too unstable.
People have died and that's not what we want, is it? Far
better to hook them and keep them than to lose them.'
Several of the older and more experienced men smiled to
themselves. 'Look at it this way, Charlie,' Marcus said to
the young man, 'if an infection kills its host, then it will
kill itself, won't it?'

Coffee was served, the men talked among themselves
and then the atmosphere changed, just like at the coming
of a storm.

'Gentlemen,' said Marcus solemnly, 'we have a problem;
a very serious one. One that could, if it's not dealt with,
severely undermine, if not cripple what we have taken so
long to build up.' He paused to relish the effect of his
words. 'It seems that one among us is not satisfied with
his lot.' There were more murmurs. 'So dissatisfied that
he's passing on information to those who could destroy
us. Gentlemen, we have a traitor.'

Several of the men frowned at one another.

'Who? When? What?' clamoured the voices, indignant
and outraged as all heads turned back to Marcus.

'When I find out, and believe me I will,' and he slowly
ran his fingers down the length of a pencil and then
snapped it in two, 'I . . . will . . . wipe . . . him . . . out
and I don't have to tell you what that will mean.' His dark
menacing eyes surveyed the room.

There was more hushed talk among his audience.
Marcus clicked his fingers at his secretary who jumped up
and poured him another coffee. There was silence as the

steam from the cup gently curled up in the warm, still air. Marcus took a sip.

'This traitor,' he announced levelly, 'cannot hope to remain undetected for long. It is dependent on all of us to do everything we can to winkle him out because, as you all know, an organization like ours will not survive unless we all pull together.' He took a pristine white hanky from his breast pocket and patted his sulky lips. He had shaved that morning but already his chin was blue with stubble. 'I have, have I not, gentlemen,' he continued, 'taken care of you after my stepfather died? I stepped into his shoes and built the business up to what it is today, advancing the ambitions of all of you so that now you are individually rich and successful men. This is why I find it so difficult to understand why one of you should be so ungrateful.' His gaze slowly circled the room, boring into each of them one by one. 'However, the traitor has been careless, attracted attention. His cover has been detected, but then that's the wonder of modern technology and –'

But suddenly Marcus stopped and spun round. The doors had been flung open and there stood Camilla, wearing only a pair of silk camiknickers underneath her kimono, and a pair of stiletto-heeled shoes. She was carrying a bottle of vodka in one hand and a cigarette in the other. She was gently swaying and smirking to herself.

'Oh deary, deary me,' she smiled, lips thick with scarlet gloss. 'Have I interrupted one of your meetings, darling Marcus?' and she tottered into the room, eyes veering around as she smiled at the assembly.

Some of the men audibly gasped. Marcus's jaw tightened. Her dishabille left little to anyone's imagination, and the erections alone could have supported the table.

She sashayed down the room, one breast visible as the material of her garment slipped, holding out her hand to the men, who despite themselves, smiled back.

'Hello, Michael, hello, James. And Steve, well, fancy seeing you here.' She turned back to the head of the table,

73

took a swig of her vodka and wiped the back of her hand across her mouth leaving a red weal of lipstick across her cheek. 'Marcus, you should have told me,' and she grinned aimlessly.

Marcus's secretary got to her feet.

'I wouldn't if I were you!' cried Camilla, her face suddenly hardening. The secretary, an efficient and prudish woman, halted in her tracks, unable and unwilling to take on Camilla.

'You know,' said Camilla with relish as she looked the woman up and down, 'I always thought green suited you better. It would go with your pasty complexion,' and she laughed to herself. 'Oh by the way,' she added, 'did my darling brother tell you he's bought an extra large horse?'

The secretary turned to her boss. 'Mr Killington –'

'It's all right, Veronica,' he said darkly, 'I'll deal with this.'

'He didn't?' expounded Camilla, screeching. 'Then you won't know there's now something in the stable strong enough to take your weight,' and she laughed cruelly again.

Marcus pressed a button on his desk. Camilla saw it but it didn't frighten her.

'Fuck you, Marcus,' she sneered and ambled over to the young man who was sitting nearest. She stood as close to him as she could, pressing herself up against him so that his face was buried in her voluptuous breasts. The other men sweated, loosening ties and staring. She was tantalizing.

'You like that?' she asked, her voice dripping with sex. All the time she watched Marcus. His eyes met hers, challenging. The room became silent. No one moved.

Then: 'Please, miss –'

She pressed the young man's head tighter against her flesh. 'Feel that,' she whispered. 'It's wonderful, don't you think? Wouldn't you like something like that to fuck each

74

night instead of your pallid little girlfriend?' and she leant back and cackled. 'I bet she couldn't do half the things I can.'

The door opened. It was Patrick. Marcus and he exchanged a brief glance and the game was over. The ex-soldier marched down the room, grabbed Camilla around the waist and bodily carried her out while she screamed and yelled and rained continuous blows on him.

'You fucking bastard! You fucking, fucking bastard!' but he ignored her.

The doors were shut behind them and Marcus smiled as her screams faded away.

'Children,' he said. 'They will have their little games, won't they?' He looked down at his paperwork. 'Now, gentlemen, where was I?' and the young man who had been imprisoned in the sexiest and most frightening embrace of his life, sighed with relief and wiped away the sweat on his brow.

Afterwards, as the gathering left for their helicopters, one of the older men took the younger one to one side and, in a fatherly way, put his arm around the other's shoulder.

'Liked that, did you,' he said smiling, 'the way she rubbed your nose in it?'

The young man smiled nervously and licked his lips. 'A bit,' he admitted, and then, realizing that no one could overhear them added, 'God, she's something else. I could have that morning, noon and night.'

The older one smiled. 'Do you know what happened to the last one of us who tried that with her?'

The younger one frowned. 'No.'

'Exactly,' replied his colleague, 'and neither do we.'

Hildegard was sitting with old Mrs Killington in her apartment watching her feed snippets of smoked salmon to her over-indulged Yorkshire terrier, Sabre.

'So she's back then?' said the old woman, her words

hissing slightly because since the beginning of her illness, her dentures didn't fit properly. She eyed Hildegard with small, greedy eyes, her nonexistent lips pulled together like a tightly drawn purse string.

'Yes, Frau Killington. Miss Camilla has returned.'

'Bleeding hell! That means chaos will be let loose. God knows why he puts up with her. Why the hell he just can't let her go and marry one of those men, I don't know. After all, she's had enough of them. There can't be a man left in Europe she hasn't had.'

Her voice lost its hard edge as she fed some more salmon to her dog. 'Here you are, Sabre,' she cooed. 'Does my darling boy want some more?' and the dog snapped it up, just missing one of her wrinkled fingers.

'You know,' she continued, 'that Camilla is just like her mother. She was the town tart as well. See, runs in the blood, Hilde, runs in the blood,' and she nodded her shrunken white head.

'Yes, Frau Killington.'

Hildegard valued her job too much and was, in any case, far too discreet to ask what else ran in the blood.

Marcus was about to ring his bank in Switzerland when the door crashed open and there stood Camilla. She waved at him with an exaggerated flourish.

'Well, well, if it isn't the mighty, the glorious, the magnificent all-time fucking bastard, my stepbrother, Marcus.' She almost fell into the room. 'You did rather ask for that little scene, didn't you? Been having fun at my expense again, haven't you? Been messing about with my life again where it's none of your fucking business, haven't you, you bastard?'

She had now almost reached him, her eyes glittering with emotion and a heady cocktail of drugs. She took a swig out of the bottle, nearly missed and sent a fountain of the liquid down her already stained kimono.

'Go back to your room,' he said without looking up.

'Ooops! Silly me!' she giggled. 'I spilt my drink all down my front and onto your very expensive, hand-woven carpet. Oh dear, what a shame,' and she pulled an apologetic face, all fat lips and girlish winsomeness. 'Shall I pour some more on it, Marcus, really ruin it, 'cos then you'll have to buy another one, won't you? Then you'll have to go and spend some more of your millions and show the world what a big man you are.' She made as if to tip the bottle up, all the time watching him, waiting to see if he would react. She smiled and tapped some cigarette ash onto the carpet instead. Her hand went to her mouth. 'Oh dear. Now look what I've done.'

'Camilla, you're drunk.'

'My goodness!' she exclaimed with mock horror. 'You mean you've only just noticed? Well, I am amazed. Such perception! Such powers of deduction!' She turned away and then, with all the rage of her being, she spun back and threw the half-empty bottle at him. It flew past his head and crashed into the wall, spilling vodka down the plaster work and across some rare seventeenth-century books.

'Fuck you, you bastard!'

Marcus rose to his feet, his eyes as black as his mood, his violence about to surface. After the humiliation of the meeting, she had gone too far and he had had enough. He came to stand in front of her.

'You will leave this room, Camilla, go to your apartment and stay there until you have recovered your good manners and then, when you have sobered up and changed your clothes, you will come back here and clean this mess up, after which you will apologize to me. Understand? What happened today was disgraceful and I won't have it and if it ever happens again, you will surely live to regret it!'

'Oh yeah?' she laughed defiantly. 'And what will you do about it, eh? Spank me like a naughty little girl? But then you'd like that, wouldn't you, you pervert?'

'I'm warning you –'

She spat at him, the globule of spittle running down his cheek. For a moment nothing happened. The air positively shimmered with anger. Then he hit her, a backhander so powerful that it knocked her off her feet and sent her tumbling across the floor, her hand to her mouth.

She whimpered but didn't move. He said nothing, only the slight heave of his shoulders giving away his inner turmoil and a vein throbbing in his neck.

'Get out,' he said eventually, turning his back on her. 'You're making a fool of yourself.'

He did not see the look of utter hatred she gave him as she struggled to her feet.

Four

Sian stood in the junk shop browsing through a table covered with bric-a-brac. She was looking for something to go on the dressing table back at the cottage. She liked having personal things around her and for that reason missed the hotel, where she had a veritable gallery of stuff all over the walls and covering all the spare windowsills and shelves. Mainly she collected small china pieces — nothing especially valuable, just things that caught her eye.

There didn't seem to be anything to suit her on the table. The choice wasn't especially good and no matter how much the owner of the shop kept glancing at her with a hopeful expression, she didn't feel the need to buy any of his wares. Newton Abbot was a reasonable sized town and she felt sure that on this, her afternoon off, she could find refuge from the sweltering sun in another such place.

She turned away and let her gaze fall on a book shelf. There was the usual collection of motley old titles, long out of print, and among the musty spines she saw nothing exciting until her eye fell on something rather unusual. It was small, unobtrusive and, if she hadn't taken a second look, she would have missed it altogether. She took it off the shelf and looked at it. On the front, in spidery hand-writing, she read, 'Isobel Warrener, A Journal'.

Intrigued, she opened up the slim volume with its slight burn marks around the edges and took a closer look, and there, on the flyleaf, was something that really interested her. It was an ink drawing of The Grange. Not an exact picture because the place seemed to have been bigger then, with what looked like an extra wing, but it was definitely The Grange.

'How much?' she asked the proprietor, holding up the book.

The old man smiled kindly, took off his glasses and gave them a wipe. She handed him the book. 'That's an interesting one you've picked out,' he said turning it over in his hand. 'The Grange is a well-known house around these parts. The lady that wrote this used to live there.'

'So I gather. Do you know anything about her or her family?'

He shook his grey head slowly. 'No,' he answered. 'It all happened a long time ago now.'

'What did?'

'Oh,' he said looking up, 'the fire, you know.' He opened the book and pointed out where it was damaged at the back. 'As you can see, it's not all here. Some of it must have been destroyed.'

She looked to where he was pointing. 'I see. And do you know anything else about the place? The family? What they were like?'

His brow puckered as he concentrated. 'Not really,' he answered at length. 'It was a bit of a to-do by all accounts but, well, you know, people in those days kept things more to themselves than they do now so I can't really tell you anything. There were rumours, of course, but like I say, things were hushed up. I do know though, that the old man Warrener were alive until a few years back.'

'Really?'

'Dead now, though.'

'Oh.' Sian was disappointed. The prospect of finding out something really positive about the place and its owners had seemed suddenly really important, but if they were all gone . . .

'Well, never mind,' she said. 'I expect I'll find out any exciting family scandal by reading this.'

'Oh no, dear,' he said. 'I've read bits of it and there's

not much in there, you know. Hints, of course, but then it being a diary, a person's most private thoughts need not be fully explained. People have said all sorts about The Grange over the years; how it's supposed to have all this hidden treasure and so forth . . .'

'Hidden treasure?' Sian gave a small laugh. 'Surely not?'

'Yes, but I don't think so. Lot of old nonsense, if you ask me. Just the sort of stuff folks gossip about when there's nothing else of interest. Local legends and no more.' The man took a paper bag and slipped the book into it. 'That will be, what shall we say, a fiver?'

'Okay.'

'And remember,' he said as she went to leave, 'it's just a fairy tale really. There's nothing up there but a load of old ghosts,' and his eyes twinkled over the top of his glasses.

It was even hotter out in the street. Pedestrians were wilting in the sun, even fanning themselves. Sian decided to find herself a cool place and sit down to read her new acquisition. She wandered off down the high street, straw hat and new sunglasses keeping the sun off her. It was then she saw Andrew.

He was walking on the other side of the street, absorbed, concentrating. His eyes were seemingly fixed to the pavement in front of him as he marched along, oblivious to anything around him. Sian was behind and on the opposite side of the road, and, for some perverse reason, decided to see where he was going. She had nothing better to do.

For about fifty yards she followed him along, observing other women's reactions to him. It made her smile the way old, young and middle-aged, they all seemed to notice the handsome blond with his long purposeful strides and determined manner. But he didn't see any of it. Neither did he go into any shops or window gaze.

When he did finally slow down and mount some steps, Sian could see why he was so thoughtful. So would she be if she were going there. It was the bank.

'Hello. My name is Andrew Mann. I have an appointment with Mr Kendall.'

The bank teller smiled and indicated a chair. 'Would you like to sit down, Mr Mann? Mr Kendall will be with you in a minute.'

He sat but he didn't want to. He wanted to go home, to be out of this place. Despite the number of times he had been here in recent months, his stomach was in knots. Partly because it was his natural inclination to dislike any kind of authority, especially one that stood in the way of his business, and partly it was because he was perilously close to the edge. He was here to plead one last extension to his overdraft; to try to make his bank manager, a man who ordinarily he would liked to have shared a drink with, understand that everything depended on his letting Andrew go a while longer until he turned the corner and the business started to make money.

He sighed and sat forward in the chair so that his shirt didn't stick to his back. Damned bankers and their bloody bits of paper, he thought. He had heard all their arguments, all their reasons and all their options, but they just didn't understand. His business and The Grange were all he had left. He had to make the stables work; he couldn't afford not to. Kendall would have to be made to listen, just this one last time.

'Mr Mann?'

Andrew looked up as a hand was extended in his direction.

'Come in, Mr Mann. Hot, isn't it?'

Andrew smiled briefly and as he walked into the manager's office he wondered if walking into a lion's den would be a more attractive alternative.

'I'm sorry, Mr Mann, but any way you look at it, you really are in an impossible position. I mean, consider it from our point of view.'

Andrew ran his hand tiredly through his damp hair. He

had been in Kendall's office for what seemed an age and they were getting nowhere. They were going round and round in circles and still they hadn't found any solution. Whatever he suggested, Kendall came back with a negative response. The situation was looking hopeless and the longer it went on, the hotter and more irritable they were both getting.

'So you're telling me I have no alternative but to sell up? Is that what you're saying?'

Mr Kendall, a corpulent man in his forties, smiled wearily. He had heard it all so many times before and it still wasn't any easier despite his years in the job. As much as he would like to help all his customers, there came a time when there was nothing more to be done.

'Basically, yes.'

Andrew uncrossed his legs, stood up and walked away from the desk. Mr Kendall watched him passively.

'I'm sorry, Mr Mann, but really there is little more I or the bank can do when you have both an overdraft and unpaid loans. You have got to be able to service your loans and at the moment, that doesn't seem feasible. We cannot lend you any more. All I can give you is a bit longer for you to decide either to sell up or find someone to bail you out.'

Andrew faced him, hands in pockets, a resigned expression on his tanned angular face.

'That's it then?'

'I'm afraid so. I can give you six months, no more.'

'What happens after that?'

Mr Kendall sighed. This was the one thing he hated saying more than any other. 'We will have to repossess. I'm sorry.'

'No, I am.'

When Andrew left the bank, demoralized and depressed, he had no idea of where he was going or what he had to do. He wasn't a loser, he knew that, but why it was that fate kept turning things against him he had no idea. He had fought so hard to get where he was. Everything he had now had been got by the sweat of his brow and his determination to see things through. It all seemed so unfair that just when he thought he had seen the back of his troubles, this should happen.

He walked down the street, ignoring everything with only one word going through his mind: repossession.

Sian was sitting in a pub garden underneath an umbrella. Nearby there was a stream and she was enjoying the babbling of the cool water over mossy stones and the jerky flight of dragonflies and other insects as they darted and swooped in the sunlight.

It was too hot to do anything except doze quietly behind her sunglasses and her new book remained unread on her lap. It was good to be here, to be able to enjoy the summer afternoon with young children running around in their noisy games and all the talk and noise of the distant traffic melting together in a hum.

She finished her orange juice and lemonade, glanced at her watch and decided she would have another one. She got up and went into the pub.

The long dark wooden bar, so cool after the heat of outdoors, welcomed her with cigarette smoke and the thump of a juke box. As she stood waiting her turn, she glanced around. At first she didn't see him because of the dimness after the bright sunlight and because she was wearing her sunglasses, but then her eyes became accustomed to the gloom. There he sat, long legs stretched out in front of him, arms folded across his chest with an almost melancholy look on his face. Andrew.

She hesitated, not knowing if she should or shouldn't.

'Yes, miss?'

'Oh, um, another orange juice and lemonade, please, with ice.'

'Of course. You need it in this weather, don't you?' smiled the painted landlady.

Sian's drink was handed back to her along with her change. She turned round, expecting to walk over to Andrew, but he had gone and on the table stood his half-finished pint of beer.

'Oh.'

'Something wrong, dear?' asked the landlady.

'No, nothing. I just thought I'd ... well, it doesn't matter.'

Sian left the cool interior and went back out into the garden. Maybe he hadn't seen her after all or maybe, she hesitated to think, he didn't want to see her.

She sat down at her table and thought about him. He looked so lost, so unhappy ... And then she smiled at herself. She must be getting soft or something. She had no reason to feel sorry for him, though in her heart of hearts, she couldn't help it. He looked so alone, so hurt, and no one, however brusque they had been to her, deserved to be like that.

Andrew walked briskly back to his Land Rover. Sian? What the hell had she been doing there? She was the last person he wanted to see, especially now.

He opened the door and the heat hit him. He jumped in and wound down all the windows. He then sat back against the hot leather, closed his eyes and breathed deep.

'Sod it!'

Everything was going wrong and on top of it all, she was there with the face, body and soul he found so hard to resist. But he couldn't allow himself to get carried away. If he had spoken to her back there in the pub, God knows where it all would have ended and he didn't want that, not at a time when he was under such pressure.

It was no good, he told himself. This was not the time for sentimentality. He had to think straight. He had to get it all sorted out. Then and only then, could he relax.

And so, with heavy heart, he started up his vehicle and drove away, determined to put as far between himself and her as he could.

Five

'Is Camilla ready yet, Hildegard?'

Marcus turned from the huge rococo mirror and glowered at his housekeeper. Hildegard descended the last two stairs with her usual stately carriage.

'I do not know, Herr Killington. I could go and look if you like?'

He gave a barely perceptible nod and then turned back to the mirror to check his tie.

'Do it, and tell her I'm getting impatient.'

'Yes, Herr Killington.'

Hildegard reached Camilla's door and knocked loudly. She was well aware of Camilla's habit of taking pills to sleep and then having to take pills to wake up. There was no reply so she knocked again.

'Yes?' came the faint reply.

Hildegard tried to open the door but couldn't.

'The door, Fräulein. It is locked.'

There was a laugh from inside. 'Tough titty.'

'Open the door, Fräulein. Please. Or Herr Killington will come and get you and I do not want that.'

There were footsteps, a click and the door opened. Hildegard felt relieved. The last thing she wanted was any more ugly scenes. She didn't like having to use psychological warfare, but sometimes it was a necessary evil when dealing with this capricious young woman.

'There, satisfied now?' pouted Camilla, flouncing away in her nightie. She was unwashed, her hair unkempt and she had no makeup on. Hildegard watched her, unmoved by the petulance. She was well used to it by now.

'Your brother is waiting for you downstairs. He is getting impatient.'

Camilla swayed over to her dressing table, its top littered with potions and perfumes, pills and powders. She poured herself a drink. She had no inclination for self-constraint.

'Screw him,' she said sullenly. 'He can wait,' and she watched Hildegard's reflection in the mirror, waiting to see what the big woman would do now.

Hildegard was not going to be dragged into yet another one of Camilla's temper tantrums and chose instead to start clearing up the mess. She bent down and picked up discarded clothes, all expensive, designer items that Camilla treated with the utmost casual contempt. Hildegard adored good clothes and hated to see Camilla's disregard for them.

'I will run your bath,' she said, disappearing into the *en suite* bathroom.

'I don't want one. I'm not going anywhere, least of all down to Devon, of all places. Might as well go to the far side of the universe.'

Hildegard appeared at the doorway, her mouth set.

'You are going, Fräulein, because your brother has said so and we are not going to argue about it. Now,' she said rolling up her sleeves, 'get undressed.'

Camilla stood up and let her wrap fall to the floor. She was naked, but that wasn't what Hildegard saw. It was the bruises. Her eyes flickered back up to Camilla's face. The woman was smiling.

'There's no need to look so surprised,' and she walked past into the bathroom.

'Do we have to go to Devon, Marcus?' Camilla's voice was plaintive, childish even. Already they were well on the way, the powerful Rolls devouring the miles.

He stopped his tape recorder and laid it down on his lap. He smiled tightly. 'Yes, my dear. Business.'

'Business, business,' she echoed, sighing heavily and helping herself to a Scotch. She drank greedily and then poured another. 'Always fucking business,' she continued with a sneer. 'It's all you're interested in, isn't it, dear brother, that and your precious racehorses?'

Marcus firmly took the glass out of her hand, finished the drink and then put the bottle and glass away.

'No more, I think,' and he resumed his work.

Camilla lunged at him, her hands flying wildly.

'Don't you bloody well tell me what to do, you pig! I'm not one of your employees and if I want a drink, I'll bloody well have one!'

Marcus patiently put his work aside and with all the ease of an elephant swatting an irritating fly, took hold of her delicate wrists in his vice-like grip.

'Stop it, Camilla. We don't want another drunken exhibition, do we?'

He didn't like raising his voice. He took it as a sign of weakness. Emotional outbursts of the kind Camilla employed embarrassed him. So much better to be self-controlled. A steel hand in a velvet glove had always been his preferred style.

She sat limply. Fighting would be useless. His strength far outweighed hers. He squeezed her wrists even tighter, his knuckles white, his heavy gold signet ring digging into her flesh.

'Ow!' she whined, her face contorting. 'You're hurting me!'

Bains ignored them.

'Now listen to me,' Marcus said hoarsely through clenched teeth, his eyes flaming. 'We will have no more of these immature little outbursts, will we?' and he bent her wrist backwards.

She glared at him. The pain was excruciating.

'You will behave yourself,' he continued, his voice lowering, each word laden with a threat. 'Just one more of these temper tantrums and I will get really angry. Do you hear me? Just one more and I don't have to tell you what might happen, do I?'

His face was inches from her own, his spittle hitting her skin.

'Please, Marcus . . . please . . . you're hurting me!'

'Promise me, Camilla?'

She couldn't reply. The pain was so great. She nodded wordlessly.

'I didn't hear that.'

'Yes . . . yes . . . ! I promise! I promise!'

He threw her back into the seat with utter contempt, a dishevelled heap, slumped and miserable. He then rearranged his tie, swivelled his ring round and sat back. Everything was as it should be. He resumed his work, Camilla unheeded and unnoticed by his side.

Coming up to Exeter along the M5, she spoke.

'I need to stop, Marcus.' It was the first thing she had said in over an hour.

Without looking up from his papers he said, 'Pull in at the service station, Bains.'

'Sir.'

The place was packed. Tourists, their children, caravans, cars.

'Over there, Bains, away from all this rabble.'

The car pulled to a stop.

'Five minutes, Camilla. We're late as it is.'

She snatched up her bag and flounced out of the car. If Bains hadn't opened the door for her, she would have slammed it in Marcus's face. Anything to wipe away that supercilious look.

Once in the ladies', Camilla locked herself in a cubicle, opened her handbag and took out a small plastic bag full of white powder. It was her saviour, her sanctuary. If there was to be no man in her life, then she would have this. It never let her down.

She emptied a small amount onto a vanity mirror, shaped it into a line and then sniffed it up through a silver tube, a good deep snort in each nostril.

She shut her eyes and relaxed. The hit was instantaneous. Everything became easy again. She could cope with it all. None of it mattered. The pain went away and then she laughed quietly. Good old Marcus. He did have his virtues after all and a regular supply of cocaine was one of them.

When she got back to the car, Bains was leaning against the door smoking a cigarette. Marcus was still working. He didn't say anything until she had settled down.

'Next time don't keep me waiting so long, Camilla. Unlike you, I have a tight schedule.'

She ignored him.

They arrived at the Stoneygates Hotel mid-afternoon. Eddy was nowhere to be seen when Marcus marched into the foyer. Marcus didn't like that. It showed disrespect and he expected his managers to be ready and waiting when their boss called.

He fixed the receptionist with an icy glare.

'Killington. Where's your manager?'

The woman glanced nervously from him to Camilla to Bains, who followed in with the luggage.

'I'll get him at once, sir.'

'Do it!' he snapped.

She smiled briefly and turned to her companion who was manning the switchboard.

'Mr Williamson?' she asked hopefully, with panic in her eyes.

Her colleague shrugged. No one had seen him since lunchtime. The first receptionist turned back to Marcus.

'Perhaps you would like to go through to the lounge, sir, while we find Mr Williamson?'

Please go and sit, she thought, please. We haven't a clue where Eddy is.

Marcus paused, eyeing the woman up and down. He made it an unwritten rule that only the most attractive female staff were to serve as receptionists. He was glad to see that Eddy's were more than up to standard. The young

91

woman blushed. She found such close scrutiny unnerving.

'No, I think not. I've spent long enough sitting down today. I think I'll go and look round the kitchens. An unannounced inspection always gives a much truer picture, don't you think?'

The receptionist could only agree.

He moved purposefully off and disappeared behind a swing door marked 'Staff Only'. With him out of the way, all relaxed.

'My room key,' demanded Camilla holding out her hand and clicking her fingers. She had no intention of going anywhere except to bed. Suddenly she had a ferocious headache.

'Yes, madam.'

Without a thank you, Camilla disappeared into the lift. She didn't wait for Bains, who was left standing with all the luggage and the stairs to negotiate.

Fingers touched tip to tip.

'I love you, Eddy.'

He said nothing. He couldn't. In the dimness of the warm, musky bedroom, the afternoon light peeking in between the drawn curtains, he stood in silence, beads of sweat tingling down his naked spine and his eyes fixed on Rowena's fleshy body. His heart pounded. She was everything he desired: firm, bold, lavish, and all his. Each part of her — her luscious breasts, her slender waist and her rounded and smooth thighs — invited him onwards.

'Do you want me?' she asked huskily, watching him through half-closed eyes, her lips moist. She put a hand on each of his shoulders and pulled him towards her. 'How much do you want me, Eddy? Show me.'

He needed no more words. Hungrily, he latched onto her, his greedy lips pressed hard against hers as his tongue probed inside her mouth. His hands, almost besides themselves, took handfuls of her flesh and kneaded it. He couldn't get enough of her and all the time the throbbing in his groin grew harder and more insistent.

'Rowena . . . Rowena . . .' He kissed her throat, her shoulders, her ears. 'Rowena,' he whispered through wet lips.

'This way, baby.' She took him by the hand and smiling in the half-light, led him to the bathroom. 'Let's shower.'

The cool water cascaded down on top of them as, entwined in each other's arms, they kissed and caressed. They knew each other well now. She knew how to tease him; how to entice and excite him. Ever eager, she sought to slow him down, to stop his enthusiasm getting the better of his technique.

'Stand still,' she ordered, rivulets of water running down her face and plastering her blonde hair to her skin like white patent leather. 'I'm going to do something for you,' and he sighed, anticipation heightening his desire. Down and down she went, touching, tasting, brushing and nibbling. Finally she was on her knees, the hard enamel of the bath pressing against her. It was then, faced with his engorged vermilion-tinged manhood, that she took it in both hands and very, very gently, eased it into her mouth.

He shuddered, a trembling running right through him and escaping as a languorous sigh. 'Oh . . . baby.' He held her head in both his hands, his fingers entwined in her hair. 'Rowena . . . Rowena . . .'

She held him loosely between her thumb and forefinger, pulling and retracting his stretched foreskin. Eyes closed, lips over her teeth, she let his scent fill her up as backwards and forwards she went, his muscles tightening beneath her touch. Then she started to go faster. Eddy, panting and breathless, opened his eyes and looked down. On the brink of exploding, her sudden halt had brought him crashing back to the present. He stared, bewildered at her. She stood up and smiled lazily.

'My turn,' she murmured, kissing him through the water's spray. She took his hand. He was shaking. Guiding him downwards, she homed in on the centre of her sex. His fingers slid against her swollen wetness. She sighed. 'Ah . . .'

She closed her eyes and leant back against the white tiled wall, hands outstretched, mouth open as he masturbated her.

He watched her intently, ignoring the water that ran into his eyes and blurred his vision. She never failed to amaze him the way she was so at one with herself.

'Faster, lover . . . faster,' she urged.

He did as instructed. Her whole body was now rigid, her fingers, toes, limbs straining against the wall as he stimulated her. Beneath his ravenous fingers, her clitoris slipped and slid as she pushed against him, her pelvis grinding against the tiles.

It was too much for Eddy. Overwhelmed by the sight and sound of her pleasure and the knowledge that he was responsible for it, he felt a surge of sexual predation unleashed. He was going to have her right now, right here whether she liked it or not. But he didn't. Rowena, despite her limp exhaustion, stopped him.

'No . . . not here, baby . . .' she said, her finger pressed against his anguished mouth. 'The bed.'

He picked her up in his arms and still kissing her, his hot mouth stuck on hers, he carried her into the bedroom and dropped her onto the bed. She immediately rolled over onto her stomach.

'I want it this way,' she smiled at him over her shoulder, 'the way you like it best.'

No further encouragement was needed. Without preamble, he spread her tanned legs, crouched over her white buttocks and slid into her dark, hot, velvety insides. 'Uh . . .'

Together they moved; slowly at first but then the intensity grew. He had had to wait long enough and it was more than he could endure. Supporting himself by his arms, their skins wet with perspiration, he licked his lips as he moved inside her, his eyes fixed on the back of her head.

She rotated beneath him, grunting and groaning as she too moved towards her orgasm. Then, in a flurry of heaving, writhing, hot flesh, they came together.

'Oh, God!'

'Rowena!'

'Yes!'

'Ah!'

Time and again, he thrust inside her. On and on it went, seemingly endless, as their contracting bodies reached the heights of pleasure.

Then it was over. Exhausted, detumescent and replete, they lay sprawled across the bed, too tired even to speak.

The receptionist knocked on the door to Eddy's suite. Nothing. He must be in there. She had searched everywhere else and no one had seen him. She had even checked the garages, but his car was still there so he couldn't be out.

She knocked again, louder this time. At last; footsteps. The door opened and there stood Rowena with only a towel held to her breasts. She blinked several times and screwed up her eyes against the light.

'What?'

The staff all knew about Eddy, Sian and Rowena. By way of a peculiar osmosis that only occurs when people live and work together under the same roof, the whole tacky episode had been relayed through the entire staff almost before it had even ended.

The two women glared at each other. There was no love lost between them. The receptionist had been very fond of Sian.

'Mr Killington is here.'

Rowena blanched and the receptionist smiled. 'What? Eddy!'

She spun round and slammed the door in the receptionist's smug face. The woman sauntered off down the corridor, highly delighted. She couldn't wait to see how the pair of them were going to talk themselves out of this one.

Rowena dashed to the bed. 'Eddy! Eddy!'

She roughly shook him, at the same time throwing the towel to one side. They had to get dressed quickly.

'Uh . . . wha . . . what's up?'

He was just getting into a good dream and objected to being woken so abruptly.

'Killington!' said Rowena, pulling on her bra. 'He's here!'

Eddy's brain recognized only one word and it was enough to make him jump out of bed.

'Shit!'

Sex forgotten, afternoon slumber dismissed, all hell broke loose as the pair of them hurried into their clothes.

'Your tie! Your tie!' exclaimed Rowena, running over to straighten it before he could leave the room. 'There,' she said, patting his shoulders, 'all done. Right, you go down the front stairs and I'll go down the back. Then I'll come along as though nothing's happened, okay?'

Eddy nodded distractedly. He had to move it. God only knew what Killington was up to downstairs.

'Sian!' reminded Rowena sternly. 'What are you going to say about her? You know what Killington's like.'

'Don't know. I'll . . . Oh God, I'll think of something.'

'Tell him she's ill. Woman's problems. He won't question that,' she assured him. 'Men never do.'

'Okay, right. All set? Do I look all right?'

She smiled. 'Fine. See you downstairs,' and they set off in their separate directions.

Eddy first went to reception, checking himself in the hall mirror as he did so.

'Where is he?' he whispered, leaning over the desk, wishing to God he and Rowena hadn't got carried away. Afternoon sex always did that to him: knocked him out better than a sleeping pill.

The receptionist nodded towards the kitchen. 'In there,' she said.

The swing door opened and there stood Killington. He

was rubbing his thumb and forefinger together, musing. He smiled when he saw Eddy but Eddy knew that meant nothing. Killington's smiles were like the one a snake might give you before he wrapped you up in his coils for lunch.

'Eddy!' he boomed good-naturedly. 'How good to see you at last. So, where have you been? You know I like to be met by my most senior staff when I come to visit.'

Eddy could feel his back prickling with beads of sweat. He rubbed his hands down the seat of his trousers.

'Mr Killington, how nice to see you.' He shook his boss's hand. 'Busy, you know. To be honest with you, I was just looking over tonight's menu.'

'Oh?' Killington put his arm around Eddy's shoulders and guided him through to the lounge. 'With who? The chef?'

'Yes, yes.' Eddy nodded, his smile in place.

'That's strange,' said Killington, smoothly, 'because I've just been talking to the chef and he said he and you discussed the menu thoroughly only two days ago. Is there a problem with it?'

Eddy didn't falter. Lying for him was as easy as breathing. It was just another version of the truth as he saw it.

'My own copy, Mr Killington. I was checking my own copy with the commis chef.'

'Really?' replied Marcus, not believing a word of it. He knew Eddy of old, ever since he was a commis chef himself in another of Marcus's hotels. He didn't like him much but he liked the way he operated, especially with the guests. The man had charm – never obsequious but always the flatterer – and the guests lapped it up. Marcus had taken a chance on Eddy and promoted him into senior management. When Sian came along, the pair were, in Marcus's view, the perfect match. Whatever Eddy's shortcomings, Sian more than made up for him. She was the grafter, the one who got things done. By herself she would have done extremely well except that she was a woman and Marcus didn't employ lone female managers. The guests didn't like it either. Sexual equality didn't come into the equation. He was the boss so his managers were all men.

'Coffee?'

Eddy, knowing he was on a sticky wicket, was trying to make amends. 'We use a particularly fine blend here, Mr Killington. Brazilian. Very good. I discovered it. I'm sure you'll like it.'

Eddy's temperature was increasing and he could feel beads of sweat on his forehead. A waitress arrived with their coffee.

'Well then, Eddy,' said Marcus, relaxing back in a leather chair, 'I don't see Sian anywhere and you know how much I like your charming wife.'

He watched Eddy closely. He could see exactly how uncomfortable he felt and he was enjoying every minute of it. Then Rowena appeared.

'Mr Killington. How are you?'

Eddy let out a silent sigh of relief. Thank God. Marcus stood up and held out his hand. Eddy hardly dared look at either of them but when he did he was relieved. Spotless, elegant, unblemished and in a stunning dress, Rowena was more than enough to take Killington's mind off asking awkward questions.

'And you're Eddy's new assistant, I believe?' Marcus smiled. 'He told me over the telephone that you were a particularly capable young woman and by the looks of things,' and he shot Eddy a smiling glance, 'I'm sure he is right.'

Rowena blushed. 'Why thank you, Mr Killington,' she fluttered, pulling down her tight skirt.

'Are you settling in all right?'

'Yes, thank you.'

'Well in that case perhaps you could tell me what's happened to Sian?'

Rowena glanced at Eddy but he was studiously avoiding her.

'Didn't Eddy tell you? She's gone away for a few days. She's not well, you know. Female problems. I'm just standing in for her,' and she smiled brightly.

'Yes, and I'm sure you're doing a wonderful job, my dear. Eddy would be especially appreciative of your help, wouldn't you, Eddy?'

But Eddy only smiled briefly.

'Well,' continued Marcus, 'let's hope she returns soon because I wouldn't like it if she didn't.'

Eddy belched, his hand shooting to his mouth to hide his embarrassment. 'Excuse me,' he spluttered. 'Lunch,' and he tried to smile. Rowena looked as though she was going to kill him.

'Anyway, after that unsolicited testimonial to the quality of the food in this place,' said Marcus smoothly, looking at Eddy, 'down to business. Your office, I think,' and he stood up. Then he turned to Rowena and flashed her a charming smile. He took hold of her hand and slowly brought it to his mouth where he gently kissed it. 'So nice to have met you, my dear. No doubt I will see you for dinner?'

'Of course, Mr Killington.'

Rowena watched the two men go, inwardly melting. She found it hard to understand why Eddy was so in awe of Killington. Anyone would think he was frightened of him. She wasn't. She thought he was delectable, and she ran her fingers over the back of her kissed hand. Yes, very attractive. And then she thought of Eddy. Trust him to spoil things. He had the manners of a pig sometimes, and no idea how to behave when it really mattered. She would have to tackle him about this. No partner of hers was going to let her down so publicly again.

'Why weren't you at the meeting, Eddy?'

'Work, Mr Killington. Honest, I did try and get there but

you know how it is: guests, things to sort out, crises,' and he laughed nervously. 'We businessmen have to keep on top of things.'

'Like Rowena, you mean?'

Eddy puffed rapidly at his cigarette. 'No, no, not at all, Mr Killington.'

'Don't,' said Marcus through gritted teeth, 'and I mean don't, let it happen again. When I say be there, I mean it.'

'Y-Yes, Mr Killington.'

'You have the latest figures?'

'Yes.'

Eddy unlocked a grey filing cabinet. He reached into the back of a drawer.

'I keep them in here. That way I get rid of any paperwork that may fall into the wrong hands. They're all on disk. Don't worry,' he said, noticing Marcus's disapproval, 'Sian doesn't go in here. She can't. She hasn't got a key.' He switched on the personal computer and inserted the disk. After a few minutes, Marcus had what he wanted. Eddy waited while Marcus read the figures, scanning them quickly, a lifetime in business allowing him to soak up information like a sponge.

'Good, good,' he muttered. 'A bit down in the winter, I see.'

'Bad weather. Tourists all gone. Not much demand.'

'How about Exeter, Plymouth and Bristol?'

'Picking up. We have to be careful, though, not to tread on anyone's toes. We don't want any trouble, especially not with the police.'

'Mmm . . .' and Marcus continued reading. 'The quality?' he asked. 'Holding up?'

'Very. With upfront finances and prompt payments, there's no argument. Everyone's happy.'

'When's the next shipment due?'

'Couple of weeks. There's no moon but that doesn't really matter. It all takes place well away from shore.'

'Good. And the fishermen? They're quite happy with the arrangements, are they?'

'More than happy. They can't fish because of these new regulations so a bit of smuggling comes in handy for paying the mortgage.'

Marcus turned and smiled, a genuine one this time. Eddy relaxed.

'I think we deserve a drink, Eddy. I'll have some of that excellent five-star brandy of yours.'

'I'll ring over to the bar.'

'And while you do, I'll get out my latest plans.'

'Oh?'

By the time a waiter had delivered their brandy, an architect's blueprint was spread out over the desk.

'So, what do you think?'

Marcus swirled the dark amber fluid around in the crystal balloon. He loved this drink.

'I've got to move my centre of operations because it's getting to be noticed by the wrong people and I don't want that. It's too dangerous running drugs from Oxford.' He jabbed a finger at the plans. 'This place will do perfectly. It's extremely convenient for dealing with the middle men like you on this part of the coast, but it's way out in the middle of nowhere, is surrounded by acres of moorland and has only the one exit.' He smiled. 'By the time I've got it sorted out, no one – least of all the Drugs Squad – will know about it. It will be a front, of course. As far as everyone is concerned, it's the headquarters of my property empire and nothing else. You and the others, though, will know different and I don't want it getting around.' He pointed a finger at Eddy. 'Remember that.'

'Yes, Mr Killington.' Eddy took a mouthful of his drink. 'What's the name of this place then?'

'The Grange.'

'And the nearest village?'

'Leighford. Only there's one small problem.'

'Yes?'

101

'The chap who owns it doesn't know he's going to sell it yet,' and he gave another small smile. 'But he will soon.'

I bet, thought Eddy, and if he knew Killington, there was no way the owner would be able to refuse.

Marcus finished his brandy in one mouthful and indicated he wanted another.

'I shall get what I want, Eddy,' he said, the menace in his voice unmistakable. 'I always do. Nothing ever stands in my way.'

Eddy shrank from his gaze.

That evening at dinner Marcus was at his charming, urbane best and kept them all amused with his stories and witticisms. They dined on Brigham's finest and freshest lobsters, washed down with a selection of excellent wines.

Camilla was the only one who didn't join in the good humour. She ate little, spoke even less, but drank copious amounts. By the time they were on the cheese course, which she waved away dismissively when the waiter asked her if she wanted any, all could see how drunk she was. Luckily they were dining in a private room. Eddy and Rowena were both acutely and uncomfortably aware of the awkwardness of it all but neither knew what to do.

'That was very nice, Eddy, very nice. Compliments to your chef,' said Marcus.

'Thank you.'

'And you, my dear,' he said, looking at Rowena, 'are looking very attractive.'

She tried to smile but her face only twisted. Camilla was threatening to fall off her chair any minute. Eddy was staring resolutely at his plate as if it held the answer to their quandary.

'Well,' said Rowena, her smile forced, 'it's been a lovely evening but I really think I ought to retire.'

Marcus smiled slowly. 'Oh no,' he said. 'I can't have anyone leave yet. We haven't finished our meal, have we, Camilla?'

The woman looked at him but her eyes were unfocused.

'Please, Mr Killington . . .' but Rowena never did get to finish her sentence.

'Wine!' yelled Camilla, thumping her glass down on the table.

'Now, my dear,' soothed her brother. 'There's no need to shout. I'm sure the waiter can hear you from here.'

'Please, Mr Killington,' said Eddy, jumping to his feet. 'Let me. I'm sure we have another bottle down in the cellar.'

Marcus laid a restraining hand on his arm. 'Not at all, Eddy. You sit. I can't have my senior manager running around the cellar. The waiter will do it.'

The atmosphere was deadly by the time the waiter returned. Eddy and Rowena sat like condemned people while Camilla could barely stay awake. Marcus smiled to himself.

'Your wine, sir,' said the waiter, holding out the bottle.

'Open it,' Marcus replied without looking, 'and give this drunken bitch a glassful.'

'Yes, sir.'

Eddy and Rowena exchanged glances.

'And these two,' added Marcus.

'No, no, Mr Killington,' protested Rowena. 'You've been too kind as it is. It really is getting late,' and she yawned rather obviously, as did Eddy.

'No. I insist,' Marcus answered darkly. 'I want you to see just what a useless, spoilt, wasteful slut this female is. Wonderful, isn't she?'

Neither of them answered.

'Fuck you,' said Camilla, wine dripping down her chin.

'My goodness! It speaks,' and he started to laugh. 'You poor drunken cow,' he said, cupping her face in his hand. 'What an appalling sight. I can't believe you would behave like this in public. Still, mud will always find its own level, won't it?'

Eddy and Rowena were beyond salvation. Transfixed with horror, they could only look on this sordid scene as passive spectators. Then Camilla fell off her chair. Eddy tried to be the gentleman but Marcus stopped him.

'Go to bed,' he said. 'Both of you.'

'But what about her?' said Eddy, looking at the prostrate figure on the ground.

'What about her?' smiled Marcus, taking him and Rowena by the arms and leading them out of the room.

Rowena saw now what a ruthless man Marcus Killington was. She vowed to herself to keep out of his way – or keep her wits about her.

Six

It was mid-afternoon. Sian lay flat out on the floor with a cushion underneath her head. The radio was playing softly in the background and she was gradually drifting off into that wonderful restorative sleep that eventually comes only when anxiety begins to recede. She hadn't felt so at peace with herself for some time. With hindsight, she could see how she had been running about for weeks getting more and more stressed. No wonder she hadn't seen what was going on right underneath her nose. The discovery of Eddy and Rowena had been the final straw and it had almost broken her.

She was glad she was here with Helen. Getting that job at the stables wasn't the most interesting career move but, as Helen said, she needed the money and it kept her mind off her problems, which was her most important consideration. She had space to relax, time to unwind and eventually, maybe, time to heal a little.

She rested her hand on her belly. She must take care of herself. She had someone else to consider now. She smiled. A baby; her baby. She could hardly believe it. Even after all she had been through, nothing was going to dampen her excitement about that.

She had returned from the stables about an hour ago, hot and thirsty. It was hard work, made even more difficult by Eck's slow speech. Sian found him almost painfully shy and every time he spoke to her, he blushed. It was difficult for him to look her in the face, but by gently coaxing him, she was overcoming his reluctance.

She stretched out along the floor. She was still stiff, even after two weeks of such work. The trouble was, she was so tired she couldn't be bothered to do anything when she came home except collapse. The book she had bought in Newton Abbot was still sitting on her dressing table unopened. She must get round to it before long. It might have something interesting to say about The Grange and the people who lived there. A private journal, never designed for public view, could give a valuable insight. She wondered if there would be any connection with the present owner.

Andrew was a strange man. She knew that wasn't the right word to describe him, but it was the only one she could think of that came halfway to fitting him. If asked what she felt about him, she would have had no hesitation in saying hostile indifference except, of course, after seeing him in Newton Abbot, maybe that wasn't true. Even Helen obviously liked him, despite all her protests to the contrary.

Sian could see he exuded an air of mysterious attraction that under other circumstances she might have found hard to ignore and it was difficult not to feel his presence all around the stables, but she was vulnerable, too hurt and far too angry even to think of trusting him, or any man, at the moment. She must remember her vow and steel her heart against any of them but especially Andrew. Anyone that could affect her the way he did on their first meeting could only spell danger.

If she had any lingering doubts about that then all she had to do was remember Eddy and Rowena and that scene in the linen cupboard. Their naked abandon and blatant betrayal had cut her so deep that she honestly doubted if she would ever love a man again. And then that little scene in the stable office with that woman and Andrew . . . it was all too much. All the pieces of her that she had welded to her husband had fractured with such violence that she couldn't even begin to know what she felt beyond her immediate rage. She knew he had done it before and had known all the pain that had induced, but witnessing it had

106

made it so much worse. She felt skinned. All her defences had been ripped away.

Now, quite unexpectedly, she rolled over and started to cry. It had all been so horribly squalid.

Eddy wasn't happy. The dinner that first evening and Killington's presence unnerved him. Three days he had been there and he still showed no signs of leaving.

Eddy was in his office reading about the day's racing but he couldn't concentrate. There was a meeting on at Newmarket today and if he could only think straight, he might have a bit of luck for a change. He did a lot of losing.

From where he sat, he could look straight out across the courtyard to the kitchens and watch all the young nubile waitresses he employed. Normally he enjoyed his harmless pastime but lately it didn't lift his sour humour. Nothing would do that.

He cast a listless eye over the paperwork that lay on the desk. Sian would usually do all this. He hated it; it was so routine and boring. Worse, Killington kept asking awkward questions which only Sian could answer.

Damn Sian! Everything had been going so well. The money was good and he had regularly seduced each new female member of staff. He couldn't see why she had made such a fuss. To him it was just part of the job – one of the manager's perks. Whether they were staff or guests, his friends' wives or complete strangers, he drew no distinction between any of them. Women were women as far as he was concerned and it was a bit much for his wife to expect lifelong fidelity. After all, how was he, a red-blooded male in his prime, supposed to resist the call of his hormones? Sian expected too much of him. Being unfaithful was as normal to him as breathing.

He thought he loved Sian but if she wasn't going to understand him, then thank goodness Rowena was so handy. She knew exactly what he wanted.

The door opened.

'Morning,' chimed Rowena, smiling at him, a dimple showing in either cheek.

He grunted.

She came around his desk and put her arm across his shoulders. Eddy's old secretary, who said nothing and saw everything, studiously ignored them.

'Something wrong, darling?'

He could smell her strong scent. As usual, she was made up to look her absolute best, not a long blonde hair out of place and her face perfectly painted. She was a natural beauty anyway, in a heavy sensuous way, but she always enhanced her looks with a thorough application of makeup. As she leant down to him, her large breasts strained against the flimsy white material of her blouse.

He shook his head. 'What are you so damned happy about? He's still here, isn't he?'

'My, my, we are in a good mood, aren't we?' she teased. 'Anyway, *he's* going out this afternoon, if you want to know. Still, I don't suppose it will make you any more pleasant.'

'I'll speak to you later, darling,' he relented with a tired smile. 'I'm too damned stressed at the moment.'

'Oh, and is that why you couldn't get it up last night?'

'Rowena!' and his face flushed as he glanced at his secretary.

Rowena stood up and straightened her tight black skirt, designed specifically to show the curves of her buttocks and thighs. When she walked, she liked to make sure men watched.

'I'll see you later,' she said, with tight-lipped restraint.

He waved his hand flippantly. 'Fine.'

She left in a huff, slamming the door. He winced; his headache was still pounding. He needed another cup of coffee. He looked at his secretary and smiled tepidly. The thin, dried-up woman with a disapproving mouth like an anal sphincter didn't smile back.

'Get me some coffee, Maureen.'

She sighed. She didn't like it when he interrupted her at her typing. She took the cup and left, Eddy watching her spindly varicosed legs as she tottered across to the kitchen. It was then he realized he couldn't put off the inevitable any longer. He was going to have to find his wife and bring her home whether she liked it or not.

Sian had been asleep. How long she didn't know, but the telephone had woken her, its insistent ringing breaking through her black dreamless exhaustion.

She blinked her eyes a couple of times, trying to rid the sleep from her body and then she sat up. She was still so tired and the aching muscles felt even worse. The telephone still rang.

'Okay, okay, I'm coming. Just hang on, will you?'

She staggered to her feet and half walking, half stumbling, tried to run out of the door to the hallway. She grabbed the receiver, sending the telephone flying off its small table and onto the floor.

'Hello . . . hello . . . are you still there?'

'Sian.'

'Mum. Oh, it's you.'

'Well, don't sound so pleased to hear me, will you, dear?'

'I'm sorry. I was asleep and you woke me.'

'Well, I have some news that will cheer you up. We've just had that delightful husband of yours round here demanding to know where you are.'

Sian was suddenly wide awake. 'You didn't tell him I was here, did you?'

'No, of course not, dear, but he took some persuading I can tell you. And he smelt of booze. Tell me, dear, is he a lunchtime drinker because he looked decidedly the worse for wear.'

Sian closed her eyes and slid down the wall until she was sitting on the floor. It was so typical of Eddy. The slightest bit of stress and he started to drink. He had never been that way at the start of their marriage, but she had noticed how much worse he had got over the last year.

'What else did he say?' she said tiredly.

'Oh the usual, dear. You should know what men are like by now. If there isn't someone to cook, clean, wash and iron for them, then the poor dears instantly fall apart. They're so bloody useless. I mean, look at your father. The only thing he can cook is a boiled egg. He'd starve if I wasn't here.'

'Did he say sorry?'

Megan was quiet for a moment. 'No, dear, he didn't. In fact, he seemed to be treating the whole thing as a minor inconvenience, as if you had gone off for an extended shopping expedition or something. Not a word about his major indiscretion in the broom cupboard.'

'Linen cupboard,' corrected Sian.

'Linen cupboard then, whatever, he said nothing. He seemed more concerned about his paperwork and the fact that your boss, Killington, wants to know where you are.'

'Typical!'

'Exactly, my dear, but that's men for you. All the sensitivity of a rhino and about as stupid as one as well. You know, I have a theory that the Y-chromosome and intelligence are incompatible so let's hope to goodness that you're having a girl.'

Sian said nothing. If only he had said sorry – just a little apology – it would have made all the difference.

'So, my dear,' continued her mother, 'how are you and how is the bump?'

Sian reluctantly answered. Her heart was so heavy. 'Fine,' she replied. 'There's no bump yet, of course. It's far too early but otherwise, I'm feeling okay. Helen's looking after me and I have a small part-time job at the local stables.'

'Are you sure you should in your condition?'

'Mum, I'm not ill, you know.'

'I'm not saying that, dear, it's just . . . well, you've been

110

under a lot of stress lately and we wouldn't want anything to happen to the baby, would we?'

'Heavens! When I first told you, you were really indifferent about it. What's made you change your mind?'

'The idea that you might come to your senses and divorce that husband of yours.'

'Mum! How can you say that? Just because we've had a . . . a disagreement doesn't mean we're going to get divorced.'

'A disagreement! Is that what you call this?' Sian could hear her mother breathing deep indignant breaths. 'He's a lecherous bastard, always has been and always will be. Did I ever tell you what he said to your sister at your wedding? *Your* wedding, note.'

'No, but no doubt you're going to enlighten me.'

There was an expectant pause. 'He only suggested that he and Rhiannon should get to know each other a bit better.'

'He was drunk, Mum,' said Sian tersely. 'Look, I'm tired and depressed and I really don't want to talk about it, okay? So if you have nothing else to say, I would like to go now.'

Megan, knowing that she had gone too far, tried to soothe things over. 'Listen, my dear, I'm old and a bit crabby and I shouldn't have told you that. I'm sorry.'

'That's okay.'

'It's just that I've only got your best interests at heart and I would dearly like to see you settled with a man who treated you like you deserve because it's hurt me so much to watch Eddy and the things he's done to you. Next time, dear, take a bit of advice from your old mum.'

Sian smiled. 'Oh yeah, and what's that?'

'If he hasn't got brains, breeding and brass and anything else you can care to think of, then leave him well alone.'

Sian chuckled. Trust her mother to think of that one.

'I'm going now, dear. I've got my bridge class at four. I'll ring soon. Take care, won't you?'

'Yes, I will. Bye.'

After another shower and a late lunch, Sian got out the sun lounger and fell asleep in the back garden. She woke with a start when an ice-cold drink was plonked on her bare stomach.

'Oh!'

'Come on you, wakey, wakey. Have some of this. It'll put hairs on your chest.' Helen sat down on the end of the lounger while Sian sat up moaning slightly.

'What's the matter?'

'I'm sore. Too long out of the saddle.'

'I'm not surprised. You look a bit pink as well.'

Sian touched her face and flinched.

'Ouch! Oh no!' she wailed. 'I'm burnt!' She looked at her arms and legs with dismay. 'Look at me!'

Helen smiled. 'Not a pretty sight. Why didn't you use that sun cream I lent you?'

'I don't know. Just forgot about it, I suppose.'

'Well, have some lemonade. It will help cool you down.'

They drank quietly, the early evening sun filling the scented air with a golden hue.

'Don't know what's wrong with his nibs today,' said Helen, lighting a cigarette. 'Right pain in the butt. Even the two Jayne Mansfields couldn't get him to cheer up and believe me, they really tried. Snappy so-and-so. I'm telling you, Sian, he'll drive people away if he carries on like this.'

'Why? Is he like it all the time?'

'No, not really. Most days he's fairly grumpy. Occasionally he smiles, but today . . .' she trailed off thoughtfully. 'Today, he was positively revolting. Damned if I know what makes him tick but sometimes he's impossible. Stupid sod! Maybe,' she added, a mischievous smile playing across her lips, 'maybe it's all these female tourists. Perhaps he can't keep up with them all, if you catch my drift.'

'You're exaggerating, Helen,' Sian replied, remembering

the scene in the office and thinking that perhaps she wasn't. She was keen to change the subject.

'I don't suppose you got round to asking Andrew if I could bring Bracken over?'

Helen beamed. 'Yes, I did, and he says no problem although he doesn't want her interfering with your work.'

'Of course she won't. She'll just be there for me to ride out when I feel like it. You can ride her if you want. You always liked her.'

'Thanks, I'd like that.'

'Good. I'll have to talk to Andrew about the cost. When will we get her?'

'The weekend?'

'Okay.'

They drank their drinks in the warm sun. Helen stood up and walked along her flower borders. They were full of summer colours.

'Mum rang earlier,' said Sian. 'Eddy's looking for me.'

Helen bent down and pulled out a weed. She chucked it onto the compost heap. The action seemed symbolic.

'Oh yes?'

'She didn't tell him where I am. Apparently, he's upset because there's no one to do the paperwork.'

'Poor dear,' said Helen sarcastically, 'my heart bleeds for him.' And they both smiled.

The telephone rang while they were watching the news on television. Helen answered it, her face full of hopeful expectation that it was one of her admirers. She returned looking tired and irritated.

'That,' she said, slumping into the chair, 'was your delightful pig of a husband. Nice turn of insult, hasn't he?'

'And what did you call him then? I'm sure you must have come up with something appropriate.'

'How did he find out where you are, Sian?'

'Oh dear. Now that is a problem. What did you tell him? You didn't confirm that I'm here, did you?' The words rushed out, one on top of the other.

Helen held up her hand.

'No, no, no. Nothing like that. I just told him to get lost and to stop annoying me. I also said that even if I did know where you were, whatever gave him the idea that I would reveal it to a swine like him?' She grimaced. 'I don't think he liked that too much because after that it just degenerated into a slanging match. He called me an overweight dyke and I called him a brainless moron who was all mouth and no potential.' Then she laughed. 'I also asked him whether it was true that he was as hopeless in bed as you had said he was!'

The pair of them giggled loudly.

'He didn't know what to say to that at all. Just spluttered inanely!'

Sian bit her lip. It was all very well for Helen saying things like that to Eddy but if he came down here, it could get very unpleasant. He didn't lose his temper often, but on the odd occasion he had done, it was not a pretty sight.

'Why the hell did he ring here?' she asked, more to herself than Helen.

'Why not? Sounds to me as if he is determined to track you down. He must be ringing all your friends systematically.'

Sian's face puckered with concern. Helen reached over and grabbed her arm.

'Don't be so worried. You've got me to protect you, and believe it or not, I pack a mighty punch.'

Sian didn't look convinced. 'Great, that's all I need.'

'Oh come on, cheer up. If he turns up, just tell him to piss off or something. I would.'

Sian gave her a resigned look.

'He can't make you go anywhere, Sian, not if you don't want to. You're a free woman now and just you remember that.'

Marcus and Camilla were in Exeter. They were on their way to see Frank Jessop, a dealer in antiquities. Camilla

114

was sulking. She sat with her arms folded over her white silk shirt, bottom lip sullen and dark glasses hiding her bloodshot eyes. She didn't want to be here and would have preferred to have stayed at the hotel with a line or two of cocaine for company. Anything was better than accompanying Marcus on one of his interminable business meetings.

She glanced sideways at him. Seemingly relaxed and debonair, he looked every bit the successful entrepreneur. In his lightweight linen jacket and classic Savile Row trousers, he sat still and complete in the comfort of his leather seat. Nothing was going to ruffle his day or so it would appear, except Camilla knew better. His little finger, with its heavy gold signet ring, tapped the armrest. A small gesture, it spoke volumes.

He was on his way to do a deal. She knew it. She knew what he was like when his blood lust was up, when he caught the scent of his prey. With other men it was golf, fishing or hunting. Not Marcus. With him if it wasn't race-horses, it was gold, and as hard as he tried, he could never keep still. There would always be one tiny part of him betraying his inner turmoil.

She turned away and smiled. It wasn't the first time during this visit he had got so wound up. The aftermath of their ghastly dinner with Eddy and Rowena on the first night of their stay had been quite amusing as well because she knew how much she had humiliated him even if he would never admit it. Poor Marcus, such a temper on him and so desperate not to lose it. How she loved to provoke him, watching him seethe, watching his eyes bulge and his complexion darken. It was a game with her; a dangerous, exciting game and she enjoyed it even if she did have to pay the consequences later.

'Park here, Bains.'

'Sir.'

The Rolls pulled over next to a three-storey half-timbered house whose upper windows hung out over the lower ones. There was a jeweller's shop on the ground floor with an iron grille across the windows. It looked shut.

Bains held the door open for Camilla. She stretched out her long legs with all the grace and elegance of a gazelle. Marcus turned to her and spoke over the roof of the car.

'Run along and explore the shops, my dear. I'm sure you can find something on which to waste more of your money.'

'I don't want to.'

His eyes hardened. He was beginning to lose his patience with her and her little tantrums. Without any change in the tone of his voice, he said, 'Move it, Camilla.'

They glared at each other.

'But I thought you wanted me to come in with you. Isn't that why you dragged me along?' she said petulantly.

'No,' he answered with a smile. 'I just brought you along so that you would stop poking around the hotel office and interfering with things that are none of your concern.'

She looked away. Someone must have said something.

'Bains will accompany you if you like,' he continued.

'Oh really?' she drawled. 'How bloody interesting, eh, Bains? Bet you know all about *haute couture*, don't you?'

The chauffeur remained silent. He knew better than to answer.

'Camilla,' said Marcus tightly, 'if you're going to behave like a spoilt brat, then I'll have to treat you like one and the way to deal with little girls who don't behave themselves is to . . .' He let the threat hang in the air.

She looked contemptuously at him. 'Really, Marcus, you're just an inadequate little bully with a big man's car, aren't you,' she said with a grin, before flouncing off, her hair swinging around her triumphant face.

She wandered idly around the city. She simply wasn't in the mood for shopping, nor had she seen anything that particularly interested her. With money enough to buy all that she wanted and more, shopping had become tiresome. She didn't really have to go to the shops at all nowadays.

She could simply order goods over the telephone and they would be delivered. And then there was the choice of venues: Paris, Rome, London and New York. Shops that most people only ever heard of were her hunting grounds. A small cathedral city, she thought, could hardly provide what she wanted.

Bored and indifferent, Camilla found herself window shopping near the cathedral and was just admiring a particularly interesting piece of jewellery when she felt a swift and hard tug on her arm. She didn't even see the thief until he had her handbag and was already out of reach.

'Stop him!' she shrieked, beginning to run after the teenage boy. 'Stop him! He's stolen my bag!'

The boy sprinted away across the green, interested spectators watching, but nobody doing anything.

'Come here you!' she cried. 'Come here! Give me back my bag!'

But, younger and much fitter, he was easily outrunning her. He even had the gall to laugh. Then suddenly a tall man with blond hair grabbed him by the arms as he sprinted into his path, and was holding him tight. Camilla ran up to them. She was furious.

'You little bastard!' she yelled at the now contrite boy. 'You selfish, stupid little boy! I've got half a mind to knock your ill-bred, ill-mannered head off! How dare you steal my handbag!'

She snatched it off him and quickly opened it to check all was there.

'What shall I do with him?' asked the man. 'Would you like me to call the police?'

Camilla looked up. It was the first time she had really taken any notice of him. He smiled at her.

'Well . . . I suppose . . .' She smiled back.

'The police?' he suggested.

'Sorry?'

'I said the police. Shall I get the police?'

'I won't do nothing like it again, miss. Honest.'

Camilla noticed how the boy's clothes were dirty and torn and he didn't look as though he had had a decent meal in ages.

'No,' she said, relenting, 'not the police. Not this time,' and to the astonishment of the boy, she reached into her handbag, took out a tenner and gave it to him. 'You should have just asked, you know. Now get lost,' and without a moment to lose, the boy ran off, unable to believe his luck.

'That was a very generous thing to do,' commented the man.

'Well, yes. Can't say I'm usually in the habit of doing such things. I can't think what came over me,' she laughed. 'Must be the sunshine or something.' She held out her hand. 'My name's Camilla Killington and thank you for what you did. It really was most kind.'

'I'm Andrew Mann,' he shook her hand, 'and it was nothing.'

She smiled again, feeling excited. He was so very handsome.

'Can I get you a coffee or something? I feel I ought to thank you properly for what you've just done.'

He shook his head. 'No, there's no need to buy me a coffee. I'm sure you have loads of other things to do.'

'Oh not really,' she said too quickly. She couldn't let someone like him just walk out of her life like this.

'Well, maybe another time. I'm afraid I have to get on. I've got a business to get back to.'

Her face fell but then she smiled brightly again. 'Perhaps our paths will cross again? I hope so.'

'Yes. Maybe. Bye.'

She watched him as he walked off through the summer crowds. Whoever he was and wherever he lived, she was going to track him down. He was one man Marcus wasn't going to get rid of.

'Very nice, Mr Jessop, and what did you say it was?'

In the dark room, curtains pulled against any casual

intruders, Frank Jessop, short, round, shiny bald head and quick acquisitive eyes, suspicious and intent above a thin-lipped mouth and fleshy nose, turned the anglepoise lamp so they could get a better look at the coin. He handed a magnifying glass to Marcus.

'Take a good look at it, Mr Killington. You won't see none better than that.'

Marcus peered closer.

'Clodius Albinus, AD 193–197. A gold Aureus,' said Jessop with awe, his voice a strangulated whisper. After years as a dealer, he liked to keep his negotiations as quiet as possible. Never knew who was out there ready to get one over on him.

'Clodius Albinus,' repeated Marcus, turning the heavy gold coin over and over in his hand. The exquisite pleasure it gave him to hold it, to possess it, to feel its history, its richness in his hand, was almost better than anything he knew.

'What's its provenance?' he asked casually. He was trying to keep his excitement under control.

'There are some more,' said Jessop carefully, watching to see Marcus's reaction. 'It belongs to a hoard that went missing back in the twenties. Exactly how much more and where it is – well, I have my contacts working on that – but I know it's part of the collection. There's been rumours about it for years and then this turned up.'

'When?'

Jessop's mouth turned down. He wasn't about to give away all his information, not without some sort of recompense and he knew that Marcus could pay him very well indeed if he played his cards right.

'How much?' said Marcus getting out his chequebook.

Jessop pinched his lips together. Cash not cheques was his fashion. He didn't trust bits of paper unless they promised to pay the bearer the sum of lots of pounds.

Marcus, seeing his doubtful look, put away his cheque-book and took out his wallet. It was stuffed full of high denomination notes. Jessop's eyes only partially hid his respect.

'Why don't we have a drink, Mr Killington?' he said, smiling greasily. 'I always likes a drink when I'm doing a spot of business.'

Camilla was walking back to the car quite dumbfounded. A complete stranger had rescued her from a thief and in the briefest of moments had stolen her heart.

As she neared the car, Bains came over to her. He must have seen that something was wrong by the look on her face.

'You all right, miss?'

Silence.

'Miss Camilla, you all right?'

'Mmm . . . oh yes,' and she fleetingly smiled. 'I'm fine, thank you, Bains.'

The journey back was very strange, Bains noted. Neither Mr Killington nor Miss Camilla said a word, both staring out of the window, smiling to themselves. Whatever had happened in Exeter, they each seemed well pleased with their morning.

Seven

'Much further, Bains?'

'No, sir. Just ten miles.'

Marcus relaxed back in the Rolls' comfortable upholstery. It was a hot day, the sun's glare worsening his headache, a headache born out of anticipation and acute annoyance. The closer he got to The Grange, the closer he was getting to the Roman treasure.

Today, Marcus had gladly left Camilla behind him at the hotel. Always challenging, she was now pushing him to his limits. He could control her by pure strength if he had to, but he didn't want that. He wanted her love and because she wouldn't give it he felt himself to be on an emotional north face of the Eiger, hanging on by his fingernails. One false move and there would be nothing between him and oblivion. He didn't know who he trusted less – himself or her.

She wasn't his only problem, though. That buffoon Eddy Williamson and his marital problems could upset things. A couple of years ago this wouldn't have happened. Then Eddy was the best of his employees; the most astute, the most industrious, the most inventive. It would appear, however, that success had bred complacency and that was something Marcus didn't approve of. He wanted commitment from his staff. One hundred and ten per cent. It was obvious that Eddy was not applying his full attention to his job and mistakes could be made. Already too much information was getting into the wrong hands, which could jeopardize everything. As Marcus saw it there was only one thing to do: Sian would have to be brought back. She didn't know anything about the drug smuggling but she was

Eddy's anchor. Without her, he just wasn't up to the job.

Time for a drink, Marcus decided, and he poured himself a large whisky. It would help restore his good humour.

He reached out for his briefcase and extracted a newspaper cutting. Marcus had paid Jessop a lot of money for this, amongst other information. The cutting dated from August 1920, and despite the jeweller's careful preservation, had yellowed and become brittle. Marcus read it through once more.

> The plot thickens in the curious case of the long-lost Roman treasures recently unearthed by a ploughman working on Lord and Lady Middleton's estate at Norton.
>
> The hoard, which included several fine pieces of gold jewellery, silver tableware, statuettes and a huge engraved plate, as well as many gold coins, was being kept under lock and key at the local constabulary. In due course it was expected that Professor Edward Hamilton of the British Museum, who specializes in Roman antiquities, would visit Dismundham to study the find, which is of enormous importance, being the largest of its kind this century. However, much to the local constabulary's embarrassment, a forced entry was effected at the police station over the weekend and the entire hoard removed without trace.
>
> Lord and Lady Middleton have expressed their deepest regret and outrage at such a despicable event, and their son-in-law, Captain Hugo Warrener, who is staying at the estate with his wife, Isobel, has put up a not insubstantial reward which he hopes might lead to information about the theft.
>
> The Dismundham Constabulary have refused to comment on the case except to say that Scotland Yard will be investigating.

* * *

It had taken quite a lot more cash to buy from Frank Jessop the fact that the Warreners were the former owners of The Grange near Leighford. Apparently Roman treasure being hidden at The Grange was a long-standing local legend. But Frank Jessop's contact had found the coin at a sale in a box of studs and cufflinks that could be traced back to Hugo Warrener himself. If there was this coin, somewhere there had to be more. Hugo Warrener had never expected to pay over the reward for recovering the artefacts because he knew exactly where they were all along. Marcus liked that. Perhaps he and Warrener were kindred spirits. In any case, Marcus forgot the expense of Jessop's information as he marvelled at his luck. The Grange was the very place he already had in mind for his operations. He'd made enquiries with a view to persuading the current owner to sell, and now it seemed that Andrew Mann, the owner of The Grange, was the only person standing between Marcus and the Warrener Hoard.

The car pulled smoothly along as Bains negotiated the narrow lanes. Soon they were in Leighford. Marcus gave it a cursory glance. Small villages and their even smaller inhabitants were of no interest to him. Another four miles and they would reach The Grange. Upwards towards the moor went the car, through speckled sunlight that shone between the overhanging trees, but all of that was lost on Marcus. He didn't see nature, only the amount of profit he could make from it.

At last the overhanging foliage gave way to a wide open space. The hedge carried on down one side but on the other, set back behind a wide grass verge, was the gateway to The Grange. No lions rampant or any other decoration, just two grey granite columns with an iron gate propped open to one side.

'Stop the car, Bains.'

For a few minutes, Marcus sat and looked. He could see thick bushes of rhododendrons on either side of the drive leading up to the house, their pink and red blooms hanging like Chinese lanterns in the morning heat. The place was secretive, hidden. It was just what he needed.

'Up there, Bains.'

'Sir,' and the large car slid powerfully along the drive.

He hadn't met his adversary yet, although he had a small file of information about him. It had proved surprisingly difficult to dig up Andrew's past even with Marcus's contacts. It was almost as if there was something Andrew wanted to remain hidden. Marcus rubbed his chin. This 'accidental' meeting that he was engineering with Andrew, must not arouse any suspicions. He had to be careful. He wanted no mistakes. His instincts told him to be wary.

'Go knock on the door, Bains.'

He watched patiently as his chauffeur crunched over the drive and banged the large ornate knocker against the huge wooden door. He waited but there was no answer. He tried again but still nothing. He came back to the car and got in.

'No one there, sir.'

Marcus was disappointed. He had been looking forward to meeting Andrew. He sat and thought for a minute. 'Well,' he said, 'I'll just look around for myself. I'm sure the owner won't mind.'

Bains got out and opened the door.

'You stay,' ordered Marcus.

'Sir.'

Marcus looked up at the large house. It might not be as big as his Oxfordshire mansion, but it was just as impressive in its own way. Three storeys high and made with the local granite, it was an imposing structure with a crenellated wall surrounding the roof, giving it a castle-like appearance. Huge windows, becoming smaller with each floor, reflected the sun's bright rays. At the front was a massively carved and arched front door with a family crest and motto carved into the grey stone above it. He liked the place and his determination to have it was only increased by actually seeing it.

Marcus walked towards the front door. Maybe Bains hadn't tried hard enough. He pulled the large old-fashioned bell but it didn't work so then he tried the heavy brass knocker. But Bains was right. The place must be empty. But a house this size had to have more than just one entrance and if there was a way in, he was going to find it. It was far too interesting simply to walk away from.

Andrew was down by the river cantering along the bank on Sebi, with Blaize running alongside. It had been a while since the horse had been properly exercised and Andrew could feel the way the animal pulled beneath him.

'Steady boy, steady,' and they slowed down to a walk.

Sian. He couldn't get her out of his mind. No matter what he did, she still kept coming back to haunt him. She had a mystique about her: the tilt of her head, the set of her eyes, the way her hair shone like heavy silk over her shoulders and down her back. And then there were her more obvious womanly features. Any normal male could appreciate those and he was no exception. There was only one problem: after their initial meeting, she seemed to have taken a dislike to him, going out of her way to ignore him. Since he'd seen her in town the other day, she had become even more aloof. He hadn't felt like talking to anyone in the pub, and wasn't sure Sian had even seen him. If she had, and was offended, she was certainly over-reacting. Unless, of course, it was something to do with that scene in the office that she walked in on, but he couldn't think that it was. He had been in the process of gently rebuffing one of the Levi sisters, nothing more. Sian was at the very least indifferent and at the worst, hostile. She had been offhand, abrupt, terse, rude even. Maybe he should have spoken to her in the pub. It wouldn't have done any harm, but he then rejected that idea. If things didn't improve soon, he would have to get rid of her anyway so there really wasn't any point in it all.

'Get on, boy!' and the horse sped off faster and faster.

The trees, the ground beneath their feet, the air across their faces — it all rushed by, sweeping away the uncertainties.

Sebi, at long last given his head, galloped as fast as he could, his hugely muscled hindquarters thundering through the grass. Upwards they went, climbing the hill towards The Grange, the trees flying past and Andrew having to duck the lowest branches. Blond on black, they became a blur as they swerved around the trees, twigs and leaves thrown up by the horse's hooves.

'Come on! Come on!'

They shot out from the trees and onto the drive. The horse swerved to a halt, gravel flying into the air. Blaize raced ahead dementedly barking at the strange car. Andrew looked suspiciously at the vehicle while Bains smiled nervously from the front seat, thankful that the dog couldn't get at him. Andrew trotted over.

'Shut up, dog!' Blaize ignored him. 'I said shut up!

A sudden silence, the dog casting timid glances at his master.

'Who are you and what do you want?' Andrew demanded.

He glared down at the sweating man who had now opened the window. Blaize jumped up and firmly planted his huge feet on the Rolls' pristine paintwork.

'Oy! You!' shouted Bains, pushing the dog off. 'Get your bleeding feet off this car!'

Andrew drew alongside. 'Who are you and what do you want?' he challenged, staring with contempt at the chauffeur.

'I believe it is me you want,' came a cultured voice from behind them.

Andrew swung the horse round and Blaize came bounding up.

'Down, Blaize!' yelled Andrew and then more quietly. 'I don't think Mr . . . Mr?'

'Let's just say I may be able to do business with you and —'

'Blaize! Get down!'

Marcus smiled much like a viper would and glared at the growling dog.

Andrew dismounted and walked over. He regarded the stranger with barely concealed contempt.

'So,' said Andrew, tying the horse's reins to an iron hook in the house brickwork, 'what exactly is it you want from me?'

'Please, I'm sure it would be far more convivial if we talked inside your splendid house. Lutyens, isn't it?' said Marcus in friendly tones, holding out his hand.

Andrew ignored it. 'I prefer not to, if you don't mind.'

Marcus looked up at the house.

'Like I said, it's a magnificent building. Needs a bit of work though, doesn't it?'

'That is none of your concern.'

'Oh, but it might be. Would you mind if I were to look around inside?'

Andrew's eyes narrowed. 'Why?'

'Well, I'm very interested in buying something like this –'

Andrew interrupted. 'I don't know who you are or what you want and what's more, I don't give a damn, but there's no way you're coming inside so get back to your car and get out of my sight.'

'Mr Mann,' replied the unfazed Marcus, totally ignoring Andrew's building anger, 'I'm sure if I were to explain what I represent, I –' but he didn't get time to finish.

'I SAID OUT!'

'Mr Mann, really –'

'Look, are you deaf as well as stupid?' Andrew grabbed Marcus by the lapels and marched him backwards towards his car. 'Over the past year I have had God knows how many of you people coming up here and trying to look around my house,' and with a heave he flung Marcus back against the vehicle where, with the force, he slid over the bonnet and onto the ground. He picked himself up and

127

brushed himself down while Bains, who stood even taller and broader than Andrew, got out and was preparing to defend his employer. Marcus restrained him.

'No. Get back in the car.'

'But, sir —'

'No!' he snapped and Bains retreated. Marcus looked back at Andrew, regarding him with faint amusement.

'You seem to take great exception to anyone who wishes to do business with you, Mr Mann. I wonder why?'

'None of your business. Now go and don't let me ever see you or any of your scum around here again.'

Marcus turned away and then stopped. He looked up at the house once more and then he looked at the glaring Andrew who stood with hands on hips, his blue eyes ablaze. 'You know, you didn't even stop to hear what I had to offer you.'

'I don't need to. The Grange is not for sale, to you or to anybody. Period.'

Marcus smiled wearily and brushed some dust off his sleeve.

'That's a pity, Mann, because I could make you a very serious offer and believe you me, I don't intend to give up.'

Andrew advanced and stood directly in front of him. 'Am I not making myself quite clear? I said no and I mean no, so get into this poseur's machine and clear off otherwise . . .' and he called to the dog. 'Blaize!'

The animal came snarling. Marcus retreated into the car and rolled down the window, secure that the raging dog couldn't get him. His eyes were burning.

'I'll be back.'

The car roared off, dust and gravel thrown up in its wake.

'Stupid bastard,' said Andrew under his breath, watching the car until it had disappeared.

*   *   *

128

'Back to Leighford, Bains. We'll stop there for coffee and see what more we can find out about this Mr Andrew Mann.'

Marcus wasn't at all perturbed by his encounter with Andrew. In all his years of business, he had met tougher opponents. It was just a matter of biding his time. But he didn't like it when someone made a fool of him, as Andrew Mann was just about to find out.

Camilla stretched out on a lounger in a secluded part of the grounds of the hotel. The noonday sun was beating down on her bare back out of a dazzling blue sky. Above her, seagulls swooped and screeched, their piercing cries mingling with the distant shrieks of delight from children on the marina beach.

She dozed quietly, unperturbed, undisturbed and drugged. It was when Marcus was away from her that she really relaxed. He had gone to some dreadful and no doubt dreary little village today and she was pleased to be left behind.

A fly buzzed. She brushed it away without opening her eyes. Then there were footsteps, quiet ones, sneaking through the bushes. She smiled to herself. She was well used to being admired and it didn't occur to her that it wasn't a man. Without moving her head, she opened one eye. A familiar pair of legs hove into view.

'What do you want?'

'Oh!' said Eddy with feigned surprise. 'I didn't realize you were here.'

'I bet. Given that I told that oh-so-charming assistant manageress – what's her name?'

'Rowena.'

'Rowena, and within earshot of you, that I was going out to sunbathe, I'm really amazed that you're here. You're so bloody transparent,' and she turned away.

Eddy just smiled, squinting in the sunshine.

'Well,' he said at last, 'I always did have a bit of bother

129

with my ears. Don't hear as well as I should, you know.'

'Then get them syringed. Who knows, might clear your brains out at the same time.' Camilla sat up, clutching her arms across her breasts. She didn't like having her afternoon siesta interrupted. It was annoying, especially when it was only a fool like Eddy. She put on her sunglasses, pushing them up her tanned nose.

He looked her over appreciatively. Naked except for the smallest of bikini bottoms, she was a fine sight to behold. Long slim legs, fine ankles, curvaceous hips, flat stomach and generous breasts. His throat began to tighten and the sweat ran freely underneath his shirt.

'Pass me my shirt,' she ordered, holding out her free hand.

He obediently sprang forward and picked it off the ground where she had thrown it.

'Here,' he said, turning it the right way out.

She patted his arm. 'Good doggy.'

'Let me help you,' he said, ignoring the jibe, and he slid the shirt over her chestnut hair. Once it was around her neck, he stopped. She stared back at him, unflinching. She knew exactly what he wanted. The throbbing vein in his neck was giving him away.

'You're a very beautiful woman, Camilla,' he said thickly, his eyes flickering across her face.

'Really? How clever of you to notice.'

'I mean it,' he insisted. 'I've always thought so, you know. Always. Ever since we first met.'

'How nice. And what, pray, are you going to do about it?'

He moved her arms away from her breasts and let his eyes feast on her. There was a slow intake of breath. 'I know what I'd like to do so, so much. Yes,' he whispered, 'you're very, very beautiful.'

She put her arms back and his face fell.

'Like me then, do you?'

Eddy nodded.

'Well, as you like me so much and as you've been especially attentive, I'm going to let you in on a secret.'

His eyes lit up. He was almost panting.

'What?'

She let her arms fall and his gaze was instantly fixed on her breasts again, his tongue running greedily around his top lip.

'This, Eddy,' she said slowly, 'is the Fort Knox of bodies and do you know what that means?'

His glinting eyes remained steadfastly on her chest. 'What?' he whispered, breathless.

'It means little boys like you, who don't know how to treat a woman properly, don't get to touch any of it. In other words, Eddy, you can look but nothing else.'

'You mean . . .' and his eyes were crestfallen.

'What I mean is this,' and before he could say anything she put her hand between her thighs and started to caress herself. 'This is what I want. Someone who can really give me a good time.'

Eddy's mouth fell. He had never seen a woman do that before, at least not in person. Men's magazines, yes, but . . . this was out in the hotel garden in the middle of the day, and there were other guests around. His head quickly swivelled around. Thank God, no one could see them here.

'Oh Eddy . . .' she moaned, her hand moving underneath her bikini bottoms, 'it's so good.' She opened her eyes and looked at him, smiling slowly. 'So good.'

He stared. He didn't know what else to do. He was electrified by her: her hand, her breasts, the sweat running down between them, her beautiful legs. He was desperate to have her. He reached out . . .

She slapped him back. 'Tut, tut, little boy. Remember what I said. Fort Knox.'

He sighed. He was going to burst.

'Mmm, are you watching, Eddy?'

Her eyes were closed as her hands started to move faster and faster.

Eddy was stupefied. His mouth hung open and his eyes stared as there, in front of him, as brazenly as anything he had ever seen, she masturbated.

He watched closely, aware only of the thumping of his chest and the way beads of sweat rolled down his back.

'Know . . . who . . . I'm . . . thinking . . . of?'

He couldn't answer.

Her fingers shot in and out. He could hear the small sucking noises and could see her intense concentration. He wanted so much to be there. His trousers were strained to their limit but he didn't dare do anything. Not here. Not in the public gardens.

'Oh God, Eddy . . . I'm coming . . . I'm coming . . .' and her face contorted, her back arched and her legs stuck out rigidly along the lounger as quicker and quicker she moved, her hips grinding into the chair.

Then she came, crying aloud with the sweet, sweet agony of it all, her hands busily clutching at herself.

'Eddy . . . Eddy!'

He threw his hand over her mouth. 'Shhh!' and sweat, more of anxiety than anything else now, dripped off his nose and onto her gorgeous sexual flesh. He was in despair. So close and yet . . . yet . . .

And then, she stopped, all energy dying away. She smiled brightly at him, still panting.

'Enjoyed that, did you? Well, that's your lot for one day. Now run along and don't bother me any more. You're giving me a headache.'

'But –'

'Go on. Disappear. God, you're the last person I want.'

'But why?' Eddy was confused; flustered; uncomprehending.

'Because, stupid,' and she held his pained face in her cool hand, 'if I want to fuck something around here, it's not going to be some flunky of my stepbrother's. So piss off, there's a good boy, and just in case you're thinking of saying anything about it to anyone, or giving me a hard time because I won't let you sample the goods, I'll make damned sure that whore of yours, what's her name?'

'Rowena.'

'Rowena. Ah yes, forgettable little name, isn't it? So ethnic, I suppose. Anyway, I'll tell her and then I'll tell Marcus what you did to me this afternoon; how you came and pestered me and tried to have your wicked way with me, and he won't like that one little bit,' she grinned.

Eddy stood up carefully, his groin in agony. His legs were weak.

'I'll . . .' and he swallowed hard, 'go.' Muttering to himself he staggered off, her laughter floating on the wind behind him.

Rowena was watching television when he came to their room, white-faced and sweaty. Without a word, he slumped down into a chair.

'What's the matter with you?' she asked. 'You look awful.'

He shook his head. 'Nothing.'

'Are you sure? Maybe it was something you ate for lunch?'

He looked at her. 'Yes. Probably.'

She smiled. 'Why don't we go and lie down? That usually makes you feel better.'

Eddy thought about this and then decisively stood up. It would be a shame to waste an invitation like that, especially when he had had such an appetizer with Camilla.

He grabbed Rowena by the arm and pulled her to him. He kissed her deeply, his hands finding their way beneath her blouse with all the instincts of a homing pigeon.

'Well, well, well,' she laughed softly. 'And what's got into you today?'

He kissed her again. 'Just be quiet, woman. I want you now.' Together, their arms tightly embraced, he walked her back to the bed until they fell over in a heap.

They rolled around hot and breathless, arms and legs

entwined like ivy around a tree. Bit by bit, grunting and groaning, they excitedly removed each other's clothing.

He massaged his shiny face between her breasts, rolled her big pink nipples in his mouth and sucked like a pig.

She ran her fingers down his torso, feeling his pulse race beneath his hairy skin. She wanted him so much. Over and over they rolled, kissing and licking, his fingers digging into her ample white flesh as she pushed against him, rubbing herself up and down his body, her wet hot flesh opening for him.

'Take me, Eddy, take me,' and so he did.

'Well,' she said afterwards, as she dressed herself, pulling the zip of her skirt up with a decisive frustrated yank, 'that was different. I never realized it could be so quick. How novel.'

He said nothing, his face buried in his pillow. He just wanted the ground to swallow him up there and then as she left the room in a huff.

Eight

Hildegard replaced the receiver with a heavy heart. All morning she had been on the telephone and still she couldn't find who she was looking for. Someone should know; someone out there amidst all the millions should know where he was.

She walked over to her sitting-room window and stood gazing out across the immaculate lawns of her employer's Oxfordshire mansion. Why couldn't she find him? she asked herself; why was it so impossible? She turned to one side and picked up a small fading black and white photograph. There was a man with white hair with his arms around a very blond little boy, dressed in a pair of shorts, a jumper and wellingtons. She smiled fondly at it. Such a chubby little boy. About two years old, his knees grazed, smiling shyly at the camera safe in the arms of his father. The man was her uncle and the little boy, now adult and somewhere out there, her cousin. She looked up again and squinted in the sun, her plain, strong-boned face sombre. Her cousin was all she had left, her only family, and she was determined to find him.

The telephone rang, shattering her contemplation.

'Yes?'

'Hildegard! Why aren't you here? What are you doing in your room when you should be looking after me?'

'I am very sorry, Frau Killington. I will come at once.'

But the old lady rattled on. 'I should have had my medicine half an hour ago. It's not good enough, you know.'

'I shall come at once,' and the phone went dead.

Hildegard sighed. The old lady, like elderly patients everywhere, could be extremely fractious.

'Right then, Camilla, it's all been arranged.'

'What has?'

She looked at Marcus with puzzlement. They were having lunch on the hotel terrace, enjoying the sunshine and gentle breeze.

'I told you yesterday. Don't you remember?'

She frowned. He told her so much sometimes. How was she to remember, especially when she was stoned out of her mind.

'No. I don't.'

He patiently laid down his napkin and sat back in his chair.

'We shall be returning to Oxford today. I have some research to do as well as other business commitments –'

'I'm not coming,' she announced, interrupting him. She had her own agenda.

'I beg your pardon?'

'You heard.' She took a bite of some salad. 'I want to stay. I like it here. Well, not *here* exactly, especially not with that tiresome Eddy, but . . . well, maybe nearer Plymouth perhaps,' and she smiled at him.

His suspicions were not allayed.

'For what purpose?' he asked.

She shrugged. 'Sailing?'

'Sailing,' he repeated, running the word around his mouth. 'Really? And I'm supposed to believe this, am I? You can't sail. You never have done. You get seasick.'

'Then maybe it's time I learnt how to, isn't it?' and she glared at him. 'Anyway, I'm not going back. Not yet. Not until I'm ready.'

He said nothing, but she could see he was clearly annoyed.

'And what if I say no?' he said.

'Why the bloody hell should I always do as you want, Marcus?' she cried, flinging down her napkin. 'I'm old enough to make my own decisions, you know!'

He leant forward, his massive hand covering hers, which he squeezed possessively.

'Yes, my dear,' he said quietly, 'but I do know what's best for you, don't I, and we both know why you should stay with me, don't we?'

She snatched her hand away.

'Well, not this time, brother, dear. I want to stay and I will stay! You don't own me!' she hissed.

He stroked the back of her hand with a forefinger, a lingering smile hovering around his lips.

'You forget, Marcus,' she continued, 'that I'm every bit as important in our business as you are. I own fifty per cent and without my co-operation, you won't get what you want. I could so easily foul things up for you, so don't push me about, okay?'

'Is that a threat?' he asked incredulously, 'because if it is, I rather think that of the two of us, you would come off so much worse.'

Her nostrils flared angrily with each breath and her lips, usually so generous, were thin and bloodless.

'No, of course not,' she sniped.

'So what exactly does it mean then?' he asked.

'Whatever you like,' and she smiled.

He got up and came to stand behind her. She watched him warily. He laid his hands on her shoulders and started to knead.

'My dear girl,' came his deep velvety voice from behind her, 'we are one. Always have been and always will be.' His grip tightened. 'And you will do as I say because if you don't, or if you have any ideas about messing things up for us . . .' He squeezed even tighter. He was hurting her and she winced with the pain as his fingers dug into her but there was nothing she could do. 'I might get really angry and we wouldn't want that, would we?'

She couldn't answer. She was in agony.

'I will let you stay here,' he said, his voice deceptively smooth once more, 'provided you do something for me.'

She didn't reply. She felt sick.

'And if you do as I want, and I'm sure you will . . .' he leant down, his face inches from her ear, '. . . you can have whatever you want, within reason, of course.' He paused. 'Is that a deal?'

His last words were a deadly whisper.

She closed her eyes. The pain was excruciating but she was not going to cry. There was no way she was going to give in to him by showing any weakness. She bit the inside of her mouth. That stopped the tears.

'Well, my dear, I'm waiting.'

She nodded silently.

'Pardon?'

'Yes . . . yes. Please let me go, Marcus, please.'

He stood up, stroked her head as he would a child and then pulled her to her feet. She turned around to face him, her mouth wavering. He took hold of her hands and kissed her on both cheeks. She flinched.

'Now, you go and tidy yourself up, Camilla. You look a mess and you know how I don't like that. I'll be in to see you later. I've got to see Eddy first.'

'Yes, Marcus,' came the mumbled reply.

'And now the full SP of the 2.30 at Ascot. First number 10, Colonel Bogey, 5—4 on favourite. Second number 1, Neversaydie, 6—1, and third, Malley's Girl, 15—1. The distances were a short head and three lengths. Seven ran.'

Eddy looked miserably down at the floor.

'Shit!'

Lost again. No favourite, especially one at that short price, had won over the mile when the ground was so fast. How could he be so wrong? He rested his chin disconsolately on his hand. More money down the drain; money he couldn't afford and money he couldn't do without. If only Sian hadn't left. She had twenty thousand sitting in the bank and God, he could do with it right now. He had so many debts and it was getting desperate. He couldn't think what she needed it for.

He flipped off the television and looked at his watch. It was an expensive Swiss-made one, a present from Sian on his last birthday. It must be worth quite a bit. He could always sell it if things really got bad. That or ask Rowena.

His telephone rang.

'Yeah?'

'Killington here,' said the cold voice.

'Mr Killington!'

Eddy immediately sat upright, straightened his tie and tucked in his shirt.

'Sorry about that, Mr Killington. Didn't realize it was you,' and he laughed nervously.

'Downstairs in the office,' said Marcus unamused. 'Right now.'

'Yes, Mr Killington. Right away.'

When Eddy entered the room, his hair hurriedly brushed and his suit changed, he was slightly out of breath. The lift had been in use and it was a bit of a sprint from his room to the office.

'Sit, Eddy.'

He did. Marcus was standing at the window, hands clasped behind his back. Their aftershaves clashed; one prohibitively expensive, Eddy's mass-market, so he lit a cigarette. Funny how it was his office and yet there was no way he would even begin to think of usurping his boss.

'Eddy.'

'Yes, Mr Killington?'

Marcus swung round, a small smile on his face. 'The National Hunt season starts in a couple of months and I have a few plans for it.'

Eddy remained silent. Now what was Killington up to?

'Did you know, Eddy,' said Marcus, seating himself in Eddy's chair behind the desk and pouring himself a cup of coffee, 'that the first person who doped a horse was a man called Daniel Dawson. He used arsenic. Apparently, it's a good stimulant if used in the right quantities. Unfortunately, for Mr Dawson, he used too much of the stuff and the horses died.' He looked at Eddy and smiled smugly. 'So the authorities hanged him.'

He paused, watching Eddy closely. Eddy began to perspire.

'What's this got to do with me, Mr Killington?' he asked tentatively.

'Well, you're a man who likes the horses. You gamble a bit, don't you? In fact, I think you probably gamble too much. Am I right?'

Eddy didn't answer.

'I'll take that as a yes then, shall I?'

Both men looked at each other.

'Anyway,' said Marcus, 'I'm about to shorten the odds considerably in your favour, so much so, that you'll be able to make quite a profit if you're prepared to go along with my plans.'

Eddy knew all about doping. Everyone did who had anything to do with racing and it was the only thing that Killington could be referring to.

'And you want me . . .' he began.

Marcus smiled briefly. 'Maybe. I don't know yet. You see, I only have a couple of jumpers as most of my horses are running on the flat, so the game is new to me. They're fairly moderate animals but with a little help in the right direction, I don't see why I can't tip things more in their and my favour. A small three-horse race at a modest meeting with the usual lax security could guarantee that my animals win. And you, Eddy, would be just the man to do it.'

Eddy glanced up at him. He was to take all the risks, like he always did.

'Of course,' continued Marcus, 'you would be generously recompensed. That goes without saying.'

Eddy didn't understand sometimes. Why should Killington, with all his millions, want to do this at all? What did it matter if one of his animals lost? He owned some of the best two-year-olds in the country. They had picked up more than their share of top-class sprints this season. Why he should want to risk it all like this seemed pointless to Eddy. His thoughts must have been entirely evident on his face.

'I can see,' said Marcus, 'that you're not really sure about this; that you're wondering why I should want to do it, maybe? After all, I already have so much.'

Eddy was embarrassed. He didn't like being so transparent.

'Well, I'll tell you why – why it is that I'm a success and you never will be – because I'm the one that grabs each and every opportunity, Eddy, while idiots like you wouldn't know where to begin.'

Marcus's face had hardened, his usually handsome features coarsened with anger.

'You're a nobody, Eddy,' and the other man bristled but the quiet onslaught didn't stop there. 'There was a time when I thought that maybe you could be really valuable to me. I'm now beginning to realize that my faith in you was misplaced. You have turned out to be mediocre, *vin ordinaire*, as they say. It looks suspiciously to me as though Sian has left you, and if this were so, I would be very displeased. I thought I made it clear I want her here. Just remember that I'm the one who gives the orders around here and if I tell you to do something, and I'm willing to pay you extra for it, you will do it without question, understand? This may very well be your last chance to prove to me that I can rely on you after all.'

Eddy reluctantly met the dark brooding eyes and shifted uncomfortably in his seat. He should have known better than even to think of questioning Killington.

'Sorry, Mr Killington. I just thought –'

'Well, don't,' snapped Marcus. 'You're not clever enough for it.'

'Yes, sir.'

'You will, of course, keep quiet about this as you do all of our business arrangements.'

'Yes, Mr Killington,' answered Eddy, a bit too quickly, anxious to make amends.

'I hope so, because you wouldn't like it if I found out you had been talking, because then you really would be in trouble. Do I make myself clear?'

Eddy tried to smile but it was impossible. He lit another cigarette instead. This attack was so unfair. He was a reliable middle man for Killington's coastal activities and had never let him down.

Marcus watched impassively. He enjoyed others' discomfort. It was more than likely this plan to fix the races would never come about, but he liked to exercise his power, to bully.

'I have my reasons for doing this, Eddy, because as you know, it's not just racehorses that can be doped,' and he suddenly stood up. The interview was over.

'I have other things to see to now,' he said. 'Much to your relief — and don't deny it, Eddy — I shall be leaving later.'

Eddy looked at the floor.

'Camilla will be staying on for a while, however, and you will see to her every need, understand?'

Eddy stood up. His knees were unsteady. He nodded dumbly. When Marcus had gone, he slumped back down in the chair. He couldn't wait to see the back of that man.

If only Sian were here. It was all getting too much; all this hassle, all this tedious paperwork, all this organizing. He needed her, he couldn't do without her. The bloody place was coming undone at the seams and she was the only one who could put it back together again.

'There you are, Bracken, off you go.'

Sian slid the halter off the horse's neck and watched contentedly as the chestnut mare with her four white socks, galloped away across the paddock, her proud head

142

held high and her nostrils quivering at all the new smells.

'She looks really good, Sian,' said Helen.

'Yes, she does. I've missed her, you know.'

Helen came to stand next to her. 'Well, what do you expect? A fine animal like her, full of get up and go, and no one to give her the proper attention. I mean, I'm sure your friend looked after her well enough but she belongs to you and you're the one she really needs.'

They stood watching the mare as she frolicked about, snorting and stamping. The other horses looked positively dull by comparison.

'Look at her!' laughed Sian. 'It's wonderful.'

'When shall we go for a ride then?'

'Give her time to settle down a bit, a couple of days perhaps, then we'll go.'

'What exactly is she?' asked Helen. 'She looks a bit of a mixture to me. Some Arab, some Thoroughbred?'

'Yes, something like that. She can be a bit of a madam sometimes too, which must be the Arab side of her. She's been known to really play up if she wants to, although with me she's no problem. I don't think she'd dare.'

The mare ceased her careering around and started to nibble at the grass.

'By the way, Helen, where's Sebi?'

'Oh, Andrew's got him up at The Grange. He keeps him there most of the time, especially when the covering season's over. Stops him getting any ideas and gives him time to recover. We could ride up there if you like. It's a lovely place. Bloody huge. God knows why he lives there. It must be like a pea rattling around in a saucepan.'

'Why doesn't he sell it?'

'I don't know,' shrugged Helen. 'It's something to do with his past, and it's not worth asking.'

'I saw him in Newton Abbot the other day.'

'Did he say anything?'

'No, just looked really miserable.'

'Ah,' said Helen with a smile, 'that's our Andrew.'

'Why doesn't he like talking about his past?' Sian asked. 'Does he have something to hide?'

'Not that I know of. He just doesn't. He won't talk about anything personal. Just clams up. For all I know,' she chuckled, 'he could be an escaped convict or something. You never know.'

Sian lowered her voice. 'I think I might be able to find out something about him.'

'Oh yes?' Helen smiled, her eyes lighting up. 'What?'

'Well, when I was in Newton Abbot the other day, I was in this junk shop just browsing and I came across this journal written by someone called Isobel Warrener and she used to live at The Grange. I haven't read it yet. I keep meaning to, but I'm so tired in the evenings.'

They both looked out over the paddock.

'I wonder if there's any connection between Andrew and her?' said Sian.

Helen shrugged. 'Who knows? Like I say, he's a closed book. Keeps everything close to his chest. Nothing would surprise me about him. Absolutely nothing.'

'He couldn't really be a criminal or anything, could he?' queried Sian.

'Well, he could be.'

The two women looked at each other and then both shook their heads.

'No way.'

'Of course not, but then . . .' and Helen let the idea hang in the air.

'Anyway,' said Sian, 'I can't say I really care about that. What with one thing and another, Eddy and the baby, I'm far too preoccupied to spend my time speculating over Andrew. Emotional upsets like I've had are hardly conducive to daydreaming, are they?'

'Suppose not.'

'Mind you,' she mused, 'I suppose if I were really put on the spot, I'd have to agree with you that he is just a tiny bit good-looking. Not that it means anything,' she added hurriedly. 'Let's just say that in the general run of things, purely objectively you understand, he does have a certain . . . well, attractiveness.'

'Is that all?' drawled Helen ironically. 'Wow! you're really generous.'

'So what do you expect me to say? Remember, one I'm still married to . . . to that bastard, and two, I'm pregnant and in a very short time, it'll start to show and then what am I going to say to Andrew? He's bound to be annoyed about it because I won't be able to work, and I'll look like a beached whale.'

'He might not be,' countered Helen.

Sian shot her a disbelieving look.

'Anyway,' she demanded, 'what is this? Why do you want to know what I think of him? I thought you said to keep well away from him? You're not matchmaking, are you?'

'No.'

'Because if you are, forget it. I've told you, I'm not interested. I couldn't care less about men at the moment. As far as I'm concerned, they're a pain in the butt that I can do without. I can manage perfectly well without any of those morons messing up my life, thank you, and after the way I've been treated, it will be a very long time before I want to be even civil to one of them!' and her mouth shut tight with determination.

'Okay, okay,' surrendered Helen, 'no need to bite my head off.'

Sian's eyes filled with tears but she just about kept herself in check.

There was silence between them, each lost with her own thoughts. Helen was the first to speak.

'He really did hurt you, didn't he?'

'What the hell do you think, Helen?' came the pained reply.

'I'm sorry.'

'Oh, damn it!' exclaimed Sian, furious with herself and

angrily wiping her face. 'I'm sorry. I didn't mean to snap.'

'That's all right,' said Helen smiling. 'It's your hormones.'

'Oh dear. Does that mean I'll be an emotional wreck for the next seven months?'

'Of course not. Anyway,' resumed Helen, as if nothing had happened, 'how long will you keep riding for?'

'Don't know. I'll see how I feel, I suppose, and how big I get. I don't think I'll be able to work here too long. Maybe until the end of the season.'

'And then?'

Sian looked at her. Even though she was wearing sunglasses, Helen could see she was worried.

'Then I don't know. It depends.'

'On what?'

'Eddy, I suppose.'

Eddy stood at one of the upstairs windows and watched Killington's Rolls being loaded up.

'Come on, Camilla. Get a move on.'

Killington appeared with Camilla reluctantly following. She looked unhappy about something. Even Eddy could see that. The set of her mouth and the way she held herself suggested that something was very wrong. He wondered what it was, but then he wondered quite a bit about the relationship between Killington and Camilla. He just couldn't work it out. He saw how when her stepbrother leant forward to kiss her on the cheek, she seemed to freeze.

'Now remember, Camilla, Patrick will be down tomorrow to take care of things. I can't relax unless I know that you are okay.'

'I'm all right, Marcus, and I don't need Patrick or anyone else to stand over me. Don't you trust me?'

There was no reply.

'Yes, well, I'm off now. I'll ring you tonight.'

'But I don't need Patrick!'

146

He wasn't listening. He never did. He turned towards Bains.

'Everything set?'

'Yes, sir.'

'Right then. Now Camilla,' and he took her rigidly clenched hands in his, 'behave yourself and I'll be down soon. Goodbye.'

Eddy noticed how she forced herself to smile. She waited until the dark blue car had disappeared through the hotel gates before turning on her heels and marching back indoors, rubbing the palms of her hands against her trousers.

Camilla knew exactly what she was going to do. She was going to run a very hot bath, get very, very drunk and take some cocaine. By that time, she would be so stoned out of her head, she wouldn't care about anything. It would be the only way of getting him out of her system.

'Where are you going tonight?'

Sian was sitting at the kitchen table reading the evening newspaper when Helen had walked in.

'Oh, just off to Plymouth,' answered Helen casually. 'Why don't you come?'

Sian shook her head.

'No, thanks. I'm too tired to do anything much tonight except collapse in front of the TV. Are you going to meet anyone special? Billy, perhaps?' and she chuckled to herself. 'Honestly, Helen, you were a bit mean to him. Poor chap. He didn't deserve that.'

Helen stood in front of the mirror, checking her makeup. 'Oh please, spare me.' She turned around, lipstick poised. 'You don't know what he's like!' and she returned to the mirror. 'He's a bloody limpet, that man. Hangs on like grim death and it doesn't matter what you say, he still comes back for more. You're welcome to him – and his spots.'

'Mmm, perhaps I won't,' and Sian smiled. 'So who is it, then, that you're meeting?'

Helen grinned. 'Just someone.'

'I see. Well in that case, it's a good thing I'm not coming. I'd only cramp your style. What's his name?'

Helen seemed not to have heard at first. Then: 'Darryl. He's a builder.' She put her lipstick away. 'He's not much to look at, I suppose. Bit short. Fairly ordinary but he's okay, and let's face it, beggars can't be choosers.'

Sian smiled.

'You're not fair to yourself, you know, Helen. That's not true at all.'

'Bollocks!' came the sharp retort. 'And don't you say otherwise.' She paused, thinking, her hairbrush in mid-air.

'Darryl is more your Mini Metro than your Rolls, if you know what I mean.'

Sian chuckled. 'Well, so long as his "big end" works.'

Helen laughed. 'So apart from watching the TV,' she said, 'are you going to do anything?'

'No.'

'It must be all the aggro you've been through,' she explained as she rooted through her handbag. 'It's finally catching up with you. Plus, of course, your pregnancy. That's bound to make you feel different. One of the neighbours had a baby last year and I remember her saying how totally exhausted she was for the first four months.'

'I can hardly keep my eyes open.'

'Yes, but you look well on it. Must be all the extra hormones. It's bloody unfair, you know, even when you've got morning sickness you still look attractive. I bet if it were me, I'd look terrible. More like an uncooked potato than pale and interesting. I don't know why I bother sometimes.'

Sian laughed. 'Rubbish. Look at you tonight. You look lovely.'

Helen did a twirl. Her black ski pants were stretched to their maximum and her white cotton T-shirt made her bust look like the Alps on their side.

'Well, let's hope Darryl thinks so.'

Left on her own, Sian made herself comfortable on the sofa, feet up to watch a film. After a while she got bored, so she switched channels. That bored her too, so she turned it off. She put on some music, something quiet and melodic; something to dream to; something to sit out in the garden with, to gaze up at the pincushioned night sky. It was a beautiful night, a magical night, a night for love and romance – but not for her.

She sighed. She wished more than anything that there was someone out there who would love her and hold her and whisper sweet words to her. There just wasn't anyone. She lay back on the grass, her hands behind her head and closed her eyes . . .

. . . The man held her face in his hands, looking deep into her eyes.

'I love you,' he said. 'I always have done and I always will do. You're all that a man could wish for,' and then he kissed her.

She answered his kiss with passion of her own. Standing there in the tropical surf, the warm sea rippling around their ankles, the air filled with the fragrance of night blooms, she couldn't believe how happy she was. This man, this wonderful handsome man, was holding her in his powerful arms and wanting her, something that she had never thought would happen.

He kissed her neck. There was an urgency in him now, something she recognized and wanted as badly as he did.

His mouth covered her. His kisses were hot and demanding. It was all she could do to breathe. Her stomach tightened and there was a familiar tingling deep inside her. They pressed hard against each other, their deep instincts pushing them closer and closer.

'Sian . . . Sian . . .'

His voice was calling her and she couldn't ignore him, didn't want to ignore him. He was everything to her. More male, more man, more animal than anyone she had known before.

He laid her down on the sand, softly and gently. There was no impatience. He smiled at her as she lay in his arms.

'What was it that brought us together, my love?'

She shook her head slowly. 'I don't know. I only know I can't live without you.' She held his head. 'Love me. Take me. I'm yours for ever,' and again they kissed.

His hands ran over her body, brushing and caressing her skin, drawing her to him. Sometimes he kneaded her, sometimes he kissed her, but always he tantalized her. Her breasts, her stomach, her shoulders, her thighs. She was getting hotter and hotter, the heat inside burning her up. She wouldn't be able to stand it much longer.

And then . . . his hand slid her thighs apart. He was getting closer and closer. She wanted him so much. She was aching for him.

'Please . . . please . . .'

She held him tighter. She was breathless, sweat prickling her skin.

He was pressing against her, his hardness rigid against her flesh, setting her alight.

He touched; she quivered, a frisson of delight running up her spine. At first it was slow, teasing, and leaving her only wanting more. But then . . . faster and faster, all thoughts banished from her mind as all she could concentrate on, all she wanted, the overwhelming deep-seated explosion started to build inside her.

He smothered her face with kisses, his breath hot against her face.

'Sian . . . I love you . . . I love you.'

Then he took her, filling her inside with every last bit of him, eating her up with all he had to give.

They moved together, ripples of water running over their bodies as the moon shone down on them, their silvered flesh highlighted against the shore.

On and on it went; deeper, faster, harder and then, just when she couldn't bear it any more, just when she thought she would die from it, she –

She sat up, panting and embarrassed. She looked around her. All was silent. In the distance she could hear the church bells ringing out midnight.

She must have been dreaming but it was so vivid. Every touch of his fingers, every kiss of his lips, the very smell of him, she could recall it all and it shamed her. She wiped her brow.

She stood up, weak-kneed and surprised. An erotic dream, in her condition! It was ridiculous. She went into the kitchen and ran the cold tap until the water was really icy, and then filled a glass. She drank thirstily. She stopped and thought for a while, staring out of the window. She knew who it was who affected her like that and it dismayed her. She ought to have more control. Her dream had betrayed her.

Up at The Grange, Andrew couldn't sleep. The heat, the sultriness, the clammy sweat that covered all of his body.

He was standing by the huge bay windows of his bedroom, letting the warm night air caress his bare skin. He had a drink of iced water in one hand, which he periodically held against his wet brow.

Out there, somewhere in the valley beyond the black trees and the scorched fields and tucked away in that small cottage, lay the woman he couldn't stop thinking of. Every time he lay down and closed his eyes, it was her face he saw.

He sighed. It was a full moon tonight. It hung in the deep, dark sky surrounded by myriad stars and casting its silvery light across the sleeping land.

A slight gust caught his hair and lifted it off his forehead and with it came the faint aroma of honeysuckle and lilies that grew in the gardens. It reminded him of her scent that first time she came into his office; a scent that touched the core of his being and one he would never forget.

A vixen shrieked, her timeless eerie call echoing through the valley and a shudder went through him. Here he was, so desperately alone. He wondered if the loneliness would ever end. He wanted to relax, to let the stars shine down above him the way they used to do so long ago, at a time when he was happy and could appreciate them. Strange how after all this time he was starting to notice them again.

'Well, boy, what do you think of it?' Blaize was lying at his master's feet and when his name was mentioned, he looked up and cocked his large intelligent head on one side. 'Lovely, isn't it? All this and no one to share it with.'

The dog's tail thumped.

'I wonder what it would be like if she was up here now? Do you suppose she would like it?' but Blaize only licked his hand. 'I don't suppose you care one way or the other. Just so long as you get fed every day, that's all you're bothered about, isn't it, boy? Well, I don't blame you. Ordinarily my needs would be much the same, but . . . something's changed and she's the one that's changed it.' He sighed heavily. 'Thing is, what the hell am I going to do about it, especially as she doesn't seem to like me too much?'

He patted the dog's large head. He wasn't going to find any answer there.

Nine

From the drawing room window Mrs Killington watched Marcus walking in the grounds. She sighed.

'Is something wrong, Frau Killington?' Hildegard came over to join her. She knew at once that she had asked the wrong question. She really ought to know better by now.

'Oh, nothing you can do, Hildegard.'

Mrs Killington's smile was lopsided and did not improve her untidy lipstick.

'I just wish that son of mine would find himself a decent wife, you know, a proper one, like. I know Camilla acts as his hostess – I do as well sometimes – but it's not right. He really ought to find himself a proper wife; a good woman who would be a credit to him. I mean, that Camilla . . . well, she's never been right, you know. Always been a strange one. Her mother was the same. Between you and me,' she whispered conspiratorially, 'they used to call her all manner of names in the pub and none of them nice ones, if you know what I mean.'

She raised her thin pencilled-in eyebrows at Hildegard, fixing her with a narrow stare.

Hildegard watched Marcus with complete detachment. She felt nothing for him. Then she turned her attention back to the old lady. She was long used to Frau Killington's favourite topic of conversation. She groaned inwardly.

'Sabre!'

Hildegard swung round as Mrs Killington screeched. The Yorkshire terrier was scuttling off across the carpet like a hairy miniature torpedo, short legs a blur under his dark coat.

'You little rat!' yelled Mrs Killington. 'Just you wait till I get you! I'll skin you, you little bleeder!'

'What has he done?' asked Hildegard, coming over with concern.

Mrs Killington pointed, her bony hand shaking with indignation.

'He's done that, he has. Look at it! All over that bloody awful rug!'

'That, Frau Killington, is a handmade Persian silk rug and it is very expensive.'

'I don't care what it is. It looks bloody terrible to me!'

The corner of Hildegard's mouth quivered. She despised all animal life except humans and she only liked a very few of those. Frau Killington wasn't one of them. It was very difficult, however, not to laugh out loud at the sight of her outraged and wrinkled puce face.

'Perhaps you should have let him out earlier?'

'Oh yes? And have him doing those horrible things with that cushion he found in one of the sheds?'

She wrinkled her nose in disgust.

'Did you see him the other day, Hildegard?'

'No, I did not.'

'Well, it was so embarrassing.'

'It was?'

'Yes,' and she shuddered at the memory, her scrawny body encased in yet another of her vibrant blue shell suits. Then her small piggy eyes, encrusted with matching makeup, widened with horror.

'There, in front of all my ladies from the bingo club, he began to ... well, you know,' she spluttered uncomfortably.

'You mean,' said Hildegard loftily, 'he began to masturbate?'

'Exactly!' Mrs Killington's mouth was a pinched dark red smeared hole. 'Bloody little thing! I didn't know where to put myself.'

'Perhaps, Frau Killington, you should think of having him castrated?'

Hildegard smiled sweetly, her huge bulk looming over Mrs Killington.

The old lady recoiled as if she had been smacked in the mouth.

'Castrated!' she cried. 'Absolutely not! A male is not a male if he has that done. Oh no,' she shook her head firmly, 'not my Sabre. He's got to have his sex drive.'

Pity, thought Hildegard.

Marcus wandered down the baize-green lawns of his house unaware that the two women had been observing him.

He was a purposeful man of singular intent and ambition, and despite all that he owned and all that he controlled, it wasn't enough for him any more. He had an irritating sense of dissatisfaction that refused to go away; a feeling that whatever he had achieved in the eyes of others, by his own exacting standards, it wasn't enough. Had he been a man of gentler emotions, one with an eye for beauty of form, his wanderings across the perfectly manicured lawns with their speckling of mature oak and beech trees, might have restored his sense of wellbeing. But it didn't.

He was troubled, irritated and hungry, and there were several reasons for this.

First of all Camilla. The business was wasted on her. She had no interest in it, never concerned herself with its day-to-day affairs and mostly just sat there gathering in his hard-won profits that she then squandered on frivolous things.

Then there were the police. He was walking on thin ice and he knew it. One of his drug couriers had been arrested at Heathrow and there was every chance that he might spill the beans to the authorities. Marcus was going to have to act swiftly if he was going to contain things. A damage limitation exercise was called for. He would get one of his

London associates to visit the man in detention and point out to him the benefits that would be gained if he were to remain silent. If the courier still didn't listen, then he would simply be eliminated. Marcus didn't like waste, or people who wasted his time. He liked to think of himself as a decisive individual who got things done.

The Grange – he had to have it. It was imperative that he moved his operations as quickly as possible. Mann had been unnecessarily difficult. Camilla should change things there. Marcus didn't always use force. He knew only too well the difference a pretty face could make. It was one advantage he was going to make the most of. Others had been just as easily beguiled and so it would be with Mann. Camilla could be quite devastating in her own little way.

He smiled to himself and then stopped. A young black-bird, newly fledged from the nest, its feathers still downy in places, was struggling to get to a nearby hedge out of harm's way. It appeared to have broken one small unused wing and was dragging it along the ground. It flapped pathetically as the large human peered down at it.

Marcus cupped his hands over it and picked it up. It lay warm and trembling in his palm, its tiny heart fluttering wildly in its breast, its bright eyes nervous.

'Poor bird,' he whispered. 'You poor, poor bird,' and then with its head between his thumb and forefinger, he broke its neck. There was no place for anything weak in Marcus's life. Those faced with life's injustices who didn't fight back, deserved all that they got.

He dropped the tiny warm carcass in a nearby shrubbery that was covered in pink scented blooms. Of what sort, he couldn't say, but then he employed a gardener and left the garden entirely up to him. Nature's beauty was something he never bothered with.

'Mr Killington!' It was Patrick. 'Where do I have to go, sir?'

'Leighford, Patrick. Near Newton Abbot. Bains will tell you.'

'Sir.'

Patrick's punched-in face screwed up in the sunlight. He stood still, subservient yet distant.

'Take the Range Rover. I've rented a place called Belvedere Cottage just outside the village. You and Camilla will stay there. And Patrick?'

'Yes, sir?'

'Keep a close eye on her this time. I don't want her getting any strange ideas.'

'Anything else, sir?'

'Yes. There's a chap called Andrew Mann who owns a house called The Grange on the other side of the village. He keeps a stable. Anything you hear about him – anything at all – you report back to me, understand? Directly to me. Nothing to Camilla.'

Patrick nodded. He asked for no explanations. What his boss did was none of his concern. He just did as he was told.

'Right then, off you go and keep in touch. I will be visiting.'

'Sir.'

With Patrick gone, Marcus looked out across his land, the sunlight sparkling off the lake, a flotilla of ducks bobbing across its surface. Then he put his hand into his trouser pocket and pulled out the Roman coin he had bought from Frank Jessop. He held it up to the light and marvelled that something that was this old could have such a fascination for him. He had always been interested in the past and the treasures that could be found. Roman treasure was a particular luxury that he allowed himself. A sideline, he called it; something to invest all his money in; something to hoard and gloat over when no one else was around. He prided himself on the fact that he owned one of the biggest private collections in the country, which he was convinced, if he got his hands on The Grange, would become *the* biggest. The coin he was holding belonged to the Warrener Hoard – Jessop had been quite informative about that, especially when he had seen just how much money he would get out of the deal. Marcus smiled. This coin had come to light and there would be others; plenty of others, and not just coins either. Plates, jewellery, statuettes, the newspaper cutting had said. All of it sitting there just waiting to be discovered. No one was going to deny him it, least of all some small-time stable hand.

'So there he is, Hildegard. My little boy as he used to be. Sweet, wasn't he?'

Hildegard picked up the photograph and peered closely at the small child. She could hardly believe that the round angelic face with its button-bright eyes, mop of coal-black hair and cheeky grin was Marcus.

'Of course,' said Mrs Killington, taking the photograph from her and smiling fondly, her hard eyes softening and the wrinkles smoothing out, 'he were a little moppet in those days. Wouldn't say boo to a goose. Quiet like, if you know what I mean. Always going off to his room or down to his den. Used to spend hours alone, he did.'

There was a pause.

'And then she arrived.'

'She, Frau Killington?'

'Camilla. Huh!' she snorted contemptuously. 'Camilla! I ask you. What a stupid name for a little girl. It was all down to that mother of hers, you know. I always did think she were no better than she ought to be. Camilla! Bloody snooty name. No wonder I didn't like her.'

She pulled a mean face and taking out a cigarette, lit up and inhaled deeply, her perm soon wreathed in clouds of blue smoke. Hildegard discreetly waved the smoke away.

'I cannot believe, Frau Killington, that you did not like Miss Camilla simply because of her name? That is illogical.' She turned over a page in the photograph album. 'Here,' she said, pointing to a picture, 'is Miss Camilla and very pretty she looks.'

They both looked at the snap. Camilla must have been

158

aged about seven. She wore a Sunday best dress of light blue cotton with a trim lace collar and cuffs. Her shoes were shiny black patent leather and she had long white socks. She gazed sidelong at the camera, her thumb being chewed pensively. Whoever was taking the picture was not getting any co-operation from her.

'I remember that day,' said Mrs Killington. 'Little madam had given me non-stop trouble all day. The four of us, me, her Dad, Marcus and her were out at the seaside. I had her all dressed up, looking smart and you know what she did?' Her small venomous eyes pinned Hildegard down.

'*Ja?*'

'She wet herself.'

Hildegard pressed her lips together in order to stop the laugh that threatened to explode.

'I couldn't believe it!' continued Mrs Killington. 'I asked her if she wanted to go, like, when we were about to leave but she said no. Then, when we got in the car, she just spread her legs and went. God, I went spare. 'Course her bloody father, as always, took her side. As far as he was concerned, she was the best thing that ever happened to him. Butter wouldn't melt in her mouth, or what? Didn't matter what she did, he always defended her.'

The old woman fell quiet as she sifted through her memories. When she spoke again, her voice was reflective. 'Don't know why, but she always got away with it.'

'Surely not, Frau Killington. She was only a little girl.'

Mrs Killington looked at Hildegard with tired disbelief.

'You don't know her, Hildegard. That one was never just a little girl. Never! She always knew too much. Don't ask me to explain,' she said, seeing her companion's questioning look.

'I don't know why, but that's how it was. And it was the same with Marcus, you know. Once she and her Dad moved in with me and him, that were it. Marcus was never the same again. Went from being a nice little boy into something else completely.'

'Why?'

The old lady pulled hard at her cigarette. 'You tell me. I couldn't understand it. He just seemed . . . fascinated with her. Right peculiar, if you ask me. Anyway, it wasn't anything I did, you know.'

She suddenly stood up. 'Let's have a drink,' and before Hildegard could say anything, she had tottered very slowly and very unsteadily to the sideboard and helped herself to a generous measure of Scotch. Sabre watched from his fur-lined bed, his beady little eyes following his mistress's every move.

Mrs Killington sat down again, rearranged some of her rings and then absently picked at one of her dentures.

'So, it was never the same once that miss had come to live with us. She and Marcus were as thick as thieves. Everywhere he was, she was right behind.'

She gulped her drink noisily, drops escaping down her shrivelled chin.

Hildegard did not approve. Drinking at this time of the day was not a good idea, especially when the doctor had expressly forbidden it.

'I find it hard to believe, Frau Killington, that Miss Camilla could have been a burden. She looks such a beautiful little girl,' and she picked up another photograph from the album. It showed Camilla swinging upside-down from a climbing frame, her father in close attendance.

'You don't know what it was like!' exclaimed Mrs Killington. Then suddenly she smiled, the lines around her eyes clustering thickly together.

'Mind you, she didn't have it all her own way. Sometimes my Marcus would get the better of her.'

'How?'

'Oh, he had his way. She used to tease him unmercifully, called him names and things. You know what kids are like – dead mean when they want to be. Well, one day he disappeared into the garden shed. Camilla was on the swing as usual. She always swung on the swing. Hardly

160

ever gave Marcus a go. Well, he came out of the shed with his hands behind his back. I was hanging out the washing so I saw all of this. Well, he came up to her and said, "Guess what I've got?"'

Mrs Killington chuckled. 'She always was a nosy little thing. Couldn't keep out of anyone's business so when he offered her what looked like a bag of sweets, she put her hand straight in without thinking. It was only when she pulled out this bloody great spider that she realized he had played a trick on her. My God, did she shriek, or what? She was so damned angry, she chased him all the way across the garden and into the pub car park. She had a look of real evil on her face, I can tell you, and if she had caught up with him, heaven knows what she would have done.'

She paused in her tale, her eyes softening with the memory. 'Mind you, she got her own back later. Oh yes, she always got her own back that one. She waited for him in his bedroom where she had broken every last one of his model soldiers. All the Roman ones and their forts, which he had spent hours making, she had smashed up. What a mess! He went berserk. Threw a real paddy. I'd never seen anything like it because he wasn't one to do things like that. I never had any of that tantrum bother like most mums do, but this time I truly thought they were going to kill each other. When my husband came home though, he soon sorted them both out. Gave them what for and that was that – or so it seemed.'

'There was more?'

'Well, I wouldn't exactly say more, except that it was never the same between them again. They seemed to get the measure of each other that night. It was as if they knew that if one stepped out of line, the other would fight back. Marcus certainly never played another trick on her, although he did throw some funny turns when they was teenagers.'

'How?'

The old lady curled a lip. 'Don't know really, but I think – and I know this is going to sound silly – I think he used to get jealous of her, especially during the school holidays which was the only time he saw her, what with them both being at boarding schools and all. She were so pretty, and of course all the boys came sniffing like they do.' She inhaled deeply so as to expunge the disgust out of her system.

'Well,' she added, 'I can't say I ever approved, and her father certainly didn't, although he were so damned busy by then, I never saw him from morning till night. No, it were Marcus who got really bothered by it all. Got all moody and sulky like. Damned if I knew why. I mean, it's not as though he didn't have his own admirers. Those looks of his could get any woman on earth if she had the sense, except he never bothers with anyone as far as I know. You don't think . . .' and she looked at Hildegard uncomfortably, 'you don't think . . . ?'

Hildegard smiled. 'No, Mrs Killington, I don't. It is simply that he hasn't found the right woman yet, that's all.'

Mrs Killington's shoulders relaxed and she let out a small sigh. 'Oh well, I hope so. I would like it, you know, if one day I had some grandchildren. Some proper ones. Marcus's kids. I know Camilla is one of the family but . . . well, she's not mine. No blood ties – or love lost between us, I can tell you.'

'Herr Killington has many years before him, Frau Killington. He will meet someone one day. Of this I am sure.'

'Good,' and the old lady smiled.

'Another one, I think,' and she returned to the sideboard for some more drink.

'You got any family then, Hildegard?'

The other woman smiled gently, her fulsome mouth tinged with sorrow.

'*Nein*. I am all that is left. My parents died young. They suffered, you know. The war. It was terrible for them. I was their only child.'

Mrs Killington sat down again.

'You're all alone then?'

Hildegard nodded.

'Oh pet, that's sad. That's really sad. Fancy having no one. Not even a distant relative?'

'I do not know, Frau Killington,' she answered quietly.

'Surely there must be someone somewhere?'

'I don't know. It . . . it is too painful,' and her large blue eyes filled with tears. She took out a pristine handkerchief from her cuff and dabbed her eyes.

'I would very much like to have someone.' She blew her nose daintily. 'Anyone. It is not nice being all alone. Having no roots, no point of reference. I need that. I need a connection.' Her thick lower lip wobbled precariously.

'There, there, pet, don't take on so,' said Mrs Killington. Then she got up from the table and went to the sideboard where she opened a cupboard.

'I was keeping these for his nibs' birthday but I don't suppose it'll matter if I give him something else. He never says thank you anyway.' She took out an ornate box. 'Chocolate,' she announced with a grin, 'handmade from that place in town. Shall we open them?'

'Oh no, Frau Killington. It is not right. They are a present for Herr Killington.'

'Stuff 'im!' came the sharp reply. 'What say you and me pig out and have some fun? Bugger that son of mine and the bleeding doctor. I've had enough of both of them.'

With a chuckle, she began tearing away at the box. When the top was prised off and laid to one side, both of them looked down at the contents.

'You first, Hilde.'

'No, after you, Frau Killington.'

'Ta.'

With mouths bulging, they sat chatting amiably like old friends. The large white swan and the tiny grey chicken.

Marcus was coming down the corridor towards his

mother's apartment when he heard their laughter. He stopped. He wasn't pleased. His mother's high-pitched cackle irritated him. More to the point, she was enjoying herself with a member of his staff.

He marched into her room without knocking. The two women looked round, startled.

'Mother!'

'Marcus,' and she popped another chocolate into her mouth. 'So good of you to knock.' She licked her fingers while Hildegard slowly rose to her feet under Marcus's disapproving gaze.

'Leave us, Hildegard.'

The housekeeper turned to Mrs Killington to thank her, but Marcus interrupted.

'Leave us!' he yelled. 'At once!'

'Nice to have someone to enjoy the chocs with, Hilde. We'll do it again sometime,' and the old lady smiled warmly at the retreating figure before pointedly glaring at her son.

'What d'you want?' she snapped when they were alone. 'Don't you know it's rude to barge into someone's room without knocking, or didn't that expensive public school of yours teach you any manners?'

He walked over to the table and took the box of chocolates off her.

'You will have no more of these. You know what the doctor said,' and without waiting for her to reply, he shut the box. 'And another thing, you will not fraternize so much with the staff, understand?'

Mrs Killington's mouth tightened. 'You pompous stuck-up git!' she spat. 'How dare you tell me who I can't and can speak to! If I bloody well feel like talking to Hildegard, then I damned well will, and if you don't like it, tough!'

Marcus opened the door, peered outside and then closed it again. He walked over to his mother, bearing down on her with menace.

164

'Dear Mother,' he said, 'let's get something straightened out, shall we?'

'No we won't!' she yelled defiantly, brushing him aside. 'Once upon a time, you, your father, Camilla and me were as poor as church mice and don't you forget it. It was your father –'

'Your husband, mother dearest. He was, thank God, no blood relation of mine.'

'My husband, then, that built up all that we have today. Not you. And if I want to enjoy myself, I will!'

For a while there was silence. She sat glowering at the floor and he stood looking at her. He casually picked a piece of invisible fluff off his linen jacket before strolling over to the window.

'I'm told,' he said, 'that there's a residential home in Oxford run by some money-pinching old nurse who feeds her clients on the cheapest food possible and keeps the heating off during the day. She gets away with it because the authorities are stretched to the limit and can't keep an eye on everybody.' He slowly smiled.

'Don't you threaten me, my lad,' she hissed. 'You're not so old or so big that I can't take you over my knee and give you the hiding you deserve.'

'Really, Mother, don't you think you're a bit old for this kind of histrionics?'

The woman lit another cigarette, her hands trembling.

'Where do you suppose you'd go if I kicked you out?' he asked. 'After all, you only have a grace-and-favour apartment here. This isn't your house, it's mine, and that small sum of money that he left you is hardly going to cover the cost of a house, is it?'

She rose unsteadily to her feet. 'But you wouldn't do that.' Her voice was hushed.

'Oh? And why not?' He advanced slowly, deep-set eyes glittering at her, brittle with suppressed rage. She was paralysed, like a rabbit in the glare of car lights. 'You're here under sufferance, no more and no less, and I would prefer

165

it if you remembered that, Mother dear,' and he took hold of one of her cold shaking hands and kissed it softly. 'When your husband unfortunately passed away, it was Camilla and I who inherited the business, not you. Of course, had you shown any kind of business acumen, then who knows? Maybe you wouldn't be in this position. But it's one thing I do have to thank that nasty old man for: he certainly showed me how to treat people. All that love and kindness he handed out. What a charming man, wouldn't you agree? So let's not get above ourselves, shall we?'

He tightened his hold. She blanched. Then he slowly pushed her backwards into her chair again. She was helpless to resist.

'Listen to me, you disgusting old hag,' he whispered. 'Do you know what it's like in an old people's home?'

She couldn't answer because her throat was dry.

'Well, I'll tell you. Lots of old sods just like you, unwanted, unloved, incontinent, gaga. All just waiting to die. Now,' he added more brightly and standing up, 'if you don't do as I say, I will personally arrange for you to go to one of these delightful places. As you have few assets, you will, of course, have to apply for state benefits and that will mean, I suppose, that you will end up in one of those places where nobody cares about you or visits you. So, how would you like that?'

The old lady, who seemed to have shrunk before his eyes, said nothing.

'You see, Mother, life outside these walls, especially for decrepit old crones like you, is extremely unpleasant. Without me to help you and protect you, you will have nothing. Think it over.'

After he had gone, taking the chocolates with him, she sat very, very still. What had she done to deserve this? Hadn't she loved him, taken care of him? Where had it all gone wrong? She shook her frail head. Whatever it was, she didn't understand.

Then it hit her – the searing, jagged pain she knew and

feared so much, like a thick shard of glass tearing at her guts. She crumpled in two, hugging herself, gasping for air. Her fingers grasped at the carpet.

'Hildegard . . . Hildeg . . .' but no one was there to hear her. Then she blacked out.

'Mr Killington.'

Marcus turned and smiled at the middle-aged man and his plump wife, who beamed from ear to ear.

'Marcus, please.'

'Then you must call me Martin and not,' and at this point he lowered his voice, 'Chief Constable,' and both of them shook hands.

'We just came to say how much we're enjoying ourselves,' twittered his wife through an over-made-up face. 'It really is most kind of you to entertain us so . . . so . . .'

'Lavishly?' supplied Marcus benevolently, with the air of one used to accepting and even expecting praise. 'Think nothing of it, my dear,' he added with a twinkle in his deep dark eyes, and picking up her gloved hand, he kissed it. She fluttered amid her rouge, her thickly mascaraed eyes inviting him to take whatever he wanted.

'I think,' said the Chief Constable with a nervous laugh, 'that you really ought to get down to the ring and look over Mr Killington's – I mean Marcus's – next winner,' and he tried to steer his wife away but she wouldn't be moved. 'Marcus is a very busy man, my dear.'

'Do you have many racehorses, Marcus?' she asked, ignoring her husband. She only had eyes for her host. After all, it wasn't every day she got to meet someone who was so rich and so handsome.

'A few,' he answered, with yet more smiles. It's all so damned easy he thought. He could have her with no more than a click of his fingers and there wouldn't be a thing her pompous little husband could do about it. He was enjoying the Chief Constable's discomfort.

'You're being very modest,' said her husband. 'I was told . . .' but then he trailed off. There had been a flicker of hostility, of boundaries passed that shouldn't have been. It was only the minutest change in the atmosphere but it had definitely been there and the Chief Constable smiled briefly and looked at his watch.

'Is that the time?' he asked his wife who was still staring at Marcus. 'Come along, Cheryl. We don't want to miss the start of the next race. Thank you again, Marcus. We'll see you later,' and he ushered her away.

It was mid-afternoon before the Chief Constable managed to leave Cheryl enjoying the free hospitality, and sneak over to where Marcus stood alone. 'About our little talk . . .' he began.

Marcus smiled. 'To your satisfaction, I hope?'

'Oh, yes, yes,' and he flushed. He was so hot in his morning suit. 'The money is untraceable, isn't it?'

'Of course. No one, but no one, will ever find out about it. Swiss banks are very good. Client confidentiality is paramount and they refuse point-blank to co-operate with any government agency that tries to get information out of them. Believe me, Chief Constable, you're as safe as the Bank of England,' and he smiled.

The other man bit the inside of his cheek. Marcus put a comforting arm around his shoulders. 'Come along, Martin,' he said jovially, 'surely if anyone knows how to avoid trouble, it's you,' and the Chief Constable smiled wanly.

'Got to go,' he said, indicating his wife. 'She'll bet it all away.'

'Of course,' agreed Marcus, 'and we don't want that, do we?' and he watched them escape out of the back of the hospitality room on the main stand and then smiled to himself. Such silly people. He looked around, acknowledging others also in his pay or under obligation. He was like a king, he thought, and these were his serfs. It had been a productive afternoon, one way or another. He'd hardly

168

had time to give a thought to his mother, now confined to bed.

'Marcus!' and there was a firm slap on the back. Marcus lowered his binoculars slowly. He didn't like familiarity, even from James Fordton-Smythe, resplendent in silk cravat and matching grey silk suit. 'Absolutely splendid!' he chortled, bright blue eyes shining in his round fleshy face, his premature jowls wobbling after too many House of Commons lunches. 'And how are you, dear boy? Haven't seen you around too much lately. When are you coming up to town again? I look forward to our little tête-à-têtes on the terrace. Lots of good work done there.'

'Nice to see you too, James, and how's your wife?'

'Buggered off with some frog actually. Went off to Paris to do some shopping with the mater and damn me, if she didn't get a surge of hormones and take up with some Jacques or something. Still,' and he smiled good-naturedly as he stuffed yet another caviar canapé into his mouth, 'can't complain too much. Least it's a bloody man she's with,' and leaning closer he said, 'don't suppose you've heard the latest about the Home Secretary's wife?'

Marcus looked suitably blank. Such trivialities bored him.

'Well,' continued James, 'seems she's very friendly with this artist woman. I mean, lesbians! Bad enough when it's another man, but a woman!'

'Exactly.'

'Talking of women,' said James, looking around the room at the select gathering, 'I was hoping your gorgeous sister would be here today.'

'I'm afraid not, James. She's down in Devon at the moment. On holiday, you know.'

'Shame,' and his large moon-shaped face lost its happy smile.

'If I were you,' said Marcus, offering James his binoculars, 'I'd go and spread my assets in that direction,' and he pointed out a champagne bar where a gaggle of long-legged lovelies had herded together. 'More your scene, don't you think? Just say I sent you.'

James smiled and after enough time to appreciate what was on offer, and all at Marcus's expense, lowered the binoculars.

'Can I take my pick?' he asked, eyes bright and expectant as beads of sweat covered his upper lip.

'Isn't that what hospitality is all about?'

'Marcus! You old sod.'

'Before you go though . . .'

James stopped in his eager tracks. 'Yes?'

Marcus leant closer. 'We need to talk. There's a problem. Nothing we can't handle,' he added quickly, seeing James's reaction, 'but it might, how shall I say, endanger your position.'

'Now see here, Marcus –' began James sharply, but then he stopped as Marcus stared at him with bullet eyes.

'See here nothing,' replied Marcus quietly. 'We have a deal, a very profitable one, one that sends your daughter to Roedean, your son to Eton and your erstwhile wife shopping in Paris, so don't give me any of your crap, okay?' He then smiled to reassure the big man, raised his binoculars to his eyes and said, 'A bit leggy, that chestnut filly, don't you think?' but James didn't answer. He was sweating even more now.

'Get the money out of the country,' continued Marcus in a level voice as though he were discussing the weather, 'and don't do anything about anything until I say so, and remember, success relies on trust and we wouldn't want anything untoward to happen now, would we?'

James blanched, the colour draining from his usually florid face.

'Quite,' he spluttered, wiping his forehead with a hanky. 'My goodness, it's very hot in here, isn't it?'

'Is it?' replied Marcus, his attention switched back to the horses. 'I tend not to notice such things. I must have ice in my veins, I suppose,' and he raised his binoculars again and scanned the colourful crowd. James took the hint and left.

Now Marcus was on his own again, just the way he liked it. Business could be such a bother when there was a good race card to enjoy. There was a mass of people all dressed in their finery. This was a royal meeting and everyone who was anyone had turned out to see how they measured up. The relentless sun beat down on them all but it didn't stop the hubbub of laughter, chatter and the chink of glasses.

He looked them over like an eagle from his eyrie looking for prey. Grey morning suits, dresses and hats of all colours, expensive men and women strutting around confident in who they were and how much they were worth.

He sighed with satisfaction. It had taken so long to get here. Deviousness, intelligence and the killer instinct were his assets and he had no intention of letting anyone take his success away from him.

The public address system broke his reverie. 'And now the runners and riders for the next race, the 2.30 Killington Stakes, sponsored by Killington Associates . . .'

Marcus supposed he ought to be down in the ring with his racing manager, jockey and trainer, but that would only compromise the air of mystery that he preferred to cloak himself with. Those who mattered knew he was here and that he was watching them from his private box, and he preferred it that way. Mixing with the wealthy and the wannabes did not appeal to him. Crowds only served to remind him of his childhood and the smelling, heaving crush of unwashed men downing as much as they could before chucking out time. He was above all that now.

'Mr Killington?' It was Veronica, his secretary.

Marcus didn't put down his binoculars. The horses were parading now, the excited punters trying to pick out the winner while the ticktack men did plenty of business.

'Yes?'

'There's a gentleman here to see you. He said he had an

171

appointment. He's from America,' and she handed him a card. 'Some sort of computer fraud analyst.'

Marcus read the card with a smile. 'Good. See that he gets a drink and tell him I'll be with him when the race is over.' It was the man he was waiting for: the one who would find out once and for all who was betraying him.

Ten

Eddy stopped at the service station. He was hungry. He needed some breakfast. The place was crowded. Holiday-makers of all shapes, sizes and various shades of sunburn filled the snack bar, their children playing noisily in the play area. It didn't put him in a good frame of mind. He didn't like children. They were, in his opinion, something that other people had. He didn't want the responsibility or the expense. Sian felt differently and so did his mother, both of whom had done their level best to change his mind, but he was adamant. Sian's miscarriage the previous summer had been a blessing in disguise as far as he was concerned.

The pleasing aroma of a good old-fashioned English breakfast filled his nostrils as he walked through the doors. At the hotel, Rowena stood over him like a hawk, making sure he stuck to his diet. He wondered sometimes if having a girlfriend and a wife was worth all the hassle. They were as bad as each other when it came to his diet.

He helped himself to a large greasy plateful and sat down to gorge. He was oblivious to everything for the next ten minutes until his immediate hunger was satiated, and then his problems began once more to intrude upon his con-sciousness.

Sian; Rowena; Killington. Eddie stopped eating and wiped some egg yolk off his chin. There was a lorry driver sitting opposite him, cramming the food into his mouth as quickly as possible and then washing it down with mouth-fuls of strong tea. Eddy watched him with a kind of detached horror. People like that would never be allowed into his restaurant. The man was fat, balding and tattooed, wearing a too small red vest over a large sweaty torso. He looked up, his suspicious little eyes embedded in folds of flesh.

'What you looking at?' he challenged, his nicotine-stained teeth smeared with chewed bacon and eggs. 'Something wrong?'

Eddy hurriedly looked away. 'No. No, nothing.'

The man pointed a fork at him. 'Good. 'Cos it's rude to stare,' and he continued eating.

Eddy silently sipped his tea. He wasn't a happy man. The threat from Killington, if not explicit, had been obvious enough, and then there was Rowena. She was starting to make demands on him, demands which he felt he couldn't fulfil. She wanted him and Sian to get officially separated. She wanted to get engaged. It did nothing for his libido. Why couldn't she just leave things the way they were? She was great in bed and nice to dangle on his arm but that didn't mean he wanted to be stuck with her for life. Couldn't she understand that? He already had – did have – a permanent attachment and hopefully, by the end of this trip, his wife would be back where she belonged. Quite what he was going to do with Rowena was another matter.

He looked at his food. He wasn't hungry now. His guts had started to cramp. He stood and, avoiding the eye of the surly lorry driver, left the restaurant. Women, he thought; they cause so many damned problems. He pushed open the door to the gents. What he needed was a good bowel movement. That would help him think more clearly.

It was raining, a warm mist of water gently falling and covering the landscape. Sian and Helen were sitting on the bench in the village square, waiting for Andrew to pick them up for work. Unusually, he was late. Helen looked at her watch.

'If I'd known his lordship was going to be this late, I wouldn't have bothered getting up so damned early.' She sighed and rubbed her sore eyes. She looked as if she needed another good eight hours.

Sian smiled. 'Where were you last night? You came in very late.'

'Out dancing. There's a club in Plymouth. It doesn't really get going until the pubs shut.' She smiled. 'And then, of course . . .'

'You had to go back to his place and play Scrabble?' suggested Sian with a grin. 'Or maybe even chess?'

'Something like that.'

'So did you get any sleep at all?'

'No, but that's the trouble with chess late at night,' she grinned. 'It's too demanding!'

They both laughed and then Helen went back to staring at the road. She could barely keep her eyes open.

She sighed. 'Maybe I got the odd half-hour at about five or something, but then he does have his compensations.'

'What?'

'He pays for everything. He's got loads of dosh and boy, does it make a change from all the tight-fisted sods around here.'

'Like Billy, for instance?'

'Absolutely! Every last penny he earns goes on that awful car of his. I don't know why he doesn't take it down to the scrap heap, but then again perhaps they won't want it.'

Eck appeared, lumbering along the road in his heavy rolling gait. As usual, he was smiling amiably at everyone.

'Talking of men,' commented Helen, 'here comes the missing link.'

'Helen, that's not fair!' exclaimed Sian. 'He can't help it.'

Eck stood in front of them, his vast bulk almost as big as one of the horses.

'No Andrew?' he lisped.

'No, Eck,' said Sian kindly, 'but he'll be here soon. Sit down and wait with us.'

His whole face lit up, revealing his mouthful of missing

175

and rotten teeth. He squeezed in between the women. He didn't smell clean.

'Eck,' said Helen, pulling a face.

'Yes?'

'Have you ever thought of having a bath now and again? I mean, that yearly dip you take in the water trough doesn't seem to be having much effect, does it?'

'Eh?' He blinked slowly a couple of times and nodded his woolly, unkempt head. There was a piece of straw stuck tucked in behind one ear. 'Nay. Why?'

'Never mind, Eck,' sighed Helen.

'Look,' said Sian, 'here's Andrew.'

They watched as he pulled up to the kerb. He looked very tired. Helen and Sian exchanged glances.

'Wonder where he spent the night?' whispered Helen. 'Maybe he's got another one of the tourists.'

Sian didn't want to know. The very idea conjured up too many unwanted and uncomfortable feelings. They climbed into the Land Rover.

'I'm late I know,' Andrew said gruffly, 'but I got held up.'

'I bet,' said Helen with a sneer, 'and I bet she's got long legs, big tits and a irresistible smile if past behaviour is anything to go by.'

'Really, Helen, is that all you can think of?' he exclaimed with exasperation. 'Some of us do have other things to think about, like business matters, for example.'

Andrew ignored them all after that, his face pinched and drawn. He drove quickly along the lane.

'Right,' he said, pulling into the yard with a skid, 'we're late so we all need to move quickly this morning. Eck, you and Sian get the horses in. Helen, you do the feeds and I'll fill the water buckets. Well, come on then,' he snapped briskly. 'Move it!'

Helen and Sian walked off down the yard.

'See what I mean?' said Helen quietly. 'Such charm, such graciousness. Leaves you breathless, doesn't it?'

Sian said nothing. If that was the worst he could do, it was little compared to Eddy's behaviour. Anyway, she didn't care. Nothing surprised her any longer.

The work was soon done. The few horses that were needed that day were saddled up and waiting for their riders. Helen was tightening the girth on her horse and Sian was sweeping the final bits of straw and dung down the yard when Andrew came out of the cottage followed by Blaize.

'Given we've only got five tourists this week, Helen, I want you to take them out without me.'

'What!' she exclaimed. 'That's all I need. I'll be left coping with them all while you piss about here, I suppose?' Her stare was unrelenting.

'Nope. You can take Sian, whom I'm reliably informed has passed her BHS certificate.'

He smiled at her. 'Why didn't you tell me this before? Your friend who was looking after Bracken just rang to see how she was getting on and she told me quite a lot about you.'

Sian felt herself blushing. 'I just didn't think it was that important, that's all. Anyway, it was a long time ago and I didn't come here to teach, did I? You said you only wanted a part-time stable hand and that's what you've got.'

'Yes, well, that's as maybe, but I would appreciate it in future if you were totally honest with me. I don't like being kept in the dark about anything, and what's more, while you're keeping that horse of yours here, we might as well make as much use of her as possible. If she doesn't get any exercise she'll grow fat and lazy,' and with that he turned on his heel and marched back into the cottage.

Sian turned to Helen, her eyes blazing. 'And what damned business is it of his anyway? God, he makes me want to spit acid! And what's all this nonsense about Bracken? Bloody man!' She renewed her sweeping with extra vigour.

A car pulled up and stopped her short. To her horror and surprise she saw it was Eddy's. Her stomach lurched.

'Helen, now what?'

Helen turned to Sian, her chin defiant. 'Just one word out of him and I'll be ringing for the vet, so don't worry.'

'I'm not.' But then she added more quietly, 'He's bound to make a scene or something. I just know it. Oh to hell with him! Why on earth did he have to come here?'

'I'll go tell him to get lost, shall I?' offered Helen with a smile.

She mounted her horse and trotted towards Eddy. She pulled to a halt in front of him, blocking his way.

'What d'you want?' she asked, stony-faced. 'You're not needed here. Sian doesn't want to see you, so get back in that flash car of yours and go.'

He glanced up at her. He didn't like her one bit and had no time for her. He pushed past the animal, ducking under its neck.

'None of your damned business, Helen. This is between me and Sian.'

'Oh no it isn't!'

Helen urged her horse forward. By now there were a couple of interested spectators as the tourists were beginning to arrive.

'Going to be a row,' whispered one to her friend.

'Oh good,' said the other. 'I like a bit of excitement.'

'Get out of this yard, Eddy,' shouted Helen.

'Bugger off, Helen,' he snarled. 'This, as I have already explained, is none of your business.'

She pushed the horse onwards, coming alongside him, her crop poised in her hand. She whipped him hard across the shoulders. He yelped like a kicked dog.

'Now do as I say, Eddy. I won't repeat myself.'

He scowled, his once-handsome face dark with pouchy rage.

'You bitch!' he spat, rubbing his shoulder. 'Don't you ever do that again or, by God, I'll hurt you!'

'Oh yeah?' she answered scornfully from the safety of the horse's height. 'Like hitting defenceless women, do you? Bit of a gutless coward, are you?'

'Eddy! Helen!' cried Sian. 'Stop it, the pair of you!'

But neither of them listened and before anyone could stop him, Eddy grabbed hold of Helen, pulled her off the horse, which panicked and ran off across the yard. Picking her up by her lapels, he pulled her after him and threw her unceremoniously into the water butt. She disappeared for an instant and came up coughing and spluttering. Eddy thought it hugely funny. Sian didn't.

'What the hell do you think you're doing, you idiot?' she yelled at him, helping Helen out of the water, where she stood dripping and humiliated.

'You bastard!' she coughed, wiping her face clear of water. 'You bloody, bloody bastard!'

Eddy smirked. 'Now perhaps we can have a word in private, Sian,' and he sauntered away.

Sian walked after him. 'You and me,' she said through clenched teeth, 'have got to sort things out.'

'I don't think there's anything to sort out, is there? Why don't you just come home? It's where you belong, Sian.'

They stood glaring at each other. Then she became aware of their audience. She took hold of his arm and walked him out of earshot.

'If you think that after all this, and your appalling behaviour with that tart of yours, I am going to even consider coming home to you, then you are hugely mistaken.'

Eddy remained impassive.

'How dare you,' she continued, 'think that you can come here, insult my friend and embarrass me and then . . .' her voice rose again with indignation, '. . . and then think that I will come home with you? You must be the most insensitive, pig-headed moron that's ever walked this planet!' She shook with fury, two bright pink spots showing up in either cheek.

He thoughtfully rubbed his chin as if none of this had

occurred to him. He glanced back towards Helen, who was rubbing herself dry with a towel.

'It's her, isn't it?' he said accusingly. 'That bloody great dyke? If it hadn't been for her, you wouldn't be staying here. I know you wouldn't. You'd be back with me, back at the hotel.'

Sian looked away with disgust. It wasn't even worth losing her temper. 'No, Eddy, it isn't. Just go back to your floozy and don't come back. I don't want to see you, okay? Not now, not ever. And what's more, I'm beginning to wish I'd never even met you!'

'Oh yeah? Well, we'll soon see about that, won't we? What's the name of your boss? I'm going to have a word with him, make him see sense.'

Sian ran after him. 'Please, Eddy, no! Don't make a scene!'

He stopped. 'Right then, are you coming back, or what?'

'No. Get out of here. Just go!' she cried. 'Can't you see how much you've upset everyone? I won't come back to you under any circumstances. Not even when the baby's born!'

He grabbed her arm. 'What did you say?'

'You heard! You heard!' Tears were rolling down her face, the pain of it all overwhelming her.

'You're pregnant?' He looked her up and down. 'You mean, I'm going to be a father?'

'Yes,' she cried, 'you're going to be a father but only in the biological sense. There's no bloody way I'm having you anywhere near me again. Ever! I can't stand the sight of you. You repel me. You're . . . you're repellent, and just in case you still don't understand . . .' She had to stop, breathless with the exertion of it all.

'And just in case,' she continued more quietly, suddenly aware that everyone was listening, 'you think that you can worm yourself back into my life ever again, forget it! I'm through with you. You betrayed me so cruelly that I could never trust you again! Do you understand? Do you?'

He nodded dumbly. A father? He was going to be a father. It was unbelievable.

'But why . . .' he began, struggling to get his thoughts into some sort of coherent order. 'How? Why didn't you tell me before?'

'Because, Eddy, it was to be the surprise on our wedding anniversary. Remember that? Our wedding anniversary? It wasn't long after I found you with that female when you had promised me . . . You promised me and I, like the stupid fool I was, I believed you!'

'But I thought –'

She angrily wiped her face dry, her beautiful features transformed by her agony. 'You thought what?'

'I thought that you were going to get me . . .' He stopped himself. 'It doesn't matter,' he added, shamefaced.

He stood helplessly in front of her, completely at a loss as to what to do next.

'Look, Sian,' he said eventually, 'I'm sorry, okay? I didn't realize. I'm really, really sorry.'

'It's too late for that now, Eddy,' she answered flatly.

'But, Sian –'

'Go away! The damage is done.'

'Sian, you don't understand!'

'Oh yes I do! Only too well! Come on, Helen,' she turned to her friend, dripping a discreet distance away, 'let's go and get you dry.'

They hurried towards the cottage with Eddy trailing behind them. He grabbed Sian by the arm again but she wrenched herself free.

'What about us?' he asked plaintively. 'What about the baby? You can't leave me now. We've got our whole lives together. You can't bring up my child on your own. I won't let you.'

Sian stopped. It was more than she could bear.

'Don't you tell me,' she said through clenched teeth, 'don't you even think of telling me how to bring up this child! I'm carrying it, not you; I'm the one who will give

181

birth, not you, and I'll bring it up as *I* see fit. It doesn't need some adulterous, gin-soaked, greedy pig of a father like you whose idea of having a good time is to spend hours propped up at the bar drinking with his cronies, okay?'

'But what about Killington?' he cried.

'What about him?' she shouted, incensed. 'Do you think I care what that Machiavellian creature thinks? I couldn't care less. He's your problem, not mine, and if as my mother says, you can't do the paperwork any more, get your darling Rowena to do it. I'm sure she'd love to help.'

'But if you don't come back, he'll sack me.'

She stopped. Helen smiled tiredly at her and walked on.

'See you in a minute,' she said.

Sian, fixing Eddy with a steely gaze, went right up to him.

'Let's get something quite clear, Eddy,' she said, her lips barely moving. 'The only reason you married me was so you would get to be the manager of one of Killington's hotels.' She held up her hands ignoring his protests. 'Shut up, Eddy. I don't want to hear any more of your lies and excuses.'

'But it's not true. I did love you.'

'"Did" being the operative word here, Eddy. It's no good denying it. I can see it all now – how when it looked as though you would never get that promotion, it suddenly appeared out of the blue when Killington knew we were getting married. Convenient, eh?'

'But that's not true. I swear it. Honestly, Sian, we can still get together again, I know we can. Please, if only for the baby.'

For a moment she said nothing. She was worn out with him. Then: 'Get lost, Eddy,' and she turned on her heels.

'Sian!'

She ignored him.

'Sian!'

Andrew came to the door of the cottage. 'What's been

going on? Why is Helen soaked and why is there all this shouting and who are you?' he demanded, looking at Eddy.

'I'm Eddy Williamson, Sian's husband.'

'And he's just about to leave, Andrew,' interjected Sian, pushing Eddy away.

Andrew advanced down the path. 'Was it you who threw Helen into the water butt?'

Eddy smirked. He wasn't afraid of this man. Andrew might be bigger than he, but he could stand his ground.

'So?' he asked, confident.

Sian sighed. She had a horrible sense of foreboding. 'Eddy. Please go.'

He ignored her. The two men now faced each other, angrily staring one another down. Andrew was the first to speak.

'Don't you dare step foot on these premises again, understand? Because if you do, I shan't be held responsible for my actions. Now, on your bike before I lose my temper because I don't like it when strangers come into my yard and start throwing their weight around.'

For a moment Eddy hesitated. Then he backed off. He could have taken Andrew on. Another time maybe. He put his hands in his pockets and turned to his wife.

'I shall be back.'

'If you do, Mr Williamson,' warned Andrew, 'I shall take the greatest pleasure in breaking every damned bone in your body.'

Eddy left, the wheels of his car skidding out of the yard.

'I don't think he'll pester us again, do you?' said Andrew watching the car roar away.

Sian didn't reply. She was emotionally exhausted. Andrew turned his attention to the tourists.

'Right oh, folks, it appears we're going to have a small delay. Perhaps you'd all like to come into the cottage and have a coffee. After all the excitement, you'll need it.'

Sian didn't go out with Helen and the tourists. Eck went

183

instead. He was delighted to be asked and sat on top of the largest horse in the stable, a huge grin on his face. Andrew spoke to a now dry Helen.

'Keep an eye on him,' he said, gesturing with his head towards Eck. 'You know what he's like when he reaches open ground – head down and he's off. I swear there's a five-foot jockey inside that six-foot-four frame, eh, Eck? And don't go near the reservoir! You know what he's like with water.'

The big man grinned and nodded. It was a special treat to be allowed out.

Helen smiled. 'Don't worry. He'll be safe with me.'

The small convoy of riders trooped out of the stables, one behind the other, the rain falling gently on their backs. Andrew watched them go, standing in the middle of his yard, his hands on his hips.

Sian could see him. She was sitting in the tack room polishing a saddle with vigorous, energetic strokes. Anything to keep her anger at bay, though the tears still threatened to fall.

Damn Eddy! How dare he come here and upset her like that and be so nasty to Helen! How dare he cause a scene in front of all the others and embarrass her so much! But most of all, how dare he rip off her scab and expose all the raw pain which she had tried to hide away.

She rubbed the saddle extra hard. Would she ever be rid of him?

There was a knock at the door. 'Can I come in?'

'Of course. It's your stable.'

Andrew settled himself down on the other side of the table. She could feel him watching her. Tears of humiliation were lingering on her cheeks and she brushed them away.

'It's not been a good day for you, has it?' he asked.

'Well, we all have our problems, I suppose.'

She glanced up from her work and he could see how vulnerable she was.

184

'I'll go if you want.'

'No.' She smiled gamely through her misery. 'No, please don't. I would like to talk.' She paused, searching for words, her face puckered with an uncharacteristic frown.

'What was it all about out there, with you and your husband?'

'Nothing.'

'Nothing? In that case then, what is there to talk about?'

She looked up at him. It was so hard to explain, especially when his was the face that kept appearing in her dreams at night. It was difficult to shrug off the images in the light of day.

'It's everything and nothing, except of course that none of that makes any sense, does it? It was just another display of how your sex treats mine but then we shouldn't be surprised by any of that by now, should we?' and she returned to rubbing the saddle.

'You're very angry with all of us men, aren't you? Maybe if you told me why he was here I could understand better?' he asked.

'I don't know,' she answered reluctantly. 'You don't want to hear about it.'

'Isn't that for me to decide?' Andrew watched her closely. He could see she wanted to talk, but was held back by her distrust. 'Look,' he began, 'I know it's none of my business but it would help to talk, you know, and as you do work for me and this is my stable, I'd prefer it if my staff were happy. I can't really afford to have emotional outbursts in front of the tourists. It doesn't look good, does it?'

'My goodness,' she laughed drily, 'you're just full of the milk of human kindness.'

'You've taken it the wrong way, Sian. I didn't mean to sound so harsh, but you've got to admit, I am right.'

She polished; he watched. The atmosphere was tense. She wanted him to go away. Talking to him about her problems would be a mistake. Andrew confused her.

'I mean, why the hell should I expect any sympathy from you?' she continued. 'After all, you're a man too. You're all the same: just completely selfish. God knows why any woman should get herself mixed up with any of you.'

'We're not all like your husband, you know,' he said patiently and with forbearance.

'Aren't you?' She looked at him steadily, her green eyes wary.

'From what I hear, there's absolutely no difference between you and Eddy. Both of you bed hop. Probably had more women than I've had hot dinners!'

She glared at him, challenging him to answer her accusations; to prove her right. He had to be like Eddy, had to be. Then she could deal with him so much more easily.

'That,' he said sternly, 'was totally uncalled for. First of all, Helen – and I presume it's Helen – knows damn all about my private life. It's just gossip based on wild speculation. And secondly, just because your uncouth, overweight slob of a husband comes here and starts throwing his weight around, it doesn't give you the right to judge and condemn me.'

His voice was even but his eyes were fiery. She glanced at him. She wasn't so sure of herself now. She put down the chamois, sat back in her chair, her arms folded across her chest and stared steadfastly at the table top. He watched her. Then she suddenly stood up and turned away from him. When she spoke her voice was anguished.

'Do you have any idea what he did to me?' She leant against one of the wooden roof supports, her long red hair sprayed out across her shoulders, her hands behind her as if she didn't trust them.

'He promised me . . . I mean . . . last time. He said it wouldn't happen again and I believed him. I thought that if we had a baby, it might . . .' and then she started to weep quietly. She covered her face with one hand while she searched for a tissue.

Andrew sat waiting for her to calm down. He could have gone over and comforted her but something stopped him. A feeling that he hadn't experienced in years was welling up inside him, a vulnerability that he had hidden away, and it frightened him.

When Sian's sobs became quiet sniffs, he prompted her again. 'What did he do?'

'I found them. Naked.' She looked away, embarrassed. Mentioning sex around Andrew made her feel naked herself. 'Funny really, walking in on them like that. I still can't believe it, because you know what?'

He shrugged.

'I was just about to go and tell him I was pregnant. Can you imagine it? I'm so happy, having got the one thing I wanted more than anything else and that . . . that husband of mine is having a good time with our bloody assistant!' As she started crying again, she slowly slipped down the wooden support until she was sitting on the dusty floor, her arms wrapped around her knees and her face buried.

This time Andrew couldn't sit still. Her pain was too much for him to bear. He walked over to her. Kneeling down, he put his hands on her arms and gently pulled her to her feet. She didn't protest. With his fingertips, he wiped her face dry.

He smiled to himself. What did she look like? Face all wet and blotchy, hair all over the place with odd bits of straw in it. Dust all over the back of her jodhpurs and T-shirt splashed with tears.

'Here,' he said gruffly, 'blow your nose,' and he gave her his large handkerchief.

She accepted it wordlessly and did as she was told. He then led her back to the table and sat her down. She wiped her eyes and sniffed quietly.

'Pregnant eh?'

She nodded.

'How long?'

'Two months. I suppose this means the sack. I mean, it's

not as though I'm going to be much use around here, is it?'

'No, but then you don't look pregnant and until you do, I don't see why you can't stay.'

She smiled feebly, the corners of her mouth still firmly pointing downwards.

'Is that why your husband came here today, because of the baby?'

She shook her head and wiped her cheeks. 'No. He came because if I don't go back, he'll probably get the sack.'

'The sack?' Andrew was incredulous.

'You don't know our boss,' explained Sian. 'There's no such thing as unfair dismissal in his book. He'll get you one way or the other.'

'And all because you're not there?'

'So Eddy says, but to be honest, I think he would say anything to get me back to do the paperwork. That's what he really wants, someone to do the paperwork.'

'What will happen then?' asked Andrew. 'Will you go back to him?'

'No. He didn't even say sorry when I found out about him and Rowena. Not one damned apology. That's the sort of man he is and I've had enough, especially after this morning and the way he treated me and Helen. It was unforgivable.'

'And the baby? Surely he must care about that?'

She snorted with contempt. 'I don't think he really cares one way or the other. Okay, he might have kicked up a fuss about it today, but that won't last. Looking back last summer when I had a miscarriage, he wasn't too bothered about that so I don't think he'll be too bothered about this either.'

She stared glumly at the table, her face propped up by her hand.

'And the future?' he asked.

'Heaven knows. Haven't a clue except for one thing,' and she looked up and smiled.

'What?'

'No men. I obviously have no taste when it comes to the male sex and I don't want any more pain. I'll take care of myself and my baby. I don't need a man messing things up again.'

'So what about the nice guys?' he asked.

Sian glanced up at him, her eyes alight with irony. 'What?' she asked rhetorically. 'You know some, do you, some or even one that would genuinely care about a woman instead of just wanting to own her or possess her as if she were just another thing to be thrown to one side when a newer, more exciting model comes along?'

'Maybe.'

'Well, I don't,' she said quietly. 'No one is going to do this to me again.'

Andrew smiled slowly. 'You're very angry, aren't you?'

'Wouldn't you be?'

'Maybe, but then I think I would tell myself that someone out there, among all the thousands and millions of women, would be the one for me and that even though I had been through a bad experience, that didn't mean that it would happen again.' He reached out across the table, his fingers just touching hers. 'Remember, Sian,' he said softly, his voice a gentle murmur, 'there is a man for you somewhere, a man who wouldn't dream of hurting you, a man who would love you and cherish you and –'

'Anybody home?' called a voice from outside. 'I've got some feed stuffs here!'

'I'd better go,' Andrew said, quickly glancing over his shoulder.

She watched him leave the room, her anger beginning to subside. He'd seen off Eddy, he'd confirmed he'd have to sack her, and yet just now he'd been really quite kind and gentle. He was a chameleon, Sian decided, and she didn't understand him – or trust him just yet.

Eleven

The Range Rover pulled to a stop outside the thatched cottage. For a few moments, neither of its occupants said anything.

'This it, then?'

'Uh-huh. Belvedere Cottage.' Patrick took the bunch of keys off the dashboard. 'This is where we'll stay until further notice.'

They both looked at the house. It was a traditional Devon long house with white painted cob walls, small deep-set windows and a vibrantly coloured front garden alive with buzzing insects that flew from bloom to bloom. Normally it would have been a city dweller's dream come true, but Camilla wasn't impressed. It wasn't what she was used to and she didn't see why she had to stay in such a small place. She sat looking at the house from behind her sunglasses, face impassive, mouth sullen, arms crossed and her tapping foot signalling her impatience. For the time being, it would just have to do.

She had done her homework since Marcus's departure for Oxford. Andrew Mann — so different from Marcus. Blond and blue-eyed; a small-time businessman instead of a tycoon. In fact, in every way, he was her stepbrother's opposite.

The name had begun to haunt her. Lying in the sun gently roasting herself at the hotel, she had had plenty of time to think of him. It was a name and a face that was taking up all her waking hours. He was in her mind, her body, her every breath. When she fell asleep, the last thing she thought of was him. When she woke, he was the first. A man she had met only once and then only briefly and yet . . . But she had to be careful. Marcus must not find out.

It was ridiculous she told herself in her more lucid moments, but that didn't stop her. And now she had tracked him down. She had an address, a telephone number and all she had to do was to stroll into his life as easily as he had strolled into hers. To make sure she was at her best, she had cut down on her drinking and, much to her amazement, stopped taking drugs. Here was an opportunity she told herself, just for once in her life, to really love a man. It had to be, because if it wasn't, why had fate decreed that they should have met like they had? He was her destiny, she decided. This was her chance and no one, least of all Marcus, was going to stand in her way. Whatever it took, however long, however far, whatever the expense, she was prepared for it. She wasn't going to let anything go wrong. Time was running out and she couldn't spend the rest of her life running from one man to another.

Marcus was the one she really had to watch. It was his interfering which had put paid to more of her future happiness than anything else. Whichever way she turned, there he stood. Whatever way she decided to evade him, he always found her out. He just wouldn't let her go.

But not this time. This time she had made her plans. She had thought long and hard and she was determined to have her way.

'Better get out, miss.'

She glanced at Patrick. He was smiling at her. God knows why. She opened the Range Rover door and climbed out. She came round to Patrick's side.

'Nice place,' he remarked. 'I wouldn't mind a house like this some day. What about you, miss?'

'Rabbit hutches are for rabbits,' she replied haughtily, holding out her hand for the key.

He gave it to her and she walked to the door while he saw to the luggage.

'Which room is yours, miss?'

'The one furthest from you. You snore like a pig.'

He took the bags upstairs without a backward glance. It was pointless arguing with her. When he came downstairs, she had already opened a bottle of wine. He sighed and glanced at his watch.

'It's only eleven thirty, miss. Couldn't you at least wait until lunchtime?'

'It's not breakfast, is it?' she sneered. 'And don't tell me what to do. I get enough of that from Marcus.'

'Yes, miss. Well, I'll just finish unpacking the car.'

'Yes, you do that and while you're at it, find me a deck chair or something. There must be one in this hole somewhere.'

'Yes, miss.'

Helen was off with the trekkers, Eck was putting away some feed bags and Sian was sweeping down the yard.

She couldn't concentrate on anything. That conversation with Andrew in the tack room and the way he looked at her and the way their fingers touched . . . It kept coming back to haunt her. There was something intriguing about him, something that made her, despite all her reservations, want to know more about him. Perhaps the journal would at least throw some light on his connection with The Grange.

She stood leaning on the broom, daydreaming. It was Eck who broke the spell, making her jump with his sudden appearance.

'Hello,' he said shyly.

Sian held her hand against her pounding heart. 'Oh Eck, you made me jump.'

He blinked slowly, looking upset. She was immediately contrite.

'It's all right. Don't be worried,' she soothed. 'You didn't do anything wrong.'

He smiled broadly again and nodded.

Sian resumed brushing, and this time she was humming.

'Let Eck help,' he said holding out his hands.

'Thank you. That would be really nice. I was getting pretty tired.'

'Andrew said we must,' he explained as she sat on a nearby hay bale. 'He says we have to look after you.'

'Oh?' She was surprised. This she hadn't expected. 'Well, that's very nice of him,' and she smiled. The man carried on brushing.

'Do you know him well?'

'He's good to Eck,' he nodded cheerfully.

'Has he ever been married?'

'Don't know,' he frowned. 'Maybe.'

'Does he have a girlfriend now? Maybe one of the tourists?'

'Don't know. Maybe.'

She sighed. 'You don't know much at all, do you, Eck?'

He grinned in reply. 'No one tells Eck nothing,' he announced proudly, 'but he can keep a secret.'

As he swept the yard enthusiastically, Sian idly wondered just what secrets Eck knew. But soon her thoughts returned to her employer. There was only one thing for it, she decided looking over the valley to Andrew's house, she would have to visit The Grange.

'I'll see you later, Eck,' and she left him to it.

Bracken was down in the main paddock. When the mare saw her, she trotted over, eyes alert and ears forward, looking for a titbit.

Sian fished an old mint out of her pocket and held it out. The horse took it gently and then, with her intelligent head over the rail, blew horsey breath into Sian's face. Sian stroked her nose.

'Fancy a ride then, do you?'

Bracken threw her head around.

'Men,' she mumbled into the animal's soft coat, 'you

don't know how lucky you are, Bracken. None of this emotional merry-go-round for you, eh?'

The mare flicked her ears against the flies.

'Come on, you and I are going to pay our boss a visit.'

The ride up to The Grange improved Sian's spirits no end. The lush green fields around the moor's edge were full of ripening crops or contented animals grazing in the shimmering, sweltering heat. Swifts screeched on the breeze, swooping around on the thermals as they chased after their prey. Smaller birds flittered among the hedgerows, their songs giving them away. Apart from the occasional car or a dog barking in the distance, she saw and heard only what nature intended.

Sian always wore a hat when riding, but the sun's heat was making her sweat so much that she removed it after a while. She ran her fingers through her damp hair to try to relieve her discomfort but achieved little. It was too hot.

Soon she came to a bridleway. Here it was a grassy track, and Bracken, sensing a time for a canter, began to toss her head.

'Okay, girl, calm down,' but the horse didn't. She was too impatient. Sian just had time to replace her hat and then they were off.

She had forgotten the thrill of galloping flat out – the way the adrenaline surged through her body. She leant forward, her hands flush to the mare's neck. Faster and faster they went, the Thoroughbred in Bracken giving her the power and speed to cover the ground in long, fast and easy strides.

The track wound gently upwards. On either side were thick impenetrable hedges and behind them were a field on one side, which went back down into the valley, and woods on the other, which went up to the top of the hill. Bracken was slower now, the slope defeating her. Eventually she slowed to a walk. Both horse and rider were hot and sweaty.

'Good heavens, girl!' Sian breathed heavily, removed

her hat, the reins hanging loose, and wiped her brow with the back of her arm. 'Some gallop that was!' But the horse only flicked her ears and plodded on.

They came to a five-bar gate. A notice said, 'The Grange. No entry.'

Sian dismounted and led Bracken through. Now that she was so close to her destination, she was starting to feel apprehensive. She told herself not to be so silly, he wasn't going to bite her head off, but her admonishments did little to calm her fluttering stomach.

The path wound between trees, oak, beech, and others Sian recognized but couldn't name. It was a cool, green-dappled corridor that led her onwards and upwards. Sunlight danced all around her, butterflies hovering in its light, lifting and diving in the rays. A woodpecker hammered, the thuds of its workmanship echoing through the trees. Another bird sang, its trilling whoops and whistles answered by a neighbour and everywhere, from the leaves, from the bark, from the muffled ground, came the aroma of the undergrowth, old and atmospheric, of things living but unseen. She felt an instinctive need to be as quiet as possible.

The horse walked on while Sian sat in the saddle looking about her and marvelling at all this undiscovered beauty; the unspoilt naturalness, the sumptuous greenery. Then, quite suddenly, the trees ended and horse and rider were out on a broad drive. To the right of them stood The Grange, a vast grey monolith on the edge of the valley.

Sian was surprised. She had expected something big, but nothing had prepared her for this.

The vet closed the stable door. He was a small, wiry man who, with a sharp pointed face and sparse grey hair, had the appearance of an elderly Jack Russell terrier. Only his shining blue eyes showed how kind he was.

'A bad case of colic, Andrew. We're going to have to watch him very closely for the next twenty-four hours to make sure he doesn't twist a gut.' He snapped shut his bag. 'Make sure he has plenty of water to drink. I've given him some liquid paraffin and I'll want to know how quickly it goes through him, so you'll have to stay with him. Has he eaten anything he shouldn't?'

'No, not that I know of. I fed him myself yesterday and, as you know, there's nothing in his paddock that would upset him. I cleared out all of the ragwort last year.'

The vet turned back and looked at Sebi over the stable door. 'Well, I don't know. Something's going on.'

The two men contemplated the stricken horse, who stood pathetically in his box ignoring everything except the pain in his guts.

'Right, I've done all that I can. If there are any developments, ring me at once.'

'Okay.'

'And don't worry,' he added, seeing the look on Andrew's face, 'he's a fine strong animal and he'll pull through. I'm sure of it. A bout of colic like this isn't going to knock him over.'

Andrew smiled ruefully. He wasn't so sure.

The vet gone, Andrew leant on the top of the stable door looking at his stallion. If he were to lose him there would be no way to replace him.

The noise of trotting hooves brought him back to the present. He turned round and there was Sian. She pulled Bracken to a halt and smiled.

'Thought I'd come and visit,' she explained, fiddling with her reins, unsure whether she should dismount or just turn round and go. He didn't look to be in a very welcoming mood. His eyes were guarded. 'You don't mind, do you? I mean,' she hurried on, aware of how nervous she must sound, 'I can always come back another time.'

He still didn't reply so she plunged on. 'I thought I'd . . .' and she stopped.

'Yes?'

He stood arrogantly against the door, his black jodphurs

and matching shirt contrasting dramatically with his blond hair and blue eyes.

'I'd heard so much about your wonderful house, I just thought . . .' she trailed off again under his staring blue eyes. 'I'll go,' she suddenly announced. 'I can see this isn't a good time.' He looked so damned angry, his mouth surly and unwelcoming and his whole demeanour dismissive. He was draining all the strength out of her. She pulled Bracken round and walked away.

'Sian!'

But she kicked the horse on.

'Sian!'

She stopped and turned round slowly. He was walking towards her. When he reached her, he took hold of Bracken's reins and stroked the animal's face.

'I'm sorry. I shouldn't have been so rude. It's Sebi,' he explained. 'He's ill. The vet's just been here. It's been a bad day. Forgive me?'

Sian hesitated a moment and then said the only thing she could say.

'Of course.'

They smiled at each other.

'What's wrong with him? Is he going to be okay?' she asked.

'Yes, probably. Well at least I hope so. He's a valuable animal and I'm very fond of him. I would hate it if anything were to happen to him,' and then a smile replaced the concern on his face. 'Stay for a while?' he asked. 'Come up to the house and have a beer with me?'

'Okay.'

But as Sian was dismounting, she missed her footing. With a cry of alarm and pain she crumpled into an undignified heap on the floor.

'Ouch! My ankle! I think I've sprained it,' but before she knew what was happening, Andrew had helped her to her feet, his strong hands underneath hers, standing her up.

'You okay?'

She smiled briefly, somewhat embarrassed. 'Yes, fine.'

'Perhaps I should get the vet back,' Andrew teased. 'Maybe you need his services.'

She went to put her weight on her foot and cried out. The pain was intense.

'Ow!'

'Here, let me help you,' and he picked her up in his arms.

'You don't have to,' she protested feebly, instantly aware of his overwhelming maleness. 'I can manage, honestly I can.'

'Rubbish. I insist,' he smiled. 'A gentleman should always help a lady in distress.

So she had no choice but to hold on. He smiled at her, his face barely inches from her own. There was no mistaking how handsome he was. Pregnancy or no pregnancy, she was beginning to feel in a way she had long forgotten.

'I must have twisted it,' she said, trying to cover up what she thought was her obvious discomfort as Andrew carried her towards the house.

'Probably,' he smiled. 'We'll need to get it into some icy cold water as soon as possible. It will help alleviate any swelling.'

He carried her along as if she were no more than a bag of feed. He looked ahead but she allowed herself, just now and then, and only for the briefest moments, to study his face again. She was aware of his sheer animality; his strong muscularity, his aroma. He was all male.

They went into the kitchen where he sat her on one of the chairs while he drew a bowl of cold water.

'Take your boot off,' he said, laying the bowl on the floor.

She did, but only with much wincing. In just those few minutes, her foot had swollen considerably.

'Nasty,' he said, examining it gently.

'Mmm, not very nice.' She looked up at him. 'How many sick days do I get for this?'

'What? You want sick days?' he smiled. 'I think not. I can't see how the stable is going to function without you, you know.'

'Rubbish.'

He sat back in another chair smiling. 'I feel honoured,' he said.

'Why?'

'Well, after what you said about men in the tack room I hardly expected to see you up here.'

'Oh that,' and she looked away. 'I was just . . . well, I'm sorry about it, that's all. You know what it's like when you get carried away,' and she smiled apologetically. 'Anyway, you weren't exactly polite yourself the other day.'

'Oh, when was that?'

'The pub in Newton Abbot and don't say you didn't see me because I couldn't have been more than ten feet away from you.'

His face clouded. 'Ah, that. Problems, that's all,' he explained. 'I just didn't want to talk to anyone at the time. I would have been terrible company.'

'That's okay,' she smiled warmly. 'It's not as if I have a right to know anything about you. Heavens, I've only been here five minutes.'

'Does that mean,' he queried gently, 'that I'm an honorary exception to the rule of horrible men?'

Sian laughed. 'Perhaps. I'll let you know sometime.'

'Well, maybe I should get that beer.'

'And then please could you show me around the house? I'd love to see more of it.'

'Okay.'

She looked about her, at all the heavy old furniture, the cupboards, the Aga, the old cooking utensils hanging up along one wall with the huge pots and pans.

'It looked very impressive coming up the drive,' she said, 'but . . . well, if I had to be really honest with you –'

'And no doubt you will be.'

She smiled inwardly. 'I'm not sure I'd want to live in something as large as this. I mean, it must get really lonely sometimes.'

His eyes, she noticed, stopped smiling but only briefly.

'Anyway,' she added, trying to brighten the sudden heavy atmosphere, 'think of all the housework you've got to do! No thanks, not for me. The hotel was big enough for that and I had a whole team of cleaners working for me. I can't imagine what it's like cleaning this place.'

'Well, I have a solution for that,' Andrew said, handing her a beer. 'I simply don't do that much of it.'

He picked up her foot, examined it and then replaced it in the water.

'How's it doing?'

'Better thanks. It's going down already.'

'Most of the house is uninhabited,' he said, going back to his chair. 'I only live in a couple of rooms and until I get round to doing the place up, I can't see things changing much.'

'But surely it will take thousands to do up a place like this?'

'Exactly,' he sighed.

'Don't you have any relatives, anyone who could help you? Or how about the banks?'

He laughed hollowly and the sound echoed around the vast room.

'To answer the first part, apparently, I have some distant relatives in Germany, although what they'd say about me landing on their doorsteps, demanding money to do up a place they had never heard of, is anybody's guess. And as for the banks . . .' He shrugged his shoulders. 'I might as well ask for the moon as get anything more out of them.'

'Oh dear. Like that, eh?'

She took her foot out of the water and moved it around. It was swollen but the pain had subsided.

'I think maybe I can get my boot on now,' she said hopefully.

'Great, and then I'd be delighted to show you around.'

'Only go slowly, won't you?'

'Of course.'

It was a struggle to get her boot back on, but they did eventually.

'Thank goodness for that,' Sian said. 'I was beginning to wonder if it would ever fit.'

They went slowly round the house, she limping and he supporting her by the arm. He showed her all the rooms that she wanted to see: the study; the billiard room with the huge snooker table covered with a dust sheet; the hallway with its magnificent carved ceiling; the day rooms; the bedrooms – she only glanced briefly at his. The big four-poster would only get her wondering. They were on the top corridor, about to descend to the ground floor when a painting of a woman and child caught her eye.

'Who are they?' she asked. 'They're very beautiful.'

He looked at it too with a wistful expression and the merest of smiles. 'My father did it. He was on the U-boats during the war. He was very young when he was called up,' he explained seeing her questioning expression. 'It ruined his lungs and he could never breathe properly after that so he took up painting.' He paused. 'That was one of his favourites.'

'Members of your family?'

He smiled. 'Yes,' but there was no further explanation. 'Shall we continue?' he said, holding out his arm.

He helped her round the rest of the house, filling her in with as much history as he knew. Finally they came to the great ballroom. When he opened the double doors, she was truly amazed.

'My God!'

'Impressive, isn't it? So what do you think of the place now?'

Sian hobbled into the middle of the large oblong room

and turned slowly around, taking in all its empty majesty. Even without any furnishings, it was still magnificent.

'Capable of holding at least two hundred,' Andrew said, coming to join her.

Tall windows ran the length of one side, giving panoramic views of the nearby woodland, and behind that, the moor and its grey granite tors. Above her, in the carved alabaster ceiling were trumpet-blowing cherubs with tiny wings, dancing across the white landscape, interspersed with garlands of flowers and ribbons in bows. Three massive crystal chandeliers hung along the middle, dusty now but their timeless glory still shining through.

She limped slowly towards the windows, her feet echoing on the parquet floor.

'This really is something else,' she said with a grin. 'I've never seen anything like it, not even in all my years working in hotels. It's truly splendid.'

Andrew watched her. She was beautiful yet strangely unaware of herself. But it was when she smiled that her face really came alive. Up until now she had been so serious, so pensive but now, looking around her, her smiles had transformed her from the attractive to the stunning. And then there was her hair: long, waved, red. So few people had hair like that. She was glorious, standing there in his house, in this room, just being herself and quite, quite unaware of what she was doing to him.

'Imagine,' she said suddenly, her face animated and her eyes shining, 'what it must have been like in the olden days, all the ladies dressed in their finery and all the men looking like penguins.' She closed her eyes and began to sway to some silent symphony. 'It must have been wonderful,' and then she tried to waltz but having forgotten her ankle, she only fell over again.

'Oh help!'

Andrew came over and stood her up.

'Well, that was clumsy of you,' he said, laughing.

'I know,' she agreed. 'Terrible, aren't I?'

The smile faded from his lips as he looked deep into her eyes. 'No,' he said solemnly, 'you're not terrible. You're anything but.'

For a moment time stood still. He had hold of her arms and could, if only he wanted to, lean towards her and kiss her perfect kissable lips. So he did and it was a moment of sublime beauty.

'Why did you do that?' she whispered. That touch, that tenderness, that feeling that she was about to find out something about herself and the way she could feel about a man, but then it all went.

'I . . .' He turned away. 'I'm sorry. I shouldn't have.'

'I've . . . I've got to go,' she said, flustered. She brushed some stray hairs away from her hot face. 'Helen will be wanting something for tea and I've got to get it ready.'

'Of course.' He turned around and smiled at her. 'I'll walk you back to Bracken.'

'Fine,' and they left the room.

Why did you do it? he kept asking himself as he followed her down the corridor. What on earth possessed you to take hold of her and kiss her? But he couldn't answer that one. He only knew he could never feel the same about her now as before the kiss.

She walked on ahead, feeling his every breath behind her, hearing his every step, acutely aware of his being. She momentarily closed her eyes. How could she possibly expect to sleep tonight?

They were adjacent with the overgrown rosebeds when she stopped. They were her favourite flowers.

'Roses, I love roses. Can I look around?'

'Certainly.'

She limped along the grassy path looking, touching and most of all, breathing in the scent.

'What beautiful, beautiful flowers,' she said. 'So perfect, so utterly exquisite.'

He followed behind her.

She turned round, her face enraptured. The awkward-

203

ness had gone. 'You must have some really old ones here and they always smell the best. Modern ones look nice and bloom for ages but they don't have the scent that these do.' She leant down and sniffed a particularly deep, dark red rose. 'Here, try this.'

He did.

'See what I mean?' she said, smiling at him and then her face suddenly saddened.

'What is it?' he asked.

'All this,' she said, her voice cracking. 'Why is all this so beautiful and people sometimes so . . . so . . . horrible?' and her eyes filled.

He searched for a handkerchief and offered it to her.

'Your husband, I take it?'

She nodded, wiping her face. 'You know, I really thought I had it all worked out. And then, just when I thought life was wonderful, fate came along and knee-capped me.' She sniffed noisily. 'It's so unfair!'

'But life's like that, Sian – arbitrary; wanton; unpredictable – and we all get our fair share of it. We're all lined up just waiting for something or someone to boot us where it hurts. That's the way it goes. We all get it.'

She looked up at him, her face tear-streaked. 'And you? Did you ever get your share?'

'Yes, oh yes, I got my share and like you, I thought the world had fallen apart. But it hasn't, you know. You will get better. You will get over him and you will love again.'

'I don't know. I don't think I could ever do that.' She shot him a quick glance. 'Back there, in the ballroom . . . It mustn't happen again, Andrew.'

'Why?'

'It's too soon. I can't, that's all. Please.'

He took her hands in his and kissed them both lightly. 'Okay, I understand.'

'Do you? Do you really know what it's like to love someone and then to have it taken away from you?'

He let go of her hands. His smile was thin. 'Yes, I know

only too well.' Then he smiled brightly. 'Come on. It's not the end of the world. It might feel like it right now, but it's not.'

'How can I believe you?'

'Because I know, that's why.'

But there was no joy in her. 'Your house,' she said. 'It's a bit like my marriage. It looks good, but it's an empty sham really.'

Andrew looked up at The Grange. 'A house but not a home,' he said gently.

'Exactly.'

'Well,' he said, 'we'd better get you back to Bracken. She'll be wondering where you are and I have to see to Sebi. He's got colic, you know. Can you walk on that ankle?'

'Yes, it's a bit sore, but I'll manage.'

'Here, take this with you,' and he leant down and, with his penknife, cut her a red rose.

'For you, the most perfect bloom, and remember, there are some things which are so precious we're frightened to touch them in case they break.' He watched her carefully as she took the rose and held it close to her nose. 'I'm not frightened, Sian, and there's no need for you to be either.'

'Where were you?'

Rowena stood at the bathroom door, arms folded across her heaving bosom, her mouth clasped shut with rage. She was tapping her foot. Eddy brushed past her. He was in no mood for this. She shut the door with more force than was necessary and hurried after him.

'I asked you a question, Eddy Williamson, and I expect an answer. Where were you that day I was away at my mother's? I've been told you were out all day. I've been told that no one knew where you were. What's going on, Eddy?'

He stopped in his tracks. He was getting mightily fed up

with Rowena. The sex was one thing, but she had no damned right to interrogate him like this.

He turned to face her. He realized she could look quite ugly when she lost her temper, especially the way her jaw jutted out like that.

'Did you know,' he said, pointing at her face, 'that you have a huge spot coming up on your chin?'

'What!'

Her hands flew to her face and she scurried off to the mirror to look. Eddy turned away with amusement. She was such a vain creature. He fixed himself a drink, loosened his tie, pushed off his shoes and stretched out on the sofa. It was a few minutes before Rowena came back, still sulking.

'Thanks for the drink,' she said, flouncing past him.

He raised his glass in slow ironic salute. 'No problem.'

She sat down in one of the chairs, scowling.

'You'll get wrinkles, you know, if you carry on looking like that,' he observed.

She turned away, bottom lip prominent. 'Tell me where you were, Eddy, and all this silliness can be forgotten.' She turned on a smile, long and suggestive. 'I know what would cheer you up, darling, but if you're not going to be fair with me, then I might not be fair with you. I can think of plenty of other men who would find me very attractive.'

She got off the chair and crawled on all fours across the carpet until she was sitting between his legs. She ran a perfectly manicured nail along his flies.

'Please, darling, tell me. Tell little Rowena where you were. I can be very appreciative if you want me to.'

She undid his flies, smiling all the while. Eddy knew only too well what was going to happen next.

'Come on, darling, speak. I'm waiting.'

She pulled down his trousers and then his pants. By now the anticipation had done the trick and he was more than interested in her.

'My, my Eddy, what a big boy you are.'

She took his erection in her practised hand and kissed its tip – small, butterfly kisses that felt like touches of fire. She watched him respond, his eyes slowly closing, his mouth parting as his breath got faster. But still he said nothing.

'Eddy ... Eddy ...'

He took hold of her head and started to move it against him at the pace he wanted.

'That's so good, baby. So good.'

With her mouth full of him, she didn't reply. Faster and faster she went, one hand cupping his balls, the other holding his shaft, full and engorged. And so she continued until suddenly she stood up, her hands on her hips.

'Speak or forever be frustrated, my darling.'

He opened his eyes, his desire fading.

'My God,' she said, laughing as she looked him up and down. 'What a prime specimen of manhood you are.'

'Bitch!'

'Bastard!'

He did up his trousers.

'Stop teasing, Eddy, and tell me where you were and then maybe, I will finish where I left off.'

'If you must know,' he said reluctantly, lighting himself a cigarette, 'I was seeing Sian and what's more, she's pregnant.'

Rowena's face fell. 'What?'

Eddy shrugged. 'I know. Bloody terrible, isn't it? Well anyway, there's no need for hysterics about it.'

Rowena started to cry, blubbing noisily.

'Now what's wrong?' he demanded. 'What the hell are you crying for?'

He watched helplessly, perplexed. He just didn't understand women at all sometimes.

Rowena wouldn't answer and she wouldn't be comforted. Instead, she stood up and ran to the bathroom where she locked herself in.

'Bloody hell!'

It didn't matter what he did, he just couldn't win sometimes.

Helen sat by the telephone, waiting nervously. He said he was going to ring her and arrange a meeting as soon as he arrived in Plymouth.

She glanced at her watch. Six o'clock. He should be in Plymouth by now. She chewed her thumbnail. She thought about another cigarette but the ashtray was already overflowing. Anyway, she only had one cigarette left. If she smoked that, she would have to go out to buy some more and then she might miss his call.

'Are you sure you won't have anything to eat, Helen?' It was Sian in the kitchen. She had made them a huge salad to go with some smoked mackerel and fresh wholemeal bread. 'There's plenty here.'

'No, thanks. I'm not hungry.'

'But you've got to eat, Helen. You can't go on like this, only picking at your food.'

It was true. Helen had lost her appetite. Normally so enthusiastic about her food, she had changed completely during the last week and her weight had plummeted.

Sian came out carrying a filled plate. She offered it to Helen.

'I hope he's worth it, this Darryl. Can't I tempt you just a little bit?'

She was worried. This behaviour was quite unlike Helen. Normally so cheerful and relaxed, she was anything but at the moment.

Sian scrutinized her closely. Helen's brown eyes shone with a brittle intensity that made her look perilously disturbed. Underneath were shadows as though she were drawn and ill.

'Are you sure you're feeling all right, Helen?'

'Yes, yes, I'm fine. Don't nag so.'

Sian put the plate down on the stairs. 'Just in case you change your mind,' she explained with a smile.

Helen smiled back and took hold of Sian's hand.

'Thanks. You're a pal. I don't know what I'd do without you sometimes.'

'Shouldn't that be the other way round?'

'Rubbish!'

'I hope he realizes what he's doing to you, this Darryl,' and she helped herself to a piece of tomato. She offered the food to Helen again. 'Go on. Have some. You'll fade away otherwise.'

'You must be joking!'

'I'm not.'

'Oh, all right then, but I'm not the least bit hungry, you know. I'm only doing this because you want me to.'

'It's this falling in love business – a temporary insanity, as I once read. It plays havoc with the guts.'

Helen grinned sheepishly. 'I'm that obvious, am I?'

'Yes.'

'Oh dear.'

'Come on, move over and tell me all about it.'

Helen shuffled to one side of the stairs. Sian sat down and waited patiently.

'Well?'

Helen shrugged. 'Nothing to say really . . . I love him so much it hurts.'

'Mmm, that bad, eh?'

'Yes.'

'So when am I going to meet this paragon of male perfection?'

'Don't know.'

'Why? Is he too busy or something?'

'No.'

'Married?'

'No.'

'Then why? I don't understand.'

'We just want to keep things quiet for a while, that's all.'

'Oh.' Sian paused and then said, 'Where did you say you met him?'

'I didn't but it was in Leighford.'

'He's local then? I thought you said he came from Plymouth.'

'I did? Well, he doesn't.'

'Sounds mysterious. What's he like?'

Helen's eyes sparkled. 'He's unlike anyone else I've ever met. He makes me feel special; feminine.' She shrugged. 'Wanted.' She lowered her head and chuckled. 'I know, I'm being silly, but there you are, that's the way it is.'

'That doesn't sound like the Darryl you were talking about the other day. Are you sure you've got the same man?'

The phone rang, saving Helen from answering. She was off the stairs and picking it up before Sian even had time to react. She looked at Sian. She didn't have to say anything for it to be understood that her presence wasn't required. Sian picked up the plate of food and shut the kitchen door firmly behind her. She didn't want to hear any of this.

Eddy finally got Rowena to open the bathroom door.

'What are you playing at, Rowena?' he asked gently.

She came towards him, her face a mess of tears and ruined makeup. She held out her arms and embraced him. They stood silently for a while, rocking gently.

'I'm sorry,' she mumbled into his shoulder. 'I couldn't help it. It's just . . . it's just . . .' and then she started to cry all over again.

'Now come on, Rowena, that's enough of that,' and he wiped her face dry with his hand before kissing her on the lips. 'Don't cry, darling, please. There's no need for it, you know.'

She pouted and looked at him coquettishly. 'You're not angry with me, then?'

'How could I be if I don't know what all this is about?'

She snuggled up to him again. 'I want a baby,' she whispered.

Eddy inwardly sighed. Not her as well.

'Please, Eddy. We can afford it, you know. What with my salary and all that bonus that Killington is going to give you.'

'I don't know about that,' he corrected her darkly, and moved back to the sofa where he picked up his drink. This was not what he wanted to hear.

'Well, he said he would if you did those little extra jobs for him.'

'If I did them. They're not certain yet.'

She came over and cuddled up to him, holding on tightly. She felt like a clamp to him.

'Please, Eddy.' Her voice was small. 'Wouldn't you like to have a son?'

'No,' came the immediate reply, only to be met with her wailing.

She angrily stood up. 'You're a pig, you are!' she shouted, 'an absolute bloody pig!' and she stormed out of the room.

What Rowena had described as Killington's 'little extra jobs' were constantly preying on Eddy's mind. Since Sian had left, his life had been getting increasingly out of control. He looked ruefully at his glass. It was empty.

Camilla came out of the shower. She had one large white towel around her wet hair and another wrapped around her bust.

Marcus was visiting tonight. He had phoned her earlier. She wasn't particularly looking forward to it.

She sat down in front of the dressing table and stared indifferently at her reflection. He was going to come round for dinner so she supposed she had better make an effort. Her Chanel dress or a Valentino? She didn't know. Nor did she care. She just couldn't be bothered.

There was an unopened bottle of champagne sitting in an ice bucket on a side table.

'Patrick!' she yelled, not bothering to get up.

She heard his heavy footsteps on the stairs and coming down the corridor. He knocked on her door.

'Come in.'

He entered at the same time as she undid the towels. She stood up as he came in and the towel around her fell on the thick carpet. She turned to face him, a full frontal nude. He only looked her in the eyes, his gaze not flickering. He was well used to her stunts by now. Nothing surprised him any more.

'You wanted something?' he asked. She pointed to the champagne. 'Open it.'

'Miss.'

He stepped over to the ice bucket and took out the bottle. As he untwisted the wire, she came over to him. She started to run her hands over his trousers, a small, teasing smile playing around her lips.

'My goodness, Patrick, I always wondered about you and now I know. Pretty impressive, I'd say.'

The cork popped. He replaced the bottle in the bucket, and pushed it down into the ice.

'Anything else, miss?'

'Oh, I'm sure there could be if you really wanted it.'

His strong hands stopped hers, his grip tightening. 'I don't think so, miss.' He pushed her away. 'Mr Killington wouldn't like it, miss.'

'He would never know. Of course, I could tell him that it was you who made a pass at me.' She smiled again, the tip of her tongue running between her moistened lips.

'And you think he'd believe you, miss?'

Her face hardened. 'You're not being fair, Patrick. Here we are, just you and me, stuck away in this boring house . . .'

'Don't you think you've had enough men, miss? Isn't it time you started behaving like the lady you are?'

She stepped away from him and slumped down onto the bed. 'Pour me a drink,' she said dully, picking up the towel and wrapping it around herself. 'And then go. I don't need your preaching.'

'Yes, miss.' He handed her a glass of champagne. As usual there was no thank you. 'I've prepared the vegetables for dinner and it's time you got ready for when Mr Killington arrives.'

'Fuck you, Patrick.'

'Quite, miss,' and he left the room.

He felt profoundly disturbed as he walked down to the kitchen. He had never known anyone like her. She was incomparably attractive but so spoilt. She had everything she wanted and yet she was never satisfied. If only she wasn't such a bitch. It would make all the difference. No man in his right mind could ignore her but she poisoned everything. Pity really.

Camilla wasn't smiling now. There used to be nothing better than teasing Patrick but recently it had become boring. Anyway, he had an unfortunate habit of reminding her of who she pretended to be and that only dredged up all her feelings of inadequacy.

She took a large mouthful of her drink. She didn't taste it. Like all the other expensive things in her expensive life, she no longer noticed it. It had all become mundane and irrelevant. What she needed, she decided, was something, or even better, someone, to make her feel alive again; someone who could bring a sense of wonder back into her life.

She lit a cigarette. Screw Patrick and Marcus. She didn't need them, either of them. She wanted Andrew. She just knew he was the one for her even though they had barely exchanged more than a few words. There was just something about him, something she could feel that gave her whole life a new meaning. She would have to meet him soon. She wouldn't be able to rest until she did. But just now she had Marcus to see to. He would be here any time and he didn't like to be kept waiting.

Camilla dressed in a dark blue jersey dress split to the

213

thigh down one side, figure-hugging and showing her off to her best advantage. She went downstairs to wait for Marcus. He arrived as punctually as ever.

'You look particularly fetching, my dear,' he remarked, helping himself to champagne.

She sipped her drink and said nothing.

'I have a present for you,' he said.

'What?'

He threw her a heart-shaped velvet box. 'To make up for our recent disagreements. Open it and see.'

She reluctantly put down her drink and did as he suggested. The box contained a magnificent diamond necklace, each stone perfectly matched and shining to perfection.

'Nice,' she commented, throwing it casually to one side. Later it would join all the other expensive jewels that he had bought for her over the years. She made a point of never wearing them, much to his annoyance.

Marcus picked the box off the floor and took out the necklace.

'Come here, my dear, and I will put it on for you,' he said.

'Do I have any choice?'

He took hold of her arm and pulled her to her feet. He then fastened the necklace.

'You look wonderful,' he said, turning her round.

'Was it expensive, Marcus?'

'Very.'

'Well, in that case – and just this once you understand – I'll wear it.' She ran her fingers over the exquisite gems. 'I suppose,' she added, looking straight at him, 'that it's my reward for staying with you, and the price you pay for perfection?'

'Exactly, my dear.'

Twelve

Sian was cantering around the paddock. She was feeling confident with Bracken again. After an initial awkwardness, the mare had settled down. She would always be a challenge to ride and would regularly throw her head and stamp her feet, but she suited Sian, who liked the animal's unpredictability. It made for an exciting ride.

Sian was loving every minute of it: the sun on her face, the wind in her hair, the feeling of power, of live flesh and blood power between her legs. After the months of stress and strain she had been under working at the hotel and putting up with Eddy, it was good to feel so alive and fit again.

She turned the corner of the field and kicked on up a gentle slope. Bracken started to gallop over the dry ground, faster and faster, so that by the time they reached the gate, both of them were hot.

Andrew appeared, bronzed, relaxed and smiling except there was a tiredness around his eyes that Sian hadn't seen before. He leant against the gate, arms across the top rail, one foot on the bottom.

'She's a fine animal, big topped, strong. Make a good brood mare,' he commented.

Sian smiled shyly at him. She was so aware of him now in every respect since their kiss. Her visit to The Grange and the way he had treated her had subtly changed everything.

'Is Sebi better?' she asked.

'Yes. As the vet thought, just a touch of colic.'

She's so beautiful, he thought, here in the sunshine, the breeze blowing a few hairs from her chignon around her face. All he had to do was reach out and touch her, if only she would let him.

'Would you like to come out for a ride later when the tourists have gone? We could go up to the reservoir. There's some good rides up there,' he suggested.

'Maybe,' Sian said, stroking Bracken's neck.

She's feeling awkward, he thought, they both are.

'Don't worry,' he assured her with a small laugh. 'You'll be quite safe. Nothing will happen.'

She wasn't at all sure if that was what she wanted to hear, even if he was teasing her. It was all so confusing. There was an element of caution about her and she still wasn't sure.

'I'll see.'

'Okay,' he said with patient good humour. There was no point forcing the issue. She would come round in her own sweet time, he reasoned.

'I'll see you later if you like, when I come back with the trekkers.'

She smiled and nodded her assent.

'Later then.' He turned to go.

'By the way,' she called out. He stopped. 'Were you any relation to a Major-General Warrener? I meant to ask yesterday only . . .' and she blushed.

'Why do you ask?'

'An old journal I bought in Newton Abbot. It mentions the name, that's all.'

'I'll tell you what,' he said, leaning on the gate again, 'you come to the painting exhibition at the Church Hall with me and maybe, just maybe, we'll talk about it.'

She remembered her pledge to avoid men — all men — until her emotional wounds had healed. Andrew could be so difficult, so puzzling. Better not risk further hurt. 'Thanks, but I think not,' she said kindly.

He shrugged, smiling to show no hard feelings. 'I'll see you later, then,' and he walked back up the yard.

'Andrew!' It was Helen.

216

'Yes?'

'There's someone here to see you,' she said mysteriously, with a grin.

'Who?'

'A woman.'

'Oh for God's sake, Helen, don't play games with me. I'm not in the mood.'

Her smile faded. 'How the hell should I know who she is?' she retorted. 'She's some skinny thing with far too much makeup, okay? A Camilla something or other. One very classy broad, judging by the gear.'

Andrew frowned. He had heard the name somewhere before, but for the life of him he couldn't remember where.

'Camilla?'

'Yeah. Like I said, a very attractive lady – if you like that sort of thing,' she added under her breath. 'Anyway, she's waiting for you in the cottage.'

He raised his eyebrows. 'Why did you let her in there?'

'I didn't. She just let herself in.'

He didn't stop to answer her but set off to the cottage. He knew who she was now. It was the lady he had rescued in Exeter that day. He had never expected to see her again. Prompted by Helen's description of her, he remembered what she looked like now: the pleasing features, the wide blue eyes and childlike nose. She was certainly the kind of woman that men would find attractive, especially from the neck down, but she hadn't made a big impression on him. Sian was the only woman who had done that. Camilla's was altogether a different kind of attractiveness, the sort that would be looking out at him from every glossy magazine arranged along the newsagent's shelves. It was a shallow, skin-deep beauty, and as such left him indifferent.

He opened the door and stepped into the cool interior of the cottage.

'Hello.'

He stopped in his tracks and instantly all his assumptions about her were binned. This wasn't at all the woman he remembered. She held out her cool hand.

'Andrew Mann? I'm Camilla Killington. You remember, we met under somewhat unfortunate circumstances at the cathedral in Exeter when you stopped that young man who stole my bag?'

'Of course.'

He shook her hand, trying to take in all that he saw in front of him: the smiling face with inviting eyes and warm, full lips, the tender expression of good manners, but above all, the powerful scent of woman. If Sian had engaged his most honourable feelings, this woman was appealing to something altogether more basic.

'Would you like a drink?' he said at last, regaining his composure. He wasn't sure he liked her, but given the state of flux that he had found his emotions going through recently, she was an interesting diversion.

'I would love one, thank you.' Her voice was honeyed.

'This way then.'

He led her through the house and into the garden where there were a couple of easy chairs for them to sit on.

'I'll be back in a minute,' he said. 'Make yourself comfortable.'

'Thank you.'

He rushed back inside and then stood for a moment by the open fridge thinking of her. She was tall, elegant, her jeans and white shirt were casual and very expensive. Even he could see that. Helen's description of her was very apt: she was one very classy act. With her short lustrous hair and those magnificent kingfisher-blue eyes, she was quite dazzling. He wondered what she was doing in this part of the world.

'Here you are. They're nice and cold.' He handed her a can of beer and sat down on the chair next to her. Blaize came over and sniffed the newcomer. He didn't welcome her and Andrew noticed she was nervous of him.

'Don't worry about him,' he said. 'He's a big softie.'

'Rather like his owner, then,' she answered with a smile.

'That's a matter of opinion,' he laughed. 'Anyway, to what do I owe the pleasure?'

'Well, I wanted to say how much I appreciated your help the other day and I also wondered if you would help me again.'

'How?'

'Is your phone working properly?' she asked.

He frowned. 'Yes, I think so. Why?'

'I've been trying to reach you for the last few days and each time it was either engaged or you were out.'

He shrugged. 'I'm very busy. I do a lot of work from home. That way I can keep it out of sight of prying eyes.'

'And do you have many things to keep secret, Mr Mann?'

'Andrew, please.'

'Andrew?'

'No, not really. Just the usual businessman's hassles, that's all. That was why I was in Exeter that day.'

They both smiled.

'You were saying something about me helping you?' he prompted.

'Ah yes. I'm going to be in the area for a while and I've been told that you're the best riding instructor around here so I thought it might be a good opportunity to start lessons again.'

'I see. Where are you staying?' he asked.

She was wearing diamond studs in her ears and when she moved her head, they sparkled in the sun, giving her face a haunting luminescence.

'Belvedere Cottage. Do you know it?'

'It's beyond the other side of the village, isn't it?'

'Yes, and I thought that while I was here, it would be a good idea if I brushed up my riding skills.' She gave a small, musical laugh. 'I'm not very good, I'm afraid. I have been riding for years, ever since I was a little girl, but some of us are made for equine pursuits and some of us aren't and I think that maybe I'm not. Although,' and she looked at him coquettishly, 'I'm sure someone of your eminent skill can soon straighten out any imperfections and bad habits I might have fallen into over the years.'

She watched him closely over the rim of her can while she sipped her beer.

'So, Andrew, what do you say?'

'Riding,' he repeated. 'You want lessons?' and he smiled. 'Well, I don't see why not. I'm sure we can come to some sort of arrangement.'

'But of course we can. Anything's possible if you want it.'

It was then that Andrew realized that they might not be talking about the same thing.

Camilla turned to look out over the undulating land, parched and shimmering in the early morning heat. It was going to be a very hot day.

'I think I'm going to like it around here,' she said, and fixing him with a slow smile she added, 'especially as some of the locals seem so accommodating.'

'Well, let's see what we can fix up, shall we?' he said, smiling briefly and rising to his feet. 'I'll just go and fetch the diary.'

The holiday-makers left the yard, their horses following obediently one behind the other. Helen was out in front on her favourite gelding. There was no doubt about it, thought Sian from inside one of the stables where she was mucking out, Helen had lost quite a bit of weight recently. It was so unlike her, and Sian was worried for her friend.

She soon lost sight of them, and then couldn't hear them either as the sound of their hooves disappeared into the moorland.

After a few minutes of gathering up wet pungent straw and putting it into the wheelbarrow, she became aware of the sound of a man and woman laughing together. Sian

220

stopped and listened. They were very happy. The voices came closer. It was Andrew and a woman.

'No, no, it was fate,' insisted the woman, half laughing. 'Just one of those strange events that happen now and again. The planets, you know.'

'Really? And you believe all that astrological stuff, do you?'

'Maybe. Anyway, what are you?'

'Apparently – and I don't believe any of it, you know, I'm far too much of a sceptic – but apparently I've been told that I'm an Aries with my Venus in Taurus, whatever that means.'

'Venus in Taurus, eh?' she mused. 'That means a strong sensuous lover and a mite possessive. A jealous streak, even. Mmm, sounds very interesting.'

'Is that so?'

'Uh-huh, a ram, you see, and as they say with rams, very impulsive and very sexy,' and then there was more laughter, his as well as hers.

Sian stood still and listened in quiet amazement. She found it difficult to reconcile the man who had the previous day kissed her so tenderly, and this morning asked her out for a ride, with this one, who was so obviously enamoured and flirting outrageously with somebody else. Duplicity was not a virtue in her eyes.

She let the pitchfork fall to the floor. She had lost all her incentive for mucking out. Yet again disappointment filled her heart. She had come so close to opening up to him and now this.

'You all right?' Eck appeared, his massive gormless face a mask of concern.

Sian gave him a thin smile. 'Yes, Eck, I'm fine.'

He grinned, a line of dribble running down his stubbly chin and came forward to pick up the pitchfork.

'Eck'll do it,' he said. 'You go sit.'

He gently pushed her to one side where she gratefully sat down on a hay bale and watched him for a few minutes.

The laughter from the yard had died away so Sian turned her attention back to Eck. He was a huge man of immense proportions, slow and lumbering, but his heart was of pure gold. His clumsy attempts to be nice to her touched her heart. His baby-blue eyes would follow her wherever she went.

'Eck?'

'Yes?'

He looked up and blinked in his characteristic slow way.

'Where do you come from?'

'North.' He returned to his chore.

'Where in the north?'

'Dunno,' and he grinned.

'Well, do you want to know something?'

The big man looked at her. 'What?'

'I'm a fool, that's what. A real idiot.'

He frowned and then slowly shook his head. 'No. You can't be,' he said in all seriousness. 'You're nice.'

She sighed.

'Am I? I don't know any more. It's all these men, you see. They just mess up everything, absolutely bloody everything.'

'You sad?' he asked, his face forlorn.

'Yes, Eck. Well, not sad exactly, just . . . I don't know. I wish I did, then maybe I wouldn't be in this mess.'

'Eck like you,' he said cheerily.

'I know you do and I like you too, but we'd better get on, hadn't we, and clear all this mess up otherwise Andrew will get cross.'

Eck's huge frame shook with silent mirth. 'Naw,' he said, 'he won't get angry. He likes you too.'

'Does he?' she answered quietly. 'I wish I could believe you, you know. I just wish I could.' She sighed. She was going round and round in circles, her emotions on a path all of their own, swinging her one way and then the other. It was most unsettling.

She abruptly stood up, resolving to pull herself together.

'Come on then, give me the brush and I'll finish up here.'

A car horn blasted in the yard. Blaize was barking. Eck followed Sian out into the sunshine. It was the vet, his dirty car full of medicines, and his own dog, a feisty terrier, attacking the window as he tried to get at Blaize. The bigger dog ignored him. It was beneath his dignity to acknowledge such a canine scrap. He bounded over to the vet, wagging his tail.

'Well, hello there, Blaize, and you two. Any sign of the old man?' he beamed.

Sian turned towards the cottage. 'I think he's in there.'

'Could you go and get him for me, dear, because Eck promised to show me the swallows' nests, didn't you, Eck?'

Andrew was in there with his visitor and Sian didn't want to interrupt them, but it was too late to do anything. The vet had taken Eck by the arm and was steering him off down the yard.

This is stupid, she told herself as she neared the cottage. Just because she had heard him laughing with some strange attractive woman didn't mean anything, and what's more, she had no right to feel cross about it. Surely she had enough problems of her own without adding to them?

She opened the door and stepped in. 'Andrew!'

No answer. She tried again. 'Andrew! The vet's here!'

'Through here, Sian!'

They were in the back garden, sitting under the tree. As soon as she walked out to them, she could feel herself being closely scrutinized by the woman. She only glanced briefly at her.

'Andrew, the vet's here.'

'Right,' he said getting to his feet, 'I'd better go.' He turned to Camilla. 'Sorry about this. Perhaps Sian would like to keep you company until I get back.'

'Well, actually, Andrew,' said Sian hurriedly, 'I've got loads of things to do out in the yard and I'm sure I'll only bore your visitor.'

'Not at all,' came Camilla's smooth reply.

Sian took her first real look at Camilla. She was sitting there as casually as if she owned the place, one bejewelled hand lying along the arm of her chair; long legs crossed, a gold sandal flapping against her foot as she habitually waved it up and down. She had put on dark glasses and it was hard to tell what she was thinking, although Sian instinctively felt unease in her presence.

'I would very much like your company. What did you say your name was?'

'Sian.'

'I'm Camilla and if you don't mind me saying so, you have a very pretty name. Welsh, isn't it?'

'Yes. My mother's side.'

'Lovely.'

'Well,' said Andrew, 'I'll leave you two to get to know each other. I really must go and see the vet,' and with a smile for both of them, he left.

'Do come and sit down, Sian,' said Camilla, patting the seat of the other chair. 'You're making me feel uncomfortable standing up there like that.'

Sian moved over to the empty chair. She wasn't liking this one little bit. She felt like a butterfly being asked to dinner by a hungry spider. Irrational she knew, but that didn't make it any better.

She obediently sat.

'Well,' purred Camilla, 'and how long have you worked here?'

'Not long. I came a few weeks ago.'

'Oh really, and what were you doing before that?'

'Hotel work.'

There was a brief silence as Camilla thought this one out.

'How wonderful,' she said at last in a tone that asked what sort of a low-life was she talking to.

How patronizing, thought Sian.

'And what exactly did you do in the catering trade?'

asked Camilla, again not even trying to hide the contempt in her voice. 'Were you a waitress or did you work in the kitchen or maybe,' and for some reason she seemed to find this amusing, 'or maybe you were a chambermaid?'

'No,' said Sian slowly, enjoying every minute of this, 'not at all. Actually, I was the manageress.'

Camilla's smile froze for only the briefest moment. 'Oh,' she said. 'How nice,' and that was the end of that topic.

The insects buzzed, a skylark twittered above them, hovering on the still, hot air and so they sat, each aware of the other and neither saying anything. It was Camilla who broke the ice first.

'I'm here to have lessons, you know.'

'People do that at a riding stable,' replied Sian levelly. She wanted Camilla to understand that whatever she might think of her, however much she might try to belittle her, it wasn't going to work.

'Quite,' was the tight reply with the tiniest flash of venom in Camilla's feline smile.

'You're a grockle then,' said Sian, feeling better now she had established her credentials.

Camilla raised a perfectly arched eyebrow. 'A grockle?'

'Yes, a tourist. It's what the locals call visitors around here.'

Camilla nodded with a kind of bemused comprehension. 'How quaint,' she muttered. 'And you're a local, are you?'

'No, I'm not, as it happens. My father was an army officer so we travelled around a fair bit. He's retired now and lives down in Brigham, which is where I managed the hotel. The Stoneygates.'

There was an instant but almost imperceptible reaction. Somehow that name had subtly altered things, although Sian didn't know how or why. Camilla, who had been in the middle of taking a sip of her beer, had held the can to her mouth for just an instant too long. Even if Sian hadn't been looking at her, she would have known that something was amiss. It was the sudden atmosphere that had sprung up out of nowhere; a change of temperature.

'Ah, Brigham,' said Camilla slowly, seemingly relishing the name in her mouth.

'Do you know it?'

Camilla smiled a neat cautious smile and shook her head. 'No.'

Sian didn't believe her.

'Where are you staying?' she asked, letting the moment pass.

'I've taken a cottage beyond the other side of the village. Pretty place. Obviously very old. Not quite what I'm used to but one has to make do, of course.'

'Of course,' echoed Sian.

'I'll be here for some time I expect,' added Camilla, her voice full of hidden meaning, and then just in case Sian hadn't got the message, she spelt it out for her.

'Andrew's quite handsome, don't you think?'

'Can't say I've noticed,' said Sian turning away and staring out over the paddock.

'Does he have any family?'

'Not that I know of,' and she felt Camilla's eyes boring through the back of her head.

'Any girlfriends?'

Sian got to her feet knocking Camilla's can of beer over as she did so. She hurriedly picked it up.

'I've got to go,' she said, pushing her hair back from her face. 'I've got loads of things to do, so if you'll excuse me,' and she went to leave.

'But you haven't answered my question,' Camilla protested and when Sian looked back at her, she smiled innocently enough.

'I don't know,' replied Sian patiently. 'You'll have to ask somebody else. I don't know anything about him. I only work for him.'

Camilla smiled to herself. Poor little girl, she thought, wearing her heart on her sleeve like that. Someone was bound to step on it. First Eddy and now . . . well, she might, especially when she got Andrew right where she wanted him.

'Damn her! Damn her! Damn her!'

Sian marched home as fast as she could in the suffocating heat. That insufferable Camilla had made her so angry she would have knocked her head off if she had asked any more of her impertinent questions. Who did she think she was? She had only been there five minutes and already she was ruling the roost as though she owned the place.

She slowed down. It was too hot and the sweat was pouring off her. She wiped her hand across her forehead – hot, wet and uncomfortable, and her thick hair only made the problem worse. Behind her neck, tendrils of hair were sticking to her skin.

Camilla. Camilla who, and where did she come from, and what was all that stuff about Brigham that made the air crackle between them? She didn't know, but she knew one thing: she didn't like her one little bit. Every sinew, every nerve was screaming at her and there was that primitive hard lump of immediate dislike sitting in her guts.

It was obvious, though, that Andrew didn't share her view. He felt quite differently.

Sian stopped marching and ruefully smiled to herself. What did it matter? Nothing was going to come of it. Nothing could come of it. She was pregnant, and yet here she was getting all het up because the man she worked for – someone she had only known for a few weeks and didn't even like when she first met – was making eyes at another woman! It was utterly stupid and totally ridiculous and she had absolutely no right whatsoever to feel like she did. There was no justification for it, no rationale, no nothing. Just idiotic emotions and even they couldn't be trusted any more. She had to face it; she had no taste where men were concerned. She had married an adulterer who had done nothing except destroy her self-confidence and now she was allowing herself to fall for a man who didn't care for her. It had to stop.

She ambled on, now at peace and full of good intentions, the sweat running down her back and around her neck. She grabbed at a grass stem and chewed it thoughtfully. As she went past the empty brown fields, not a thing stirred. The breeze had died completely and the air hung still and heavy. She would forget about Eddy; she would forget about Andrew and she would get on with her life. She would put them both behind her and that's where they would stay. Neither one of them was going to upset her any more.

'Where's Sian?' asked Andrew, when he returned.

He wiped his forearm across his damp brow, sun-bleached hairs sticking to his forehead.

'I don't know,' replied Camilla sweetly. 'She just took off. Things to do, she said.'

'Yes, well, it wasn't what I wanted her to do. I'll have to have a word with her when I next see her. Pregnancy or no pregnancy, that doesn't give her the right to take off before her hours are up.'

He opened a fresh can of beer and sat down next to Camilla.

'Pregnant, is she?' asked Camilla slowly. 'She doesn't look it.'

'Only a couple of months, she said.'

'So she won't be here much longer then?'

'I don't know. I suppose it depends on how she feels.'

'Well, she can hardly work with horses if she's the size and shape of a barrage balloon, now can she?'

He smiled. 'We'll see.' He paused and took a mouthful of beer, squinting into the sun. 'Now, where were we? Lessons. When?'

Camilla laid her hand on his arm and smiled. 'Whenever you like. How about tonight?'

The invitation couldn't have been more obvious.

'Can't,' he said, ignoring her advances.

'But I mix a very mean salad,' she said, playfully running a nail along his arm.

'"A mean salad"?'

She nodded, her face quite serious except for the glint in her eyes.

'I'll be too tired,' he said.

'Well, how about tomorrow then? Surely busy people like you have to take some time off now and again?'

He looked at her with guarded eyes. 'You're a very persistent lady, aren't you?'

She smiled slowly. 'But of course. Only those who go after what they want, get anywhere. Surely you can appreciate that?'

He stood up. 'Look, Miss Killington —'

Her face lost its softness. 'My name's Camilla,' she insisted.

'Okay, Camilla. I think it's best that we don't meet socially for the time being.'

His face was friendly but she wasn't comforted. He was refusing her.

'It's nothing personal, you understand,' he added with a smile, 'but . . . well, at the moment things are difficult. Under normal circumstances, I would jump at the chance, but not now.'

She seemed to accept this gracefully. She too stood up and then took a step closer to him, so close she could smell his musk. She rested a finger lightly on his lips.

'I think, Andrew, and it's only my considered opinion, you understand, that it's high time you changed your working practices. All these hours; it's no good. You know what they say; all work and no play makes for a very boring person.'

Their eyes locked. Then he removed her finger.

'I think not,' he said.

Her eyes only briefly registered her disappointment but

then she smiled and stepped to one side. She picked up her handbag and swung it over her shoulder.

'You know something, Andrew?'

'What?'

She walked towards the back door and then stopped. 'I never, ever give up.'

Patrick couldn't understand it. He had cleaned the house, cooked a meal – her favourite – and done the washing and she was still in a foul mood. Now he was cleaning up the broken crockery that she had flung against the wall.

'Look here, miss! Stop it! If you do any more damage around her, Mr Killington will go spare!'

'Fuck him, Patrick! Just fuck him!' and she threw the rest of her drink down her throat, most of it missing and spilling onto her shirt. She was getting violently drunk.

'Now look what you've done, miss,' he said reaching for a cloth. 'That wine will stain, you know.'

'I don't care!'

'Come here, miss. Let me wipe it off.'

'Leave me alone!' she yelled, brushing him aside.

For Patrick, it was nothing he couldn't handle. He was more than used to her outbursts. As the blows rained down on him, he simply carried on, until she caught the side of his nose.

'That's it, miss!' he bellowed, his eyes bulging and veins standing out of his bull-like neck. 'Now pack it in!'

She stared hard at him, more in surprise than anything else. 'I'll tell Marcus!' she threatened. 'I will! You wait!'

'Then tell him, miss, because I don't think he's going to take much notice of you.'

She remained rigid in his arms, then fell against him, limp and defeated.

'Oh Patrick . . . why? Why?'

'Why what, miss?'

'Why can't . . . why can't . . . doesn't anyone love me?'

'Of course they do, miss. Mr Killington does,' but that

didn't cheer her up at all, which only perplexed him. Normally she kept her distance from him but now she was actually leaning against him for comfort. He tentatively put his arms around her.

'It's not fair!' she whispered. 'No one loves me! No one!'

'Now come on, miss. That's not true.'

They stood for a few minutes; he baffled by her completely uncharacteristic behaviour towards him, and she too upset to do anything else. He wondered what on earth had brought this on. It must be something to do with that man up at the stables and if it was, he wasn't sure he liked it, which surprised him even further.

'There, there, miss. You'll be okay. It will all come out in the wash. At least that's what me granny used to say.'

Her voice was warm and muffled when she spoke, mumbling against his shoulder. 'Will it? How do I know that?'

He rocked her gently. 'It will, miss. Trust me. Just you wait and see.'

Thirteen

'Happy birthday to you!
Happy birthday to you!
Happy birthday, dear Sian!
Happy birthday to you!'

'Helen! How lovely!'

Sian kissed her friend on the cheek, both women smiling broadly. Helen handed her her post and a small package.

'Nothing much,' she mumbled, 'but it's the thought that counts.'

'Thanks, Helen. That's really nice of you.'

'Here, you open all your cards and I'll make some coffee.'

Sian sat down at the table, sifting through the envelopes, recognizing most of the writing immediately.

'To tell the truth,' she said, 'I've had so much on my plate recently, I'd clean forgotten about my birthday. It was really kind of you to remember.'

'Well, I could hardly forget my oldest and bestest friend, now could I? Come on, hurry up and open my pressie. I want to see if you like it.'

Sian tore open the package and beamed. It was a small enamel brooch of a prancing horse exactly the same colour as Bracken.

'It's lovely!'

Helen gave her a small hug. 'I know it's not much, but you know what the wages are like working for Andrew.'

'It doesn't matter. I still think it's very pretty,' and she put it on.

'Anything from that Neanderthal husband of yours?'

Sian looked through the envelopes again. 'No, nothing.'

'Typical,' replied Helen. 'You're married to him for what – five years? – and he can't even be bothered to get you a birthday card. What a pig!'

Sian sighed. She had been half expecting something; just a little thing; just the smallest of cards would have sufficed. But nothing, not a bean – it just made the heaviness in her heart more noticeable. But then what did she expect? He had Rowena. He wasn't in the slightest bit bothered with his wife any more, or his baby. He just didn't care less and what's more, she didn't either. Not now.

'Well, it's not as if we're on the best of terms, is it?' she said, standing her cards up along the dresser.

'No, but he could have done something, couldn't he?'

Helen picked up a card and read it. It was from Sian's parents.

'Anything from Andrew?' she asked casually.

'No. Should there be?'

Helen shrugged. 'I just thought there might be, given that you two seem to have reached some sort of . . . how can I say . . . an agreement?'

'Meaning what?'

'Meaning that you've been a lot nicer to each other recently and I just thought –'

'Well don't, Helen,' interrupted Sian. 'Whatever you might have thought, hasn't happened.' Realizing she might have been a bit too defensive she added, 'I just went up to The Grange to take a look around, that's all.'

'So you have been up there then? Kept quiet about that, didn't you?'

'Nothing happened, that's why. He just showed me around the place and then I left, okay? Satisfied, are we?'

'If you say so.' Helen grinned lasciviously. 'That would explain why he's been in a better mood lately.'

'No it doesn't! Anyway, after yesterday when that female arrived —'

'You mean that skinny one with the big chest?'

Sian sipped her coffee. 'Exactly. I left without finishing my chores and I strongly suspect I'm going to get an earful when I get in.'

'Rubbish! He won't do that. He likes you too much.'

Sian snorted with disbelief.

'Still,' said Helen, 'what are you going to do to celebrate?'

Sian's face was full of patient irony. 'Like what? Be whisked off my feet for a champagne balloon flight over the moors? Be picked up by my chauffeur and taken off to Paris? What exactly did you have in mind?'

'Well, we could have a meal here only . . .' and she pulled a rueful face, 'it can't be tonight. I'm seeing someone.'

'Let me guess, the wonderful Darryl?'

'Something like that.'

'It doesn't matter then. We can always celebrate another time,' and she smiled warmly at Helen. 'And thank you for the lovely brooch.'

The telephone rang, its piercing tone cutting through the early morning quiet.

'Who the hell's that?' asked Helen, going to answer it. She returned a few moments later. 'Eddy,' she said, standing in the doorway. 'Shall I tell him to bog off, or what?'

Sian stood up, a look of surprise on her face. 'No, it's okay. I'll handle him.' She picked up the receiver.

'Hello.'

'Tell Helen I heard everything she said,' grumbled a familiar voice.

Sian smiled to herself. If nothing else, he was always consistent.

'Bit early for you, isn't it, Eddy? Rowena kicked you out of bed, has she?'

There was an intake of breath down the other end while he resisted the temptation to bite back.

'Actually, Sian, I was ringing you up to say, well . . . I wanted to say how unfortunate things were at the stable the other day.'

She looked at her reflection in the hall mirror. There wasn't any trace of emotion in her clear green eyes.

'Unfortunate?' she queried. 'Are you sure you got the right word there?' She paused. 'How about bloody awful, Eddy? How about dreadfully embarrassing? How about you being abjectly and totally sorry for your appalling behaviour?'

'Okay,' he began slowly, 'maybe I did just . . . well, maybe we both got a little bit heated.'

'A little bit?' Sian cried. 'If that's what you call a little bit then God help you when I really blow my top because there won't be anything left of you by the time I'm finished!'

Silence. He didn't have an answer for that. She glared angrily at the mouthpiece.

'You still there, Eddy?'

'Yes. Just thought it politic if I waited until you had calmed down a bit. I had no idea you could be so unreasonable, you know. Must be all this baby stuff, upsetting you like this.'

'Don't you patronize me, Eddy!' she yelled. 'Me, unreasonable? ME? How dare you! You're the one who doesn't know how to behave himself, not me! You're the one who screws around, not me! Don't you bloody dare tell me how to behave!' She slammed down the phone.

Helen was standing in the doorway, a cup of coffee at the ready. 'Being his nice gentlemanly self, was he?' she asked smiling.

Sian screwed up her face and clenched her fists in sheer frustration.

'Damn stupid man! He always gets to me. Always!' and

then she laughed, the tension draining out of her face. 'Honestly, when am I going to learn?' She gratefully took the coffee. 'I hate him, you know,' and she burst out into a broad grin, 'swine that he is.'

'That's my girl,' said Helen, laughing.

They were saddling up the horses for the day's trekking when a van pulled into the yard. 'Petal's Flowers,' it said down the side. The two women looked at it as the young driver, overalled and spotty, got out.

'See,' said Helen, 'Andrew did know.'

'How?'

'From your P45, silly.'

Sian's stomach fluttered. Maybe, she thought, just maybe. . .

'How do you know they're for me?' she asked. 'They could be for you from Darryl.'

Helen looked at her with disbelief. 'Well, of course, Darryl sends me flowers all the time, and as for my secret admirers, well, there are legions of them.'

The man stopped, a huge bouquet of roses in his arms. He read a small piece of paper.

'Sian Williamson?' he asked, looking at both women.

'See,' nudged Helen excitedly.

Sian smiled and held out her hands. There was a blush to her cheeks. Roses . . .

The man handed them over. 'Someone loves ya,' he teased.

'Thanks,' she muttered. The roses were beautiful, a wonderful bright yellow. Not her favourite colour, and they didn't have much of a scent, but they were lovely.

'Let's have a whiff,' said Helen, 'and hurry up and read your card. I want to see who they're from.'

Sian quickly opened the small envelope. Her smile froze, withered and then faded altogether.

'What's the matter?' asked Helen.

Sian didn't answer. Instead she took the roses off Helen,

marched across the yard and dumped them in the rubbish bin.

'Here,' she said, coming back, handing over the small card to the astonished Helen. 'Read it. How could he?' Her lips quivered with indignation. 'How could he?'

' "To the only woman I have ever loved, Eddy",' read Helen.

Sian leant against the horse she had been saddling, breathing hard. Helen put a comforting arm around her.

'Come on, pet, it's not the end of the world.'

Sian looked at her, eyes swimming with angry tears. She took Helen's offered tissue and wiped her eyes.

'You know,' she said, 'just when I think I'm coming to terms with it all, he goes and pulls a stunt like that and it's back to square one again.'

'I know, but then they're like that, aren't they? Absolute sods.'

'I know, but at least you've got Darryl.'

'Yeah, well, he's different.'

Sian's face collapsed again. 'That's what I thought Eddy was!'

Footsteps. Helen looked over her shoulder just as Blaize came up to her, his tail wagging. Andrew appeared close behind, frowning.

'What's going on?' he enquired, not unkindly but simply because it wasn't every day that a member of his staff stood in the yard bawling her eyes out.

'It's her birthday,' explained Helen.

'But shouldn't that be a reason to celebrate?' he asked.

'Not when you've had an earful from your husband before breakfast.'

Sian gathered herself together and looked at him with red eyes.

'I suppose you're now going to tell me off about yesterday?' she said wearily. 'Well, go ahead. Things can't get any worse than they are already.'

He looked at her beautiful pale tear-stained face, which

237

looked so incongruous on this wonderfully sunlit morning.

'No,' he said gruffly, 'not unless you want me to.' Then he glanced from one to the other, 'But I will lose my cool if the horses aren't ready on time. We haven't got all day, you know. Birthday or no birthday, there's things to do and little time to do them, so get a move on. After you've done here, you go home, Sian. I can't have you falling to pieces in my yard just because your husband has forgotten your birthday or something.'

Both women stared at him and then Sian marched off.

'Thank you very much!' blazed Helen, her eyes flashing with anger. 'You're all heart, you are! Real sensitive!'

Without a word, Andrew turned and walked back to the cottage. When he reappeared, he went straight to his Land Rover, got in and took off. He caught up with Sian a short distance away down the lane. He sounded the horn. There was a slight stiffening of her back, but no other response. He drew level with her and wound down his window.

'Get in, Sian. You can't walk home in that state.'

She ignored him, her mouth clamped shut with hurt determination and her head held high.

'Sian.'

Still no response. The Land Rover shot forward and slewed to a sudden halt in front of her. Now she had to stop as the lane was blocked. He got out to face her.

'Now get in and do as you're told!' he ordered.

She stood her ground, arms folded, lips pressed shut. Her glittering eyes were hard and unwavering.

'Get in that Land Rover, Sian, or I won't be responsible for my actions!'

An arched eyebrow rose sceptically.

'Right!' he said, grabbing her arm. 'That's it!' and he frogmarched her in before she could even summon up an outraged refusal. She sat fuming. He climbed in and started up.

238

They drove in indignant silence to Helen's cottage. When Andrew turned off the engine, they sat like statues, neither prepared to make the first move. Eventually she opened the door.

'Don't.'

They glanced at each other.

'I'm sorry,' he said. 'I shouldn't have ... I mean, I didn't – shouldn't have spoken to you like that. Not on your birthday. It was unfair of me. I should have thought before I opened my big mouth.' He smiled ruefully. 'Business problems. Makes you a bit ratty sometimes.'

She sat back in her seat, rubbing her wrist.

'Did I hurt you?' He tried to take her wrist and examine it. She pulled away. 'Give it here, Sian.'

'No. I'm all right.'

'Give it here,' he repeated wearily.

She reluctantly gave in. As he gently turned her hand over in his, she found herself examining the top of his blond head. His touch made her skin tingle. If it were her breast, her thigh ... She stopped herself.

So fragile, he thought. This wrist, this slim fragile wrist, the colour of light golden butterscotch and covered in the finest layer of tiny blonde hairs. He didn't let it go. When he looked up, his eyes met hers.

'You okay?'

She hurriedly looked away and nodded. Then she gave a tired smile. 'Yes, just silly and pregnant I guess.'

She removed her hand from his and inclined her head towards the cottage. 'I'd better go. You've got to take the trekkers out.'

'Well ...'

She looked at him, half hopeful, yet simultaneously chastising herself. Forget it, said a voice, forget it. But it didn't stop her wanting.

'Coffee?' she said.

The look on his face said it all.

'I can't. I've got to go and give some private tuition this morning.' He glanced at the dashboard clock. 'And I'm late enough as it is.'

The spark of hope was instantly snuffed out. Of course. Camilla. How silly of her to forget.

Sian scrambled out of the Land Rover as though she couldn't get out quickly enough.

'Thank you for the lift,' she said.

He watched her walk briskly up the path. There was no doubt about it: she had left her mark on him and he couldn't rub it out.

Maybe he ought to fire her. That way he would be rid of her and the constant irritation she had unwittingly become. That way he might be able to sleep at night instead of lying awake and thinking of her, dreaming of holding her in his arms, kissing her, caressing her, tasting her skin and getting to know all the woman in her. It would be so much easier if she weren't around. With all his problems, she was the last thing he needed.

Sian sat nursing endless cups of tea for most of the morning. She tried reading the paper but she couldn't concentrate; she wandered out into the garden to sunbathe but was restless so that in the end she slumped listlessly onto the sofa and stared out of the window.

What a birthday, she thought. On her own, pregnant and with no one to celebrate with. If it wasn't for that Camilla, she felt sure Andrew would have come in. It made her irritated just to think about it. The telephone rang, breaking her thoughts.

'Hello.'

A pause and then: 'Hi, it's me again.'

She sighed heavily. 'Look, Eddy, why –'

'Sian,' he interrupted, 'please hear me out. Please.'

She hesitated. She really wasn't in the mood for any more of him.

'What?'

'Jo and Robby are having a party at the yacht club and I thought that, as it's your birthday, and as she's a good friend of ours, the very least we could do is go together and, well, just behave ourselves for once. No scenes, if you like. I promise.'

'And why the hell should I? Why should I do anything at all for you and what's all this stuff about "we" behaving ourselves? As I understand things, you're the one that needs to learn some manners around here.'

He didn't answer at first. 'Okay, okay,' he said eventually. 'I'm sorry. It's all my fault and it won't happen again, all right?'

'No, it's not all right. What if I have another man by now? What if I don't want to be seen out and about with you any more?'

More silence while he thought this one over, followed by a cautious, 'You haven't, have you?'

'And why shouldn't I? Contrary to what you think, I don't look like the rear end of an elephant yet.'

'Yes, I know, but you're pregnant!'

She laughed with derision. 'Oh God, Eddy, you do say the dumbest things sometimes.'

'Yes, but you are. Surely you don't, I mean, it's not . . . not . . .'

'Natural? Heavens, what on earth do you know about anything, Eddy?'

There was a silence of hurt ego.

'Well, are you going to come or not?'

'What about Rowena?'

'She's gone,' he said airily. He'd worry over what to do about Rowena when Sian made up her mind to come home.

'What, left the hotel? When?'

'Two days ago.'

'I see. So she's only just given you the heave-ho?'

'It wasn't like that, Sian. You're far too suspicious, you know.'

241

'And with good reason as I see it.'

'Did you get my roses?' he asked, after a moment's reflection.

'Yes, I did.'

'Nice, weren't they?' There was a smile in his voice.

'I don't know. As soon as I read the card, I chucked them in the bin.'

'You what?' he spluttered. 'They cost me a bloody fortune!'

'Tough. Right, here's the deal, Eddy.' If she was going to stomach him for one evening so she could see her friends in Brigham, she wanted to sort out the fundamentals right from the start. She wasn't going to stand for any of his messing around. 'You get drunk, show me up or in way embarrass me and I'm coming home immediately. Got that?'

'Do I have any choice?' he asked wearily.

'No.'

'Okay, I'll see you at six.'

'Good, and don't be late,' and she put down the receiver. An evening out. It wasn't what she wanted, but it was better than staying in and moping – and for the first time since she had returned home, she smiled.

'How am I doing then?'

Andrew was standing in the middle of the paddock, hands on jodhpured hips, grimacing in the sun and watching Camilla as the horse trotted by. If she had had previous lessons then he couldn't see any evidence of it. She was all out of balance and as the horse went one way, she went the other.

'Well?' she persisted.

'Fine, fine.'

She scowled at him. Pretty and spoilt, he thought. Almost too attractive in a brittle kind of way – a false artificial gloss that was unnecessary really given her natural good looks.

242

'Is that all you can say?' she asked, bouncing awkwardly.

'Keep going, Camilla. Stop talking and concentrate. Now feel the mare's rhythm. Up and down, up and down.'

She tried another circuit.

'Is that better?' she called, still bouncing in all directions.

'Look,' Andrew said, an edge of irritation entering his voice. He was beginning to wonder why he had agreed to this. 'Feel the mare's movement. Squeeze with your thighs and push yourself up in the stirrups. Come on. You can do it.'

She smiled suggestively. 'I'd rather squeeze something else than a horse,' but he ignored her.

'I don't know about this, Andrew,' she said a few minutes later. 'I don't think this horse knows how to walk properly. I've never had such a problem before.'

'Less gas and more action, Camilla,' he ordered. 'You'll find it easier to concentrate that way.'

'But I am!' she whined. She pulled the horse to a petulant halt. 'Are you sure this is the best horse you've got? It can't be my fault if the damn thing won't trot properly.'

Andrew walked over to her, quietly counting to ten. By the time he reached her, the mantle of professional charm was firmly in place. He took hold of the horse's reins and patted the animal on the neck.

'Look, Camilla, this mare, Kitty, is the best one I've got. She's a real old trouper. She's taught more beginners than I've had breakfasts and I haven't got a better animal than her.'

'But what about that one over there?' was the accusatory query accompanied by a pout.

Andrew turned to where Camilla had pointed. It was Bracken.

'That's owned by a member of my staff and no, you can not ride her. Anyway,' he added, 'she's a real handful and from what I've seen this morning, I don't think you're anywhere near ready enough to ride an animal like her.'

'Huh! She doesn't look special to me,' sniped Camilla.

'Well, she is. She's a good quality Arab/Thoroughbred cross and needs an experienced rider – and you, whatever else you might be, are not that.'

'Oh?' she smiled, her face lighting up and her voice dropping. 'And what else am I?'

Andrew brushed some flies away from Kitty's dozy face. 'Time we got on,' he said, refusing to be drawn.

'Well, that's not nice,' she said with feeling.

He walked away from her taking the lunge rein with him.

'You know,' she said, 'you shouldn't turn your back on a lady,' but he only smiled. One way or another, she was determined to get a reaction out of him and equally, he was determined to resist her.

'Let's get on,' he replied, trying to keep the brusqueness out of his voice. 'You're not my only client. I do run a business here.'

She glanced around her. The place was eerily quiet.

'I don't see much business,' she said.

'Well, I do, and delaying tactics such as yours aren't going to get us anywhere.'

'Oh, but they are.'

He was reaching the end of his patience.

'How?' As she obviously had no intention of continuing the lesson, he went along with her.

She smiled and glanced at her watch. 'I think it's time that we called a halt to this and did something far more interesting.'

'Such as? I don't mix business with pleasure.'

She took hold of the other end of the lunge rein and pulled him gently to her. When she spoke, her voice was velvety soft and full of promise.

'You ought to now and again, you know. It would add an extra dimension to your life and believe me, some business clients are full of all kinds of unexpected surprises.'

He watched her warily. She just didn't give up.

'Another time,' he said, walking back to the middle of the paddock. 'Walk on, Kitty.'

Camilla sulked.

Another half-hour and their time was up.

'I've got to go now,' Andrew said.

'Oh do you?' Camilla asked. She looked around. 'I can't see anyone yet. Maybe your next pupil has been delayed?'

He took Kitty by the reins and led her to the gate.

'It's not a lesson,' he said.

'What then?'

'Business.'

They clopped into the yard.

'What business?'

'None of yours,' he answered shortly.

He stopped the horse by one of the stable doors and tied her up.

'Come on, off you get.'

She pouted. 'You haven't answered my question.'

He said nothing and, seeing he wasn't going to, she held out her arms. 'You'll have to help me.'

'Really?' and this time he couldn't hide the sarcasm in his voice.

She though, ignored it. 'Uh-huh. Too big, this Kitty. I might hurt myself and we don't want that, do we?' She made a great play of looking down at the ground. 'I can't possibly jump down from here.'

Andrew stepped towards her and reluctantly held up his arms. After all, she was a private client and was paying very generously for her individual lessons.

She took her feet out of the stirrups, swung both legs towards him and slid down into his arms; her arms lassoed his neck. She smiled triumphantly. 'This is nice.'

He didn't respond. 'You'd better go,' he said, about to remove her hands.

'But I don't want to,' and her clasp tightened. Pressed against each other, feeling each other's warmth, thigh to thigh, breast to breast, she was all his for the taking. She misconstrued his hesitation.

'Come on, Andrew, why don't we go inside? No one's here. We could get to know each other a little better.'

This time he didn't hesitate. He firmly but gently undid her hands and stood back from her.

'Like I said, business comes first.'

'Well, later then,' she pressed.

'I can't. I'm all tied up tonight.'

'With who?'

He started to undo Kitty's girth. 'I really don't see how that's any of your business.'

She wasn't listening. 'The dinner's still on, you know.'

He pulled the saddle off and removed the blanket. 'I'll remember that, but now I have to go.'

'How about this weekend?'

'I'm busy.'

She followed him across to the tack room. 'Are you always busy?'

He nodded. 'Anyway,' he added with a smile, 'your lift is here.'

Camilla spun round, instantly annoyed. There was Patrick in the Range Rover. She hadn't asked him to come.

'Damn!' she muttered.

'Anything wrong?' asked Andrew, amused at her irritation.

'No,' she answered curtly, 'nothing at all.'

'Maybe he thinks you need looking after,' suggested Andrew.

'Hardly,' she replied, her lip curling with a sneer. 'He's the last thing I need.'

'You'd better go,' said Andrew, anxious for her to leave.

'I'll see you tomorrow, won't I?'

'I'll be here,' and he disappeared into a stable.

Camilla flounced off across the yard, glaring at Patrick.

'Did I tell you to come and pick me up?'

'No, but I thought –'

'Well, don't. Thinking won't do you any good at all, especially as you're so damned stupid.' She got in the car. 'Now drive!'

From inside the stable, Andrew watched them disappear. She was incorrigible.

He glanced at his watch. There was still time to get a surprise meal organized for Sian if he hurried. A birthday treat would be just the thing to thaw her out, he thought. He would ring her first, though, just in case she had other plans. He didn't want to foul things up with her again.

Sian was having a bath, the radio playing loudly to accompany her. She stopped singing when she thought she heard the telephone. Then, sure that it was ringing, she raced downstairs, only for it to stop when she reached it. She regarded it balefully.

'Stupid thing!' Wet, hot and dripping, she was doubly annoyed, and sent the phone flying to the floor. She didn't notice that she had knocked the mute button, and it would ring aloud no more. Contrite, she replaced it, and went back to her bath, leaving a trail of perfumed bubbles on the stairs.

Eddy arrived promptly an hour later. He grinned at her when she opened the door.

'Hi, you're looking great,' he enthused, advancing on her, arms open.

She stepped to one side, avoiding him. 'Hands off!' she ordered. 'I agreed to the party, not to you handling me, so keep those grubby adulterous paws to yourself.'

His grin faded and she walked past him to stand waiting for him to open the car door.

'Where's your wedding and engagement rings?' he asked, looking at her finger.

She fixed him with a level gaze. 'Give me one good reason why I should wear them?'

'Because we're married?' he asked hopefully.

'Just so long as you don't bank on it for too much longer.'

They drove off in silence. Eddy didn't attempt any small talk, seeming to know full well that he was on probation. Sian simply enjoyed the early evening weather. Hot, sunny and with the air full of insects and birds, it was turning out to be a splendid summer even if she didn't appreciate it all the time.

When they reached the yacht club in Brigham, Eddy parked the car and, reaching into the glove compartment, handed her a jewellery case.

'For you,' he said. 'Happy birthday.' He wasn't entirely at ease. The evening was all turning out to be more difficult than he had anticipated, so far.

Sian looked suspiciously at the flat box. 'What is it?'

'Open it and find out.'

It was a multicoloured gold rope. She took it out of the box and held it up. She couldn't help smiling.

'Here, let me help you,' Eddy said, taking it from her.

'It's beautiful, Eddy, really beautiful,' and for the first time since she left him she gave him a genuinely warm smile. 'Thanks.'

'Ummm,' he began, hesitantly, 'don't suppose I can have a kiss for my efforts?'

'I suppose so,' she said, grudgingly.

There was a knock at the window. 'Come on, you two lovebirds. The party's started!'

'In a minute, Phil.'

Eddy held on to Sian. 'Come back,' he whispered. 'The place isn't the same without you. We all miss you. I miss you and I want you and the baby back where you belong.'

Sian looked at him. She felt nothing.

'And Rowena?'

'She's gone. Over. Finished.'

Sian ran her fingers along her necklace. 'I'll think about it.'

The party was bursting at the seams when they walked

248

in. Streams of garish bunting hung from the ceiling and was festooned around a multitude of coloured lights. A disco was blaring in the corner although the floor remained resolutely empty. It was still too early and people were too sober to make fools of themselves.

'Sian! Sian! How lovely to see you.'

A hand grabbed her arm and a pair of lips were firmly planted on her cheek. It was Robby, one of their hosts.

'Welcome to the birthday bash, dear girl. For you and for me.'

'Hello and happy birthday.'

'Now, you'll want a drink, won't you?' and Sian let herself be guided through the mêlée, saying her hellos to her friends. Robby's wife, Jo, took her to her ample bosom when they reached the bar.

'Where have you been, my darling?' she boomed, a walking chandelier of silk, gold and hairspray, her kaftan hiding everything except her huge personality.

'I've been on holiday!' shouted Sian above the din.

'On holiday, eh? Is that what you call a bust-up nowadays?' and Jo's suntanned faced twinkled under the flashing lights.

Sian smiled. She couldn't hide anything from this lot.

'So,' asked Phil, taking Eddy to one side, 'did it work?'

Eddy sipped his drink, a smug look on his face. Then he puffed at his cigar. 'Most certainly did.'

'There you are, old boy,' smiled the older man, relaxed and bronzed in his polo shirt and white slacks, 'I told you it would. Baubles and trinkets, baubles and trinkets. Always do the job. A woman can't resist them. Damned good thing I know that jeweller lady friend of mine. There's no need to worry about paying for it yet, by the way.' He nudged Eddy. 'When you're ready and all that.'

Eddy's smile was uncertain. He honestly had no idea when or where he was going to find the cash. Things were a bit perilous at the moment. He changed the subject.

'Is that how you keep your wife quiet then, you old fox?'

Phil smiled broadly. 'You could say that. Have you seen her latest car? Ferrari. Cost me a fortune. Blood money, I call it.' He sighed. 'But there you are. If a man's going to have his fun, he damn well has to pay for it, I suppose,' and he sipped his Pimm's. 'So how's that delicious Rowena then?' he asked, his eyes twinkling.

'Hands off, Phil. She doesn't like older men,' and they both smiled, men of the world.

Two weekenders were discussing the shiny new yacht moored just yards away.

'Why don't you come on board for drinks on Sunday, then?' said the owner. 'Pamy cooks a wonderful lunch, don't you, old girl?' and the two men smiled at the well-dressed woman, whose own smile was as rigid as her hair-sprayed hair.

'Actually,' said the other man, 'I was thinking that we might go out for some fishing. I hear there's a wreck off the Point where you can catch shark if you're really lucky.'

Pamy's eyes widened in the gloom so that the whites were startling. 'Fishing?' she repeated tightly. 'You want to go fishing?'

The man looked at her with alarm and then at her husband. 'Well, isn't that the whole point of having a boat?' he queried.

'It most certainly is not!' she retorted. 'Especially as far as I'm concerned,' and she snorted indignantly. 'If you think you're bringing maggots on to my boat, then you've got another think coming,' and before her husband could say anything, she flounced off into the crowd.

. . . 'You're pregnant! But that's wonderful! Absolutely wonderful!' A group of delighted friends gathered round Sian and kissed her.

'Well done, my dear, and may the little darling turn out to be as lovely as yourself.'

'Thanks, Jilly.'

250

'What do you want?'

'When is it due?'

'Have you thought of any names yet?'

'Of course, in my day . . .'

'Was that the Dark Ages?'

'Very funny.'

'So, how are you feeling, Sian? Make way, Johnny! Woman with child here and she needs your seat . . .'

. . . 'You know if you stand down on the breakwater you can hear everything.'

'What's that, Mark?'

'I was explaining to Dave here how much you can hear with one of those VHF scanners. They can pick up absolutely everything and recently, it's been really interesting.'

'So what have you been hearing, then?'

'Lots of hush-hush stuff, I can tell you,' and he lowered his voice to the small crowd of men. 'Drugs. It seems the police are mounting some sort of surveillance operation and I wouldn't be surprised if there were arrests soon . . .'

Later, when everyone had eaten at the buffet and had more than they normally drank, the dancing started. Hot, drunken, perfumed and sweaty bodies swayed and gyrated under the lights, while the booming of the disco was heard right across the harbour. Sian soon got tired. She wasn't used to such late nights and she wanted to go home. Fortunately, Eddy had kept his word and was still sober. They said their goodbyes and left.

The drive back was warm and companionable. A selection of love songs played on the stereo as they wound their way back along the deep dark lanes of the Devon countryside. High above them, a blanket of stars was throwing an eerie light across the sleeping land. They reached the cottage just as the clock struck one. It was dark inside, the curtains were drawn. Helen still wasn't back.

'I'd better go,' Sian said. 'Thanks for the lift and for a wonderful evening. To tell the truth, I didn't think I was

251

going to enjoy myself, but I did. And thanks for the neck-lace. It really is beautiful.'

'Look,' Eddy said, 'I've got something to say.'

'Yes?'

He picked at the leather-covered steering wheel. 'I know we haven't got on too well recently.'

'Yes.'

'And I know I've behaved abominably.'

'Yes.'

'But I have been good tonight, haven't I? I mean, I didn't get drunk or play up or show you up, did I?'

'No.'

'And I did give you that lovely necklace, didn't I?'

'Yes. What's all this leading to, Eddy?'

'Well . . . I was thinking . . .'

'Yes?'

'. . . As I've done everything you asked me, could I, I mean, could we have sex?'

It was much later when Eddy got home to the hotel and Rowena, who was waiting up for him. She was in a foul mood.

'You bastard!' she shrieked. She advanced on him like an enraged Valkyrie. 'Where the bloody hell have you been?' Then she stopped abruptly. 'Oh my God, what on earth have you been doing?'

Eddy stood pathetically by the door, his hand over a large throbbing eye. It would be a real shiner by breakfast. Sian was far stronger than she looked.

'Got hit by a drunken sailor,' he lied. 'I didn't stand a chance. Got me from behind.'

'Oh baby, let me clean you up,' and he willingly gave in to her warm embrace.

Just for now he was relieved to shelve the problems of Killington and his worrying bonus jobs, the paperwork, his rapidly increasing insolvency – and especially how to get Sian back.

Fourteen

Eddy snuggled up to Rowena's hot body. The throbbing in his eye had ceased in the last couple of days. Nor was he tired. There were other things than sleep on his mind.

'Rowena?'

'Mmm?'

'You awake?'

'Yes. I am now,' she grumbled. 'What d'you want?'

He kissed the back of her neck.

'You know what I want.'

His hands cupped a breast, tweaking the large nipple between thumb and forefinger.

'Come on, Rowena, come on, baby.'

He kissed her ear and throat. She smelt divine, her skin smooth and perfumed after her bath. He was getting excited, his hard penis throbbing against her backside. His hand ran up her thigh, under the silken material of her nightdress towards her crotch.

'Rowena,' he whispered. She was turning him on so much, he wanted to roll her over and have her right now.

She moaned. 'Eddy . . .'

'Yes, baby.'

A pause and then: 'Piss off. I don't fancy a repeat performance of the other afternoon.'

'You what?'

'You heard. Now go to sleep and stop messing me around. I can't be bothered with any of that at this time of the night – even if it would only take a couple of minutes. I need my beauty sleep.'

'But, baby –'

She turned to face him. Even in the dark he could make out the lustre of her eyes.

'I said piss off and if you don't stop annoying me, then I might lose my temper. So stop it.'

He moved away from her, his penis rapidly retreating.

'Well, thank you,' he muttered.

'Think nothing of it,' and she settled herself down again.

'Of course,' she added, 'this might have nothing to do with the fact that you won't buy me an engagement ring, but on the other hand, it might. After all, if you won't do nice things for me then you can hardly expect me to do anything nice for you, can you? Now, goodnight!'

He lay in the dark, listening to her rhythmical breathing. What with Killington and Rowena and Sian, and now a baby on the way, it was all getting a bit too much for him. He only wanted a peaceful life, and all he got was hassle. He gazed thoughtfully at the shadowed ceiling, the outside lights from the car park shining through a gap in the curtains. That was the trouble with women, he thought angrily as his desire ebbed away. They didn't just want sex, they had to have all the trimmings that went with it. At this rate, he'd have been better off with Sian. At least he knew where he was with her, even if he was going to be a father. He must get her back. Things couldn't go on the way they were. Killington and Rowena between them were seeing to that.

He tried sleeping but it was impossible. He was too uptight. He needed something to relax him. What he needed was a woman, a real flesh-and-blood one who wouldn't turn her back on him. There was nothing for it, he decided. If Rowena wasn't going to oblige, then he would have to find someone who would.

Eddy glanced at his watch. It was one thirty. There was a new waitress who had just started work for him. Small, brunette and delightfully dimpled, she had made it perfectly clear that she liked him right from day one. With a bit of luck she might still be awake.

He smiled to himself as he got dressed. If Rowena wanted to play hard to get, now was not the time to do it. She could find herself some other sucker. He tiptoed to the door, his anticipatory desire already returning.

'And where do you think you're going?'

The bedside light snapped on and there was Rowena, fixing him to the spot with a steely gaze. 'Well? I'm waiting.'

With his shoes in one hand and the other on the door handle, his mind fumbled for a plausible explanation.

'Just thought I'd go and do some paperwork.' His grin was cheesy and unconvincing.

Rowena glanced at the clock. 'Paperwork? At this time of night? Do I look as if I was born yesterday?'

He put his shoes down on the carpet. He was a rabbit caught in her headlights.

'So why were you creeping out like some guilty thief?' she asked imperiously.

'Didn't want to wake you up, darling.'

'But I was awake already, dearest. Remember? You woke me with your pawing.'

'But I thought –'

'You thought, Eddy, and woe betide the rest of us when you think, but you thought you could sneak out on some nocturnal activity just like you used to do with Sian, didn't you?'

'But, baby –'

'Don't baby me!' she boomed.

His shoulders slumped. There was no point in arguing. She could see right through him. He walked back to the bed under her relentless gaze. Even before he was undressed, the light was off and her back was to him again. He lay quietly in the silent blackness, too annoyed with himself even to think of sleep.

'By the way,' Rowena said.

'What?' He wondered what missile she was going to torpedo him with this time.

'That new waitress, the pretty brunette one with the big cleavage.'

'Who? I don't know who you're talking about,' he non-chalantly replied.

She ignored his feigned innocence. 'I gave her her marching orders tonight.'

He shrank further under the duvet with a groan.

'I caught her in flagrante with the commis chef in one of the storerooms. Apparently, she had slept with virtually all the kitchen staff and the next man she had in line was you. Can't think why. I should have told her it was a waste of time. She'd have more fun plucking her eyebrows. Goodnight.'

Eddy was left to contemplate his problems. Earlier that day, Killington had rung. The drug courier who had been arrested coming in from the States had said too much to the authorities.

'I want the whole operation shut down, Eddy, and no mistakes. Everybody has been given the same instructions.'

'Yes, Mr Killington.'

'Now listen. I'll be in the City for the next few days. There's an SFO enquiry, and I've been called to give evidence. After that I'll be down to see you and I want everything wound up, finished and out of the way by the time I get there, okay?'

'Yes, Mr Killington.'

'And, Eddy?'

'Yes?'

'Is your wife any better yet?'

'Oh . . . Sian, you mean?'

'Yes, Eddy, that's the one. She is your wife, isn't she?'

'Yes . . . yes, she's much better, thank you.' Eddy had broken out into a sweat.

'Good. Then I'll see her when I come down, won't I?' and the telephone went dead.

Eddy stared at it for a long time. There were times when he hated Killington.

Patrick had spent the evening down at the King's Arms in Leighford, sitting by the one-armed bandit quietly nursing his pint, smoking and thinking about Camilla. Strange woman, he thought. Snappy, irrational, wilful and just when you had got used to that, she turns on the tears and behaves like a hopelessly lost little girl. He didn't have the insight to work it all out, but he did know one thing: she unsettled him. He ought to hate her; by God, he had enough reasons to. After all the scenes he'd put up with, the abuse and the tantrums, he had taken more than normal flesh and blood should bear, but he still came back for more. Not once had he turned on her. He couldn't. It just wasn't in his nature. He could kill a man in seven different ways – the army had taught him that – but he could never hit a woman. He smiled to himself. What a pity no one had taught him how to cope with her.

He finished his pint, then walked over to the bar. There were a couple of old men sitting at a table nearby. Locals, bent and gnarled from years of work, silent and contemplative. They appeared unconcerned with everything going on around them. Both were dressed in shapeless clothes, timelessly drab. There was stubble on their chins and what was left of their white hair was brushed back over well-tanned pates. They were outdoor people. Probably spent hours in their vegetable gardens picking out the weeds or chatting with their neighbours. One smoked a pipe, the stem jammed between tight lips, and the other stroked his black and white collie bitch, which rested her head on his lap.

'Can I get you two gentlemen a drink?' asked Patrick.

The man with the dog smiled broadly, but the one with the pipe turned slowly and scowled.

'We're pensioners. We can't afford to buy you one, so no thank you.'

'Please yourselves, but don't think I'll offer again,' and he turned back to the barman.

'Pint of your best, Barney.'

The barman tilted his head towards the old man with the pipe. 'Miserable bugger, that one. Name's Samuel Fletcher. He wants a drink all right.'

'What's that you said?' croaked the old man, glaring at him. 'I knows you said something about us. I'm not deaf, you know.'

'I said I'm sure you'd like a drink really. I don't see any of the other holiday-makers buying you two a round.'

The old man pursed his lips, his bushy eyebrows descending over his rheumy eyes, and petulantly turned his back on both of them.

'See what I mean?' said the barman. 'Stupid old sod,' and he smiled.

'I heard that, Barney. Don't you go calling me a stupid old sod or I'll have you up in front of a magistrate, I will, for keeping an unruly house.'

'Will you, Sam? My goodness, I'm scared.'

The barman and Patrick smiled at each other.

'Get whatever they're having anyway,' said Patrick generously.

'Okay, but don't say I didn't warn you. He's a cussed old bugger, as sharp as anything with his tongue, especially with you grockles.'

Patrick looked puzzled.

'Tourists,' explained Barney.

Patrick picked up the three glasses and put them down in front of the old men.

'Here you are, gents. One for you, one for you and one for me.'

He pulled up a chair and made himself comfortable. He might as well spend the rest of the evening with these old codgers. It would be better than being by himself. Who knows, they might have some interesting gossip.

'My name's Patrick O'Donnell.'

'Irish, eh?' the grumpy one said. 'Bunch of bloody navvies!'

'No, not quite, but my great-grandad was Irish. I'm named after him.'

Patrick decided to ignore the rude comments. He had got used to such remarks down through the years. After eight years in the Paras, he had to. He got nonstop ribbing from his mates then, especially when they got sent to Northern Ireland.

'And your names are?'

The other man spoke, a smiling and much friendlier version of the pipe smoker.

'I'm William and he's Samuel. We're brothers.'

Patrick shook William's stick-like hand, the fingers were bent with arthritis but still surprisingly strong. He held his hand out for Samuel, but was ignored.

'So,' said Patrick, 'how long have you two lived in Leighford?'

'All our lives,' said William. 'We've never lived nowhere else. We was born 'ere.'

'You must know the place well then.'

Samuel nodded sagely, clasping his pipe in his ribbed veiny hand. The offer and subsequent arrival of the pint had made him change the attitude of a lifetime towards tourists.

'Certainly do. There's nothing we don't know about Leighford. Our father were the parish clerk. His father, our grandfather, were the village blacksmith. Our family's been 'ere for generations.'

'Really?'

The two men nodded in unison.

'Thanks for the pint,' said William, his eyes sparkling in his weatherworn face.

'That's all right.'

Patrick stroked the dog, running his huge hand over the animal's silky ears. 'That's a fine dog you have there, William.'

The old man's face softened noticeably. 'That's Bess. She's an old girl now, aren't you, Bess?'

The dog wagged her fringed tail, her gentle brown eyes hanging on her master's every word.

'She used to work till a few years back – well, we both did. I kept a few sheep up on the moor. She liked going up there, didn't you, Bess?' William looked hopefully at Patrick. 'She likes crisps you know, cheese and onion especially.'

'You mean,' said his brother from deep in his chair, 'you do.'

William took on a look of hurt surprise. 'Well, so what? It don't matter.'

Patrick called to the barman, 'Two packets of cheese and onion crisps, please, Barney.'

The dog's face brightened up immediately she saw the crisps. She even began to drool. Patrick gave her some.

'Likes her grub, doesn't she?' he chuckled as the crisps vanished.

'Certainly does,' agreed William, 'but 'er teeth is going, so I can't give 'er no 'ard stuff like bones no more.'

They fell silent, all looking at the dog, her once-black muzzle now flecked with grey.

'You staying in the village then, Patrick?' It was Samuel.

'At Belvedere Cottage. You must know the place. It's a little way out.'

'Oh yes. We know that one.' He turned to his brother who was now busily eating the crisps. 'Wasn't that where Mr and Mrs Clarke lived before the . . . accident?' His voiced lowered.

'What accident?' asked Patrick. He could see Samuel was deciding whether to tell him or not.

'I shan't say anything, old man,' promised Patrick, holding up his hand in mock salute. 'I'm not really interested anyway so you don't have to tell me if you don't want to.'

Feigned indifference always worked.

'Well,' said Samuel, leaning closer and almost whispering as he glanced from side to side, making sure no one was listening, 'Mr Clarke used to run the largest farm around these parts. 'Is parents wanted 'im to marry the girl on the neighbouring farm, so bringing the two properties together under one name, if you like. Well,' and he took a replenishing mouthful of beer, ''e didn't want this. I mean, Mary Webber were a decent enough girl, but,' and he pulled a face, 'she were no oil painting.'

'So what happened?' prompted Patrick.

'Well, no matter what 'is parents said, 'e refused 'er. They were so upset about this that I swear to this day, it were the reason why 'is father 'ad that 'eart attack. Isn't that right, William?' But he didn't give William time to answer. 'So 'e died, and poor Mrs Clarke couldn't run that there big farm 'erself, so she moved into the village and left it to 'er son and before the year were out, guess what happened?'

The two old men fixed their watery eyes on Patrick.

'He got married?'

''E certainly did, an' it were that floozy from Winkleigh, weren't it, William?'

'I —'

'So, there you are,' nodded Samuel.

'But that's hardly an accident,' ventured Patrick, thinking he must have missed something.

'Oh, but it were,' insisted William, getting a say at long last. ''Cos she shot 'im!'

Samuel finished off his pint and stared meaningfully at his empty glass. 'That were a fine pint, that were.'

William finished his too. 'Ay, a real fine pint, Samuel. 'Tis rare that you find a pint as good as that.'

Patrick picked up the glasses. 'Three more pints, please, Barney.'

'They'll fleece you,' said the barman, handing back his change. 'Don't be fooled by their poverty-stricken appearance. Pensioners they may be, but those two are worth a packet.'

Patrick nodded. He knew that already, but he was an

outsider and so therefore he had to play by the rules. He was quite prepared to play the game until the pints bought some useful information. He put the fresh drinks down on the table.

'Why did she shoot him then?' he asked, when they were all settled again.

Samuel and William both glanced furtively about them before answering.

'Well, rumour 'as it, and 'tis only a rumour, mind you,' emphasized Samuel, 'that she caught 'im in the barn.'

Patrick waited. The air of expectancy was killing him. 'In the barn?' he repeated. 'Doing what?'

William giggled but stopped suddenly after a thunderous glare from his brother.

'Well, I don't like to say really,' said Samuel, ''cos it's not natural.'

Patrick tried hard to contain himself. 'What was he doing, Samuel?'

The old man blinked rapidly a couple of times. ''E was with an 'eifer,' he said solemnly.

'Friesian,' said his brother.

'No,' said Samuel. ''Twas an 'Ereford.'

'You mean to tell me,' said Patrick, incredulously, 'that he was screwing a cow?'

The two brothers looked at him, their eyes small, hard and serious.

'No, it weren't a cow, 'twas an 'eifer,' pointed out Samuel pedantically. 'Even a bull elephant'd get lost up a cow. Be like 'aving it away through an open window. Impossible!'

Patrick burst out laughing, the two men trying to shush him.

'Don't!' said Samuel, glancing round the room. 'It's not funny, you know. It were terrible at the time.'

Patrick couldn't stop laughing, even with both of them frowning at him with disapproval. But at last he did, his eyes watering.

'What was so terrible then?' he asked, wiping his face dry.

'Well, seems 'e preferred Tulip to 'is missus and that can't be right 'cos she were a right pretty girl, even if she 'ad been around a bit.'

Patrick laughed again. It was all so bizarre.

'So she shot him?' he asked at length.

'Well, wouldn't you?' demanded Samuel. 'Bloody pervert is all I can say.'

Patrick shook his head and slowly supped his pint.

'You an' your wife staying there, then?'

'Pardon?'

'You an' your wife. At Belvedere Cottage,' probed Samuel.

'No, she's not my wife.'

The two men exchanged disapproving glances.

'And she's not my girlfriend either,' reassured Patrick.

'Oh,' said William, 'that's all right, isn't it, Samuel, 'cos we're Baptist, like, and we don't approve of no living in sin,' and his small chin jutted out defiantly.

'So what is she?' enquired Samuel, unable to contain his curiosity any longer.

'I work for her. She's my boss.'

'Oh ay, is that so? 'Ear that, William? Patrick 'ere works for a woman.'

The brothers digested this news and then Samuel said, 'Is she one of they feminists then?'

Patrick smiled broadly. It was the way the word 'feminists' had been said that placed the brothers somewhere in the last century.

'Yes, I suppose so.'

'She's damn good-looking,' said William, staring into the middle distance. 'Saw 'er the other day. Moved bloody well, she did,' and his eyes glinted mischievously.

'What moved well?' asked his brother.

William held out his hands suggesting some impossibly massive bust.

'Dirty old man,' muttered Samuel. 'She wouldn't look at some decrepit old compost heap like you.'

'No harm in looking I say,' and William smiled at Patrick suggestively. 'Must be wonderful working with 'er in the 'ouse.'

'That's what you think,' said Patrick, and William sighed wistful longing.

'If you've lived here all your life,' said Patrick slowly, 'what do you know about The Grange?'

The old men smiled gummily at him and both of them picked up their now empty pint glasses.

'Mine's the same,' said Samuel.

'Me too,' said William.

Patrick rose slowly from his chair. There was a price to be paid for everything.

'Hate to say I told you so,' said the barman shaking his head as he filled up the glasses. 'I hope you have a bottomless wallet. They might look defenceless, but I can assure you, they could drink the whole pub under the table if they had a mind to, and still walk home.'

'I'll remember that,' said Patrick, taking the refilled glasses.

'Ah!' said Samuel appreciatively. ''Tis good to 'ave someone around who likes 'is beer.'

'Yeah,' drawled Patrick, 'especially when I'm paying for it, eh, old man?'

Samuel's face puckered.

'Right then, gents,' said Patrick, putting down his pint, 'let's hear what you have to say about The Grange.'

Samuel refilled his pipe, carefully put his tobacco pouch away and then slowly lit the aromatic bowl. He sucked noisily.

'Well,' he said at last, his brother waiting as expectantly as Patrick, ''tis a long and horrible tale.'

Patrick's eyebrows rose. The evening was getting more interesting.

'Major-General Warrener —'

''E was the one 'oo owned The Grange,' interrupted William, his face shining like an excited child.

'Major-General Warrener,' began Samuel again, fixing his brother with a cross stare, 'first came to The Grange just after the Great War. 'E inherited the place from 'is father. Of course, 'e weren't a major-general in them days. 'E were just a junior officer in the King's Dragoon Guards. 'E brought 'is new wife, daughter of some Lord something-or-other, down 'ere an' they settled in very well. Of course, being a regular army chap, 'e weren't around much, were 'e, William?'

The other man shook his head.

''E were off fighting in India or something a lot of the time. Well, the Second World War came an' 'e were off again, this time to North Africa.'

'Hadn't you better tell Patrick about 'is daughter?' queried William.

'Oh yes.'

'Who is this?' asked Patrick.

'Sophie Warrener. Real beauty, she were. Like 'er mother, but much more so, weren't she, William?'

'Oh yes, real beauty.'

''Cos it were she,' said Samuel, 'that caused all the bother really.'

'How?'

The old men drank their beers while Patrick impatiently searched their faces. Each had a smug look of confidence shared and reluctantly revealed.

'She got tangled up with that Jerry prisoner of war. The Major-General didn't like that at all,' added Samuel.

'Hang on a minute,' said Patrick. 'Can we back-track? What German POW?'

Samuel glared at him. 'Weren't you listening to anything I were saying?'

'I just want to know where the German comes in, that's all,' explained Patrick.

Samuel thought about this for a moment and then said,

'It were like this: the Major-General were shot to pieces in North Africa so 'e 'ad to come home. The Jerry, 'e were a submariner and were sent to work on The Grange estate. It were then that Sophie met 'im. It were the beginning of the end, you see.'

'Talking of which,' said William, holding up his empty glass, 'I've got a dreadful thirst this evening.'

'Me too,' added his brother, finishing off the last third of his pint. Patrick had barely touched his. He looked from one old face to the other, only to be met by clear unabashed eyes. They had no guilt. This time the barman just smiled. Pints replenished, Samuel continued.

'You see, the problem was The Grange were bankrupt. There were no money. They were living on tick.'

William wiped his chin with a grubby sleeve. 'And old man Warrener needed to get some money quick. 'E drank it all away, you see.'

'Otherwise, he'd lose the place.'

'And 'e couldn't 'ave that after all these years –'

'And,' interrupted Patrick, stopping the two of them in mid-flow, 'somehow this POW got involved?'

The men nodded simultaneously, like a pair of matching toy dogs in the car back window, their white crested heads bobbing up and down between scrawny shoulders.

'You see,' said Samuel, 'Sophie loved the Jerry. She ran off with 'im!'

''Twas terrible!' exclaimed William. 'A young thing like 'er from a well-to-do family, taking off in the middle of the night with a Jerry! The village didn't stop talking about it for days!'

'So what happened to the Major-General when he found out?' asked Patrick.

Samuel sucked at his pipe, releasing a huge cloud of blue smoke. ''E couldn't bear the 'umiliation of what 'appened so 'e shot the staff and 'is wife and then 'e tried to blow 'is brains out but 'e missed.'

'But not before 'e set light to the place,' clarified William.

266

'You mean to tell me,' said Patrick, 'that just because his daughter ran off with a German, and just because the place was verging on bankruptcy, that he killed everyone and tried to burn the evidence?'

'Well,' said Samuel, relighting his pipe, ''e were a very strange man sometimes, very strange.'

'Gone right off 'is head since 'e got 'is injuries,' added William. 'Proper mad 'e was. That's why 'e got off light.'

'For his sentence, you mean?'

'Oh, 'e didn't serve no time at all. Just went straight to one of they funny farms,' said Samuel.

'But that still doesn't explain why he behaved like he did in the first place,' argued Patrick.

'Simple,' said Samuel. 'Rumour 'as it that somewhere up there, hidden away, like, is 'is 'oard of Roman gold,' and he waited to see what Patrick's reaction to that piece of gossip would be.

Patrick said nothing but quietly sipped his pint. This was the first bit of interesting information he had heard about The Grange. No wonder Killington wanted him to keep an eye on the place. It was the gold he was after – the hoard of Roman gold – and if Patrick knew his boss, nothing would thwart him.

'But that still doesn't explain things properly,' he said carefully, not giving away any sudden reactions. He wasn't going to let these old boys know anything.

'Yes it does,' said William. ''E wanted to marry 'is daughter to some rich old chum of 'is. That way, 'e'd save the 'ouse without 'aving to sell 'is gold.'

Patrick sighed. Oxford seemed such a long way from here.

'You say,' he began, 'that the treasure is still up there?'

'Yes, definitely up there somewhere. 'Course, many 'ave tried to find it through the years, but . . . well, we didn't 'ave much success, did we?'

'No,' agreed his brother forlornly.

'Maybe then,' suggested Patrick, 'it's not up there and

the rumours aren't true. Surely if there was something up there the present owner would have found it by now? After all, he's been there for a while, hasn't he?'

Samuel curled a lip and William gazed morosely at the floor.

''E's too busy with 'is 'orses, that one. 'E couldn't care less about it.'

'We tried talking to 'im about it once,' added William, 'but it were no use. Said it were just a load of gossip. Quite rude 'e was.'

'So how come you two know all about it if everyone was killed?' asked Patrick.

The brothers looked as if they had been caught with their fingers in the till. There was something they weren't telling him.

'Not everything were destroyed in the fire,' said William, glancing quickly at Patrick. 'And Mrs Warrener kept a diary, a journal.'

'Yes, an' we found some of it after all the fuss 'ad died down an' she said very clearly –'

'Well, almost,' added William.

'– that there were something there.'

'She hinted at it, more like.'

'Perhaps, but she did mention something.'

'And do you still have this diary?' asked Patrick, trying to keep his excitement out of his voice.

Samuel looked coldly at William, who pursed his lips and nonchalantly looked in the other direction.

'Someone,' said Samuel, leaning forward to Patrick, 'lost it, the blithering idiot.'

'It were an accident!' protested William, his wrinkled face hurt at the accusation. 'It must 'ave gone out with all that junk we sold.'

'Bah! Accident my foot! Youse so bloody accident-prone, youse trip yourself up 'alf the time, you stupid old bugger! Anyway,' sighed Samuel witheringly, 'it's gone.'

The three men sat quietly, each lost in his own thoughts.

'Maybe though,' said Samuel quietly, his face brightening, 'we could do a deal?'

'How?'

'Three-way split,' he whispered, glancing around him. 'Now that youse here an' youse a young man with plenty of brains, you could do what we never could.'

'Oh yes, and what's that?' asked Patrick, smiling at the old man's scheming mind.

'Well, you could break in, like, look around, see what's what, 'cos we're too old for that sort of thing nowadays.' He paused, eyes alight. 'Well, what d'you say?'

Patrick considered for a minute. If there was as much gold as they seemed to think and as Killington seemed to think, it could be the answer to so many problems. After all, he had no intention of spending the rest of his life as a gofer for Killington. He had his ambitions too.

'Another drink, gentlemen?'

Samuel and William beamed at each other.

Fifteen

'Was that Eddy on the phone again?'

Sian nodded.

'Bloody man!' fumed Helen. 'Why the hell can't he leave you alone? I'd have thought when you belted him in the eye he'd have got the message. How many more times do you have to tell him it's over?'

Sian poured herself a fresh cup of tea. 'Until I'm blue in the face, I expect. He always was a stubborn man.'

'And it's only seven thirty in the morning. I'm too tired to cope with Eddy.'

'I thought it was me who was supposed to be tired. You pregnant too?'

Helen pulled a face. 'God, I hope not.'

'So when am I going to meet this Lothario of yours who seems to have such carnal appetites that you don't get any sleep?'

'Don't know. Soon I expect,' and she avoided Sian's eyes.

'Helen,' said Sian with a smile in her voice, 'this is me you're talking to, remember? Your old friend. So what are you hiding?'

Helen blushed. She didn't like being found out. 'Nothing,' she said too quickly.

'Look, if there's a problem –'

'There isn't, okay? Nothing I can't cope with. I'll have to be like you – strong and resolute. I'm pretty feeble with men you know,' she murmured. 'They push me around and you know what? I let them get away with it.'

Sian looked at her. She was troubled. The tone of Helen's voice made her sit up and take notice.

'Are you talking about Darryl here?'

'No. I'm not,' she said, subdued and thoughtful. 'Things between me and him . . .' She shrugged. 'I'm sorry, but that's the way it is,' and reaching for her cigarettes, she lit up. Sian wrinkled her nose. Helen usually didn't smoke this early in the day.

'You love him, don't you?'

Helen nodded slightly, shamefaced with her confession.

'Must be one hell of a man, this Darryl.'

Helen drew deeply on her cigarette. She didn't answer.

They were late for work and Andrew wasn't in a good mood. He hadn't been for some time recently, not since Sian's birthday when he had given her a lift home. She wondered what it was all about. He seemed perfectly all right with the others but with her, he was short-tempered and snappy.

After grooming, she went to see Bracken. The mare trotted over to her in her usual manner, eager for a titbit, but not Sebi. The longer Sian waited and watched, the more she realized something was very wrong with him.

She climbed the gate and walked over to him. She didn't have to reach him to see that he was ill. She raced back to the yard.

'Andrew! Andrew!'

He came running towards her, the concern already showing on his face.

'Look!'

'Oh God, now what?'

He leapt over the gate and raced across the paddock with Sian right behind him. Sebi was standing still, his head lowered, his eyes staring at the ground and his breath shallow.

'What is it?'

Andrew ran his hand over the horse's head. 'I don't know,' he muttered.

'Doesn't look good, does he?'

Andrew turned to face her. There was something in his eyes, such hurt, that she instinctively wanted to reach out and brush it all away.

'I'll ring for the vet,' she said.

In the office, searching among the mounds of paperwork for the vet's telephone number, she noticed a document with a distinctive letterhead: 'Armitage Financial Management', but she had no time to read further and put it to one side.

The vet removed the thermometer from Sebi.

'Mmm,' he said, holding it up to the sunshine. 'I'm not sure what's going on here, Andrew. I think I might have to take some blood and get it looked at. He's definitely not right and after that bout of colic the other week, we don't want to overlook anything.' He turned and smiled reassuringly. 'How are the others?'

'Fine, as far as I know, although the only other horse in this field was Bracken. Surely if it were anything infectious she would have got it too?'

Andrew was standing at Sebi's head, holding on to his halter, his face riven with worry. It crossed Sian's mind that she had never seen him look so tired.

The vet cleaned the thermometer and put it away.

'I'll just have a quick look at Bracken, if I may. I need to be thorough about this, Andrew.'

Sian brought the mare over and Bracken stood patiently while she was inspected.

'Well,' said the vet, straightening up and rubbing his back, 'there doesn't seem to be anything wrong with this animal although she's coming into season and if you don't want her in foal, I suggest you move her out of here,' and he smiled.

Sian returned his smile with a faint blush to her cheeks. She should have noticed.

'I'll take her over to the other paddock.'

*   *   *

Not long after the vet had left, Camilla arrived, beeping her horn as she pulled into the drive. She waved out of the window. Andrew didn't wave back.

'What do you want?' he asked, his voice tired. 'Your lesson isn't until four.'

'Well, that's a fine way to greet me. I just thought we could go and have lunch together.'

Sian walked past with a barrow full of dung and the two women smiled briefly at each other.

'Attractive girl, isn't she?' said Camilla.

Andrew hung up two bridles as though he hadn't heard her and then went back into the stable. She followed him.

'Didn't you hear me, Andrew?'

He walked past her again, this time carrying a saddle. 'Who is?' he said.

'Her, your stable lass.'

'Can't say I've noticed.'

'Keeps you occupied, does she?'

He stopped and looked at her, his eyes revealing nothing.

'I think you had better leave. I have a very sick horse to look after and I'm in no mood for your catty remarks. Now, I'll see you this afternoon. Goodbye,' and he walked off towards the cottage.

Camilla, who was not so easily put off, followed him, her high heels clicking over the yard.

'Andrew!' She ran after him into the cottage. 'Please, Andrew, can't we have lunch? I promise not to say anything more about your staff. Honest,' and she smiled sweetly at him, her large aquamarine eyes clear and bright.

'No, I can't. I'm busy. I've got too much to do and, more to the point, you look the sort of woman who only likes the best in life and I don't think my wallet stretches that far, so no, not today. Some other time maybe. Now if you would excuse me –'

'But I will pay if that's all that's worrying you. Good heavens, we don't live in the Dark Ages any more. A

273

woman can pay for lunch now and again. Come on, what d'you say?'

'No.'

He began to ascend the narrow staircase. She started to follow him.

'Don't!'

It was a command of such force that she stopped in her tracks.

'I mean it, Camilla. Back off, okay?'

She watched him go. He wasn't playing the game. It hadn't happened before like this. No man had ever refused her. She couldn't understand it. Her ego was taking a pounding and it hurt. She bit her lip; she wasn't going to give up that easily. She left the cottage, slamming the door after her.

Sian was walking along the lane back down to the village when Camilla's Range Rover sped past, throwing up dust and small stones as she went. Happily there was a gateway next to Sian otherwise she would have been knocked down. As she stared after the vehicle, she wondered why Camilla had been going so fast and why she had almost run her over. Surely she must have seen her?

Marcus fixed himself a drink.

'Want one?'

Patrick nodded. 'Sir.'

He handed Patrick a beer. 'Now,' he said, sitting down, 'I want to know anything that you might have heard about the Warrener Hoard.'

Patrick opened his can. It frothed over the side.

'Haven't heard nothing, sir. If you mention it at all, you get no response. Seems that folk round here don't like to talk about it,' and he took a swig of his beer.

'So for all we know then, it could still be only a rumour.'

'Probably.'

Marcus took a cigarette from a silver box and inhaled deeply.

'Only I don't believe that for one moment,' he said, blowing the smoke out with each word. 'I've had some research done while I've been in Oxford. There's a chap I know at the British Museum who was more than a little interested when I mentioned the name Warrener. In fact, his face positively lit up.'

Patrick sipped his drink quietly, his face a blank mask. What he knew he was keeping to himself. If this hoard was worth all that Killington seemed to imply it was, then it could be his ticket to freedom.

'And there's something else.'

Patrick looked up.

'Our Mr Mann at The Grange is in serious financial difficulties. Very serious difficulties indeed. It seems he is only just hanging onto that place by his fingertips. One little accident and he'll be over the edge and that's just what I want. There's too many questions being asked about my operations in Oxford. People are poking their noses in where they don't belong and time is running out.'

Patrick nodded.

'You will visit Mann,' he said decisively, breaking out of his contemplation. 'We're going to have to get him out of there while you have a good look around the place and I know just the person to distract him.'

'Why?'

'Because I want you to.'

Camilla smiled. 'Is that all?' she asked pointedly. 'I know you, Marcus, remember? I'm the one who's grown up with you and I know exactly how that devious mind of yours works, so let's start again; why should I take Andrew out for dinner? What are you up to and why is it so much of a secret? After all, I am your business partner and therefore I should know all about it.'

She was sitting on the white leather sofa in the lounge of the cottage, one leg tucked up underneath the other. She had changed since she had come in and was wearing a sheer silk dress of an almost gossamer luxuriance. Ivory coloured, it fitted closely over every contour. She held a Campari and soda in her hand which she sipped occasionally. Marcus stood by the mantelpiece. They were playing a game of cat and mouse.

'My dear,' he said calmly, 'that is a lovely dress you are wearing. It suits you very well.'

'Don't bullshit me, Marcus. Flattery won't get you anywhere.'

He breathed deeply and a shadow of a smile crossed his face. 'My dear, we both know that as a concept you own half the business, but as a reality, you have nothing to do with it so let's not get upset over something that you can't possibly understand. Just leave it all to me and I promise you, nothing will go wrong.'

'You patronizing bastard.'

'Precisely. However, I have something for you,' he said, reaching into his pocket, 'that might make you feel a little better.'

'Fuck your presents,' she said in her sing-song voice. 'I don't want them.'

Marcus put a ring box on the mantelpiece. 'In case you change your mind.'

'I won't. You're too predictable and it bores me. In fact, everything bores me about you. Why don't you just piss off back to Oxford and leave me alone?'

'Because, my dear, I have things to do.'

'Yeah, like watching over me. Christ!' she yelled, standing up and throwing the glass down. 'Why can't you leave me alone?'

Her face was a mass of hatred but he wasn't perturbed. He slowly advanced towards her and took hold of each of her arms. His eyes searched hers.

'We both know why, Camilla, so let's not fight about it. Let's just accept the inevitable.'

'No, not this time.' She began to shake her head wildly. 'No! no! no!'

276

The slap when it came was also inevitable. Heavy-handed, powerful and stinging, it knocked her over and sent her sprawling onto the floor.

There were footsteps and Patrick appeared at the French windows. For the briefest moment, he stood poised to launch himself to her defence but just one look from Marcus stopped him.

'I heard a noise,' he said.

'Get out!' hissed Marcus.

Patrick needed no further instructions and he pulled the door shut behind him. After that, he blocked off any further noise of her screams by mowing the lawn. It was amazing how much noise an electric mower made, but it didn't stop him feeling sick. And his disgust strengthened his resolve to break free from Marcus Killington.

Sian was out walking. It was really too hot for anything much but she felt restless and just sitting down in the garden wasn't enough to make it go away.

It was a lovely afternoon. The sky was empty except for the overpowering, baking sun. Its heat drenched everything. Flowers wilted, even the usually pungent honeysuckle was drooping. Grass browned and hedges, sapped of all their juices, hung lifeless in the still air. In each field she passed, the livestock were standing under whatever shade they could find, incessantly flicking their tails and ears against the persistent flies. What was left of their pasture looked mean and dry.

She took off her sun hat and fanned it across her face as she pushed back her heavy red locks. Hairs were sticking to her forehead, glued down with sweat and trickles of it were running down the back of her neck and between her breasts. She was thankful she was wearing only the thinnest of cotton dresses.

The village was way behind her now. She was beginning to wish she had brought a drink with her. Perhaps if she called in at the next house the owners would let her have some water.

'Belvedere Cottage' said the sign on the hedge. She began to walk down the lane, turned the corner and then stopped. A quick look at the people standing by the cars two hundred yards ahead, was enough to make her back-track. She pulled in by the hedge where they wouldn't be able to see her.

She hadn't liked Camilla from the beginning and now she knew why. There she was being kissed by someone she knew only too well: Marcus Killington. What was going on?

'Right then, Camilla, I'm off to Plymouth. You know what you have to do and I expect you to do it, understand?'

She nodded dumbly. Her face still hurt from where he had hit her and there was still the taste of blood in her mouth, but at least the other bruises were out of sight under her dress.

He stood close to her, his arms on her shoulders and then he leant forward and kissed her. She remained icily still. How ironic, she thought, that he wants me to go out with a man that I want to go with, but who will have nothing to do with me. She smiled. Marcus, seeing this, took it as a sign of affection.

'That's better, my darling.' He cupped her face in his hands. 'See,' he said, his face close to hers, 'you can be so nice when you want to be.'

'Go away,' she whispered.

He smiled and kissed her again. 'I'll see you soon,' and he got into the car.

That night Sian lay in bed gazing at the window, sleep evading her. She just couldn't stop thinking about the scene outside the cottage. Should she tell Andrew what she knew? It might be nothing or it could be something really important. Nothing would surprise her. Killington was up to all sorts but what was he up to here?

* * *

Eck sat on a bank of grass just outside the village. It was very late and he knew he really ought to be at home where Mrs Tucker, his landlady, would fix him a warm milky drink just before sending him to bed but he knew he wouldn't sleep tonight.

He dug a hole with a stone in the dew-drenched earth next to him. Across the field, by the light of the waning moon, he could see rabbits hopping about, and above him in the still warm air, ghostly forms of hunting bats swooped and swished in the dark as they hunted their prey. Over in the dark forbidding woods, an owl hooted.

He sighed. He didn't know what to do. He had to keep his secret because he had promised Helen he would, but something was wrong. There were good secrets and bad secrets and he knew, even if he didn't understand why, that this secret probably wasn't a good one.

'Promise me, Eck! Promise me!' Her words frantic and urgent yelled at him again and again.

'Eck! Is that you lad?'

He looked up. It was Mr Tucker, small and wizened and standing by the gate at the bottom of the field.

'What you doing up there, lad? Come down here and I'll take you 'ome. Missus 'as been worried sick!'

Eck got to his feet and lumbered down the hill, his problem shelved. He found it difficult to concentrate and he had been glad to see Mr Tucker. By the time he got to the bottom of the field, he had cheered up considerably.

Mr Tucker smiled. 'Silly lad,' he said fondly. 'You'll get us both in trouble if we don't get 'ome smartish. She won't let us go play skittles tomorrow night and you don't want that, do you? You won't 'ave your beer then.'

'No.'

Mr Tucker took him by the hand and walked on. 'You great dafty, Eck. Honestly, you're just a baby really, aren't you?' But Eck only grinned.

Sixteen

It was two days since Sian had witnessed the scene at Belvedere Cottage and she still didn't know what to do about it. Sometimes she felt she ought to say something and then, just when she thought she had made up her mind, she decided against it. After all, it was hardly any business of hers. Camilla could see who she liked but the fact that she was on close terms with someone whom Sian knew to be a shady character made the whole business smell odd. The longer she dwelt on it, the less sure she became.

Then there was finding the time to tell Andrew. It had to be when he was alone and when she could guarantee that they weren't going to be disturbed. Normally this would have been easy, but recently they had had their full complement of tourists and he was always too busy to talk to her. Then there was Camilla. She was always there, hanging on his every word, sitting in the cottage garden drinking his beer or having her 'private' lessons. Sian wasn't that sure what the situation was. It seemed as if the pair of them were getting along fine, although he didn't always seem pleased to see her.

She laid down her newspaper. She had to make this decision by herself. It was no good asking Helen. She was so wrapped up with her Darryl that she hardly had time to wash and change before she was out of the door for another night's dancing.

No, there was nothing for it: she would have to say something, even if it were less than direct. Andrew had to know who he was tangling with. Sian went to the telephone and dialled. It rang several times before it was picked up.

'Hello, Leighford Stables.'

It was Camilla. Sian froze. To speak or not to speak; she was suddenly paralysed with indecision.

'Hello?' demanded Camilla's voice. 'Answer me, will you?'

Sian hesitated.

'Right,' said Camilla, 'if you're going to waste my time and your money, I'm going to put the phone down. Goodbye.'

Sian thoughtfully replaced the receiver and nibbled a fingernail. Right now she wished fervently that she knew nothing about Marcus Killington – or Camilla.

'Who was that?' Andrew came through the door. He didn't look pleased. 'I thought I told you to wait in here. I don't remember giving you permission to answer my telephone.'

'Oh really, Andrew, there's no need to get so shirty about it,' she smiled sinuously, unwrapping herself from his chair and walking over to him. 'I was only trying to be helpful.'

'Well, don't. I can take my own messages. I don't need you to butt in.'

She pouted, her thick red lips glossy and spoilt.

'Why are you always in a mood with me?'

'Because,' he answered, 'you take too many liberties and I don't like that. Don't you realize that a man likes to be in control of his life?' He went into the small kitchen. 'Anyway, who was it?'

She shrugged, coming in after him. 'I haven't a clue. She wouldn't say.'

'So it was a woman then?'

'Of course.'

'Did she say anything, anything at all?'

'No. Nothing, but it was the quality of the silence that gave her away. I know that silence,' and she smiled enigmatically.

'Really?'

'Oh don't tease, Andrew. I do, you know, and that was the silence of someone who wanted to speak to you and not me and I wonder who that might be? A little redhead perhaps?'

'You're imagining things, Camilla.'

'You can say as you like but, believe me, I know what I know.'

He sighed.

'Dinner then?'

'God Almighty!' he exclaimed. 'Won't you ever take no for an answer?'

She smiled broadly. 'No.'

He exhaled the breath of one who knew he wasn't going to get any peace until he gave in.

'All right,' he agreed at last. 'Just this once – and it has no significance, okay?'

'Oh Andrew, how can you say such a thing when you haven't even spent an evening with me?' She stepped closer to him, so close she could smell his aftershave, and the aroma of horse on his clothes. 'You'll get to discover what a real woman is like,' she murmured with a seductive smile, 'and I would keep my opinions for later if I were you because by tonight, you might have changed your mind.' She was so close that she leant forward and kissed him on the lips.

He didn't move, only watched.

'I'm going now,' she said. 'I have to get ready for tonight,' and she left in a swirl of perfume.

Andrew wasn't the only one going out that night. Billy, after weeks of put-downs and rebuffs from Helen had decided that if she wouldn't go out with him, then maybe Sian would. He'd finally summoned up the courage to ask her. Now he stood on Helen's doorstep, and banged the knocker noisily. There were footsteps and then there was Sian.

'Yes? Oh it's you, Billy. I'm afraid Helen's not in tonight. I'll pass a message on to her if you like.'

His face reddened even more than usual and he smiled sheepishly. 'Actually, it's you I want to see.' He looked past her shoulder. 'Umm, can I come in?'

She was so surprised that she wordlessly held the door open for him and followed his small, wiry frame into the lounge. She indicated one of the chairs, sat herself down and smiled politely.

'What can I do for you then, Billy?'

He glanced around nervously, patently unsure of his reception. She waited.

'Would you like a cup of tea?'

He rubbed his red, scarred hands together and sniffed a few times. 'Well . . . actually,' he began, 'I was wondering, that's if you don't mind, like . . . we could . . . we could . . .'

'What, Billy?'

He smiled, deep dimples in either ruddy cheek. He took a deep breath. 'I was wondering . . . if we could go to the pub?'

She sat dumbfounded.

'Well, actually, Billy –' she began, but he interrupted.

'I would like it very much, Sian. You're a real looker, you know. All me mates think so,' and he smiled again.

'Well, thank you. That's very nice of you, but I don't want to. Nothing personal, you understand, except that I'm pregnant, very tired and not at all in the mood for socializing.'

His face began to crumble.

'I'm sorry,' she added, feeling embarrassed. Seeing how hurt he was, she felt pity for him.

'Just one drink?' he asked.

She wavered and glanced at the television. One of her favourite films was about to come on.

'Okay, Billy. Just one and just this once.'

He beamed.

What did she have to lose, she thought to herself as she fetched her cardigan. To all intents and purposes, she was a single woman, a pregnant one, but single, so what did it matter? Anyway, an evening down at the local might raise her spirits. It would certainly stop her brooding over the telephone call she didn't succeed in finishing.

Billy offered to run her down to the King's Arms in his car but one look at the bright pink, souped-up Ford Capri, with its fluffy dice in the window, was enough to persuade Sian otherwise.

'I think not, Billy. I'd rather walk,' and then not to compound his feelings of inadequacy she added, 'I need the exercise.'

She was dressed in a long cotton dress with short puffy sleeves and a pair of strappy sandals. Billy's schoolboy figure sort of hopped and skipped alongside her, hands dug deep into jeans pockets. He wore a white T-shirt, patched denim jacket and a pair of outsize Doc Martens. She was painfully aware of their incongruities.

They were nearing the village centre when a familiar vehicle appeared: Andrew's Land Rover.

Sian saw Camilla was in the seat beside Andrew, and she caught a brief glimpse of their look of surprise before she lowered her head and fixed her stare onto the tarmac. Why, why, why, now of all times, did they have to see her like this? The vehicle passed slowly because of all the holiday traffic. When it was level with her, the worst scenario happened. Camilla opened her window.

'Well, good evening, Sian and . . .'

'Billy,' said Billy, with a grin.

Sian blushed fiercely. She could hardly bring herself to speak.

'Hello,' she mumbled. She looked past Camilla towards Andrew, but he had kept his eyes firmly fixed on the road ahead. Sian just knew he was angry. It was the set of his jaw and his unmistakable frown.

'Going somewhere nice?' gloated Camilla.

'The pub,' replied Billy.

'Yes,' said Sian awkwardly. 'The pub.'

'Well, we shan't keep you,' smiled Camilla, the car window rolled silently upwards and they drove off.

'To hell with you,' whispered Sian under her breath as she heard Camilla's fading laughter.

'That wasn't very nice of you, Camilla,' said Andrew, 'making her blush like that.'

'Nonsense. It was just a bit of harmless fun. Anyway,' she added with a grin, 'maybe that was what she was trying to tell you about on the telephone this morning. She obviously has a new man in her life – and what a man!'

Patrick pulled on a black polo-necked jumper and a pair of black trousers. A pair of black trainers and black gloves completed his ensemble.

He glanced at his watch. Ten p.m. Camilla should be eating her dinner with Mann right now and that would give him a good hour before he had to get back.

The old men down at the pub had been on at him nonstop since they had told him of the Warrener Hoard and with Killington on his back as well, he would do well to find something tonight, although he fully intended to keep it to himself.

He picked up his car keys and made for the door. Camilla would keep Mann occupied in her usual inimitable style and curiously enough, that upset Patrick, but he had no time for sentiment tonight. He had a job to do.

The food at the Harbour Hotel was delicious but Andrew had no appetite.

'Please, Andrew, try and at least pretend you're having a good time. I can't be that offensive.'

He looked at Camilla, put down his fork, with which he had been pushing the food around his plate, and smiled. She was looking exceptionally attractive tonight and apart from their little spat in the car on the way over, she had been an excellent companion.

She smiled encouragingly, her eyes large and bright. She was wearing the sheerest silk print dress, which hung lovingly over her figure to the maximum advantage, and he couldn't help but notice what she looked like. He must set his business problems aside for the evening. Nor would he let himself dwell on the other nagging thought that constantly jumped into his mind: Sian and that oaf Billy.

'I'm sorry, Camilla. I'm being rude and I should know how to behave in the company of one who looks so . . . beautiful.'

'My goodness! Compliments, and from one who normally only has such rough words for me. What on earth have I done to deserve this?'

'I don't know.' He smiled ruefully. 'Maybe I've just had too many problems on my plate and have let them get in the way of my good manners.'

She covered her hand over his. 'That's all right,' she purred. 'It doesn't matter now. All is forgiven. I would forgive you anything. You do realize that, don't you?'

His smile was brief. 'Did you know,' he said, 'that the name Camilla means "the huntress"?'

'Rather apt, I'd say,' she replied.

The flickering candlelight danced between them, throwing their faces into relief.

'Well, at least you're honest,' he laughed.

'That's better,' she smiled. 'You look so much more handsome when you smile. Tell you what,' she added, taking her fork and prodding a piece of lobster on to it from his plate, 'why don't you try a bit of this now? Who knows, if you can learn to enjoy my company, you might even enjoy your meal. You never know unless you try,' and she held the fork to his lips.

He took the offered morsel into his mouth and ate it slowly.

'There,' she said, 'that wasn't so bad, was it?'

From that moment, they both knew how the evening

would unfold. A timeless dance was calling them and he was unable to resist it any longer.

Sian spent an uncomfortable evening in the pub. In the beginning Billy was shy. There were long strained silences between them as she tried to coax him to talk. He smoked incessantly, which made her eyes smart, and when he wasn't doing that, he feverishly chewed his nails, not noticing how she turned away, unable to witness it.

'So do you have any hobbies, Billy?'

She had tried everything else and this was really scraping the bottom of the barrel.

'Yeah. Football.'

'And who do you support?'

'Liverpool.'

From then on he became remarkably articulate and eloquent. She learnt all there was to know about Liverpool; when the club started, who was playing where, when they won the FA Cup and who their best players were. On and on it went, a nonstop stream-of-consciousness monologue, without beginning or end. He hardly seemed to draw breath.

Sian nodded now and again, not knowing if it was appropriate, but it would have appeared rude if she hadn't made some response. She became aware that even though she was sitting with Billy and appearing to all intents and purposes to be listening, her real thoughts were elsewhere. Why did Andrew look so cross sitting in the front of the Land Rover? Where were they going and why did she feel so . . . so bothered by it? It was none of her business, she told herself. What he did and who he did it with was his concern, but it didn't make her feel any better.

'Another drink?'

'Sorry?'

'Another drink?'

'Yes, well, all right then, but it must be my last. I have to go to work tomorrow.'

'Don't worry,' he said from the bar. 'You're quite safe with me,' and he grinned.

When he got back to his seat, the same topic dominated his conversation. Yet again, it was Liverpool this and Liverpool that.

After a further ten minutes' monologue, Sian said, 'Tell me, Billy, don't you know anything about anything else? I mean, is Liverpool Football Club the only thing that you can talk about?'

He stared at her, puzzled. His dull brown eyes slowly comprehended what she was saying.

'You mean,' he said eventually, 'that you don't like football?'

'No.'

'Ah.' He shifted his nonexistent bottom on the small leather stool. 'I thought you liked football, you see, 'cos you didn't say no different, so I just sort of carried on.'

He blinked at her. She began to think that he might be related to Eck somewhere along the line.

'Actually, I don't. I can't stand it. It bores me rigid. All those men chasing a little ball around. Plain stupid, if you ask me.'

'Oh.' There followed a pregnant pause while he chewed this thought over.

'Well, what do you want to talk about then?'

'Life, art, the state of the nation?' she suggested ironically, but he failed to understand anything of what she was saying and simply looked at her blankly.

'My mum says . . .'

'Yes?' She waited expectantly while he inwardly struggled with something profound.

'My mum says that all politicians are liars and that you can't trust 'em as far as you can spit,' and he nodded as if to emphasize the point.

'Right.'

Sian sighed. It was hopeless. They might as well get

back to football. So he did. Once he had the green light, he was off.

He insisted on walking her home although by then she had such a headache, she really couldn't stand any more of his voice. By the time they got to the cottage, her temper was on a knife edge.

'Can't I come in?' he asked, as she shut the gate firmly behind her.

'No.'

'Why not?'

'Because, Billy, I'm tired and I want to go to bed,' and even in the dark she could see him leer at her. He was a bit drunk so she let it pass.

'I could tuck you in if you like.'

'No thank you,' she answered sourly. 'Just go home before I get angry,' and she walked up the path. He wasn't so easily put off and by the time she reached the door, he was standing right behind her.

'Go on,' he said, pushing her back by the door, 'give us a kiss.'

She angrily pushed him away. She couldn't tolerate being pawed by drunks. She'd had enough of that from Eddy.

'Get away and leave me alone!' She pushed him again, this time so hard, he stumbled backwards and landed in one of the flowerbeds.

'You stuck-up, hoity-toity bitch!' he yelled, getting to his feet and wiping himself down. 'You're a prick-tease; nothing but a bloody prick-tease!'

'Oh for God's sake!' and before he could answer back, she had gone, slamming the door behind her.

'And I spent all that bloody money on you, you tart!'

She went straight into the kitchen and poured herself a glass of cold water. Anything to stop her shaking. It was a hot, hot night, building up for a storm. Maybe that's why people were behaving so badly.

* * *

Up at The Grange, it was altogether different. Back from their meal, Andrew and Camilla stood in the bedroom, lit only by the light of the storm which danced around the tops of the tors, brilliant flashes of lightning heading in their direction as they slowly, slowly revealed themselves to each other.

'I wanted you,' she whispered, covering his face with light kisses, 'right from the moment I first saw you.' She kissed him some more. 'You are the only man for me.'

'Shh, don't talk.'

Their mouths met, hot and demanding as their hands caressed each other.

He unzipped her dress, easing it off her shoulders and letting it fall to the floor, a halo of material around her feet. She stepped out of it as he cupped her breasts in his eager hands. So long; it had been so long and he couldn't wait any longer.

She sighed, pressing herself against him, her insides burning. Was there ever a man like him; a man who wanted so much; a man who made her feel so alive? It was like being on the edge of her existence and not knowing whether she would survive or not. It was all she could do to keep on her feet.

He kissed her neck, his tongue licking her flesh, tasting her, smelling her, breathing in the very essence of her womanhood. It filled every crevice of his body, bringing back to life all that had been dormant. She was all woman and yet . . . But as soon as the thought entered his mind, he brutally shoved it away. Camilla was all that he needed right now. She answered all his needs and that was enough. Now wasn't the time for him to ask questions of himself; to query his motives.

'My darling . . .'

She held his head against her breasts as he kissed each one in turn, running his tongue around the nipples and making them stand erect. Suddenly, he picked her up and carried her to the bed. He threw her down and began to undress. She watched him, like a cat would watch its prey. She had him in her sights and she wasn't going to let him go.

'Come here.' She held out her arms. She was impatient. He was all that she had expected him to be and more. By the light of the storm, she could see exactly what he was and now he was all hers.

Together on the bed, they wrapped themselves around each other, greedy and without restraint. Hot, sweaty and needful, their bodies slipped and slid against each other as the heat built.

Over and over went her fingers as she explored every last contour of his muscular body, feeling the strength of him, the way he held her so close in his arms, the way he wanted her so much. They kissed passionately, unable to get enough of each other.

And then he touched her. She almost jumped, the feeling was so exquisite. Gently, gently, he stroked her, feeling her velvety softness, feeling it grow beneath his fingers, feeling her give way to him, allowing him to find his destination.

She moaned softly, panting, letting each nerve end tingle inside her. She thought she was going to explode, and still he wouldn't stop.

He lay to one side of her, looking down at her face. All desire was there – in the curve of her eyebrows, in the languid eyes too full of sex to close; in the flaring nostrils eating the air with every breath, and mostly, in the full lips heavy and ripe for him.

He stroked some hair away from her damp face and kissed her some more – her breasts, her stomach, her thighs and then . . . wet, hot, yielding, she arched her back as he tasted her, gently, delicately, each mouthful honeyed for him. She started to move against him. He knew what was happening. He could feel it . . . soon, very soon.

She grabbed his head, pressing it down against her. 'Oh God, oh God!' she moaned. Louder and louder, faster and faster until the noise of the storm inside and outside the room filled his ears.

'Ahh!'

Her legs went rigid, her thighs clamped tight against his head as each contraction grabbed her and flung her against the bed. She gathered up the bedclothes, wrenching and pulling them, her head, storm-tossed, flew from side to side, throwing itself against the pillows. And still he didn't stop.

When she had finished, he crawled up her body, smelling the sweet scent of pleasure that filled all her pores. He smiled down at her, but she couldn't answer. The riptide had washed her clean.

'Okay?'

She nodded and wiped the back of her hand against her forehead where a sheen of perspiration covered her skin. She smiled slowly. 'That was wonderful.' She covered his face with kisses. 'So wonderful.'

He lay on top of her, filling her with his musk. She pushed him away, mischief playing across her face.

'Lie on your back.'

Sitting across him, legs either side of his thighs, she gently lowered herself onto him until he filled every inch of her. Now it was his turn to be at her mercy. She rested each hand on his strong, powerful chest and started to move carefully and with precision. She wanted this to last as long as it could.

His fingers held tightly on to her flesh. Harder and harder. She watched him closely, the intensity of his face, the sweet agony of his eyes. It was close and getting closer. She took his hand and guided it to her, gasping as yet again, he made her almost recoil against him, and together they rode the helter-skelter of desire.

When he came, exploding inside her with such energy, he left her temporarily breathless but not for long. Her own orgasm was nearing the brink and just as his finished, she echoed him, pulling him deeper and deeper inside her.

'Yes! Yes! Oh my darling! Oh God!'

At last, spent and exhausted, she lay her head on his chest and listened to the thumping of his heart. Then, gently, they fell asleep.

When she woke, the storm was still crashing and banging around the moor. No rain fell but the gods spat and feuded amongst themselves.

'Suppose it will rain eventually,' he said, looking at the window. 'I'd better get you home.'

She sat up, puzzled. 'Why? Can't I stay here with you? I'm sure we have plenty more energy to burn. I know I have,' and she started to nibble his nipple.

'No, Camilla. No more. I've got work in the morning and it's very late already.'

She buried her head in his arms. 'No, I don't want to go. I want to stay with you. I love you.'

He moved out from under her and went to turn on the bedside light.

'No!' she cried, holding on to his hand. 'Please, don't.'

'Why?'

She smiled apologetically. In the dark she could hide the bruises. 'Just don't, that's all. You look far more handsome like you are.'

'Thank you, but you're still going to have to go home. Come on. Get dressed and I'll take you.'

'Is this a brushoff?' she asked, getting dressed.

He didn't answer.

'Come on, Andrew. I can take the truth. You don't have to beat around the bush with me.'

He was standing over at the window, looking out across the wood.

'I don't know, Camilla.' He turned to face her. 'I just don't know.'

'So maybe there is a chance for me?'

He came towards her, holding out his hand.

'Let's go, shall we?'

'Just one last kiss then? Please? Just to reassure me that

293

maybe, if and when you work things out, that maybe you'll come back to me.'

He held her hand and pecked her on the cheek. She didn't say any more after that.

After letting her off at Belvedere Cottage, Andrew drove back to the village, a numb void inside him. What the hell had he done? He knew why he had done it. The woman he wanted – desired more than any other – didn't want him. But that was no excuse. He should have known better. He just shouldn't have gone to dinner with Camilla in the first place. He knew what would happen and yet somehow, he simply couldn't help himself. He was weak and instead of keeping his distance, he had only made things more difficult. He would never see the end of Camilla now.

'Fucking hell!'

He drove as fast as he could through the darkened lanes, furious with himself. Lights bouncing, gravel thrown into the blurred hedges, he seemed oblivious to all as he swerved around the corners and tore along the road, the wheels hanging on as the Land Rover was thrown around from side to side like a ship in a storm. Still he couldn't assuage his anger.

Only when he screeched to a halt in front of The Grange did he realize what a fool he had been. Memories he kept well out of sight cruelly surfaced. He held his head in his hands and leant against the steering wheel.

'You bloody, bloody idiot, Mann. Don't you ever learn?'

He sat back and gazed out of the window. The electrical storm seemed to have passed, although there had been no rain to relieve the oppressive heat.

To his left was the rose garden, the blooms giving off their luxuriant aroma even in the dead of the night. On impulse he got out of the car and set about looking for the perfect flower. A deep, dark crimson one, just the sort that Sian liked. He then drove back to Helen's cottage, pulling up quietly to the front gate. He got out and stealthily walked up to the front door. He kissed the single, flawless rose, then placed it on the doormat.

'Sorry,' he whispered. 'I'm so sorry.'

Before dawn, the rain came, large, heavy drops of it splattering across the land and washing away all the dust and decay that had built up over the summer. It also washed away the rose, leaving it battered and torn in the drain.

Seventeen

'So what did you find?'

Marcus and Patrick were in the lounge of Belvedere Cottage.

'Nothing except his bloody dog. Made one hell of a racket. Luckily it was shut up in the kitchen.'

Marcus raised an eyebrow. 'Nothing?' he asked sceptically.

'No. I looked everywhere I could, at least everywhere that I could get into. Some of the rooms were locked and those doors were far too big for me to force open.'

Marcus went to the drinks cabinet. This was not what he expected to hear. He poured himself a whisky.

'Did you find anything of interest? Plates? Jewels? Coins?'

'No.'

'Well, did you look in the stable block down by the garages?'

Patrick looked uncomfortable. 'Well . . .'

'Yes?'

'Didn't get time to.'

'Why?'

'Miss Camilla. She came back a bit early, like.'

Marcus gave a small compressed smile. He walked up to Patrick and without a word, slapped him hard across the face. Patrick flinched but otherwise gave no reaction.

'You're lying!' yelled Marcus.

'No, sir.'

Another slap.

'I'm not lying, sir.' It was said patiently through gritted teeth.

'Don't insult my intelligence, you stupid idiot! I told Camilla to keep Mann away from The Grange until eleven thirty and that's exactly what she would have done because, unlike you, she does as she's told. Now, what about the stables?'

Patrick hesitated, his eyes dull. 'Didn't look, sir.'

'Why?'

'The horse. I don't like them, especially that damn great black one.'

Marcus stared disbelievingly at him. 'What?'

Patrick shrugged. 'I can't help it, sir. Got thrown and trampled on by a neighbour's horse when I were a nipper.' He touched his nose. 'It's how I broke this. Never liked the damned things since.'

Marcus laughed aloud, a harsh sound, his head thrown back. 'I don't believe this! Here you are, a professionally trained killer with two tours of Northern Ireland behind you and God knows what other skulduggery the army sent you on, and you mean to tell me that you're frightened of horses?'

'Sir.'

'Christ Almighty! This is ridiculous! How the hell am I supposed to find out where that hoard is if you don't do your job properly? Am I going to have to go up there myself?'

Patrick didn't answer that one.

'Well, I'm not, okay? You are!' stormed Marcus, almost spluttering with rage. 'You will go up there and finish off the job properly, understand?' and he thumped his glass down on the table top.

'Sir.'

'And I don't want any fucking excuses this time.'

Patrick stood his ground while Marcus paced the room, angry and impatient.

'I'm going to have that hoard, you know,' he spat, jabbing a finger at Patrick, 'it and The Grange. I know it's up there. I'll have it whatever it costs and nothing, especially not idiots like you, is going to stand in my way!' He stared fiercely at Patrick whose face remained noncommittal. 'I will have it,' he mumbled to himself, picking up his glass and clenching until his knuckles were white. The glass cracked and a small trickle of blood oozed out of his fingers, but he didn't seem to notice it.

'Now get out of here and next time you speak to me, I expect to hear some good news for a change.'

Patrick left the room and went straight out into the garden. There was a large tree stump which he was gradually removing. He picked up his axe and thumped it hard. If he pictured his employer's face on it, he would get it out in next to no time.

Marcus was making some coffee when Camilla came down. Scrubbed clean, her hair still wet, it amazed him how she could look so young. Like one of his Thoroughbred fillies, she was all legs and large eyes. She strode in dressed in jeans and T-shirt and wordlessly took the mug of coffee before seating herself at the table.

'Do you want some breakfast?' he asked. 'I could get Patrick to make you some.'

'No.'

He joined her at the table. 'How was last night?'

She glanced at him. There was no friendliness in her eyes. 'None of your fucking business, Marcus.'

He lit a cigarette. 'Really, my dear, do you have to swear like that at this time of the morning? It really is very unladylike, isn't it?'

'Why the hell should I care what time of the day it is? Anyway, what do you know about good manners? Remember, dear brother,' she sneered, 'we both spent our childhood in a pub – or don't you want reminding about that now you're a member of the landed classes?'

'Just try and behave,' he said drily. 'You let yourself down, you know.'

'Well, perhaps if you treated me like a lady instead of a whore, then maybe I wouldn't behave like I do.'

He smoked silently and the air crackled between them.

'Did you have a row or something?'

Her eyes flickered in his direction and he knew he was close to the truth. He could read her like a book.

'Let's just say that it didn't go quite the way I wanted it to.'

'Brought you home a bit early, did he?'

She ignored him and sipped some more of her coffee, then helped herself to his cigarettes.

'What do you want him for, Marcus?' Her eyes narrowed. 'What's all this about?'

'Nothing for you to worry your pretty little head about. Just business, that's all.'

'Don't patronize me, you bastard. I'm not one of your lackeys. I don't jump when you click your fingers. Now, what's going on? One of your less legal business deals, is it? Drugs?'

'And what makes you say that?' he asked smoothly, his expression remaining unchanged. 'You should know by now that all our companies are strictly above board and legitimate.'

'Are they? Well, isn't that something, and there was I thinking you must be blacker than black. Well, fancy that. You know something, Marcus? You would make a superb politician because no one can lie like you can,' and she shot him a withering glance.

'I suggest, my dear,' he said coldly, his voice betraying the beginning of his temper, 'that you learn to keep your opinions to yourself regarding my business deals. We wouldn't want it if competitors found out things they shouldn't.'

'And what might they be? That you set up companies as fronts for your real business or that you launder money through the City?'

He sighed. 'You know, Camilla, I would have thought after our last little encounter when I oh-so-unfortunately had to teach you a lesson in good manners, that you would

299

be inclined to mind your p's and q's a bit more. I can see that it hasn't made the slightest bit of difference.' He paused, noticing the change in pallor of her cheeks. He had her right where he wanted her and for all her bravado, she was still a pushover. She glanced at him, her face defensive. 'You will learn to behave yourself, my dear, and above all, you will learn to be more circumspect. Those who speak out of turn are liable not to speak at all.'

She flicked some ash onto the floor, her mouth tight shut.

'What is it all about, Marcus?'

'Tell me what you know.'

She frowned and shook her head. 'I don't know anything. Honestly, Marcus. You know me, head like a brainless chicken. To use your own words, hedonistic, sybaritic, selfish. I don't know anything and even if I did, would I be so stupid as to jeopardize anything? After all, if you go down, so do I, and that would be stupid, wouldn't it?' Her voice was quiet. There was fear in it now. He smiled at her. This was what he liked to see.

'Are you quite sure about that, my dear? Because any kind of betrayal from those who work for me or,' and he stared hard at her, 'those who are close to me, can only result in their loss, not mine. You cross me, Camilla,' he said after a threatening pause, 'and my stepsister or no, I will personally see to it that you never do it again.' He took hold of her face in his powerful hand and pressed his fingers deep into her flesh. She gasped. 'Do you understand me?'

With terrified eyes she nodded as best she could. He let go, smiled like a viper and relaxed. She rubbed her chin.

'I don't suppose it will matter if I tell you that The Grange will soon be another addition to our business. However, how and why is something I prefer to keep to myself. When all this is over, you will return to Oxford until we move and things will carry on as they have always carried on. Except perhaps for my mother. I honestly think it would be best to leave her in Oxford when we all move down here. But nothing, my dear, will change between *us*,' and he laid his hand over hers. She pulled it away from him, stubbed out her cigarette and stood up.

'So I'm just the bait, am I?' she asked. 'Is that all? Never mind how I feel, just so long as I get out there and screw for Queen and country? Lie back and think of England, so to speak.'

'Well, my dear,' he answered calmly, 'you never objected before, did you? And anyway, let's face it, it's just about the only thing you're any good at.'

'You shit!'

He ducked to one side as the coffee cup went flying past his ears, throwing its contents all over him before crashing into the sink units.

'Now, now, Camilla, that really isn't the way to behave, you know,' and he tutted. Then he walked round the table and took hold of her by the arms. She was tight-lipped, her face ashen.

'Look, my darling,' he said quietly, 'we both know what you are – I mean what you really are – and it's no good pretending otherwise. So let's just get on with the job in hand and forget all this silly nonsense, shall we? Because if we don't then I might have to have a few words with our Mr Mann and I'm sure he wouldn't want to hear the sordid details of your, how shall we say, adventurous sex life, now would he?'

'But ... but ...' She gagged, unable to get out the words.

He stroked her face. 'What, my darling? What can be so bad? Don't I give you everything that you want? Don't you live in luxury, the type of life that most people can only dream about?'

'Why do you ... do ... this ... to me?'

He held her close, suffocating almost. There was no need to answer that one.

*   *   *

301

Patrick locked the shed door, turned on his torch and went over to the old table against the wall. He pulled it out revealing the floorboards. He thought he heard a noise outside the cobwebbed window and he froze. He listened intently but could hear nothing. It must have been the shrubs brushing the walls. The whole village was asleep. He carried on working, pulling up the sawn-through floorboard. Underneath was a bundle wrapped in newspaper. He took it out and carefully unwrapped it. Inside were spoons – Roman spoons. Part of the Warrener Hoard from The Grange. If his boss wanted them as desperately as he did, then they had to be worth something. Patrick shone his pencil torch on them. They just looked small, dull and insignificant to his untrained eye, but that didn't detract from their importance. They were his ticket to freedom.

Patrick knew he had been dead lucky to find the spoons. The house had been silent and still when he entered. Then suddenly the dog started barking, and Patrick was relieved to find it was shut in the kitchen. Now he had time to consider calmly where any treasure might be if the owner of The Grange hadn't discovered it.

Patrick ignored the inhabited rooms and concentrated instead on looking in the others downstairs. He had spoken true when he told Killington that the rooms were locked, but he had not added that all the keys were in the doors.

A once-beautiful dining room had sooty and mildewed walls. A vast table and many chairs dominated the floor space, but there was no other furniture except at one end. Under a great grey sheet, next to the wall stood a long sideboard, the kind from which a substantial pre-shoot breakfast might once have been served.

At first Patrick thought all the drawers were empty, but then, at the back of one, wrapped in newspaper, were some very old spoons, dull and misshapen. He guessed their significance at once. What else would you expect to find in a sideboard drawer but cutlery, he thought, as he scooped up the bundle into his pocket. He quickly replaced the dust sheet and fled, locking the door behind him. No one need know he had been in the house, and, he was determined, no one would know what he had found either.

An owl hooted, bringing him back to reality with a jolt. He hurriedly put the treasure away and slid the table back in place. Now wasn't the time to be careless. He couldn't afford to cross Killington. Money, power, Camilla – Killington cultivated his obsessions to a dangerous extreme and Patrick knew exactly what the man was capable of.

Eighteen

Eddy was in a turmoil. He had just had a visit from the police, who had asked him lots of awkward questions. They had caught him off guard and left him flustered in their wake.

They told him that they had information from a raid they had carried out in Bideford the night before, that drugs were being smuggled into this part of the coast. The trawler they had swooped on in the middle of the night was carrying over four tons of cannabis and one of the men arrested in the raid had mentioned Eddy's name. It had taken all of Eddy's charm to get himself out of that tight corner. That, and an alibi from Rowena.

'Really, Sergeant Ellis, I can assure you that Mr Williamson was here all evening and has been all week. Isn't that right, Eddy?' She smiled engagingly at the two police officers, her head innocently held on one side. 'Any more tea, officers?'

'No thanks, miss.'

The sergeant smiled briefly but without warmth. He and his colleague stood up. Rowena and Eddy did the same.

'As you can see,' said Eddy, waving his hand around, 'we're very busy at this time of the year.'

'Quite,' answered the plain-clothes officer.

'And there's simply no way we could ever take time out to involve ourselves in illegal activities, even if we were criminals.'

Rowena looked suitably appalled.

'Anyway,' continued Rowena, in the same tone of hurt indignation, 'what sort of people do you think we are? We're professional hoteliers. We couldn't possibly get mixed up in anything so . . . so illegal. This is a highly respected and popular hotel. We have many famous and wealthy clients and, well, I just find it absolutely astonishing that you could even think that anyone here could be involved in such goings on.'

'And your name, miss?' asked the sergeant. 'I didn't quite catch it the first time. Just for the records, you understand.'

She disdainfully looked him up and down. 'Records? Are you trying to entrap me?' she asked.

'No, miss. Just asking your name, that's all.'

'Rowena Gibson,' she relented and then she smiled and, inserting her hand into Eddy's, said, 'I'm Mr Williamson's fiancée.'

One side of Eddy's face twitched.

'Well then, sir,' said the sergeant, 'that's all for now. If there are any further developments, then either myself or one of my colleagues will be getting in touch with you. We'll be going now. Thank you for the tea and for your time.' He smiled at them both. 'We'll see ourselves out. Goodbye.'

'What do you think?' he asked his colleague as they got into their car.

'Lying,' the other officer answered flatly. 'At least he is. Not too sure about her.'

'Mmm, I thought so too. We'll have to keep a close eye on them.'

Eddy and Rowena watched the policemen drive away with undisguised relief which, in Rowena's case, quickly turned to anger. The pair of them walked over to the office in silence but when they were safely behind closed doors, she flew at him.

'What the bloody hell do you think you're playing at?'

'Nothing.'

'Don't lie to me, Eddy. I know you. You might be able

to pull the wool over Sian's eyes but you're not going to do it to me!'

He sighed deeply, his shoulders drooped and he sat down at his desk holding his head in his hands.

'I'm a middle man for Killington's drug smuggling operations.'

Rowena's face froze with horror. 'What?'

'He runs most of it from Oxford but quite a bit of it comes through here so as to attract less attention,' he continued in a dull monotone, utterly defeated by the day's events. There was no point hiding anything now. Rowena was going to find out anyway, so it seemed pointless not to tell her. 'Killington said the police had started asking questions. Apparently, one of the couriers from the States got caught at Heathrow and they've been pumping him ever since. He also thinks that there's someone in the business who may be leaking stuff to the authorities only he doesn't know who yet.'

Rowena, too shell-shocked to speak for a moment, found a chair and slumped into it, her mouth agape.

'You're a middle man? And you organize it all from here?' Her voice was incredulous.

He nodded. 'The money you see.' He smiled feebly. 'I couldn't stop. I wanted to – God, how I wanted to – but you don't know what he's like. If I tried to get out of it . . .' and his voice trailed off.

'How long has this been going on?'

'Couple of years. It's a regular thing now. We have a trawler, a crew and a network of suppliers.'

'And it was one of the trawlers that the police raided last night?'

'Yeah. Christ knows what Killington's going to say about it.'

'Bollocks to him!' she exclaimed. 'What about you? What about *us*? If you're the middle man, guess who's going to have to take the fall for all of this? He certainly won't! You can bet on it!'

She got up and started pacing the small, stuffy room. 'You're a moron, Eddy. How the hell could you be so stupid as to get involved in something like this? Didn't you stop to consider what would happen if you got found out?'

'Of course I did, but you don't argue with Killington,' he shouted. 'If he says you do something, you do it!'

Her expression was dismissive.

'You do, Rowena. Anyway . . .'

'Go on, what?'

'I got in trouble –' he started.

She held up her hands and closed her eyes. 'Don't tell me,' she said. 'Horses or some such. You were up to your eyeballs in debt, with the heavies after you, and he bailed you out but only on condition that you did something for him. Right?'

'Something like that.'

'And Sian never knew about it, this blackmail?'

'No way!' He shook his head. 'You know what she's like. She would have gone through the roof.'

'So it's all in your name? All the paperwork?'

'Disk actually. I keep it on a floppy disk. The names, dates, amounts. All that sort of stuff. He likes to keep track of things.'

'Well, you'd better destroy it then, hadn't you, because if you don't and the police find out about it, then you've had it and believe me, Eddy, if you go down, you're not taking me with you. You're on your own!'

He smoked quietly, too sunk in his own misery even to think straight.

'But what shall I do, Rowena?' he asked pitifully. 'I thought you loved me. Surely you're going to help me? You can't let me down now. We're both in this.'

'Oh no we're not!' she exclaimed defiantly. 'And just you remember that.' She was standing with her back to him, her arms folded and looking out of the window with grim determination.

'You know,' she said at last, 'I got it all wrong about

Killington. He's obviously a real bastard and a very nasty piece of work. It might be a good idea,' she said, turning to face him and smiling, 'if we stopped him before he stops us. That way, we get the hotel, your debts would be wiped out and that bastard would go to prison for a very, very long time. What do you say?'

'But I'd go to prison!' he protested.

She shrugged. 'Maybe, maybe not. Turning queen's evidence could be enough to get you out of all of it because, if Killington is as big a fish as you say he is, the authorities might be very pleased to hear what you have to say.'

Sian and Eck were spreading out some fresh wood shavings in the stables. It was hot work because since the storm, the weather was just as before, cloudless and unrelenting.

'What's the matter with Andrew, Eck?'

The big man frowned and wiped a dusty forearm across his brow.

'Dunno. He's unhappy. He shouts a lot. Sebi's not well.'

'Yes, I know, but why?'

But Eck only shook his vast curly head, so Sian just got on with her work. She didn't know what was wrong, but something was. The atmosphere at the stables seemed to be getting to everyone. Helen had snapped at her at breakfast, Andrew was either scowling or barking out orders, and now the horses were starting to go down one by one with some mysterious illness. Even Eck wasn't his normal jovial self. He was saying even less than he normally did and he rarely smiled. Sian noticed he avoided any contact with Helen, scurrying off in the other direction if she came anywhere near him. Maybe it was the heat, she thought. Maybe that was why everyone was so irritable. The only person who seemed remotely happy with herself, was Camilla. Every time she turned up, she was grinning like the Cheshire Cat.

'Well, I know someone who will bring a smile to his face,' Sian said to Eck.

'Eh?'

'That Camilla woman.'

'What's that you said?'

They both swung round. Andrew stepped into the stable, silhouetted against the bright sunlight.

'Who were you talking about, Sian?'

She hesitated.

'Well?'

'Just Camilla. I was telling Eck here how she seemed to be the only one who could bring a smile to your face nowadays.'

Andrew glanced from one to the other, stony-faced, hands on jodhpur-clad hips. 'I don't think it's any of your business who I see, do you?'

'That's not what I said, Andrew, and no, of course it isn't my business. I just said –'

'I don't give a damn what you said, understand?'

'Now hang on a minute,' she retorted. 'There's no need to get angry with me! Just because your fancy bit of stuff is running you around, don't go taking it out on me!'

'You what?' he yelled. 'What the bloody hell are you talking about?'

Her mouth clamped shut as she suddenly realized she had said too much. This was not the time or the place to tell him about Camilla and Killington.

'Well?' he shouted, advancing on her. 'Would you like to explain yourself?'

She stood her ground defiantly. She was damned if he was going to frighten her.

'Nothing,' she said, holding her head up proudly. 'I didn't mean anything by it. It just came out the wrong way, that's all.'

He turned slowly to Eck. The big man looked away, confused and embarrassed.

'Haven't you got anything to do, Eck?'

He nodded.

'Then damn well get on with it!'

Eck's bottom lip began to tremble and his eyes filled with tears. It was too much for Sian to stomach.

'You bully, Andrew! How dare you shout at Eck like that!'

'And what bloody business is it of yours how I treat my staff? Remember, lady, who you're speaking to. I'm your employer and you'll do as I say.'

'Oh yeah? Well I've had it. You can stuff your damn job! I've had enough of it, what with you and your permanent bad moods lately and that . . . creature throwing herself at you every time she comes here. It's disgusting!'

He threw back his head and laughed. 'How can you criticize me,' he began, his eyes blazing, 'when you have the temerity to go out with that neanderthal from the butcher's shop!'

'What?'

They stood facing each other quite oblivious to Eck, who simply stared at the spectacle unfolding in front of him.

'I'll go out with whoever I like and if you don't like it, Andrew, then tough!'

'Interesting companion, was he? I hear on the grapevine that he only has one topic of conversation.' He smiled, his lips a colourless, thin line and his eyes unflinching. 'You must know all about Liverpool Football Club by now.'

'Well, if I do, Andrew, at least he had good manners.'

'Really? It must have been an enlightening evening for you both, although I would have thought that you had better taste than to go out with him.'

'Coming from you, I would have said that was a case of the pot calling the kettle black, wouldn't you?'

She thrust her broom at him. 'Here, take this. I quit. Maybe that way I won't have to put up with your juvenile behaviour. If I didn't know any better, I would say that you are displaying all the signs of being jealous.'

She marched out. He followed her, still enraged.

'Me, jealous? How the hell did your warped mind work that one out?'

She turned to face him. 'Well, what else would you call it?' she cried, and before he could answer her, she was walking out through the gate.

He marched into the cottage and slammed the door behind him with as much force as he could muster. It did little to relieve his rage.

'Bloody, bloody hell!'

He kicked some riding boots out of his way and stormed into his study. Blaize cringed out of his way. He slammed that door too. He then slumped into his chair and swung it round so he could look out across the paddock and beyond that to the moor.

Why had he shouted at her? He rested his chin on his hand. It had been such a stupid thing to do, mouthing off like that, especially that bit about Billy.

He covered his mouth with his hand and closed his eyes at the memory of it. He simply couldn't imagine why or how he had been so stupid as to yell at her like that. Even someone with the smallest amount of insight could unravel what he was really saying. He was furious with himself. To allow his temper to run away from him, for his emotions to spill out all over the place; it was a dismal performance.

He slammed his fists down on the side of the chair and swore silently. So stupid, he had been so stupid and all because he was jealous.

She was right when she accused him of it. He *was* jealous; searingly so, right down to the core of his being, to a place where only one other woman had ever got to him before. His evening with Camilla had only clarified the issue: she had been so wrong and had shown Sian to be so right.

He had messed it up. He didn't mean to, but he had, and the worst thing about it all was that he wasn't sure if he should try and sort it out. Sian had made it quite clear what she thought of him and it would take more than just an apology to make up for his foolishness this time. Then there were all his other problems: he was running out of time with the bank, with no sign of being able to repay his loans, and now the horses were going down with some infection. How much more was he to go through? Hadn't he had enough over the last five years? First the accident, then his livelihood and now all of this. How much longer would he have to pay the price for his one mistake? Would he never be free from his past?

As she marched home, Sian asked herself much the same things, especially with regard to Billy. Why had she gone out with him? There was no reason for it at all. She had made a promise to herself when she came to stay here that until she had had the baby, found herself somewhere to live and got things sorted out with Eddy, she was going to stay well away from all men. Handsome, rich, poor or ugly; it didn't matter. She had been too hurt to risk allowing any of them to get to her. So why she had given in so readily to Billy? Was it because she didn't see him as a threat? That because she couldn't take him seriously, she didn't stop to consider the fact that he might not feel the same way about her? Whatever the reason, it had come as a real surprise when he had made a pass at her. She just hadn't thought that any man could find her attractive when she made no effort to attract them. Why should she? She was pregnant and she was hurt – but maybe that was the problem. In her overemotional state, her judgement was unsound. Perhaps instead of declining to attend the art exhibition with Andrew, she should have accepted. He was no ogre. She knew him well enough by now. Look how he had taken care of her when she had twisted her ankle and told Eck that he had to help her because of her pregnancy. Somewhere in all the mess she had badly miscalculated and now she would never get the chance to make amends. Her pride just wouldn't allow her to go back and apologize. One man making a fool of her was enough and there wouldn't be another.

* * *

Eddy got to work early that evening. He wasn't feeling himself. The afternoon's bombshell had left him walking around in a sea of fog, unable to comprehend much that was going on.

Soon after seven thirty, as the first diners were gathering in the main bar, he found himself sitting on a stool and ordering the first of many drinks. He was joined by one of the local bookies, a man he had done a lot of business with in the past.

'How's things, Eddy?'

Eddy finished his drink and held out his glass to the barmaid.

'Fine, Jim.'

'Mind if I join you?'

'Not at all.'

The barmaid handed him back his refilled glass. 'And one for Jim, Becky.'

He smiled weakly. He needed a pal to drink with this evening and Jim was just the one for it. A short, florid man in his mid-forties, he had spent a lifetime in and around horses.

'Coming to Newmarket next week? There's a good programme. Plenty of opportunities for someone with the right contacts.'

Eddy shook his head. 'No. 'Fraid not. Too much work.'

Eddy glanced at him but Jim was still smiling, his apple-red cheeks round and shiny. 'No offence, Eddy, but I haven't seen you in the shop for weeks. Something wrong?'

Eddy groaned and finished his drink. Jim called the barmaid over.

'Another one for your boss and make it a double.'

The drinks arrived. 'Looks like you need it, Eddy.'

'You're telling me.'

'Bit of bad luck?'

Jim trod softly. As a businessman he knew only too well just how sensitive some men were. Years of dealing with

313

people who lost too much had given him a unique perspective of the fallibilities of the human race.

'No, not really.'

'Ah well then,' smiled Jim, 'in that case, it can only mean one thing: women. The bane and wonder of our lives. Those beautiful and tantalizing creatures we can't live with, yet can't live without. The quixotic and irritating; the baffling and mysterious.' He smiled at the forlorn Eddy.

'Forgive me, my son, for waxing lyrical, but whether you love them or hate them, they do have a certain fascination for the average red-blooded male. Especially,' he added, lowering his voice and winking at the barmaid, 'when they're made like she is.'

Eddy ignored this. He couldn't be cheered.

'Oh come on, Eddy, have another drink. You can't sit here all night with a face as long as that.'

'No,' he protested. 'I've got work to do.'

'What!' exclaimed Jim with mock horror. 'And waste all this valuable drinking time? You've got plenty of staff to do all the mundane stuff, so why don't you take the evening off and forget about things?'

Eddy needed little persuasion and in no time at all, he and Jim had taken over the corner table in the bar. As the evening progressed, a few of their like-minded friends joined them. The drinks began to flow very fast.

'. . . So I says to 'er . . .'

'You said what, Eddy?'

All the men were laughing, their faces red around the glass-littered table, the air now blue with smoke.

'I said . . . no, don't, you'll make me laugh!' Eddy protested. 'Let me finish!'

Quite a crowd had gathered to hear Eddy's tale. They were all watching him, eyes shining, mouths loose, glasses in their hands. He smiled at them all. He liked to be popular. It gave him a nice warm feeling. It was much better here than being upstairs with Rowena nagging him.

'Come on, Eddy, get on with the story!'

'I can't,' he said, falling back against the chair. 'I can't remember how it goes. Another drink!' he cried, holding up his glass. 'I need another drink. Where's that bloody barmaid?'

The young woman appeared. The bar should have closed an hour ago and she was tired and irritated.

'Another drink for my friends, Becky, and stop looking so damned miserable. Remember who pays your bloody wages, my girl!'

The barmaid glanced round at the group of men all of whom smiled amiably at her. She took some empty glasses, receiving a saucy remark about the size of her breasts and a slap on the rump. It was just then that Rowena appeared. She wasn't at all amused.

'That will do, Becky. You may go now. I'll deal with this.'

The girl scurried out of the room, smiling to herself. Everything would be sorted out now.

'Right then, gentlemen, as much as I appreciate your company, I feel sure that your wives and girlfriends would appreciate it even more, especially as it's so late. So perhaps if you would like to finish up your drinks and leave, I can close the bar before we have the police around here.'

Her fierce eyes swept around the assembled group who, without any further delay, quietly and obediently did as they were told.

'Night, Eddy.'

'Night.'

'See you tomorrow.'

And they all trooped out.

'Good night, gents.'

Soon all was quiet. Eddy sat slumped in the corner, barely able to keep his eyes open, his face flushed and sweaty and his tie askew, while Rowena stood tight-lipped, white with fury.

'Do you know what you are, Eddy Wiliamson?'

He smiled inanely. He couldn't give a damn what she thought. 'Pissed?' and he giggled.

'God, what a moron!' she muttered under her breath, advancing down on him. She grabbed him by the arms. 'Come on you, bed!'

'But I don't want to!'

'Look, Eddy, I'm in no mood for this. Just do as I say and then we won't have any further trouble, will we? We've got a lot to do in the next few days and I want you sober.'

She struggled to get him to his feet but once there, it didn't take too much effort to propel him upstairs.

'Stupid bugger,' she told him when she had got him undressed and into bed. She sighed as she looked down at his sleeping face with its carefree smile. She knew she shouldn't – and it was difficult sometimes – but she did love him.

Well, she would just have to harden her heart. Sacrifices might have to be made, and Rowena was determined it would not be she who was the lamb to the slaughter.

Nineteen

Andrew strode down Jack Street in Plymouth, squinting in the noon-day sunlight and feeling angry. He didn't want to be here doing this but he had no choice. Mr Dunk of Armitage Financial Management had made it crystal clear over the phone. Either Andrew started repaying the loan he had taken out or the stables and The Grange would be taken as payment instead.

Andrew had met the obsequious and oleaginous Mr Dunk only once, but the very memory of him and the hold he had over everything that Andrew held dear, enraged him. He should never have got himself in this mess. He should have stuck with the bank and stayed well away from loan sharks like Dunk. He sighed bitterly. The bank or Dunk; either way, it looked like the end.

He kicked a piece of litter out of his path. He hated this scruffy part of the city, with its nightclubs, pubs and seedy hotels, most of which were closed at this hour. There was an eerie silence to the place. Few people were about and the odd stray dog rooting around in the gutter perfectly summed up his sense of despair.

He walked on, head bowed.

'So what exactly do I have to do for this hundred?' Mike asked. He was an old friend of Patrick's who was still serving in the Paras at a nearby base. He counted out the money yet again before folding it up and slipping it into his back pocket. He settled himself in the car seat and waited for an explanation. He then rolled down the window to let in some fresh air and lit a cigarette.

'You remember that nightclub in Bergen when you, me

and a couple of others had that run-in with those Norwegians?'

Mike nodded his large square head with its close crew cut. He flexed his fingers against each other making the knuckles click. 'Yeah,' he answered, recalling the fight with relish.

'Remember that bastard that wouldn't go down and you and me had to deal with him properly like?'

'Yeah.' Mike grinned.

'Well, there's someone my boss wants dealing with and he should be around here today,' and he indicated the nearby empty street with a nod of his head. 'Big bloke, six foot plus. Looks like he knows how to take care of himself.' He gave Mike a conspiratorial smile. 'That's why we're here.' Patrick glanced back along the street as if he expected Andrew to appear any minute. 'We just have to wait for the say-so, that's all.'

Mike held up the mobile phone. 'From this?'

Patrick nodded and impatiently tapped his fingers on the leather steering wheel. He idly watched a couple of prostitutes from behind his reflective sunglasses. The women moved off when they realized that there wasn't any custom about. 'Mind you,' added Patrick, 'I've reason enough to lay out this one myself.'

Mike's face broke into a wide smile. 'I hope she's worth it,' he commented.

Patrick shrugged casually. 'I think so.'

'Now look here, Mr Mann,' Dunk, short, greasy and with a thick layer of flab around his middle, jabbed an accusing finger at Andrew, 'you and me entered an agreement.' He wiped his brow with an off-white handkerchief. Despite the whirring fan standing on a filing cabinet, both men sweltered in the small, claustrophobic room with its utilitarian furniture. 'You and me,' continued the sweating Mr Dunk, 'entered an official and binding agreement, that if I lent you a sum of money at a certain rate of interest then you would pay it back within an agreed length of time, which you have signally failed to do.' His beady eyes shone with greed as he stared at Andrew's sullen face. 'If you had bothered to read the small print, Mr Mann, you would have realized that we in the finance business . . .'

Andrew's laugh was dismissive.

'Don't flatter yourself, Dunk. You're a loan shark. Nothing more; nothing less.'

'We in the finance business,' asserted Dunk, pulling himself up to his full five foot four height, 'have a strict code of rules to abide by, i.e. if you don't repay what you owe me, I'll just take it whether you like it or not.' He smirked, his fat face topped off by a few hairs plastered over his shiny scalp. 'Do I make myself clear, Mr Mann? Pay up or you stand to lose everything.'

'But I've already told you, Dunk . . .'

'Mr Dunk to you,' the small man reminded him icily.

Andrew's stare was hostile. 'Mr Dunk, then,' he drawled. 'I can't make the payment. At least not yet, and it's no good threatening me because the place is mortgaged up to the hilt with the bank anyway so if I do go under then surely they will get the first cut, not you? And if that is the case, then surely you ought to be a bit more helpful and not so obstructive?'

Dunk sat back in his large leather chair and smiled slowly. 'You don't seem to understand, when you signed your name on that dotted line, you signed away everything.' He glared at Andrew with hard brittle eyes as he sensed victory. 'No one, not some whingeing single mum on benefit or some disgraced aristocrat gets away from me. No one,' he repeated harshly, leaning forward to emphasize his words. 'I don't care what your sob story is, I'm not interested, you hear? The only thing that matters to me is the repayment of the loan and if you can't make that, then you and I have nothing more to discuss, okay?' He looked back at the pile of paperwork in front of him signalling the end of the interview. Then, as if to underline the message, he waved Andrew away like an irritating fly. 'Shut the door on your way out.'

Andrew rose slowly to his feet, his whole body infused with indignant rage. No one treated him like this even if he was on his financial last legs. There was a time for everything and right now Dunk, even though he wasn't aware of it, was about to change his business practice and extend Andrew's repayment terms. Against his better judgement if necessary.

'You bloody little leech!' yelled Andrew, reaching over the desk and grabbing the startled man by his shirt collar. 'You!' he shouted in Dunk's horrified face, 'have pushed me too far!' and with a heave, he pulled him from behind his desk and threw him against the floor.

Dunk rolled over and came to rest against the filing cabinet. He rubbed his head and elbow in obvious pain and nervously glanced at his assailant.

Andrew stood over him, hands on hips and breathing hard. 'Get up!' he ordered.

The loan shark hesitated, so Andrew yanked him up onto his feet, marched him back behind his desk and thumped him down into his chair. Then he grabbed a handful of papers relating to his loan agreement and thrust them into Dunk's terrified face.

'You're going to change this,' he said through gritted teeth, 'because I'm not about to roll over and give up when I've worked so bloody hard to keep that place. No piece of vermin like you is going to take away all I have. Understand?'

Dunk nodded rapidly. He was sweating more than ever now, his shirt stained with large wet patches.

'Now,' said Andrew, having calmed down a bit. He took the top off Dunk's hand-engraved fountain pen and handed it to him. 'Let's see you make this an agreement I can live with. That way we both get what we want, okay?'

Ten minutes later, Andrew was shaking Dunk's soft pudgy hand. 'I like doing business with someone who plays fair, Mr Dunk. It makes life so much more pleasant don't you think?' and he pocketed his part of the agreement. Mr Dunk said nothing. All he wanted was for Andrew to leave his office so that he could pour himself a large whisky.

'I'll see you next month as agreed then?' said Andrew, his hand on the door.

'Fine, Mr Mann. Anything you say.'

'And there's no need to show me the way out of this hell hole. I know where I'm going now.'

'Of course, Mr Mann.'

As the door closed Dunk slumped back into his chair, overwhelmed with relief. Then he opened a drawer, took out a bottle of malt and poured himself a very generous measure. Once his stomach had stopped churning, he picked up the telephone and dialled a number. When the call was over, he sat back and smiled with smug satisfaction. He raised his glass in mock salute.

'Here's to you, Mr Mann,' and he took a large gulp. Andrew was about to find out just how unwise his tactics had been.

Andrew headed for the nearest pub and ordered a pint. He had to have a drink to wash away the taste of Dunk and his unsavoury office. He knew that what had happened back in the office was just a temporary halt in his seemingly unstoppable demise. In reality, it was only a matter of time now before he went under and in retrospect, it looked as though it would have been more sensible for him simply to have accepted the bank's advice and sold up. At least that way he might have been able to come out of the whole sorry mess reasonably unscathed. At least he would have – might have – kept his dignity intact. As it was, it was beginning to look as if he would have nothing; not his house, his stables, his horses. Nothing.

He took a desultory pull at his pint and wiped the drops of liquid off his lips with a clenched fist. So much effort and for what? Fate, it seemed, was still punishing him. It didn't matter what he did or how much he tried to atone for the past, it was still chasing him and destroying all that he touched. He wondered, sometimes, why he even got out of bed in the morning? After all, where was the point of it any more when everything conspired to defeat him?

Sian. He smiled ruefully. There could have really been something there if only he hadn't mucked it up but, yet again, he had gone and put his foot in it. He couldn't stop thinking about her and now he would never find out whether she felt the same about him. Maybe, he consoled himself, there was a lesson in all of this but he was damned if he could see it.

'Another pint please, barman.'

'Okay.'

Patrick and Mike came into the bar and quietly sat at a table in the far corner. They had been waiting for Andrew and now they had their quarry in sight, they didn't intend to let him go.

Mike got up to fetch the drinks, careful not to make eye contact with Andrew, but he needn't have worried. Andrew was too deep in thought to notice anything.

'Won't be long,' he said to Patrick when he returned. 'The way he's sinking them, he'll have to go to the bog in no time.'

Halfway through his third pint, Andrew did exactly as they expected and left the garish lounge for the Gents. As he stood in front of the urinal, his head beginning to weave from the unaccustomed amount of alcohol, he stared blankly at the stained wall. He heard the door open but took no notice of the two burly men who entered and quietly locked the door behind them. 'Andrew Mann?' asked one of them.

Andrew turned his head and smiled blearily. 'Yeah?' and that was the last voluntary movement he made. The hail of punches and blows sent him flying and his consciousness soon ebbed away into comforting blackness.

Patrick and Mike stood panting and glanced down indifferently at the bleeding body. Patrick wiped his hands on his jeans.

'Come on, that's enough. Let's get out of here.' Just as they were about to leave, the door rattled.

'Let me in!' cried a feeble, elderly voice. 'I need a pee!'

The two men glanced at the door. They had no need to worry. They opened the door, barring the old man's way. His stream of invective was cut short when he noticed the prone body lying across the floor.

'Who's that?' he demanded toothlessly. 'And what you been doing to him?'

'Never you mind, Granddad,' said Mike, picking up the old man as effortlessly as a bag of potatoes. He carried him across the small concrete yard and propped him up against the wall.

'One word from you,' threatened Mike, his face so close to the trembling pensioner that his spittle hit the other's face, 'and me and my mate here will come and get you and when we do, you'd better be prepared for a very long stay in hospital because,' and here he tightened his grip on the man's throat, 'we don't like people who talk. Gettit?' And just to make sure the pensioner had got the message loud and clear, he thumped his head against the wall a couple of times.

'Look!' sniggered Patrick pointing to a pool of water that had suddenly appeared. 'Dirty old bugger has wet himself!'

Mike dropped him and they left, laughing cruelly. The old man eventually crawled away. No one was going to make him talk.

Ten minutes later another customer found Andrew on the lavatory floor, his face bashed and bloodied. 'Bloody hell!' the man swore, leaning over aghast. Then he hurried back into the bar.

'Ambulance!' he shouted, and all the customers looked up. 'There's a man in the Gents covered in blood!'

Twenty

'Hi.'

Helen nodded, her face drawn, and then went through to the kitchen. Sian followed.

'What's up?' she asked.

Helen filled the kettle. 'Want a coffee?'

'Okay.'

Sian sat at the table. She was worried. Helen's behaviour over the last few weeks had become more erratic. She was seldom at home, staying out all hours, and when she was in, she was uncommunicative and moody. If Sian asked any questions, she was met with a mute, challenging stare. Except now. There was something in Helen's demeanour, a tiredness, an air of misery which couldn't be ignored any longer.

'Please, Helen, what is it?'

She looked dreadful. Her face was pale, her eyes sunken and dull. She had a cluster of pimples on her chin and her hair was lifeless. This wasn't the Helen that Sian had known since childhood.

'Please –'

'Don't, Sian. I don't want to hear!' she cried, and then seeing her friend's hurt expression, said more quietly, 'I know what you're going to ask and I'm sorry, but I can't tell you.'

'Tell me what? What's so dreadful you can't tell me? We're old friends, remember, and you should know by now that you can tell me anything.'

'Not this time.'

The kettle boiled and that was the end of that topic of conversation, at least as far as Helen was concerned.

'Any brandy left?' she asked, getting up to fetch it from the next room.

'Yes, I think so.'

When Helen came back, she already had the bottle opened and had obviously had a swig. She poured a generous amount into her coffee before throwing the top away into the bin.

'Won't be needing that again,' she said, ignoring Sian's anxious gaze. 'And there's no need to look at me like that either. I don't need any of your bloody preaching.'

'I wasn't going to say anything.'

'Good, because it's none of your damned business.'

'What is, Helen?'

'Oh for God's sake, shut up, will you?' And then, immediately apologetic, she ran a weary hand through her unkempt hair. 'I'm sorry. I didn't mean to shout. It's just that you wouldn't understand, that's all. It's . . .' she grimaced, 'complicated. Very.'

'Come off it, nothing's that bad. What wouldn't I understand?'

Helen took a mouthful of her coffee. 'All of it,' she said, waving a hand around, 'and none of it. It's all so bloody awful, a complete and utter fuckup, and believe me, it makes for very unpleasant hearing. You know, of all the things I've done, of all the men I've slept with, I don't think I've ever been in a mess like this one.'

'If you don't tell me, how will I know?'

Helen hid her despairing face in her hands. 'I can't tell you. It's . . . well, it's horrible, that's all,' and then she started to cry.

Sian reached for a piece of kitchen roll and handed it over.

'Here, take this. It's supposed to be me who cries round here, remember, not you.'

Helen sniffed loudly as two fat tears rolled down her cheeks. She didn't smile at Sian's attempt to humour her.

325

'I've run out of ciggies,' she complained. 'I don't suppose you'd be an angel and go and get me some?'

'Yes. Of course. I'll see you in a minute.'

Sian ran down to the shop. As she was paying for the cigarettes, the shop assistant said, 'Ooh look, a police car. Wonder where it's going. Looks like it's heading up for your end of the village. I wonder who's in trouble now?'

Sian glanced back over her shoulder as she held out her hand for her change.

'Thanks, Mrs Parr.'

'What do you think they police want, then?'

'I haven't a clue. Someone's parked on a yellow line perhaps?'

'Well, I don't know about that, dear. I think it's more than just a traffic offence. Probably some of they tourists again, getting lost or something. You knows what they're like.'

Sian smiled and backed out of the shop. She could do without this right now.

'Bye, Mrs Parr,' but the old lady was too busy craning her neck out of the window to hear.

Sian walked back to the cottage. When she rounded the corner, her heart stopped.

'Oh my God!'

The police car was parked outside the cottage. She sprinted the rest of the way. She found Helen and two policemen sitting at the kitchen table. All three turned to her when she walked in. The men looked professionally grim; Helen's face was pale and drawn.

Sian advanced slowly, her heart pounding, her eyes flickering from face to face, seeking an explanation. 'What's wrong?' she heard herself say.

The older man smiled and helped her to a seat. Helen wordlessly held out her hand for the cigarettes. It was shaking. When Sian gave them to her, she tore them open, lit up and inhaled like a drowning man coming up for air.

'What's the matter?' repeated Sian, glancing from face to face.

'It's Andrew,' whispered Helen. 'There's been an accident.'

Sian's soul froze. 'An accident? Where? When? How?'

'Yes, Mrs Williamson,' said the other policeman, with kind blue eyes. 'He was assaulted earlier today at a public house in Plymouth. I'm afraid he is in quite a bad way.'

'What!' exclaimed Sian in horrified disbelief.

'Yes, severe concussion plus a few broken ribs,' continued the young policeman kindly. 'The hospital are sure he will recover fully.'

Sian blinked away the unbidden tears. Andrew attacked? Who would do such a thing and why? She couldn't believe it. They must have got the wrong person.

'But are you sure it's Andrew? Andrew Mann?'

'Yes, we are, I'm afraid.' The older policeman smiled. 'Would you like the constable here to make you a cup of tea? You look as though you could do with it.'

She nodded her head, unable to comprehend what she had been told. Helen reached for the brandy again, but no one said anything. If they had, she wouldn't have cared. She was already drowning in her own despair. It hardly mattered if fate piled on some more.

Sian took the tea the constable made. 'So how bad is he exactly?' she asked, fighting to think straight through her panic.

'Well, I suggest you contact the Accident and Emergency Department at the hospital,' replied the older man. 'They'll be able to give you some more information, but our initial reports would seem to indicate that Mr Mann's injuries are not life-threatening.' He paused. 'If it's any consolation, Mrs Williamson, in all my years as a policeman, I have seen people with far worse injuries, so try not to worry too much. Drink your tea. You'll feel better in a minute.'

She did as she was told, too exhausted to think of dissenting.

'So you two work for Mr Mann?' asked the constable.

'Yes,' answered Sian for the both of them. Helen's unfocusing eyes were giving away her drunkenness. 'I used to be the stable lass, if you like, and Helen is a riding instructor.'

The two men glanced at Helen. They could see at once they weren't going to get any sense out of her.

'And how long did you work for Mr Mann?'

'Month and a half. Helen's been there much longer.' Sian dried her face with her handkerchief. 'Who could have done this, Sergeant? I don't understand. As far as I know, no one disliked him that much.'

'So he did have some enemies then?'

She shrugged. 'A jealous husband or boyfriend maybe, but certainly no one else, although he sometimes said how he got fed up with property speculators coming up to The Grange and trying to buy him out. Oh, and we suspect someone has been trying to poison his horses lately.'

The constable wrote all this down. Both men were decidedly more interested now.

'When was this?'

'This week.'

'And is it definitely poison?'

'We don't know for certain. The vet is running some tests. You'd better ask him for the latest news. I'll write his number down for you.'

'Thanks. Anything else that you might think is useful? Strange people hanging around the stables? Telephone calls? Visitors?'

She shook her head. 'Not that I can think of.'

'That's all right, Mrs Williamson. Take your time.'

'No, there's no one,' she smiled.

'It could be that it was just a mugging, Mrs Williamson,' said the constable. 'He was in one of the more undesirable areas of Plymouth and I wouldn't be at all surprised if a couple of thugs just decided to chance their arm.'

'Maybe you're right. Did he tell you anything?'

'No. He was barely conscious when the publican found him. We'll have to interview him when he's more lucid. Do you know if he had any relatives we ought to contact?'

'He said something once about having some distant German relatives that he had never met, but apart from that, no, no one. I think he might have been married at some point, but trying to get information out of him . . . Well, he's generally a very private man, so really I can't help you there. However . . .'

'Yes?' asked the sergeant.

'Well,' and she shrugged her shoulders, 'I don't know if it's of any use to you but I think he's connected to The Grange from way back.'

'How do you mean?'

'I bought an old diary in a junk shop. It was written by a lady called Isobel Warrener who used to live up there during and after the war. It's just that Andrew mentioned once that his father was a German prisoner of war and it was Isobel Warrener's daughter, Sophie, who ran off with a POW. It's probably all totally irrelevant. Heavens, I don't know. Maybe he'll tell you more about it.'

The two men exchanged glances and then stood up.

'Well, Mrs Williamson, you've been very helpful and if we have any further questions or information, we will of course be in touch with you.'

'Thank you, Sergeant, and thank you for coming to tell us.'

'That's all right. We'll see ourselves out,' and he glanced at Helen who lay slumped across the table. 'I think your friend might have had a bit too much to drink.'

'She's rather upset, that's all.'

The news from the hospital was as Sian imagined. Andrew had had various X-rays to ascertain whether his skull was fractured, but luckily it wasn't. Apart from that, he had all manner of cuts and bruises and several of his ribs were broken.

'But he's all right, is he, I mean apart from all of that?' Sian had to sit down to stop her legs from shaking.

'Yes,' said the comforting voice down the telephone. 'He's fully conscious and although he's feeling very rough at the moment, he'll be back up on his feet again in next to no time.'

'And his ribs?'

'There's not much we can do about those. I wouldn't worry, my dear. He's a strong and fit man. He'll be out in a day or two. We just have to keep him in for observation, that's all.'

Sian sighed deeply. Thank God for that. 'When can I come and see him?'

'Later on tonight, if you like. He's a bit dozy at the moment because of his concussion, but he should be better shortly. I should tell you,' she added, 'that he's not a pretty sight at the moment. Whoever beat him up did a thorough job of it and his face is badly cut and bruised. He's had quite a few stitches as well.'

'Never mind about that,' Sian replied. 'I'm just glad he's okay.'

She resolved that first of all she was going to have to apologize to him for calling him a bully and storming out on him the other day, only oddly enough, she didn't mind what he'd said to her at all now.

Okay, he had Camilla, but that didn't mean they couldn't be friends. In the space of two days, since she had walked out, telling herself he was the most unpleasant man she knew – next to her husband – everything had turned upside down. It had surprised her just how much she had been affected by the news of Andrew's injuries and she knew now, whatever attempts she had made at denying it, that he meant an awful lot to her. She went back to the kitchen, feeling much better. It was empty and the back door was wide open. Sian rushed out into the garden.

'Helen!'

Her kneeling figure could be seen down by the compost heap where she was being sick.

'Oh no!' Sian walked briskly down to her. 'Helen, you fool!'

She helped to straighten up the pallid figure and half carried her back to the kitchen. Her T-shirt was stained and she was shivering. Bloodshot eyes looked out from a pasty face.

'I think,' said Sian, standing over her, 'we'd better get you into the bath.'

Dragging Helen upstairs was no easy effort but eventually Sian got her seated on the edge of the bath where she started to undress her. Helen sat limp and unprotesting as her wet, smelly clothing was removed, her tear-filled eyes overflowing down her morose face.

'Come on, it can't be that bad,' but it was. As the shirt came off, a whole series of vile and vicious-coloured black and purple bruises was revealed.

'Helen,' asked Sian in hushed tones, 'what is all this?'

She examined the battered torso, tenderly running her hands over the skin. There were marks everywhere.

'Come on, speak to me. Who did this? Was it Darryl?' but Helen didn't answer. Her face collapsed into more tears and she cried helplessly.

'Helen, please.' Sian held on to the heaving, sobbing body, gently stroking her hair. 'What is it, what's been going on?'

'Nothing,' she whispered, her face crooked with tears and pain. 'It was my fault. I drove him to it. See, I told you you wouldn't understand.' She looked up at Sian, her brown bloodshot eyes swimming in tears. 'I love him. I always will. He means everything to me,' and she ran her hand over her shoulder, wincing as she did so. 'My fault,' she repeated.

'But why?' asked Sian.

'No, doesn't matter . . . Won't tell you . . .'

Sian sat next to her. 'Here, wipe your eyes,' she said,

passing Helen a piece of toilet roll. 'Poor you. I don't know what it's all about, but you've got to get out of it. You've got to leave him, Helen, whatever you feel about him. It's only going to get worse.'

Helen suddenly stood up, erect and indignant.

'Get rid of him?' she cried. 'How can I? I don't think you're listening to me, Sian. Just because your relationship failed, it doesn't mean to say mine will. Okay, so we have the odd fight now and again, but that doesn't mean anything. How the bloody hell can you sit there and tell me I have to get rid of him when you can't even sort your own damned life out?'

She glared at Sian, bubbles of spittle on her lower lip. 'I love him,' she added fervently. 'I always will because in his arms, for the first time in my life, I really feel alive. I become part of him. There's no one else who can do that for me and I'm not going to give him up. Not for you, not for anyone.'

She stood gently swaying, a bruised and whipped body unsteady in her underwear. She seemed not to notice anything any more.

'But I'm worried for you,' insisted Sian. 'If he carries on doing this to you, where's it all going to end? Am I going to have to visit you in the hospital as well? Think about it, Helen!'

'But I love him!'

'Yes, I know that, but he's only a builder, for God's sake. He's not Superman!'

Helen glared at her. 'Oh yeah? And what about Eddy? Some bloody dish-water hotelier, so busy fucking all his staff that you were the one who did all the work up there. Call that fair, do you?'

Sian stood up, tight-lipped and angry. 'That's enough!' she roared.

Helen slumped down on to the floor, all fight gone. 'I'm sorry, Sian. I shouldn't have said that.' She looked up and gave a thin watery smile. 'Forgive me?'

Sian knelt down over the prostrate Helen and helped her sit up. Helen started to grin and then to laugh.

'God!' she giggled hysterically. 'Have you ever seen anything so pathetic?'

'Helen, I'm so sorry.'

'Doesn't matter. Bathtime?'

'Yes. Come on.'

Helen reclined back in the hot bubbly water, nursing her gin and tonic. Sian sat on the floor nursing a coffee.

'Mmm,' said Helen, 'nothing like a hot bath to get rid of all the toxic waste except, of course, that I'm still adding to mine,' and she held up her drink in a salute.

Sian smiled. 'Going to tell me what it's all about now, I mean, all this drinking that you've been doing lately, not to mention the fact that I rarely see you except at breakfast and sometimes, not even then?'

Helen closed her eyes in the hot fragrant steam.

'No, and I know you're my best friend and all that, but –'

'But it's none of my business?'

'Something like that. Let's just say that he's a very passionate man and sometimes, and I'm not sure why, he gets a bit angry, that's all.'

Sian raised a sceptical eyebrow. 'A bit angry? I'd call those bruises of yours more than just a bit, wouldn't you? Makes you think that going out with someone like Billy wouldn't be such a bad thing, eh?'

'Don't even mention him! The thing from the black lagoon,' and they both laughed.

Sian sighed. 'Well, maybe you can tell me what's got into Eck at the moment? He's acting really strange, you know. I passed him in the street yesterday and he could hardly bring himself to look at me.'

'What about Andrew?' asked Helen, ignoring Sian's question. 'Will you go in and visit him?'

'I suppose so.'

Helen smiled. 'It's all a bit different from a few days ago, isn't it? You couldn't wait to see the back of him then.'

'Things change, you know,' said Sian defensively. She paused and then, 'I think you fancied him at one time too, didn't you?'

Helen wiped the sweat out of her eyes. She looked uncomfortable.

'Well,' she started, 'let's put it this way: if I hadn't been so drunk and if I'd behaved myself a bit better, then he wouldn't have had to refuse me.'

'You mean you threw yourself at him?'

'God,' retorted Helen, 'you do have a way with words, don't you? You know exactly how to make a woman feel better.'

'Did you, then?'

'This is just too embarrassing,' admitted Helen, blushing under her already red face. 'I fancied him like hell when he first arrived. Heavens, who didn't? Anyway, given that he's drop-dead handsome, and given that I couldn't wait to get my hands on a decent piece of beefcake for a change, well, you can guess the rest. Bloody humiliating.' She smiled apologetically. 'I'm sorry if I gave you the wrong impression. Jealousy, I suppose.'

'You jealous? What of?'

'You're pregnant. And you're beautiful and whether you believe it or not, Andrew thinks so too.'

'You're just saying that!' Sian replied, laughter in her voice. 'What about Camilla?'

'Who gives a damn about her? He certainly doesn't. She chases after him and, like most blokes, he hates it. She's just all crutch and nothing else. God, she even makes me look innocent. No,' she added, shaking her head, 'it's you he wants. Anyone can see that. Even that row you had the other day was all about it. He was as jealous as hell of you and Billy.' She smiled fondly at her friend. 'Look, Sian, never mind his past, never mind the women he's had, just

334

you go to him and enjoy whatever it is that comes your way.'

Helen held out her hand and Sian took hold of it.

'Be his future,' said Helen. 'Don't worry about me. I'll be all right. You go to the hospital and give him all my love. I'll be thinking of you both.'

Sian smiled and leant forward and kissed her on the forehead.

It was dusk when Sian got to Plymouth and the first person she met in the hospital car park was Camilla. Each was surprised to see the other.

'Oh, it's you,' said Camilla, her face tightly drawn and pale. Usually so neat and well dressed, she looked dishevelled. She quickly tried to tidy her hair. There was an air of irritability about her. She was constantly looking around, her eyes hollow, her expression brittle, hands smoothing down rumpled clothes.

'Hello, Camilla. You've been to see Andrew?'

She started to chew her lip. She wasn't wearing any makeup. She shook her head and scratched her arm.

'Yes, but . . . well, he couldn't . . . didn't . . . the nurse said . . .' and she tapered off.

'You all right?' asked Sian, taking hold of Camilla's arm.

She yanked herself free, glaring. 'Leave me alone!' she cried.

Sian stood back. 'Okay, okay, but is there anything I can do? Are you sure you're all right? Can I get you a taxi or something?'

'No,' she snapped. 'I have my car,' and rummaging in her handbag, she took out her keys. She sniffed and wiped her sore nose on the back of her hand. 'Must go now,' she muttered, and clutching her handbag tightly, she ran off across the car park. Sian watched her go. After everything that had happened today, nothing would surprise her any more.

Camilla sat in her car shaking with rage and hot humiliation. The scene in the hospital between herself and Andrew didn't bear thinking about but think about it she must. A ring of truth, a clarity of perception had pierced through her iron-clad self-absorption and cut her to the quick.

Andrew, one of the few men she had ever really wanted, had turned her down totally. He had simply and utterly rejected her, curdling her already soiled self-image.

She had gasped when she had first seen him. All that white hospital linen, his cuts, his bruises, the swollen flesh. He looked terrible. Then he had opened his eyes.

'Hello, darling,' she said, taking his hand in hers. He didn't answer. 'How are you feeling? You do look awful.'

He turned his head away, slowly and painfully.

'Does it hurt really badly?'

He stared resolutely at the ceiling.

She tried another tack. 'Have the police spoken to you yet? They'll want to know if you can identify your attackers. I can help, you know. I can employ a solicitor for you. It won't cost you anything. I can get it all sorted out,' but he still didn't say anything. 'Andrew, are you all right? Would you like me to get you some water or something?'

'Please go away,' he whispered.

'You don't mean that, darling,' she chided. 'I was really concerned when the police told me what had happened. I nearly cried.'

He faced her, his eyes black and unfathomable, stitches crisscrossing his face, with lines of angry red cuts beneath them.

'Go away.'

'But, Andrew –'

'I mean it, Camilla,' he said hoarsely. 'It won't work. We won't work.' He stopped and swallowed painfully. 'I'm sorry.'

She sat open-mouthed with amazement, half of her

hearing all that he said, but the other half refusing to acknowledge it.

'But I can't,' she said, her voice cracking. 'We love each other. I love you. I can't leave you. In Exeter that day – couldn't you feel it?'

'Feel what?'

'The specialness between us, the connection. Don't you understand, Andrew? We were meant to be and I can't leave you. Ever!'

He slowly removed his arm from her clutch. 'You don't . . . you don't know what you're saying.'

'But, Andrew . . .' She was getting desperate, her face frantic. 'No, no, you've got it wrong. We love each other. That night when we made love, surely you knew it then? How can you say these things when you know how much you mean to me?'

He looked at her through swollen, blackened flesh.

'How can you say these things?' she repeated staring at him with pleading eyes. 'Please!'

'Don't you understand, Camilla?' He took her shaking hand. 'Listen to me and listen carefully. We had a very pleasant evening and night and it was good . . . but I made a dreadful mistake.'

'But you didn't!'

He closed his eyes. 'I did,' and his voice was no more than a hoarse whisper. 'I shouldn't have done it. I'm sorry, but that's the way it is.'

She looked at him through hopeless eyes. 'No. That's not how it was. We made love and it really meant something, I know it did.'

'You're mistaken.'

Suddenly she understood. His words had got through and she was ashamed. Tears began to well up behind her eyes, but years of training forced them down again. She would not let him see how hurt she was.

She stood up and pulled herself erect. 'I'm sorry, too,' she said, smiling briefly, lips thin and eyes aloof. 'We could

337

have made it, Andrew, really we could, but you'll never know that now, will you?' At the door she stopped and turned round. 'Goodbye, my love. I'll never forget you, you know,' and then she was gone.

Back out in her car, she sat smoking and staring out of the window. She knew who was behind all this just as he was behind everything in her life. When it went wrong there was only one person to blame and this time he had gone too far. This time he had destroyed something that she had thought so precious, something that was at the very centre of her being, and she couldn't let him get away with it.

She angrily lit another cigarette, two fierce plumes of blue smoke coming out of her nostrils. The cocaine was still working but it would help if she could have a drink. She opened the glove compartment and took out a small hip flask. She downed the Scotch in one, feeling the burning amber fluid rush through her. Damn Marcus, damn him to hell.

'I won't put up with it, you bastard. Not this time.'

Sian was shown into the small side ward.

'Heavens!' she whispered, horrified at what she saw.

The nurse leant towards her and said in a hushed voice, 'He's already had one visitor and I think it was a bit much for him. Don't stay long, will you? He's still a bit groggy.'

Sian sat down, too shocked to answer, and the nurse left the room. Andrew appeared to be sleeping, his torn and tattered face at peace.

'What have they done to you?' she whispered and, reaching out with her hand, she traced a finger lightly across his chin. Unexpectedly, she started to cry. It was then that he opened what he could of his bruised eyes.

'Crying?'

'No,' she answered stiffly, 'just something in my eye, that's all.'

He closed his eyes again. 'Why are you here?'

'Well, someone had to come and see how you are. Helen and I were very shocked to hear what had happened.'

'Really? And what was it you called me the other day? A bully?'

She squirmed a little. 'I was angry, Andrew, and people say stupid things when they're angry. Anyway,' she sniffed, 'you weren't exactly Mr Charming yourself, as I seem to remember – shouting at me and Eck like that.'

Silence.

'I'm sorry,' he said, giving her a sideways glance.

'I bet that stuck in your throat, didn't it?'

He ran his fingers over his cracked lips, grimacing. 'Now look, young lady, if you're not going to accept my apology, then we have no more to say.'

'Who said I wasn't going to accept it?'

'Will you? And don't I get one in return?'

She sat back in her chair with a smirk. 'I'll think about it.'

'Typical,' she heard him mutter. 'Get me a drink, could you?'

She held the beaker of water to his lips and a few drops escaped down his grazed chin. She dabbed it away with a tissue, watching him wince with every touch.

'The police came and told us what happened. We couldn't believe it. Honestly, just look at you!'

'I'd rather not. You're much prettier.'

Sian smiled despite herself.

'What about the horses?' she asked. 'Do you want me to look after them for you?'

'Yes.' He swallowed with difficulty. 'I'm sure someone's trying to poison the horses to put me out of business. Take care of Sebi. Take him up to The Grange and look after him. Blaize will guard you.' He stopped, the sheer effort of talking almost too much for him. 'You're someone I can trust. Don't let me down.'

'Of course not.'

He held his hand to his ribs. 'Christ, it hurts!'

'Do you want me to fetch the nurse?'

'No need,' he whispered before he closed his eyes and fell silent.

Then the nurse came in.

'Time for you to go, I think,' she said. 'He'll be much better tomorrow.'

Sian looked down at him. He could be so damned difficult sometimes, but it didn't stop her from caring for him. 'He does look terrible, doesn't he?'

'Yes, but you'll be amazed how quickly it will all go. A fit young man like him will heal in no time. Come back tomorrow, dear,' said the nurse, guiding her out. 'Go and get a good night's sleep. You'll feel much better in the morning.'

Sian left reluctantly. She, too, was exhausted but she knew she wouldn't sleep. A night at The Grange wasn't something she looked forward to, especially with a malicious horse poisoner about. But if she had to do it, she would. She couldn't let him down.

Twenty-one

It was late when Patrick got back from Plymouth. He was tired and yawned as he drove. As he got towards Leighford, he saw a signpost that made him halt. In the bright light of his headlamps, it said two miles to The Grange. With Mann in hospital, it would be the perfect time to give the stables up at the house a good looking over. There would be no one to stop him and nothing to get in his way, especially not that stupid horse.

Fifteen minutes later, he parked his car at the bottom of The Grange drive, hidden behind a tree, just in case anyone decided to investigate. He got out and listened. Nothing. Only the usual night sounds of an owl hooting and a cow lowing somewhere in the dark distance. Apart from that, the countryside was eerily quiet in the light of the moon. No lights, no cars, no humans. It was ideal.

Patrick worked the loose boxes one by one. Using his small pencil torch, he didn't have to turn on any lights and attract attention. The stables could just be seen from The Grange but as he expected, there were no signs of anyone in. All of its windows were dark.

He found nothing, just musty straw, and rodents that disappeared immediately from the beam of his torch. A cat watched him from a wall, its eyes glowing a sulphurous yellow, but apart from that, there was no other life.

Patrick tapped wooden partitions, examined the old stone walls and peered into everything that might remotely contain anything.

The stables adjoined the garages. They were all empty as well.

It was looking more and more as though the stories of

the Warrener Hoard were just that; stories. Of course, there were the spoons that Patrick had found the other night, now hidden in the shed at Belvedere Cottage. Were it not for them, he'd be inclined to disbelieve the whole treasure tale by now. But the thought that there might be something more raised his hopes for a last search. There was one more stable to investigate and then he would be home to his bed.

He walked across the yard. The top half of the stable door was open and its interior looked as bleak and as empty as all the others. He peered into it, expecting to see nothing, and was met by the large dark head of Sebi, his ears forward as he watched the stranger.

'Oh shit!'

Sebi stretched out his neck to smell the newcomer. He sniffed, snorted, shook his mane and walked over to the door. Patrick backed off.

'Nice horsey, good horsey,' he whispered.

Sebi put his head over the door. He was feeling better. The vet's medicine had worked its magic and his pain had gone. He was curious to know who this person was at his door.

'Come on,' Patrick told himself sternly. 'Don't be so fucking stupid. It's only a horse!'

Sebi now stood at the door, shaking his enormous head up and down. Patrick advanced slowly, holding out his hand.

'Good boy. There's a good boy.'

Sebi's ears went back. He wasn't so sure about Patrick. He threw up his head and whinnied, only to be answered by another horse. The stable had a wooden partition down the middle and behind it was Bracken.

'Oh no!'

Patrick was getting increasingly nervous, but when Sebi seemed to have calmed down, he stepped forward again.

'Nice horse. Good boy. Just stand there, that's right and let old Patrick come in. There's a good boy.'

He eased open the door and slid through. He left it open in the hope that Sebi would leave. He didn't. Instead he followed Patrick.

'Go away, you stupid great bugger! Leave me alone!'

Patrick waved his hands in the air, making Sebi start, but he still wouldn't leave and now the other horse was coming over to investigate him. Patrick backed away as the two of them advanced, each seemingly larger than life in the gloom of the box and both now standing between him and safety. Patrick's heart thumped.

'Move it, you damn things!' He smacked the nearest one on the mouth. This made Bracken toss her head and whinny and Sebi stamp his frighteningly large front hooves and snort into his bedding.

Feeling desperately trapped, there was nothing for it but to get searching. Patrick reasoned that as long as he played it calm, the horses would remain so too.

He turned his back on them and started to scan the walls. The small beam of light traversed the cobwebbed whitewashed brickwork. He held the torch upwards and looked at the ceiling. Long wooden beams with yet more webs ran the length of the building, but there was nothing else to be seen.

He sighed. The treasure had to be somewhere. It was at this point that one of the horses acting only out of curiosity tried to take a bite of Patrick's jacket.

He spun round defensively and hit Sebi across the muzzle with the torch.

The horse reared up on his hind legs, flailing the air as he neighed loudly. Patrick shielded himself, convinced that the animal was going to brain him. When he dared to open his eyes, both horses were standing watching him. Deciding that his only option was to bluff it out, Patrick started to shout and wave his arms.

'Come on then, you!' he shouted. 'Do your worst!'

Sebi half turned and bucked, his powerful hind legs smashing into the wooden partition, sending splinters across the floor. Bracken whinnied and stamped about. Patrick was caught. He had expected them to run off but they didn't and now he couldn't get out because they were in the way. A now furious Sebi reared and stamped, his massive head thrown around as he yelled at this impertinent human.

Patrick cowered, holding up his ineffectual hands. There was nothing he could do. As the horse lashed out at him, his huge body crashing around in the loose box, Patrick backed off as much as he could. Escape was no more than a few feet away through the open door, but they were the longest few feet he had ever seen.

Cornered, he tried to stand up. Both of the horses loomed over him, fierce and menacing. Patrick fell to his hands and knees. Keeping tightly to the wall, he made his way slowly but surely towards the door, his face averted from what he thought to be his imminent demise. A hoof whizzed past Patrick's face and hit the wall, the animal's primeval screams filling the stable.

Slowly, inch by inch, the open door came closer, safety no more than a short sprint. Finally, with what seemed to Patrick to be one of the bravest acts of his life, he stood up and ran for it. Out in the courtyard he didn't stop. Sebi chased him, hooves clattering over the cobbles, while up at The Grange a dog barked and a light came on.

Patrick ran and didn't stop until he reached the car. Sitting inside, panting and sweating, he looked up the drive and there in the moonlight were the two horses: one black as the night with a white star on his forehead, prancing and tossing his head as he walked around the yard, the other following him. Then they stood still and watched, listening as the car started up.

'All right you two. I give up. You've won.'

Had Patrick gone back to the stable he would have noticed something odd. Several bricks had been loosened out of the inside wall by all the commotion. If Patrick had pulled these bricks out further, he would have found what he had spent so much time looking for.

Patrick slept late. When he woke up he had a stinking hangover, which was made worse when he recalled how ignominiously he had been chased away from the stable.

He got dressed, scowling and sulking. He didn't like being got the better of, especially by a mere animal, but he wasn't going back there again. He would have to make some excuse to Killington, something convincing, and that would take some doing. His boss was suspicious, and he was not going to be pleased at all if he found out what had really happened.

At least Patrick had his spoons. They had to be worth something. It would have been nice to have found the whole hoard. Then he would have disappeared without a trace, his future secure. A nice little bar somewhere hot and tropical had always appealed to him. He wiped the thought from his mind. At this rate he wouldn't be going anywhere.

He was having his breakfast when Camilla came into the kitchen dressed in her bathrobe, her hair unkempt. Her face was pale, there were dark rings under her eyes, and her cheekbones were standing out even more prominently. Her nose was red and she made no effort to conceal it. She wiped a hand truculently across her face, ignoring his concerned look. Helping herself to coffee, she lit another cigarette from the butt of the one she was smoking and, ignoring him, sat down opposite.

He ate his toast, but then gradually became aware that she was watching him. He looked up.

'Miss?'

'How are you, Patrick? You came in late last night.'

He didn't know how to answer her at first. She had surprised him. She had never asked how he was before.

He frowned. 'All right, I suppose.'

'Good day, yesterday?'

He looked at her with suspicion. What was this leading to?

'Yeah, okay. Why?'

She took a deep pull at her cigarette and blew out the smoke in a long blue line from her pursed lips.

'So good in fact,' she said slowly, 'that you and maybe one of your equally unspeakable cronies had a go at Andrew Mann in a pub toilet in Plymouth, beating him senseless?'

Patrick stiffened. So this was what it was all about, only how had she found out? She answered his unspoken question.

'I know you, Patrick,' she said, sipping her coffee, her eyes digging into him. 'You're a bastard just like my dearly beloved stepbrother, and when he said do it, you did because just like him, you don't give a fuck, do you, least of all for me and what I might think?'

He sat motionless.

'This coffee's tasteless. Get me some brandy,' she ordered.

He rose from the table. 'Just following orders, miss.'

She eyed him glassily. 'Just following orders, miss,' she mocked in a high schoolgirl voice. She grabbed the bottle off him and poured a large measure into her coffee. He sat down again.

'How much does my esteemed stepbrother pay you for such activities?'

The question caught him off guard. He was expecting more abuse. His look flickered towards her. She looked dangerously angry, eyes blazing, mouth tight and pinched.

'Depends.'

'On what, you moron?'

He shrugged casually. 'On what he wants me to do.'

'And if I were to pay you more?'

'For doing what, miss?'

She smiled mysteriously, her cruel, beautiful face tantalizing him.

'For pissing off, that's what.'

'Don't know, miss.'

'You know,' she said carefully, 'I could so easily turn you over to the police. Marcus wouldn't be able to do a thing about it. He's so crooked, he'd be glad to get you off his hands, don't you think? Now answer me, Patrick, how would you like to make a lot of money?'

She leant forward and helped herself to a bit of his buttery toast, licking each finger just like a cat when she had finished.

'How much, miss?'

She didn't hesitate. 'Hundred thousand, maybe more.'

Even his professionally immune face reacted to this suggestion. But why?

'And this is just for disappearing, is it, miss? No strings attached?'

'None. I just want you out of the way, that's all.'

'How do I know you can be trusted, miss, and that you won't do what you've threatened to do?'

'Because, Patrick, for all your faults – and let's face it, you're not exactly my sort of man – I've grown to like you these last few weeks. Yes, you're a bastard but only because he pays you to be. Let's just say that although we have nothing in common,' and she looked him up and down, 'we do have a common enemy and we both know who I mean. I want you out of here because before long our problem is going to be removed.' She fell silent while the possibilities of her suggestion sank in.

'I could help you, you know,' he said watching her closely. There were fine lines around her full lips that he hadn't noticed before.

'No,' she replied firmly. 'This is my battle. It has nothing to do with you. I just want you to go, that's all. For both our sakes.'

'But –'

'No, Patrick. You owe me nothing and there's no point your getting involved.'

347

He looked at her. She must be mad, but the confident smile in her eyes suggested she knew exactly what she was doing.

'When?' he asked.

'As soon as possible,' and she got up from the table and left the room. He remained seated. By the look on her face, he wouldn't put anything past her at the moment. A couple of minutes later, she was back. She placed a black oblong jewellery box on the table in front of him.

'Open it,' she instructed.

He did, glancing up at her as he did so.

'It must have cost him a good quarter-million,' she said. 'He gave it to me last year as a present. Mind you, it's a bit better than some of his other presents,' and she stopped. There was a strange quality to her voice which made him look at her. 'Do you know what I got for my seventeenth birthday?'

'No.'

She smiled. 'No, why should you? Nobody knows about that except me, him and the team at the clinic.' Her eyes were calm, her face without emotion. 'I got an abortion, Patrick. You see, he raped me and that time, I got caught.' She gave him a weak smile. 'Of course,' she added, 'it won't happen again, getting pregnant, I mean. I got an infection after the abortion, you see, so I was thoroughly screwed, as it were.'

There was a deathly hush. Patrick said nothing, his guts twisted with horror. She had said it so calmly, without bitterness or pain. She was unnaturally still, not a finger twitched, not an expression flitted across her face. She sat there in all her haunted beauty as though she were discussing the weather.

'He's been doing it for years, but then you knew that, didn't you?'

'No, miss.' He shook his head. 'No, I didn't.'

'Oh?' and she smiled, dismissing her mistake. 'That's

why I can't leave him, you see. It's why he won't let me go. He says . . .' and her hand flew to her mouth as she suddenly gagged. The moment passed and, once more composed, she continued. 'He says, that it doesn't really matter because I'm not his real sister and there's no blood tie between us . . .' Again she gagged. This time she took her time to settle down again. Beads of sweat had broken out across her brow and she had to breathe hard for several minutes. 'He would tell, you see. Everyone would know. It's how he keeps me in place or at least how he's done so up till now. But I've got him, you know.'

'How, miss?' Patrick watched her intently. Her words, her face, the things she was telling him – it was all too awful.

She squeezed her eyes together and then looked at him. 'I've . . . I've . . .'

'Here, miss, have another coffee,' and he poured one for her.

'Thank you.' She sipped her drink. 'He thinks I'm stupid, that I don't understand anything about business and I have to say that for a long time I did nothing to contradict that opinion.' She lit another cigarette. 'Then he told me I had to give up modelling and that's when I realized that if I was ever to be free of him, I had to do something to get him out of the way.'

'And?'

'Over the last two years, I have made it my business to know all of his business and everything that he's involved in, the police know about.'

'You what?'

'I'm the mole, if you like. I'm the one who's going to sink him.'

Patrick helped himself to one of her cigarettes. This was astonishing.

'How the hell did you do it? I mean, all his records, all . . . everything!'

She smiled, her eyes glazed as she stared out of the

window. 'Computers, Patrick, they're wonderful things, you know.'

'Jesus Christ.'

She pushed the jewellery box over to him. 'Take it. I don't want it now any more than I wanted it then. It's yours. Take it and do with it as you like. You must know someone who would be able to give you a good price for it.' She shuddered. 'Anything of his makes me want to throw up.'

He looked at the peerless gems that lay in the box. A string of the most perfect diamonds, all topped off with a huge sapphire in the middle. He didn't know what to say. He turned to her, stumbling for words. She held up a hand, silencing him.

'Forget it. I hate it and I've never worn it. He just buys me things like that because he thinks it will say sorry for everything. Well, it won't. I won't have it any more,' and she turned away, her cigarette burning fiercely as she inhaled for her very life.

He pushed the box over towards her.

'You don't need to buy me.'

Camilla turned around, her face taut.

'I'll stay. I can help you. I'll do whatever you want.'

She sat in stunned silence. He got up and went to take her hands in his.

'It must have been terrible for you living with him. What you said . . .' and he·shook his head. 'How any man can do that to a child doesn't bear thinking about.' He paused, searching for words. 'I know what he's like,' he said gently. 'I've watched him all this time and I've seen what he does, although I never realized how far he took things.'

Her hands were trembling in his, her face racked with pain. Then suddenly she spun away from him.

'No, I can't ask this of you. Couldn't possibly. Out of the question. Go away. I don't deserve your help – anyone's help. Don't you see?' she asked, turning back to him. 'I'm not worth anything. Nobody can help me,' and the agony in her face was almost too much for him.

He stood for a moment unsure of what to do. The only thing left for him was to go. If she didn't want his help, then he had no alternative. He strode from the room and when she turned back, her necklace was still on the table.

Ten minutes later, Patrick appeared with his holdall. He stood in the doorway.

'Yes?'

He was puzzled. 'Why now, miss?'

Camilla poured some more brandy into her cold coffee. She was worn out and yet there was still so much to do.

'Because . . . because, all my life I've had to do as I was told. I have been bullied again and again and again and I won't have it any more. Last night was the final straw.' Her voice was faint. 'Do you know what he said to me?'

'Who, miss?'

'Andrew. He said he didn't love me. Imagine that, eh?' and her small laugh was bitter.

'Happens to us all, miss.'

'Maybe, but I didn't want it to happen to me. I loved . . .' and her voice broke. She buried her face in her tightly clenched fists while yet again she fought to control herself. 'I . . . just wanted to be like any other woman. When I cried, I wanted someone to hold me; when I was sad, I wanted someone to cheer me up and when I laughed, I wanted someone to laugh with me. Someone who would love me and protect me and . . . He said – well, never mind what he said. Suffice it to say it was awful.' She looked at Patrick smiling wanly. 'Still, what else should I expect? No one's ever loved me, not really loved me. Usually it's just my money they're after. That's what the press always say. "Poor rich little Camilla Killington, so wealthy and still not married." If only they knew, eh?'

Patrick smiled ruefully. 'Well, miss –' but she wasn't listening.

'Know what I am really, Patrick?' she continued in the same tired monotone.

'What, miss?'

'I'm a C2 made good. That's what sociologists would call me. A C2 made good. My father was a publican, you know, who got a lucky break and after that, we never had to go without again.' She smiled brightly. 'Imagine that, Patrick. I'm just like you. Despite all my expensive clothes and holidays, and all my exclusive schooling, I'm nothing more than a bloody C2. We all know who we are really, and I know I'm a publican's daughter inside and all I want are the things ordinary women have. Being rich counts for nothing, does it, if no one loves you?' Her mouth wavered but she didn't cry. 'I thought I loved him, you know, but I don't matter to him at all. He turned me down and no one has ever done that before. It hurts, you know. It really hurts. I'm a nothing, a nobody and whatever that bastard of a brother of mine thinks, we never will be. It doesn't matter how much money we have or how many businesses, we haven't even got ordinary happiness out of our wealth.'

She stopped, seemingly running out of words. Then she turned and this time her voice was strong.

'Goodbye, Patrick, and take care, won't you?'

'Yes, miss, and by the way, Mr Killington wants The Grange because of a Roman hoard of coins that's supposedly hidden up there.'

She didn't look surprised. 'Well, he would, wouldn't he?'

'Marcus,' Camilla purred down the telephone.

'Camilla. And to what do I owe this unexpected pleasure?'

'I've found something for you.'

'What?'

'Something gold, old and Roman.'

Silence and she smiled to herself. It could all be so easy sometimes.

'Where?'

'At The Grange. I took the liberty of having a look for myself last night, given that you had so helpfully put the owner in hospital. Nice work by the way.'

'This is a surprise,' he said, suspicion still in his voice. 'What made you change your mind about him? I was beginning to get the impression that you were really falling for him.'

'Let's just say, Marcus, that I appreciate which side my bread is buttered.'

'Thank you, my dear. I do my best.'

'When are you coming to see it then?'

'How much did you find?' His voice had a familiar urgency to it. He was like a moth to a flame. He just couldn't resist it.

'I don't know altogether. I think it might be a good idea if we go there together, you know, have a really good search.'

'And what about Mann? Doesn't he matter any more?'

'No, Marcus, he doesn't. I was wrong to think that there could ever be anything between us. After all, he's so ordinary.'

Marcus smiled. 'My dear, at long last you're seeing the error of your ways. We may have had our differences, but we do have so much in common and it would be a shame to break it up, wouldn't it?'

'Yes, Marcus. It would.'

When she had replaced the receiver, she took a long hard look at herself in the mirror. She ran a finger thoughtfully around her reflection. After tomorrow she would be as free as a bird and then she could really begin to live. At last she would be a real ordinary person.

Twenty-two

'Who was that? Anyone for me?'

Sian shook her head. 'No, it was the vet. He's confirmed what he suspected. Sebi *was* poisoned.'

Helen's already pale face registered her shock. 'Who would do such a thing? Did he say what it was?'

'Some kind of arsenic. It appears that after a while, the toxic effects build up in the body until the animal just can't take it any more. That's when Sebi started to show symptoms. If it had gone on much longer, he would have died.'

Helen bit her bottom lip, her expression pensive. Sian was equally thoughtful.

'All this,' she muttered, 'all these things that have gone wrong for him. The mugging yesterday, the horses and that Camilla woman.'

Helen's eyes sharpened with anxiety.

'What about her?'

'Well, I didn't like to say before what with all the goings on and you not being here most of the time, but I saw her and my previous employer sharing an intimate moment, as they say.'

'Your previous employer?'

'Marcus Killington. He and Camilla must be in cahoots.'

Helen's face dropped. 'What do you mean?'

'Well, I don't know exactly but whatever he's up to, she's probably in it as well. Maybe that's why she's down here: she was acting as some kind of decoy.'

'But she can't be!' Helen was aghast.

'Why not? The pair of them were kissing right in front of me at Belvedere Cottage. They're in this together, whatever this is. I bet you anything. You don't know what Killington's like.'

'But maybe they're just friends or something?'

'Are you kidding?' and then Sian frowned. 'What does it matter? The thing is, it's a bit of a coincidence that things start to go wrong the minute she appears on the scene and then, lo and behold, she knows him, who always means trouble.'

Helen shook her head firmly. 'I don't believe a word of it. It's pure speculation.'

'Yes, well, what about the mess Andrew's in? And last night at The Grange, someone was poking about the stables. Blaize and I had to go down there and see what was going on because Sebi and Bracken were making one hell of a row, and do you know what I found? The pair of them wandering about the drive and their stable door hanging off its hinges. I'm telling you, Helen, something is going on.'

'Are you going to tell the police about it?'

'I don't know. I don't have any evidence and I can't go and make accusations until or unless I do.' She glanced at the wall clock. 'Come on, we've got to go. I promised Andrew I'd look after the horses. We've got loads of work to do this morning.'

'I can't,' said Helen, clearing away her empty coffee cup.

'What? But what about the stables?'

Helen turned round, her face impassive and her eyes unflinching. 'I can't, all right? I have something to do. You'll have to go by yourself. You'll be all right. Everything always is in your capable hands.'

'But you can't do this Helen! How on earth am I going to cope? What about the tourists?'

'Tell them to go home. Explain the situation. It will be okay. You'll have Eck to do all the heavy work. He'll do anything for you,' and she walked out of the room. Sian quickly followed.

'But where are you going?'

355

Helen bounded up the stairs two at a time. She didn't stop.

'I told you, I've things to do, important things that can't wait.'

'But don't you think your first loyalty is to the stables?'

She stopped at the top and turned round. All the pain and anguish that she had gone through showed in her eyes.

'Please, Sian, leave me alone,' she whispered, her voice cracking. 'Leave me alone.'

Sian followed her into the bedroom. 'Is this something to do with Darryl? Now look, Helen, you've got to tell me!'

Helen said nothing.

'Answer me. Is this about all the fights you two have been having because I don't see how this is the time to do something about it. Surely you can tackle it tomorrow?'

'Just shut up, Sian! Shut up and leave me alone, okay?'

There was a fraught silence. Sian was the first to break it as Helen packed a small case.

'Going away?'

'Yes.'

'Will you ring me?'

Helen shrugged. 'Maybe.'

'I suppose it's pointless me asking where or with whom?'

A glance was all that was needed to answer that question. When Helen was packed she took hold of Sian's hand.

'Do me a favour?'

'What?'

'Don't be angry with me. Please. It's not what you think.'

'What isn't? For goodness' sake, I don't know what to think about anything any more! Andrew's in hospital, Eck's acting strangely and just when I need help at the stables, you're taking off. Explain it to me, will you?' But, receiving no answer, she sighed and relented. 'Okay, what do you want me to do?'

'Tell Andrew I'm sorry. He might understand one day.'

'Sorry about what?'

'Just pass the message on, okay?'

'All right.' Helen picked up her case and left without a backward glance.

Sian's first job was to fetch Eck. She raced to his house with Blaize next to her in the Land Rover. Eck was just coming out. She screeched to a halt and ran over to him.

'Eck!'

He stopped by the gate and waited for her to reach him. He was smiling with his usual amiability.

'Eck, I've got some bad news for you.' She took hold of his hand.

'What's the matter?'

'Now you will be calm about this, won't you? There's no need to get upset.'

The big man nodded slowly, his face creased with worry.

'Andrew's in hospital. He's been beaten up.'

His face blanched. His harmless blue eyes immediately filled with tears, which rolled down his ruddy cheeks. He began to blub, sniffing noisily like a child.

'No, no, not Andrew. Not my Andrew!'

'Eck, don't cry.' Sian put her slender arm around his huge frame and tried to comfort him. 'He's going to be all right, Eck, honest he is. He doesn't look too well at the moment but, you wait, he'll be home soon.'

He pulled away from her, inconsolable, his huge shoulders shaking with grief.

'Eck, listen to me . . .'

'No! No! He's hurt my Andrew! He's hurt my Andrew!'

'Who has, Eck?' but he started to move away from her, half running across the street, not aware of what he was doing. A car coming along the road had to stop as he nearly ran into it.

'Eck!'

'Stupid great bugger!' shouted the angry driver out of the window. 'They ought to lock 'im away, the brainless idiot, back in the hospital where he belongs!'

'Shut up!' yelled Sian at the man. She ran on, desperate to get him back, but he was off across the fields and soon out of reach, his massive wellingtons clumping over the brown hillside, tears streaming down his face, and all the while calling Andrew's name.

'Eck! Eck!' She stood panting at the gateway. It was no good. He wasn't listening and try as she might she couldn't catch up with him. For a big man, he was surprisingly quick, and before long he had disappeared into a wood. She gave up and returned to the Land Rover. She sat disconsolately in the front seat trying to think what to do next. With Helen gone and Eck too distraught to comfort and Andrew in hospital, it was going to be left to her to sort things out.

'Well, Blaize,' and she turned to the big dog sitting next to her, 'it's just you and me now. Come on.'

She drove back up to The Grange. She suspected that Eck would reappear when hunger surpassed his distress, although his recent strange behaviour made him less predictable.

Twenty minutes later she pulled up at The Grange. During the night, when the horses had been disturbed, she had moved them to another stable, not stopping to examine the damage too closely. When she had left after breakfast she only briefly scanned the mess. Now was her first real opportunity to see what had happened. She got out of the Land Rover and walked along the cobbled yard.

'Good heavens!'

There was wood and plaster all over the place, littering the floor among the straw. Great jagged holes had been dug out of the plaster walls where the animals had kicked it, and there were deeply indented hoof marks where metal shoes had slid down the brickwork. Blaize sniffed the floor intently. There was something very interesting for him.

'They must have gone berserk.'

Sian knew that something must have triggered them off.

Maybe it was the poisoner again, trying to get at them. She shivered.

She walked around, picking up bits of wood from the floor and examining them, but they yielded no clues. It was all most odd.

'Time to go I think, Blaize. Come on, let's get the horses.'

She loaded Sebi and Bracken into the horsebox and set off for the stables. Both animals, whatever disturbance they had been through the previous night, were remarkably calm and unperturbed. Sian wished she was. She wasn't looking forward to telling Andrew what had happened since she had last visited him. She could only too easily imagine the kind of reception she was going to get from him.

Camilla arrived at the stables unexpectedly after lunch just as Sian was getting ready to visit Andrew. When Sian opened the cottage door and found herself face to face with the other woman, she was at a loss what to say, and shocked. Camilla's appearance was appalling. Gone were the expensively tailored clothes, the perfect makeup and the pristine hair. In their place stood a woman haggard, seemingly exhausted and by the look in those deep-set haunted eyes, quite manic.

'Can I come in?'

'Of course.'

Camilla brushed past without a word, puffing heavily on a cigarette. Sian could already smell the aroma of alcohol. She followed Camilla into the small sitting room.

'Tea?'

There was a brief nod.

'Please sit, Camilla. I'll only be a moment.'

'No,' came the urgent reply. Sian stopped in the doorway.

'Yes?'

'Don't bother with the tea. I'll just have a drink, if that's okay?'

'I don't know if Andrew has any. I'll just look.' She went away and looked in the kitchen cupboards. She found a half-full bottle of vodka and took that and a glass back to Camilla.

'Will this do?'

Camilla helped herself and drank greedily. After she had finished the first glassful, she poured out another. Sian watched her from where she sat. Was the whole of Leighford caught up in this maelstrom of emotion? she wondered.

Camilla refused to sit down, and paced up and down instead. Sian watched her steadily. Eventually she said, 'Why are you here, Camilla, and what do you want?'

Camilla stopped. There was a fearful expression in her eyes and it made Sian shudder.

'I . . . I don't really know,' and she laughed bitterly. 'Strange really, isn't it?'

'What is?'

'Life. You know, the people we meet, the men we fall in love with. The men who love us. Nothing ever goes quite as you plan it, does it?'

'Sometimes not. Sorry, but what is all this leading to? I've got lots of things to do today as Andrew isn't here and I –'

'Please,' interrupted Camilla, 'I need to explain, to talk. To tell you why. Won't you at least give me the chance to do that? I know you don't like me and quite frankly, I don't blame you, but nothing's as straightforward as it seems. There are reasons, horrible, horrible reasons which I . . . well, I'm too ashamed to talk about them, but please believe me when I say I had no choice in what's happened around here. It wasn't my fault.'

'What wasn't? You're not making sense. I don't know what you're talking about.'

Camilla scanned the room, her eyes seemingly searching for something – anything that might help her.

'Are you sure I can't get you some tea? Or a coffee perhaps?'

The fractured smile registered a brief thanks. 'No,' and she looked down into her glass. 'Drink is all I need. To get anaesthetized, you know.'

'Anaesthetized from what?'

'Oh, you don't want to know. No one does,' and she took a gulp of vodka. 'I have to do something,' she said, the words rushing out on top of each other. 'You see, I have no option. Things have been done which shouldn't have been done and it's up to me to stop them. To put the record straight.'

'What –'

'No,' snapped Camilla irritably, 'let me finish.' She inhaled deeply and brushed her untidy hair away from her anguished face. 'People sometimes hurt us when they think they're only loving us. Sometimes you don't realize it. It's what you're used to; it's what you expect.' She started pacing the floor again, wringing her hands. 'I'm one of those people. I thought – used to think – that all you had to do was have enough money and you could have anything and everything. Even people could be bought. Even love.' She went to stand by the window with her back to Sian. 'But it's not like that, is it?' When she turned round, Sian could see how much it hurt to admit that. 'People can't be bought. Love isn't like that.'

'I can't really answer that one,' ventured Sian wistfully, 'given my own mess.'

A ghost of a smile flitted across Camilla's face. 'He loves you,' she said suddenly.

'Who?'

'Andrew.'

'No, he doesn't.'

'Oh, he might not recognize it yet, but he does. You can take my word on that.'

'But I'm pregnant with another man's child!'

'But can't you see? He doesn't mind about that! That's inconsequential . . . It's you and only you he cares about. That's what real love is and it's what I've never had and never can have.' She sighed and added quietly, 'Pregnant. It's so ironic.'

Sian was bewildered. She could not make sense of anything she heard.

'I have to go now,' said Camilla brightly. 'Things to do and all that.' She came over to the startled Sian. 'Take care, and I wish you both the very best for the future,' and before Sian could say anything, she had left the room, there was the sound of the front door shutting, and then silence.

Helen hired a car in Plymouth and set out on her journey with grim determination. She knew what she had to do now that she realized the true extent of what she had been coerced into. Of all the stupid things she had done in her life, none had been as stupid as this. And all because of love. Blinded by her emotions, she had allowed herself to be used and abused in the vilest way imaginable. Now she had to make amends for it. He wasn't going to get away with it. By the time she had finished with him, she was determined he would never think of treating a woman like that again.

She cried while she drove along the motorway, tears blurring her sight, but she still kept going. They were tears of shame, of deep humiliation, tears that had welled up from a soul that had been subject to such contempt that it hardly knew it existed any more. She angrily wiped them away.

For once in her life, after all she had been through, she was going to exact a payment for services rendered. She didn't know how. She just knew she had to.

She found her destination without much difficulty. Quite by chance, she stopped at the village shop close to where he lived and as soon as she mentioned his name, the old lady behind the counter gave her directions. Everyone knew where he lived, she said. Him and his big house, but Helen didn't stop to hear the rest of it. She was impatient.

She had work to do. Twenty minutes later, she pulled up outside the large ornate gates. Her heart was pounding and she felt clammy with nerves. When she got out of the car, a stiff breeze was blowing, its chill cutting straight through her. She walked over to the gates and pressed a button.

'Yes?' answered a female voice, crackly over the intercom.

'I want to see Marcus Killington.'

'Do you have an appointment?'

'No, but I must see him.'

'I'm sorry,' said the plummy voice, 'but Mr Killington is not receiving visitors today.'

'But I've *got* to see him!' cried Helen. 'Please. Just let me talk to him.'

'I'm sorry,' repeated the intractable voice. 'You will have to make an appointment.'

'Oh, for God's sake! It's important. Don't you under-stand?' Helen was desperate.

'Mr Killington,' came the pleasant disembodied voice, 'is not in the habit of seeing anyone who turns up. They have to make an appointment first.'

'But I must see him,' insisted Helen, her voice on the edge of hysteria. 'I've got to speak to him. It's very important!'

'I'm sorry, Miss . . . Miss?'

'Tremlett. Helen Tremlett.'

'Ah, you're the young lady who's been trying to contact Mr Killington for the past few days?'

'Yes, so will he talk to me now?'

'I'm sorry, Miss Tremlett,' continued the polite voice, 'but Mr Killington has left strict instructions saying that he no longer wishes to communicate with you in any way and if you persist in trying to contact him, then unfortu-nately he will have no alternative but to resort to the law and you will be hearing from his solicitors. Goodbye,' and the intercom went dead.

Helen's shock was such that at first she didn't react, but then, with all the anger and violence inside her, she lashed out, smashing her fist against the wall.

'No, no! Please don't do this to me! Please!' she yelled, ignoring the pain. But only the wind heard her.

Hildegard was taking Mrs Killington her afternoon tea. The old lady was very ill now, the cancer spreading throughout her body steadily, choking off her life. All Hildegard had to do was to sit and wait for the inevitable.

She tapped on the bedroom door and then let herself in. The room stank of death. As each bodily process slowed down and eventually ceased, the internal rotting of Mrs Killington added to the miasma that hung like a pall in the air. Even keeping a window open did nothing to relieve it. Hildegard tried not to breathe through her nose.

'I have brought you some tea, Frau Killington,' she said cheerily as she walked towards the huge bed. As she approached, Sabre, the Yorkshire terrier, looked up from the counterpane and started to growl. He only left the bed when absolutely necessary. He also knew his mistress was dying and didn't want anyone near her, not even Hildegard.

'Be quiet, Sabre!' ordered Hildegard. 'I am here to do your mother some good so stop growling, you naughty boy,' and the dog did as he was told. 'Frau Killington . . . Frau Killington . . .'

Hildegard gently shook the old lady's skeletal shoulder. The eyes opened slowly, not registering anything. The irises were pale and the whites a greenish yellow. She tried to open her mouth, but her nonexistent lips were stuck together. Hildegard wiped them with a damp flannel.

'Frau Killington,' she whispered. 'I have some tea for you. Would you like to sit up?'

The shrunken woman, the entire bone structure of her grey face visible through her papery skin, nodded slowly. Hildegard helped prop her up on the mountain of pillows.

She poured out the tea and sat down on the side of the bed.

'How are you feeling, Frau Killington?'

'Same as ever,' came the weak reply and she winced as another spasm rent her insides. 'Bloody terrible!' she gasped.

As the pain subsided, the creases in her face softened. She held out her hand for the tea.

'You would like a biscuit?'

'No. Makes me sick. Don't want anything to eat.'

'But you must try and eat something, Frau Killington.'

The frail head shook slowly, eyes and mouth clamped shut. She was going to die the same way she lived, with determination.

Hildegard tutted, but there was nothing she could do. Mrs Killington was a very stubborn old lady.

'Where's Marcus?' she asked.

'He is away,' answered Hildegard. 'He left earlier. Business he said. He seemed very anxious about something.'

'Huh! Wasn't me, that's for sure. Couldn't give a damn about his old mother. I don't count for nothing in his world. Where's he gone then?'

'Devon, I think, to see Miss Camilla.'

The old face nearly broke into a smile and she closed her eyes. Her breathing was laboured, her voice growing quieter with every word she so painfully uttered.

'Camilla,' she repeated, 'always Camilla,' and then her eyes opened, flashing their venom. 'I never liked her, you know. Little hussy she is and always will be.' She turned to Hildegard and smiled briefly. 'I'm old,' she said, 'and I'm dying. I know it and you know it, so don't try and lie to me.'

Hildegard kept quiet. It was best to let the old woman say what she liked.

'Pass me that photograph of my husband, will you?' and a knobbly finger pointed to the dressing table. Hildegard fetched it and gave it to her. Mrs Killington held her hand.

'You've been good to me, Hilde, very good, and I hope you find what you're looking for.'

'But, Frau Killington, you haven't finished your tea yet.'

'Take it away. I don't want it now.'

'Will you want anything later?'

'Maybe, but leave me now. I'm tired.'

Hildegard cleared the tea away and quietly left the room. When she had gone, Mrs Killington held the photograph of her husband in her hands and looked at it.

Harry, her Harry. He wasn't that handsome, but he loved her, at least at the beginning before all the trouble started, before Camilla started up all her nonsense. The old lady could never believe those things Camilla said about him. How could he possibly do those horrible acts to his own daughter? It was ludicrous! She lied, that's what she did. The little madam lied just so someone would pay attention to her.

Tears squeezed themselves out of the corners of her eyes and rolled down over her temples into her sparse hair.

'You didn't do it, Harry,' she whispered. 'I know you didn't,' and she clasped the photograph to her breast.

When Hildegard next came to see her, the photograph was face down on her thin body, and the old lady was dead.

Twenty-three

Eddy and Rowena were at the local police station. Eddy was nervous and constantly fidgeted with his ring, twisting it round and round his finger. Rowena sat still, her smooth face reflecting the exact opposite of how she really felt. On the table in front of them were a folder of papers and a plastic box of floppy disks. It was all the evidence they needed to get Killington off their backs for a very long time.

Two detectives stood out in the corridor.

'We've been after this Killington for months now,' said one, sipping his coffee. 'Let's hope those two inside,' and he motioned with his nearly bald head, 'have something worth talking about.'

'Should do,' confirmed his colleague, 'his name's come up enough times in all that information that's been passed on to us.'

The first one finished his coffee and chucked the plastic cup in a nearby bin. 'Getting Killington would be a real feather in our cap,' he said, rubbing his hands together, 'so let's go and see what they've got to say for themselves.'

'We don't make deals, you know,' said the weary detective glancing from Eddy to Rowena and back again.

'We know, Officer,' said Rowena, and she looked at Eddy, her brow furrowed. He said nothing. 'It's just . . .' and she laid a hand on the folder, 'it's just that I thought it would be best for all concerned if Eddy, Mr Williamson, came down here and volunteered all the information he had,' and she smiled at them both. 'Didn't we, Eddy?'

He nodded firmly. He wished more than anything he

could be out of here and back at the hotel where he would help himself to a very large brandy. He was sweating furiously.

'And how would that be?' asked the older detective. His colleague sat a little way behind him and the pair of them looked suspicious. Eddy couldn't swallow. He tried but he just couldn't and his palms were wet. He wiped them yet again on the legs of his trousers.

Rowena took a deep breath. 'Eddy thinks he knows something about the drug smuggling that's been going on. In fact,' and she glanced hurriedly at Eddy for reassurance, 'he knows quite a lot about it because the whole business was arranged from Stoneygates Hotel and Mr Killington, our boss, is the man you want. He's the brains behind the operation. Eddy just did as he was told, didn't you, Eddy?'

There was little response from the two policemen. Plastic cups of cooling coffee stood in front of them on the table and a trio of cigarettes released their blue curling smoke up into the still air.

The detective picked up the folder. 'And it's all in here, the evidence?'

Eddy nodded. 'Yes.' It was the first word he had said since they had come into the room. He had been reluctant to go the police station, fearing that he would be the one to come off worst, but Rowena's persistent arguments for it had finally and decisively worn him down. All through the interview his legs twitched impatiently as though they couldn't wait to get him out of there — preferably at a gallop.

'Times, dates, shipments; the lot,' said Rowena. 'Everything you want, all the details, all the evidence, we have it.'

The detective pulled hard at his cigarette. 'Why have you decided to bring it in now?'

Rowena and Eddy glanced at each other.

'Two of your men came round the other day asking

questions.' Eddy paused. His heart was beating wildly. 'We just thought it . . . well . . .' and he dried up.

Rowena finished off for him. 'We just thought that if we co-operated with you then maybe you . . .'

'Would be lenient with you?'

'With Eddy,' she corrected him, smiling nervously. 'I had nothing to do with it,' she affirmed strenuously.

'That very much depends on how the Crown Prosecution Service regards all of this, although we would let them know, of course, how much you have helped us and it might make all the difference.'

Eddy's face was ashen. He knew he had done the wrong thing coming here, he just knew it. For once, he shouldn't have listened to Rowena. Her strident voice broke through his thoughts.

'Can I go now? Someone has to run the hotel, you understand, and I'm only here to offer my support to Mr Williamson.'

'No, no, Rowena,' said Eddy quickly, his face panic-stricken. 'You can't go. Not now.'

She removed his hand from her sleeve. 'But, Eddy, I don't know anything about any of this, and I'm sure the detectives here,' and she turned and smiled sweetly at the two men, 'would much prefer to talk to you alone. After all, sweetie, you're the one who knows all about it, not me.' She stood up. 'Is it all right then?' she asked.

The two detectives looked at each other.

'We'll be in touch,' said the older man.

'Don't worry,' Rowena said brightly to Eddy, her hand on his shoulder, 'I'll come and visit you. Bye.' But he only drooped further in his chair.

Sian arrived late at the hospital. It had taken her much longer than she had anticipated to sort out the stables and all the attendant problems. The vet had arrived shortly after Camilla's visit to confirm what he had said over the telephone earlier that morning. He needed to check over the horses, especially Bracken and Sebi. Announcing them both fit and well, although in need of a rest, Sian told him of the previous night's events and of Helen and Eck's disappearance.

The vet stroked his chin and looked pensive. 'Mmm,' he said, seeing how worried she was, 'try not to get too upset about it, my dear. Eck's done this before. He's a simple chap, as we all know. However, he'll come back. He always does. Last time he spent three days living in an old barn on the other side of the reservoir. If you're really bothered about him, I could go and look.'

'Oh, would you?' she gushed with relief. 'I'm sure Andrew's going to be upset about it when I tell him, and all this business is playing havoc with my nerves.'

'I'll go and try to find him after my next call. It shouldn't be too difficult.'

'Thanks,' and she patted Sebi's neck. 'You know, it's not like Sebi to go berserk like he did. He wouldn't destroy the place unless he'd been upset about something.'

'Very strange,' agreed the vet. 'Maybe he was just playing up because of something else.'

'What?'

'Well, my dear,' he said, packing away his bag, 'it's not unusual for a stallion to get a bit strange when there is a mare in season around.'

'You don't think then that it might be our poisoner?'

'Maybe. Although The Grange is rather less accessible than here, and the poisoner would have to be very determined. But I rather feel it was probably just a case of Sebi and Bracken getting to know each other in the biblical sense. I take it you don't mind if she's in foal?'

'No, not really. Sebi's a fine-looking horse, aren't you, boy, and Bracken would make a good mother.'

'Well, in that case I don't think we have anything to worry about. Just keep a close eye on them both, okay?'

Then Sian had to cancel all the bookings for the foreseeable future. She was on the telephone for ages. She also tried ringing the cottage to see if Helen had come back, but there was no answer. She was not surprised. After a snatched sandwich for lunch, she finally set off for the hospital.

She found Andrew in a general surgical ward where he had been moved after his night in the recovery room. If anything, he looked worse now than he had the previous evening, as all his bruises had come out and his cut flesh was horribly swollen. He lay on the bed with his eyes closed, oblivious to the outside chatter and noise of the other patients. Sian pulled up a chair and sat down, her stomach churning. Where did she start first?

'Hi.'

He slowly opened his painful eyes and smiled carefully so as not to break the angry scabs around his mouth.

'I hate hospitals, you know,' he said quietly. 'They've got that smell about them that you never forget.'

'Been in one before then?'

'A long time ago now.' His face, despite its wounds, was gentle.

'How are you feeling?' she asked softly.

He didn't answer but closed his eyes.

'That bad eh?'

'Yes,' he whispered.

'I've brought you something to eat. Only some grapes, and I don't think you'll be able to manage them for some time yet.'

'Thanks,' he lisped.

She looked him over. There appeared to be bruises everywhere, large, black and blue ones covering his body along with the bandages around his broken ribs.

'Does it hurt or is that a stupid question to ask?' she asked, wishing she could feel the pain for him. He looked so pathetic lying there with all his dressings. Her heart went out to him.

He nodded slowly and grimaced. 'What do you think?'

'Shall I get a nurse?' she offered. 'Do you need some more painkillers?'

'No.' He paused with the effort and then said, 'The horses? Are they okay?'

'Yes, they're fine,' she began and looked down at her hands. It was no good. She had to tell him, to get it out of the way.

'But . . . ?' He knew that something was up. He could tell by her attitude.

She took a deep breath. 'Eck and Helen have gone. They both vanished this morning.'

'What? Together?'

She shook her head. 'No, not together. Helen left after breakfast. She wouldn't tell me where or why and then when I went to fetch Eck . . . well, he just took off.'

'You told him about me?'

'Yes. I didn't know he was going to take it so badly. He just burst into tears and off he ran. Up the road, into a field and gone. He nearly got run over by some nutter because he wasn't looking where he was going.'

'Oh God,' came the groan from the bed.

'I tried to stop him, honestly I did, but it was no use. He wouldn't listen. Once I'd told him about you being in hospital, he just got so worked up and he kept muttering something about, "He's hurt my Andrew." You don't know who he could have been talking about, do you?'

'No idea.'

'Well, now what? The vet's offered to go look for him and he said not to worry too much. Apparently, he's done this sort of thing before.'

'Yes, that's right. Some time ago now. We found him after a few days. Stupid great idiot!'

'He's very fond of you, you know,' and she smiled. 'I'm sure he won't be missing for too long. He likes his food too much.' Telling Andrew hadn't been anywhere near as bad as she had feared. She decided to take advantage of his good mood.

'About the horses,' she said, 'I looked after them last night so you've nothing to worry about except that . . .'

He quickly glanced at her. 'Now what?'

'It's nothing really,' she assured him. 'Something or someone upset Sebi, that's all, and he's caused a bit of damage to his stable. It's nothing that can't be fixed. I've left Blaize looking after them all, given there's no one else to help out. They'll be okay, really they will. The vet says so.'

'You could really do with Helen now. It's not right, you know. She shouldn't have left you with all of it.'

'She said she had something to see to, although she did ask me to pass on a message.'

'What?'

'She said she was sorry and that maybe one day you would understand.'

He stared up at the ceiling. 'Oh God,' he said quietly. 'You know why, don't you?'

'Why?'

'She poisoned the horses.'

Sian's whole body suddenly went cold. 'What? Don't be ridiculous! Of course she hasn't!'

'She poisoned the horses, I tell you. She must have done. It's the only thing I can think of.'

'Surely not! For what possible reason?'

'I don't know, but why else should she apologize?'

'But I can't believe that she would do that. She couldn't. No way. She loved those horses.'

They fell into a thoughtful silence while they considered the possibility.

'By the way, I saw Camilla here last night,' she said, watching carefully for his reaction.

'Won't see her again,' he announced. 'Not after what I said to her.'

'Did you have a row then, because when I saw her in the car park, she looked terrible?'

'Oh. Well, maybe I said . . . God, I can't remember. I

was practically stoned out of my head last night. The pain-killers, you know. I really can't remember much about anything.'

'She came to the stables this morning.'

'And?'

'When she got inside the cottage, she started mumbling about all kinds of things. I don't know what she was on about and to be honest, I'm a bit concerned about her. She didn't look at all her normal self.'

'I can't remember what she said last night,' he said, 'but I'm pretty sure we had words.' He paused and then, 'I'm . . . well, I'm sorry about her.'

'Don't have to be. You're a free man. You can do as you like.'

'I know but . . . well, it's not like that, is it? And we both know it.'

'No need to explain now, Andrew. We can talk about it when all this mess is sorted out.' She helped herself to a grape and popped it into her mouth. It stopped her from saying anything foolish. She wasn't sure but maybe there would be a time for them after all.

'Have the police been?' she asked, relieved to be changing the subject.

'I couldn't tell them anything. Didn't see anything. It all happened so fast. But never mind me,' he said with a smile. 'How are you and your bump in all of this? Typical me, always thinking of something else when I should be thinking of the really important things.'

She grinned. 'Well, we're fine,' and she rested her palm over her belly.

'Good. Don't want anything happening to either of you.'

'Nothing will. We'll still be there when you come home.'

'Good.'

Her face was serious. She ought to be happy, but there was something she had to settle with him, something he might find difficult to accept. She took a deep breath.

'Andrew?'

'What?'

'I have something to tell you. Something I should have told you a long time ago.'

He frowned at the seriousness in her voice. 'Confession time? Don't tell me, but you're madly in love with the cream of British manhood, Billy?'

She laughed. 'No, no, don't be silly!' and then her smile faded. 'This is far worse than that.'

'Oh dear. Go on then; spit it out. It can't be worse than anything you've already told me.'

'Actually, I think it might be. Camilla was seeing some-one else while you and her were . . . well, while you were giving her lessons.'

'And?'

'That other person was Marcus Killington, my old boss from the hotel.'

'Do I know him? They must be related. What exactly is the connection?'

'You'd remember him if you'd met him. You wouldn't forget someone like that. I saw the pair of them kissing one day at Belvedere Cottage. I tried to tell you several times, but, well, the time never seemed right, and anyway, it was none of my business, was it?'

He ran his hand lightly over his mouth, feeling the raw flesh beneath his fingers.

'I don't suppose,' she said, 'that the horses being ill had something to do with him?'

'Why should it?'

'Because if you had something that he wanted, he'd do anything to get it. Camilla started taking lessons and suddenly so many things have gone wrong for you.'

'But what have I got?'

'I have worked for him for four years and I never have liked him. He gave me the creeps. He's into property and all that sort of thing. He's very wealthy. Owns lots of race horses.'

'But I have no interest in Thoroughbreds.'

'Suppose, though, that he wanted to get at you, what better way than poisoning Sebi?'

'But why?'

'It could be anything. Killington's business interests stretch far and wide. He owns a number of hotels of which Stoneygates is one of the smallest, and The Grange would make a fine hotel.'

'You know, at the beginning of the summer I found this man, a stranger, walking around The Grange. We had this, well, robust exchange of views, if you like, but I don't remember his being called Killington. What does he look like?'

'Tall, dark and handsome. Very suave, extremely self-confident. Drives a dark blue Rolls.'

'Oh God, it was him!'

'There you are then. That's why all this has happened. He's the one behind it all. He's the one to blame for the horses being ill.'

'And he used Camilla to get to me?'

' 'Fraid so.'

'Oh hell! This is terrible!'

'You've not seen him since?'

'No. I threw him out and that was that, or so I thought.'

'I wonder where he is now.'

'And what he's doing.'

'Look, I'd better go, Andrew. There's so much to do — the horses, Helen, Eck.'

'Of course, and Sian?'

'Yes?' She was standing up and ready to go.

'Thanks for everything.'

She smiled. 'Think nothing of it. You're a friend and I couldn't stand by and not help. I'll see you later, okay?'

Out in the car park was Killington. Sitting in his Rolls Royce, he watched the former manageress of Stoneygates open the Land Rover door and drive off. When he was certain she was quite out of the way, he got out and walked over to the hospital building.

'How very touching,' were the first words Andrew heard. He had been dozing, the result of yet another pain-killer. He turned towards the strangely familiar voice.

'Mr Killington, I presume?'

'I saw Mrs Williamson in the car park. A very beautiful young lady. No doubt she was here to offer her con-dolences?'

'None of your bloody business and what's more, you stay away from her.'

Marcus pulled out a chair. 'May I?'

'Do I have any choice?'

'I wondered how long it would take you to work things out,' said Marcus, taking off his jacket and seating himself. 'I must say, I thought you were more of an adversary than that.'

'Cut the crap, Killington, and get to the point. What have you come here for and what do you want?'

The two men stared at each other with real antipathy.

'You were behind it all, weren't you?'

'Behind what?' smiled Marcus, looking so debonair in the hot, busy ward. He wrinkled his nose with distaste when the cries of another patient echoed down the ward.

'My . . . recent misfortunes,' said Andrew carefully.

'And what makes you think that I am responsible for that? Surely, if you were a capable enough businessman, then none of these things might have happened.'

'I am a capable businessman!' retorted Andrew. 'I've just had a bit of bad luck, that's all.'

'Really?'

'Of course,' added Andrew, 'it's not helped when persons unknown try to poison my prize stallion or when persons unknown beat me senseless in a pub toilet and leave me for dead.'

'In that case,' answered Marcus with a smile, 'might I suggest that you take a bit more care? That way, these things wouldn't happen. Of course, if you're suggesting in any way that I might have had something to do with these

377

. . . tragic events, then I will take great exception to such scurrilous remarks and will fight you tooth and claw in court if needs be.'

'I don't have to, Killington. I know shit when I see it and you're it. Make no mistake about that.'

'Really, Mann, personal insults do you no credit at all.'

'Like I said, get to the point and then maybe the nurse can open a window round here.'

Marcus lifted his briefcase onto his lap and opened it. He took out some papers and shuffled them before closing the case and resting the papers on the top. He then looked up at Andrew.

'You're a hard man to keep track of, Mann.' He looked down at the papers again. 'It seems you had reason to vanish for a number of years and none of my associates could find any trace of you anywhere. I wonder why that was?'

Andrew ignored the jibe.

'Well,' he continued, 'to put it bluntly, I want The Grange. I intend to get it and am prepared to make you a reasonable offer. It will be my only offer and given the perilous state of your finances . . .'

Andrew glared at him.

'Oh yes, Mann,' smiled Marcus, 'I have my people all over the place. Mr Dunk, who runs the finance company you have used, is a useful contact of mine. The little people always are, you know, and just because I'm a successful man, it doesn't mean to say I've lost touch with the common herd. Anyway, back to business. As I was staying, you're really in no position at all to keep your business in one piece and if you wish to avoid the ignominy of becoming a bankrupt, then I can help.'

Andrew flexed the fingers of his bandaged hand. He knew exactly what he would like to do to Killington's self-satisfied face.

'You can't prove anything,' said Killington softly, with all the friendliness of a praying mantis, 'so do yourself a favour and accept my terms. It would be much better for you.'

'And if I don't?'

Marcus sat back in his chair and smiled. 'Let me put it this way,' he drawled. 'If you don't co-operate, then that dear little Sian will find out all about your conviction and sentence.'

Andrew's face hardened. 'How the hell –?'

Marcus held up a silencing hand. 'No wonder I couldn't find any trace of you. Three years for reckless driving? And you a top-class international saloon car racer? Most unfortunate,' he said, shaking his head. 'Tut-tut. Tell me,' he taunted, 'what was it like attending your wife and daughter's funeral knowing full well that you had killed them?'

The next few moments caught Marcus completely unawares. Enraged, Andrew, wounds notwithstanding, leapt out of bed and straight at Marcus's throat.

'You fucking bastard! I'll kill you! I'll bloody well kill you!'

Nurses ran from all directions, quickly followed by a burly security man who came racing down the ward and waded into the mêlée. It all ended as quickly as it had begun, with Andrew being forcibly restrained and helped back to bed on one side of the room and Marcus being looked after on the other side.

'I don't know what came over him,' explained Marcus, now installed in the matron's office, straightening his tie as the staff nurse and the security man sat anxiously listening. 'But he seemed to get very upset about something.'

'Would you like a cup of tea, Mr Killington?'

'Yes, please.'

In the ward, Andrew lay still as the nurses tucked him in and examined his dressings.

'Really, Mr Mann, a patient in your position and with your injuries shouldn't behave like that. This is a hospital, not a boxing ring.'

'And such language too!' admonished the nurse, her pleasant face creased with annoyance. 'I do have other patients in here and I don't suppose they were very impressed with your behaviour either.'

'There's nothing wrong, Staff,' said the junior nurse. 'Just some dressings need to be replaced.'

'Count yourself very lucky, Mr Mann. Your stitches could easily have burst.'

Andrew lay still while the nurses fussed over him. He felt dead; numb, empty. All this time and no one had known about Emma and Victoria until Killington. Andrew didn't care about him knowing of the prison sentence – that was simply a fact, but to mention their names, the names of the two most precious people in his life, the ones he had held most dear, was almost blasphemous. He would have torn the man's throat out if someone hadn't stopped him. His eyes filled with tears as the past came flooding back.

It was a hospital just like this one where it had all happened. Odd how hospitals, wherever they are, always look and smell the same.

The first thing he noticed when he came to was the smell: disinfectant. He blinked a few times, trying to get his eyes into focus. The white walls of the room swayed before him, the light above him swinging to and fro as he tried to concentrate. He tried to remember where he was and then he became aware of the pain in his leg, skewers of sharp agony piercing his flesh. He tried to speak but couldn't. His mouth was hellishly dry and he badly needed a drink.

Then he saw the drip in his arm. Hospital. He was in hospital. A chilling panic began to swamp him and his heart raced. He felt sick. Emma, Vicky – where were they? Bit by bit, he began to recall those fateful events.

A crash. There had been a crash. He could vaguely remember now. His wife screaming and his daughter yelling. Then there were flashing blue lights and someone pulling at him while the bright sparks of an acetylene torch hissed and spat nearby. Voices – calm, collected and then nothing.

His eyes shot open. He remembered it all now, and a cold certainty began to overwhelm him.

'Nurse! Nurse!'

Finally someone came, a pretty young starched woman oozing quiet efficiency. She stood next to the bed and checked his drip.

'How do you feel, Mr Mann?'

'A drink,' he whispered hoarsely. She helped him to some water.

'My wife; my daughter – where are they? Are they all right?'

She was giving nothing away. 'The doctor will be here in a moment. She'll tell you all about it.'

His heart ceased its frantic pumping. They must be all right then, he reasoned, because if they weren't then surely she would have said something?

She smiled briefly after writing something on a chart at the foot of his bed, then left the room.

Andrew stared at the ceiling, making a deal with himself and whoever he thought might be listening. He would do anything, he told himself, anything at all just so long as Emma and Vicky were all right. He would give up driving even, only they must be all right. They *must*.

The door opened and his heart started pounding again. This time it was the doctor. She came over to the bed and took his arm in her cool dry hands.

As he looked into those compassionate grey eyes of hers, he knew all he had to know. The certainty of it overwhelmed any hope.

'We did everything we could,' she said gently, 'but it was hopeless, I'm afraid. Their injuries were too extensive.'

A crashing coldness ran through his heart, ripping at his insides, shutting off everything around him and in an instant, his world fell apart.

He tried to speak but the words wouldn't come. Such a waste; such an appalling stupid waste, and all of it was his fault.

'If it's any comfort, Mr Mann,' came the doctor's soft voice through the blur of his emotions, 'I doubt if they had any idea what hit them. They would not have suffered. They were both deeply unconscious when they came in and never came round.'

He lay quite still, gazing at the white, white ceiling. He blinked slowly, knowing yet hardly daring to believe. They were dead? It was impossible. They couldn't be. They were with him in the car and he spoke to them and held their hands. They couldn't be dead.

'Are you quite sure?' he asked.

She nodded and squeezed his forearm. 'Yes, I'm quite sure.'

He shook his head, his eyes clenched shut. He didn't want to hear this. It wasn't true. It couldn't be true.

'Your leg . . .' she began.

'Don't care,' he muttered through clenched teeth.

'Please, Mr Mann, you've been through a terrible shock and I know how awful it must be for you but –'

'How the hell can you know?' he yelled. 'How? How? I've just killed my wife and my . . . oh God! . . . my . . .' and the words faltered as he choked on his grief.

His daughter, beautiful little Vicky. Ten months old and her whole life ahead of her, and he had snuffed it out. One minute there, the next gone. Wiped clean. Obliterated.

The doctor was speaking but he wasn't listening. All he could think of was his wife and daughter and the terrible, terrible realization that he would never, ever see them again.

'Where are they?' he asked in hushed tones.

'The mortuary.'

'I want to see them. I must.'

She looked at him, her eyes grave. 'Are you quite sure?'

'I want to see them, okay?' he demanded. 'Please, I want to.'

'I'll see what I can do,' and the doctor left the room.

No more smiles, he thought as he lay there staring out of the window, no more of anything. The days would be empty, the nights lonely and all because of his selfishness. He would never see his daughter grow up into a beautiful woman; never see any more birthdays and Christmases . . . He closed his eyes as the tears rolled down his face. It was a future of such blank, silent emptiness that he hardly dare think of it.

The door opened and there stood a porter, a young chap, thin, greasy, his hair a black quiff over his high forehead. He smiled cheerily.

'I've come to fetch you, mate,' but Andrew said nothing.

The wheelchair journey down to the bowels of the hospital, along endless corridors of official white and green, underneath rows and rows of strip lighting with people chattering in the background, all seemed unreal to Andrew. He felt strangely detached from it all as the porter wheeled him along, softly whistling to himself.

A lift came and went and soon they found themselves alone in a quiet room with two beds in front of them. There was silence. All Andrew could hear was the beating of his own heart.

'Shall I stay?' asked the porter.

Andrew didn't answer him. How could he when underneath those sheets were his wife and daughter who only a couple of hours ago were living, breathing, smiling, laughing people; the two people he loved more than his own life?

'Mr Mann?'

'What . . . ?'

'Do you want me to go?'

Andrew shook his head. It didn't matter any more. Nothing did. If the porter saw his tears, so what?

'Push me over, will you?'

The figure beneath the sheet was his wife. He hesitated before he pulled away the material. There was something so definite, so permanent, about seeing her that he wanted to delay the inevitable because when he did finally do it, there would be no going back. He would have seen her dead, would know her to be dead and would remember her as dead. He pulled the sheet back.

He gasped.

She was white. There was no colour, no blood, no nothing. It had all gone. Everything that had been her – her voice, her smell, her warmth, her touch – had completely and irrevocably left her.

He stared, stripped bare of all his thoughts, his mind, his emotions.

'Emma . . . Em . . .' but he couldn't go on. What was there to say now? He pulled the sheet back over. He turned to the porter and pointed to the other bed. There was much worse to see yet.

Her small figure, once so full of promise, and life, lay as still and as cold as marble on the bed, the sheet covering her. He wanted to see her, to see what he had done, but something was stopping him. He clenched and unclenched his fists, steeling himself. He wondered where was he going to find the strength to cope with it when he no longer had any reason to be strong. It was for them he drove himself to the edge of his life each week; for them he got up and went out and raced round and round a race track, defying and cheating death with impunity. Ironic, then, that it should be they who died first. He took a deep breath and pulled back the sheet.

At first, he wouldn't have known she was dead. She just looked asleep. She lay as she would do in her cot – serene, calm, at peace with the world, except she wasn't. Her golden eyelashes lay against her cheeks as they always did.

He stretched out his hand and as gently as he could, laid it tentatively against her face.

'My poor, poor baby,' he whispered. 'What on earth have I done to you both?'

After weeks, months, years even, he could recall in minute painful detail exactly what his wife and baby daughter looked like. They were memories that would haunt him for the rest of his days.

There were tears on his cheeks now. Someone was talking. Andrew pulled himself back to the present to see Killington was standing next to his bed.

'Ready to do business now?'

Twenty-four

The telephone call had been direct. She was to go to The Grange. Camilla was long used to Marcus's behaviour; to his orders, his bullying, his temper. There was nothing he did that surprised her any more.

She sat in front of the dressing table in her bedroom at Belvedere Cottage and idly smoked a cigarette. She looked and felt exhausted. She couldn't remember the last times she had slept or was completely sober. All she could feel and all she was aware of, was the gaping hole that had torn itself open inside her; a hole that hurt more than she could ever imagine, and it wouldn't go away.

'A drink,' she told herself, unsteadily pouring a large brandy. She then dipped her finger into some cocaine that lay in a piece of foil and licked it off. Even that didn't work any more. Nothing did.

She studied her reflection and smiled wryly. Such a beauty, she thought. Men couldn't get enough of her once, but not now. Her eyes were lacklustre, their colour dimmed and reddened by so little sleep. Her skin looked dull and unhealthy and there were even faint lines beginning to show around her lips. Such a mess. Where had it all gone? What had happened to her?

She inhaled and blew the smoke out of pursed and dry lips. She didn't know and she didn't care. There was no meaning to her life any more and if that was the case, then it didn't matter what she did. No one would care, least of all the man she once cared for the most.

Andrew; his words – she would always remember his words. They kept pounding through her brain and nothing would stop them. No alcohol, no drugs, nothing. Rejected,

386

said her mind. You are rejected, rejected, rejected . . . The word lashed her like a whip, making her writhe under each blow. How could he say such a thing? She loved him. Didn't he see that? She could help him – save his business, save his whole future – but he didn't want to know.

She blinked in the sunlight. Autumn was in the air now. There was a changed smell to everything up here on the moor, a slow decaying smell. All around her, life was coming to an end. It seemed entirely appropriate.

She glanced at her watch, time to move. Even in her despair she was aware that she had to get organized. There were things to do, a bath to run, some clothes to sort out, her makeup to fix. Whatever happened this afternoon, she had to get it right. She would only have one chance and she wasn't going to mess this up like she had everything else.

An hour later she stood in front of the mirror and surveyed herself objectively. Yes, Marcus would like what he saw. He would like it very much. Dressed in a long skirt of the finest wool with a silk blouse and jacket, she looked as beautiful as always. She took out her lipstick and added some final colour, pressing her full lips together and carefully wiping away the excess from the corners. She then ran her fingers through her newly washed hair. A spray or two of perfume and she was finally ready. She and Marcus had an appointment, one that was long overdue, and she couldn't possibly let herself down.

'You stupid bastard, Marcus. Whatever made you think you would get away with it?' she asked standing before the mirror, watching her cold, cold eyes. They remained as brittle as always, all life having been knocked out of them.

She turned away and picked up her handbag, opened it and checked the contents. Everything was there. She made her way downstairs and was about to open the door when it was suddenly opened from the other side. Startled, she leapt back, dropping her handbag and spilling the contents. Patrick stood in the doorway.

They said nothing and then both of them looked at the floor. There, in amongst all the usual things that women carry in their bags, was a handgun. Patrick knelt down and picked it up. He held it up in front of her face.

'You were thinking of using this?'

She snatched at it but he was too quick.

'What the hell are you doing, woman? This piddly little effort wouldn't knock out a fly.'

'Give it to me!'

He walked past her into the lounge and threw his holdall on the floor. She followed him through.

'What are you doing here anyway? Changed your mind about the necklace, have you? Because if you have, it's too late.' She helped herself to a drink. He saw that her hands were shaking.

'I'll have one, if you don't mind, and then you're going to sit down and hear me out.'

She looked at him suspiciously. 'Why?'

'Because, Camilla, if anyone knows what to do round here, it's me and as my Gran always said, if a thing's worth doing, it's worth doing well. Now, hand me that drink and sit.'

She did as she was told and listened.

'You and me,' he began, 'we both have our reasons for eliminating Killington.' He paused and looked into his glass. 'Of course,' he added quietly, 'what he did to you was . . . well, bloody diabolical, but he didn't treat anyone else much better either. Screwed us all one way or the other.' He finished his drink and set it down on the table. 'It's like this: I know you don't think too much of me . . .'

She shot him a wry glance.

'. . . well,' and he pulled his bottom lip, 'it's awkward. I don't know how to say this.' He shyly looked at her. 'Do you know what I'm trying to say?'

'You'll kill him for me if I go away with you?' Her voice was tinged with ice.

'No, no,' and then he stopped abruptly. 'You've got it wrong. It's not that at all. I don't want to own you like he did. I want you to be free, to come and go when you want, to trust me even if it's just a little bit.' He paused and then smiled. 'I love you, Camilla. Always did although I didn't realize it until I was on the motorway and then, well, I just had to come back. You see, I couldn't leave you behind – not after what you said, not after what he'd done to you.'

She stared at him, her eyes brimming.

'I know that probably you don't feel the same,' he gave a small laugh, 'I know for sure you don't, but you might, one day, and then who knows? Maybe, just maybe you'll come to feel the same way about me as I do about you. But I want you to know, Camilla, that whatever happens, you're free to do as you want. I won't stand in your way. What d'you say? Of course, I don't have much but I'll get by. I always have done in the past.'

She blinked a couple of times and then slowly looked around the room as if she were looking back over her life. Suddenly, it all seemed so different.

'You know,' she began, her voice uneven, 'when I was a little girl, I used to dream of someone coming along and rescuing me and taking me away from Marcus and my father. Silly really,' and she smiled as tears spilled down her cheeks. 'Who would have thought it?'

'Is that a yes then?'

She nodded. She had nothing to lose.

Marcus was standing on the battlements of The Grange gazing out across the acres of wood and moorland that stretched before him.

He so enjoyed the feeling he got when he knew he had won. He breathed in the fragrant air. A few spots of rain were beginning to fall and a strong wind was getting up but it didn't spoil his triumph. Barring the paperwork and the legal technicalities, The Grange, the stables and all the land were his. Most of it he didn't care for, as it was of no use to him, but The Grange was. Somewhere in here, maybe under the floorboards, maybe hidden behind a wall, were the things he most wanted. The Warrener Hoard. Thousands and thousands of pounds' worth of the finest Imperial Roman gold and jewellery. Soon it would all be his. Even if he had to tear The Grange down brick by brick, he would find it. He just knew it was here. He could smell it, and he had to have it. Gold for him was his addiction and like an addiction, he could never be satisfied. He wanted more and more. This was his way, and he was as powerless to deny his need as any addict with his fix.

There was something else to celebrate as well. He finally had the name of the company traitor, the one who had so badly let him down and come so near to destroying him and everything he had worked so hard to build up over the years.

Camilla. His dear, dear stepsister. At first he hadn't wanted to believe it but gradually, as the evidence was pointed out to him, it became so convincing that he just had to. He had been upset but not seriously so. He was a pragmatist, a realist, and he knew that there was only one way to safeguard his future and that was to get rid of her. This meeting would be their last.

Marcus slowly made his way back to the attic door. He would move his operations down here as soon as possible, he decided, which might take the heat off things. After all, the greater distance there was between him and London, the more privacy he had. It shouldn't be too difficult to sort things out with the police. He'd paid for their co-operation in advance, just as he had with his contacts in parliament. A few words in the right ears, a bit of blackmail to fall back on, and he saw no reason why he shouldn't have everything as it used to be.

Camilla, of course, would have no idea about this and,

although she knew what he had shown himself capable of, it would never occur to her that he would kill her. It was only natural that she would get infatuated with Mann, which was another reason why she had to go. All her previous men had meant nothing, but Mann did, and no amount of Camilla's lying over the telephone would convince him otherwise. He just knew her too well. It was a pity really, but he saw no other alternative.

He heard a noise from downstairs. A door shutting. It must be Camilla. She must have come up another way.

'Camilla!' he called. There was no answer. He bounded down the stairs, two at a time. 'Camilla!' But still there was no answer. And then he saw why. A huge man, one he had seen once before, was standing in his hallway.

'I don't know who you are or what you want,' Marcus said coldly, 'but you will leave this minute otherwise I shall have to call the police.'

Eck didn't move. He just stared. The lights in the hallway were dim and with so little furniture and a high vaulted roof, every sound was echoed. Marcus shivered.

'Get out of my house,' he snarled. Still no movement. He advanced slowly. Eck stood his ground, his simple face impassive.

'I'm warning you for the last time, you oik, MOVE IT!'

Eck stepped back, the sheer force of Marcus's voice catching him unawares, but then he stopped.

'You shouted at Helen,' he said slowly. 'Eck saw you.'

'I beg your pardon? What business is it of yours if I did?'

Eck wrung his huge hands together and his face contorted with pain.

'Helen Eck's friend,' he whispered. 'You hurt her. Eck saw. You hit her. Made her cry.' His lips quivered. 'She made Eck promise. Say nothing. Mustn't say nothing.'

'That's enough!' yelled Marcus. 'I won't stand for this any more! How dare you come into my house and accuse me of such obscene behaviour! No one, you understand, absolutely no one, talks to me like that. You're trespassing

391

and I am going to call the police. Someone should put you away where you so obviously belong!' He marched past Eck to the telephone, picked up the receiver and started to dial.

'No,' said Eck, 'please don't. Eck doesn't want to go back to hospital. Please don't!'

But Marcus was in no mood for mercy.

'Please don't!' cried Eck. 'Don't! Eck'll have to stop you!'

'BE QUIET!' yelled Marcus, his face red with fury.

'Eck doesn't want to hurt you, doesn't want to hurt you. Please stop . . .'

Marcus ignored him, continued dialling. Then as Eck became more insistent he pushed him away, and that was as far as he got.

Eck's massive forearm, hugely muscled from years of hard manual labour, grabbed him around the throat and started to squeeze.

'AH . . . AH . . . AH!'

Marcus tore frantically at Eck's arm, gasping and choking for breath but the hold only got tighter.

'You hurt Eck's friends. Helen and Andrew. You shouldn't have done that. No one should hurt Eck's friends.'

Marcus's struggling became more intense, but for Eck, built like a giant oak, it was nothing. He stood in the hallway, dressed in his blue overalls and wellingtons, bits of straw and grass stuck to him, and his eyes tightly closed as he held the dying man close to his barrel-sized chest, and all the time he cried.

'You hurt Andrew. You hurt Helen.'

Then he let go and Marcus slid to the floor, quite dead.

Eck stopped crying, wiped his sleeve across his already dirty face and looked down at his handiwork. It was as if he had only just realized what he had done.

'You dead?' he whispered, kneeling down to feel the body. 'You dead?' He shook the body but nothing happened. 'Don't be dead!' he yelled, panic starting to fill him.

'Don't be dead! Eck didn't mean it! You wouldn't listen! Eck told you not to do it!'

The doorbell sounded.

Eck scrambled to his feet and with no thought of where he was going, fled down the hall towards the back of the house.

The plan was that Camilla would keep Marcus occupied while Patrick would sneak in another way and come up behind him. After the deed was done – and Camilla was only too thankful that she didn't have to do it – she and Patrick would disappear as quickly as they could. Patrick said he had friends in Ireland who would organize a private plane to anywhere. All they needed were their passports and as much of her jewellery as they could find.

Camilla knocked again. This wasn't like Marcus, especially as he'd asked her to come.

Still not getting an answer, she turned the large carved door handle and stepped inside. It took about three seconds for her to register what had happened.

'Oh my God!' She stepped forward, her hands to her mouth in horror. There were footsteps and she looked up, afraid. It was Patrick.

'What the hell's happened? I was standing outside for ages.'

She silently pointed to the corpse.

'Oh shit!'

He went over and felt for a pulse. 'Dead, but he's still warm so it could only just have happened.'

Camilla stood over him, feeling faint and nauseous. She had never seen a dead body before and was at once fascinated and repelled. She didn't know what to feel – it was all so unexpected to find him already dead – but she certainly felt no grief.

Patrick stood up and took her by the arms. 'Come on. We've got to get out of here. Whoever did this must have been more than unusually strong, and I don't want to meet him.' He stepped over the corpse and propelled Camilla away. She went reluctantly, hardly able to tear herself away from the scene.

'Police?' she mumbled.

'Fuck them! We don't want nothing to do with them. Let's just get the hell out of here.'

'But ... but ...'

'Look, Camilla,' Patrick said sternly, holding her in front of him and making her face him. 'Someone, and God knows who it is, has done us a huge favour so let's just thank our lucky stars and go because the boys in blue might not look at it this way and we don't want them poking around where they're not wanted, do we? Now come on,' and he ferried her out of the door.

They ran down the drive. It was pouring with rain and before they reached the stable and garage block, both were soaked. Patrick opened the Range Rover door and shoved her in. She was shivering, her teeth clattering against the cold and shock. She sat silent and terrified in the seat, unable even to smoke, with drops of water falling out of her hair and down her white face. She wrapped her arms around herself and gently rocked to and fro.

'Be back in a minute!' yelled Patrick over the sound of the rain drumming on the car roof.

'Where're you going?' Her eyes were stricken. She couldn't bear to be alone.

'In there!' He pointed towards the stables. 'I never did get a good enough look because of that bloody horse. The Warrener Hoard has got to be here somewhere?'

'Don't leave me alone!' she cried. 'I'm coming too then!' and she scrambled out of the car and followed him into the dim musty-smelling stable.

'You look in there,' he ordered, indicating the second loose box. 'Anything that might look suspicious, investigate it. Damn stuff has got to be somewhere.'

She did as he asked. More than anything she wanted

out of here, away from all the death, the violence and fear, away where she would be safe and warm and wanted. But it couldn't happen yet.

She was worn out, emotionally drained and almost beyond caring about anything. Let the police come. Let them arrest her. So what? She sat back against the floury wall with its crumbling plaster and cobwebs and closed her eyes. She was so damn tired.

'Camilla! Camilla!'

'What?' She struggled to open her eyes. She just wanted to sleep.

Patrick came rushing over to her, his face excited and animated like a little boy's. 'Look what I've found!' He knelt down in the straw and held out his hand. A magnificent twisted gold torque, the colour of ripe barley, stared back at her.

'And feel the weight!' he exclaimed. 'It's bloody enormous!'

She touched it, its burnished beauty cold yet the colour so warm.

'Can you believe it!' he laughed. 'And there's loads more next door! Come and have a look. I pulled out a loose brick and it all came out. Can you believe it?' and he danced around the small room, his feet kicking up the straw. 'We're rich! We're rich! We're rich!' and he reached down and pulled her to her feet before giving her a huge kiss. 'Come on, sunshine, let's go and see what else there is!'

Eck was hungry but he knew he couldn't go home because Mrs Tucker would shout at him because he'd run away, and he didn't want to be shouted at. He had a headache and he still wanted to be alone. He was wet through as well, and she wouldn't like that either. She was very particular about him leaving his wet clothes outside before he came in and he was never allowed to walk in the house with wet boots on. No, Eck couldn't go home. He would go and talk to Sebi at the stables, but he wouldn't go yet. People might see him and ask questions and he didn't want that. They would send him back to the hospital when they heard what he'd done.

He spent the afternoon roaming the woods and staying out of everyone's way – not that he saw anyone but he did see some deer and that cheered him up. But then he felt sad again because he knew he had done wrong and he didn't know how he was going to explain it all. Andrew would be cross and so would Helen because he'd promised her he wouldn't say anything and he'd broken his promise. He had been naughty, and now he'd be sent back to the hospital for hurting that man.

At the end of the afternoon, Eck went to the stables. Sebi stood in his box, large, black and quiet. His ears pricked forwards when he saw and smelt Eck. He whinnied softly.

'Good, Sebi. Eck's come to see you,' and he opened the stable door and let himself in. He and the horse stood together in the gloom, the man's arm around the horse's neck, body leaning against body as Eck stroked the horse's velvet muzzle.

'Done wrong, Sebi. Shouldn't have hurt that man but he were nasty. He hit Helen. Eck saw him, but shouldn't have hurt him, should he?'

The horse snorted gently.

'Bad Eck, that's what he is. Very bad.'

The horse shifted his vast feet and then dozed, his ears relaxed and a back hoof off the ground.

'Got to go away, Sebi, where they can't find Eck 'cos Eck doesn't want to go back to hospital. Wasn't nice there. Andrew was nice but the hospital wasn't. He looked after Eck and promised Eck he'd never go back but . . . naughty now. Things are different. It will be back to hospital.' A tear rolled down his face. He gave the horse one last pat. 'Bye bye, Sebi. Eck loves you. Bye bye.'

The reservoir was low. The summer had been such a hot

one, and with so little rain, that only weeks of sustained downpour would fill it again.

Eck stood on the wall of the dam, looking down into the dark green depths. It was a novelty for him to be there because Andrew wouldn't allow it. He had to stay away from it because he couldn't swim, but that didn't stop him wanting to be there. He loved water – the way it sparkled in the sunshine, the way it reflected his face and the way it ran through his fingers when he tried to pick it up. There was something about it; something fascinating yet annoying. It intrigued him but he didn't understand it.

The reservoir didn't look very friendly tonight. All around Eck in the cold and the dark, the water gently lapped against the walls of the dam, hissing and spitting where it got stuck under some rocks. And it was so black like the darkest of dark nights when there was no moon and all the stars were hidden by the clouds.

Eck didn't know how long he had been there but it must have been a long time because even he was getting cold. He looked up into the lashing rain, the black thunderous sky high and wide above him, and let the rain pour down his face, running off the end of his nose and chin, and soaking into his overall. He put out his tongue and let it run into his mouth. He licked his lips and tasted it.

He looked about him. He couldn't see much in the dark. Over to one side was the wood where he had hidden, and on the other side was the open moor where he had gone riding. He would miss this place. It was the only real home he had ever had. If he looked really hard, he could just about see the nearest tor standing out like a black hump-back whale. Better to leave now than to go to the hospital. He smiled to himself and then he jumped.

Twenty-five

It had been raining for the last two days, not heavily, just a gentle mist of warm end-of-season rain that trickled over everything, leaving a sheen of wet. In a couple of weeks, when autumn took hold, then the serious stuff would arrive: heavy downpours whipped along by strong south-westerlies, battering in from the Atlantic and stripping the leaves off the trees. But this gentle August rain that fell on Leighford did no more than cloak the small village in a veil of quiet despondency.

Sian sat at the kitchen table in Helen's cottage. Opposite her sat Billy and behind him, leaning against the pine dresser, stood Helen. They didn't say anything. Their words had been all talked out hours ago.

Helen had returned to the cottage, utterly distraught after her trip, only to discover the police swarming all over the place because a body had been found up at The Grange. Andrew had found it when he returned home from the hospital with Sian accompanying him. The police arriving en masse, sirens blaring, alerted the whole village and set tongues wagging over garden fences. Sian stayed at The Grange long enough to give a statement to the police, but after that, at Andrew's insistence, she left and came back to the cottage. There she met Helen.

'You're back then?' said Sian.

As usual nowadays, Helen's eyes were bloodshot and her face pinched. 'Can't think why,' she mumbled.

'Where did you go?'

There was a deep sigh and then she spoke. The whole sorry affair came spilling out. It was as if, after all these weeks, the dam had been breached and once she started, it gathered so much momentum she couldn't stop it.

'So you see,' she said pathetically, 'that's how it was. I loved him – or rather I thought I loved him – and he used me to get at the horses.'

'I can't believe you,' said Sian. 'It's ... it's incredible. How could you be so stupid? I told you what he was like right at the beginning. Weren't you listening to me?' And Helen cried some more, burying her face in her hanky.

'He made me ... do it, I mean, poison Sebi. I wanted to stop. You've got to believe me, I wanted to stop, but then he would get angry and say he would leave me and then what was I going to do?' she wept. 'I'm not like you. I have nobody. I never had. He was all I wanted and I loved him so much, so very much. You've got to believe me!' She wiped her nose and still she cried. 'Eck saw us, you know, one night at the stables when Marcus and I were fighting.' She lowered her eyes, ashamed of herself. 'He saw us. I made him promise not to say anything. That's why –'

'That's why,' interrupted Sian, 'he was so awkward with you. You didn't tell him off for something he had done with the horses, it was so Eck wouldn't tell Andrew and get you fired.' She shook her head with disbelief. 'Good God, Helen! Do you realize what you've done? Do you have any idea of the trouble you may have caused?' She glared at Helen but the other woman looked away. 'Now Eck's gone missing, Helen, and not only that –' she stopped and looked away.

Helen stared at her. 'What?'

Sian bit her lip. 'You better prepare yourself for a shock. I should have told you when I came in, but I was so relieved to see you and then I had no idea about you and ...' She stopped and took a deep breath for courage. 'He's dead, Helen. It was he Andrew found at The Grange. I'm so sorry.'

For a moment Helen's face froze, each line, each feature refusing to register what she had heard. 'They said at his home,' she whispered, 'that he didn't want to speak to me again.' She swallowed, her eyes staring ahead unseeing. 'They said . . . but I . . .'

Sian nodded. She reached out and took Helen's hands. They were icy cold.

'No one knows what's happened yet, but . . . it looks as though he was murdered and . . . well, we can't find Eck.'

'Oh God! Oh my God!' and then the screaming started.

Later, when all was quiet, Billy turned up and for once Sian was really glad to see him.

'Come in, come in, Billy, and go into the kitchen.'

He shuffled past, his face concerned. 'Helen . . . ?' and he looked upstairs.

'She's very, very upset. The business up at The Grange –'

'I heard. Thought I'd come and see how she was, like.'

'That's very kind of you. Would you like a cup of tea?'

They sat in the kitchen, each lost in their own thoughts while the clock ticked on and the rain still fell.

After a while, Helen came down. She had stopped crying now although she looked a funereal white. She gave a tepid smile to them both and sat down.

'Billy.'

'Helen.' He reached out and touched her arm. Her face contorted into a grimace as she squeezed his hand.

Sian made her a coffee and Billy lit a cigarette for her. For a while nothing was said.

'Don't suppose Andrew's going to be too pleased to see me,' Helen said quietly.

'No, I don't suppose he will,' answered Sian wearily. Of all the emotions she felt, disappointment was the one that took precedence. That and so much hurt. She just couldn't believe that Helen, her best friend since schooldays, someone she had laughed and cried with, someone who had shared so much of her life, could be so stupid as to jeopardize everything, and all for the so-called love of a man.

But at the same time, Sian's heart went out to her. No one should feel that much pain.

Their conversation was stilted.

'How you feeling now?' asked Sian.

'Knackered, if you must know. Guilt, I suppose.'

More silence.

'I don't understand you, Helen. I thought that you really loved the horses. It just seemed so . . . so . . . idiotic. If Sebi had died, Andrew would have lost everything. That horse is the only valuable one in the stable.'

Helen held her face in her hands. 'I know. I know.'

'And as for Eck – how could you? You know what a simple trusting soul he was. God knows where he is now. We haven't seen him for two days.'

'They're trawling the reservoir,' commented Billy, matter-of-factly. 'Just heard it down at the pub.'

Both women spun round. 'What!'

'Why the hell didn't you say before, Billy?' said Helen.

'I'm going to telephone the vet. He'll know the latest,' said Sian, hurrying out of the room.

'Oh Billy!' wailed Helen. 'What have I done?'

Five minutes later Sian returned and there were tears in her eyes.

'They've found a body,' she said quietly, 'and they think it's Eck.'

The vicar's mellow voice intoned the graveside service but Sian wasn't really listening. From all the suppressed crying that was going on, hankies pressed up against sobbing faces, it appeared that neither was anyone else.

Mrs Tucker, Eck's landlady, stood like a black barrel in the squally rain, her large round shoulders shuddering with sobs. Even her diminutive husband, half her size and as thin as a rake, had a tear rolling down his lugubrious face.

The vet and his wife stood next to them, arm in arm, their heads bowed, and next to them stood some of the

401

regulars from the King's Arms who used to let Eck play in the skittles team on the infrequent occasions he was allowed out with Mr Tucker. There was no Helen. She and Billy had gone away and Sian knew it was the right thing to do. Life had become extremely difficult at the cottage since Eck's death. It had strained relations between the two women beyond breaking point, so that Sian had packed up her things and gone back to her parents. It meant not seeing Andrew but that, it seemed, was the way he wanted it.

She stood next to him now. He was tall and rigid, his face still bruised, his blond hair lifting a little in the breeze. His blue eyes were devoid of emotion. Not once had she heard him say anything. It was as if he simply wanted to fade away without contact from anyone. She had only seen him on a couple of occasions since Eck had been found, and both times he was too preoccupied to talk. There was a great sadness about him. The light had gone from him and Sian's heart went out to him. She knew how much he thought of Eck and that to stand here, in this melancholy place on this grey windswept day with the crows calling from the damp swaying trees, was heart-breaking for him.

There had been many times over the last couple of weeks when Sian had cried herself to sleep. It had been so unfair, she thought, that the one totally honest, utterly trusting, guileless person in this whole drama should end up taking his own life.

The service came to an end and the small sad party trooped away across the damp grass. At the wooden gateway, the vicar said his words of comfort to all who were there.

'I'm so sorry, Andrew. I really am. This must have been a terrible time for you. I'm at The Vicarage anytime you want, you know.'

Sian noticed Andrew didn't reply. His lips were pressed tightly together and his eyes were guarded.

They walked out to the car park. It was there that she saw Helen standing over by a wall underneath some overhanging branches, hoping, she supposed, that no one would notice her. Billy was with her. They acknowledged each other.

'Sian.' It was Andrew.

'Yes?'

'I . . . well, I need to talk to you.'

He looked into her eyes and the pain she saw made her heart miss a beat. She reached out for his hand.

'Of course, but I just need to have a word with Helen.'

He looked past her shoulder and his face hardened. 'I'll be in the Land Rover waiting.' He walked away. It would be a very, very long time before he forgave Helen.

The two women stood face to face, not knowing what to say.

'I had to come,' explained Helen. 'I know no one wanted me here. I guess my name must be mud in this village.'

'Not quite.'

Helen looked towards the Land Rover. 'He thinks so.'

'What do you expect? He loved him, you know.'

Helen's face fractured. 'Yes, I know. We all did.'

Sian did the only thing she could do, she put her arms around her friend and held her close.

'It's all right, Helen. Shh, shh. He'll get over it. I'll make sure he does. It's just that he's so upset at the moment.' Helen kept on crying. Billy came up behind her and laid his hand on Helen's shoulder.

'Come on, maid. I'll take you home and put the kettle on. Don't you upset yourself.'

'Take care of her, Billy, won't you?'

He smiled and led Helen away and Sian knew that whatever Helen had said about him in the past, there was someone who really loved her now. She turned away and headed back towards the Land Rover.

'Where are we going?' she said when she had settled herself in.

He started up the motor. 'The Grange. I want to say goodbye,' and they drove off.

'Do you know the poetry of W. B. Yeats?' he asked suddenly. They had parked the Land Rover in front of The Grange. The huge grey building looked even less welcoming in the afternoon gloom.

'Some.'

'How does that one go . . . "But I, being poor, have only my dreams" . . .'

'"I have spread my dreams under your feet" . . .'

'"Tread softly because you tread on my dreams."'

He smiled briefly at her, his face shadowed, withdrawn. 'I used to read a lot of Yeats once. I found it really comforting. Says it all really,' he added.

'Why?'

'You don't want to hear,' he replied, with a faint shake of the head. 'Pretty dreadful really.'

'Try me.'

He fell silent and to start with, she wasn't sure he was going to say anything, so she watched him. He still made her heart soar. He had the power to fill her up with a soft warmth that permeated throughout her very soul. They had only kissed once and yet . . . she knew exactly what Helen meant when she had said she would have followed Killington to the ends of the world if he had asked her to. She would for Andrew. So near yet so alone, so needful, so loved and yet keeping her at arm's length, keeping every one at arm's length.

'Once upon a time,' he began without a hint of irony in his voice, 'there was a very successful, highly ambitious saloon car racing driver. He thought he was the bee's knees. He thought he was wonderful. Everyone told him so, so he must be – or at least that's what he thought. He was fast. He was winning lots of races. He was going places, and then, even though he had more women chasing after him than most men ever dream of, because of course, he was devastatingly handsome or at least all the women told

404

him so, he fell in love.' He smiled at some distant memory. 'She was beautiful, you know,' he said softly. 'So beautiful and what's more, after a suitable length of time had elapsed, she agreed to marry him. He was hooked, well and truly hooked, but he didn't mind. However,' and his voice took on a harsh edge as he frowned, 'it wasn't enough for him because even though they had a wonderful daughter and all the money and possessions they could ask for, he still wasn't happy and when he got frustrated, he took it out on his family because he was one ungrateful, selfish wretch.' He sighed and breathed deeply, the pain etched deeply on his face. 'Then one day, it all came abruptly to an end. Very abruptly.'

She watched him closely as he stared unseeingly at the distant hills, his thoughts in the past.

'They had a row, you see, just a stupid row over the usual trivial things.' He shrugged. 'Strange thing is, I can't remember what it was about now. Her mother, I think. Anyway, the row got worse and worse so that in a fit of pique, he did the dumbest, most stupid thing he ever could do. He went to overtake a camper van on the crest of a hill because he was a racing driver and he thought he was better than anyone else on the road and this fucking van was going so damn slow, so what the hell did it matter if just this once he risked the life of his wife and daughter?'

There were tears in his eyes now and she could see that he was fighting all the way to keep them in check. But they began to roll down his cheeks.

'When . . . when they cut me out of the wreckage, Emma, my wife, was already dead. She had died holding on to my hand. My daughter, Vicky, died on her way to the hospital. I killed them, Sian. It was me.' He turned to look at her. Get away, his eyes said. Leave me. I'm not worth knowing.

'I lost everything after that because, you see, I didn't just kill my wife and daughter, I also managed to severely injure three other people. My licence, my career, all my so-called friends. I was sent for trial and found guilty of manslaughter due to dangerous driving.' He gave a snort of ironic laughter. 'Me? A dangerous driver? God, can you believe it?' He thumped the steering wheel. 'It was strange, you know, the first time I went back to the house. I stood outside and I just couldn't put the key in the lock. Something was holding me back. It was as if . . . as if I knew that once I got inside, I would have to face the utmost certainty of it all.' He glanced down at his hand and slowly clenched it tight. 'I went in and she was there,' he whispered. 'Not her body, of course, but her spirit I suppose you'd call it, and Vicky's. The bed was still unmade. Emma was going to change the sheets when we got back from the beach because Vicky had peed on it that morning.' He fell silent. 'I could smell her still. I left that sheet until the trial. I just couldn't bear to wash it because once I did, I knew it would be like losing a last faint touch of them both.' He sighed.

'You're going to think this stupid, but I once went out for a walk, just rambling along, and I came to a call box. I actually rang home, would you believe? I don't know. I guess that subconsciously, I just hadn't accepted their deaths and maybe thought that if I rang home, then Emma would still be there and would pick up the phone.' A tear rolled over his lips.

'I'm so sorry, Andrew.'

He wiped his face dry. 'You weren't to know so don't be.'

'When did all this happen?'

'Five years ago this month.' He gave her a tired smile. 'My daughter would have been six in a couple of months' time. I wonder what she would have looked like? Beautiful, I expect, just like her mother. I'm sorry. I shouldn't have cried like that. Anniversaries, you know. They never leave you alone. They always come back to haunt you so you can never forget.' He looked at her. 'Children are the most precious things we can have. As difficult as they are sometimes – and don't get me wrong, as a parent I know all about sleepless nights and nappies and such – they bring something else into your life, something so necessary, so complete. Without them you're not a proper human. They finish you off if you like; fill in the missing pieces. Stop you being such a selfish bastard.'

'And then Eck goes and dies. Oh God, Andrew, how awful for you.'

'For us all, Sian,' and he put his arm around her and held her close.

'I used to drink after I came out of prison. Really drink, not like I do now. I just wanted to anaesthetize myself, I suppose, to forget the pain, to sink into oblivion. Can't really remember how much or what kind of a fool I made of myself. Thank God really. I must have gone about as low as is possible. And then, out of the blue, came this place. Originally my mother inherited it but she wouldn't come back here. When I asked her why she refused to answer. Too many bad memories, I imagine, although I don't know what they were.' He paused. 'It's amazing how much luggage we carry around with us, isn't it?' He looked up at The Grange. 'And this place seemed to be at the centre of so much of it.' He turned to her. 'Killington, apparently, was going to use this as a base for his drugs operations.'

'What?'

'One of the policemen told me. It seems he was up to his eyeballs in it, one of the biggest dealers in the country.'

'Good grief!'

'Yes, the man was a real crook so forgive me if I don't spill any tears over him.'

'What about Helen? She really loved him, you know.'

'Odd that, wasn't it?'

'Will you forgive her?'

'I expect so, one day, but not yet.' He started up the engine.

'No, please,' Sian said, laying a hand on his arm, 'I want

to pick some roses for Eck. Would you mind if we then went up to the reservoir?'

They pulled in at the car park and Andrew switched off the engine. There was total silence. Everything about them was still and they were quite alone. Not a breath of wind disturbed the huge expanse of water perfectly reflecting the trees and hills, and the clouds that had now parted and were letting through soft yellow rays of late afternoon sun. The air was filled with a golden hue, of insects dancing and skipping above the water, of swifts diving for a drink.

'Let's walk,' Sian said.

They got out, followed by Blaize, and finding the path through the rough undergrowth, walked towards the dam where Eck took his final leap.

They stood still and gazed over the water, sparkling in the sun.

'I shall miss him,' she said.

'Me too. He just turned up one day, out of the blue, smiling his silly amiable smile and I took him in because this government of ours doesn't give a damn about people like him – the fragile, the delicate – and I thought if I took care of him then maybe . . . Well, he was my retribution, a paying back for my sins. I thought that if I looked after him then perhaps I would find a peace in my life; a reason for it all, and maybe then, I could forgive myself.'

He took the roses off her and threw them into the water.

'Goodbye, Eck, and take care, wherever you are.'

They watched them float away, the dark, dark red against the unfathomable green of the water.

'Have you found your peace?' Sian asked after a few minutes.

'I think so. At least I was beginning to think so until you came along.'

'Meaning?'

'Meaning, one look of your eyes, one smile, one touch, and all the old uncertainties came back.' He took hold of her hand and kissed it. 'Can I love you? Would it be fair to you when everything I touch goes wrong?' He turned away and shoved his hands deep into his pockets. The clouds were building up again and the rain would soon be here. 'It wouldn't be fair, Sian; not to you, me or anyone. I'm stony broke, I lost everything, and you deserve better.'

'Is that why you've stayed away from me for the last two weeks?'

He nodded. The rain began to fall. She reached out and touched his face and ran her fingers down his wet skin. She wanted to say so much, to hold him, to love him and to never let him go.

'Why don't you ask me first?' and then she kissed him.

'I thought it was a new start, my new business. I'd always liked horses. Didn't realize how much it was going to cost, of course. That's where Armitage Financial Management came in.'

'The loan shark down in Plymouth? So that's why you were in the pub.'

'Yes.' Andrew looked into the fire.

They were both soaking when they arrived at the cottage at the stables, and had made up the fire and put on the kettle before anything else. He sat in one of the chairs and she sat on the floor, leaning against his legs. Every now and again, he would run his hand over her damp red hair as if reminding himself that she was really there.

'Stupid, really. I should have known better, but I wanted desperately to hang on to the business. I couldn't fail at that as well. I'd grown up with horses,' he continued. 'My mother was an excellent horsewoman.' He paused and the pain came back to his face. 'You know I've had to sell everything? The Grange has gone to a property developer. Ironic, isn't it? I'm practically a bankrupt now. There's hardly anything left at all. I inherited this place from a grandfather I didn't know I even had because, like I said, my mother must have had some awful experiences or something because she never said anything about him.'

'I know quite a bit about him.'

'You do? How?'

'I have a journal of your grandmother's at home. Remember? I bought it in a junk shop in Newton Abbot. It's very interesting. You'll have to read it sometime.'

'I will.' And then he added, 'Must be in the genes, you know, all this bad luck following us down through the generations. God, look how it's all turned out. Emma, Vicky, Killington, Camilla, Eck. The whole year's been a complete and utter nightmare.'

'No it hasn't. We met, for a start.'

He grinned. 'Yes, but that very nearly wasn't a success, was it?'

She returned his smile. 'So, what are you going to do now?'

'Run this place and live here. With The Grange gone and most of my debts paid, I might, if I'm lucky, keep my head above water.' He sipped his tea. The light was fading fast and, with the crackling of the log fire and its shimmering orange flames, they were enclosed in a cosy, peaceful world. She looked at him and he smiled.

'What about you?' he asked. 'Where will you go?'

'That depends.'

'On what?'

'On you, actually. I could stay if you want – help you out with the horses. Somebody's got to. You won't be able to manage by yourself.'

'Is that what you want? Would you do that even though we've been through so much and I've made such a mess of it all?'

'Yes,' she answered calmly, 'because everything's cyclical and it can only get better. You said that yourself that day I twisted my ankle.'

'Yes, I remember.' He looked at her. 'I also remember kissing you and you saying that you didn't want that.' He paused. 'Do you still feel that way?'

'No,' and she smiled. 'Not any more. I made up my mind up at the reservoir.'

'So, you're willing to stay come what may?'

'Come what may, through thick or thin and hell and high water.'

He smiled at her. 'Come here.' He stood up and held out his hand. She did as he requested. Standing before her, he cupped her face in his hands and smiled gently. 'How could we almost blow it?'

'We didn't . . . we just weren't sure, that's all.'

Their lips met, a spark of recognition flowing through them, shared and wanted.

'Don't go,' he whispered. 'Don't ever go,' and this time when they kissed, the passion roared up and enveloped them both.

Upstairs she sat on the bed, naked and waiting for him. She was warm from her bath yet the emotions that swirled around inside her were making her jumpy and nervous. It had been so long. She felt like a sixteen-year-old going to be touched for the first time.

She heard a noise, a tread of feet across the landing and then the door opened. In he came, a towel wrapped around his middle. She pulled the bedclothes closer around herself. He sat down next to her and smiled. His wet hair clung to the muscles of his tanned and taut neck and she followed the swathe of blond hairs that ran across his chest, gathered at his sternum and then, in a line, ran down his tightly muscled stomach and disappeared into the towel. He reached forward and kissed her as he might a small child.

'I love you.'

She smiled and kissed his hand.

'I'm frightened,' she said. 'It's been months. I . . . oh God, this is silly!' and she giggled.

'Don't be scared,' and he tenderly stroked some of her hair away from her face. 'I would never hurt you,' and again he kissed her and this time she could feel the wanting in him.

She lay down and he got into bed. She turned to switch off the bedside light but he stopped her.

'Don't,' he smiled. 'I want to see what you look like,' and a wave of pink modesty flowed over her. 'You're so beautiful. Why hide it?'

Then all the months, the weeks, the days, the upsets, the arguments – all faded to nothing as gradually, bit by bit, they came to know each other as only lovers can.

At first it was just their lips; his strong, demanding and yet gentle, hers softer, fuller but just as greedy. They ate their fill, tasting, licking, tongues searching, wanting more and more.

His arms enfolded her, so tight she thought he might crush her but she wanted it. She wanted him to want her so much that he would never have his fill of her.

Then he started to caress her – her smooth white neck, her full heaving breasts with their erect pink nipples that shuddered to his every touch, her rounded belly and her long thighs. Everywhere his hands brushed her skin, she came alight beneath him, rising to him, wanting him more and more. Frissons of delight like needle-sharp arrows of exquisite agony swept through her, building and building as he touched and touched again. He kissed her all over, running his tongue across her velvet skin, smelling the woman in her and wanting her.

Her heart pounded wildly. She was fighting for her breath as the heat in her grew stronger. He was bringing out the woman in her, the one that her husband had stifled. Now after a long, long time, she was waking up again.

She held him close to her, her skin pressed against his, her body flush with his, her instincts flowing with his. He took one of her breasts and ran his mouth over the nipple, his breath hot against her skin.

'I want you . . . I want you,' he mumbled and she closed

her eyes. Could the sweet agony of it all get any better, she wondered. His hand slid over her belly, caressing and sweeping over her skin. He was getting closer and closer, now around her thighs. She rose up to him, moaning. How much longer?

Then he parted her legs, his warm hand easing her open for him. He smiled at her but she hardly saw him.

Fingertips, heat and wet, wet flesh all succumbing to him.

'Ah . . . oh God!' she moaned.

'I will be gentle,' he said, and he was.

He stroked her with the lightest of light touches as she writhed beneath him, feeling him against the woman in her. There were times when she wanted to cry aloud; times when she thought she would never see an end to it; times when she wanted it to go on and on. Her body was covered in sweat, her pulse was racing. She was panting, aching for him to take her and yet wanting more and more of it.

He lay on top of her and she wrapped her legs around him. This was it. There would be only this from now on – the meeting of two bodies, loved and in love.

He took her and she gasped, forgetting how much a man could feel like. He didn't rush her. He wanted to take his time, to feel every inch of her, to experience every molecule of her.

Together they moved, slowly at first but then the tempo increased. Her body was screaming at her. More and more she wanted him, the ecstasy increasing, building and building and threatening to drown her.

He was kissing her face, not gently now but with hard, rigid, passionate kisses, smothering her – her eyes, her nose, her lips, her neck – as he pushed and pushed against her.

Their time was nearly up.

She yelled. He groaned, his hands digging into her shoulders and her fingers skewered against his back. On and on this terrible pleasure went, echoes and more echoes, reverberating around inside her, reaching out through all her limbs to the very extremities of her as he filled and filled her and still she couldn't stop.

'Oh . . . ah . . . Andrew . . . Andrew!'

'Sian . . . I love you. I love you!'

Slowly, slowly, they came to a stop, limbs, hearts, lungs, all exhausted. They lay together in the dark, flesh on flesh, sweat on sweat, and couldn't move. They were spent.

He passed her a cup of tea. 'Here you are.'

'Thank you,' and she smiled. He got back into bed.

'You know something, Mrs Williamson?'

'Less of the Mrs Williamson, if you don't mind.'

'Okay then,' he smiled. 'How about Mrs Mann? Fancy that?'

She looked at him, not sure what he meant. 'Are you saying what I think you're saying?'

'Of course. You don't think I'd be daft enough to let you go after this, do you?' He paused and looked at her. 'Well, what d'you say?'

She laughed. 'Are you proposing to me?'

'Why not? You're damn good with the horses, you work very hard, you're beautiful to look at and after this afternoon . . .' and he rolled his eyes heavenwards. 'But a gentleman doesn't talk about things like that.'

'Like what?' she teased, putting down her cup and then taking his off him as well. She walked her fingers up his chest and ran them around one of his nipples. 'What doesn't a gentleman talk about, Andrew?' and her voice was husky.

He took her in his arms. 'You know, you never did apologize for calling me a bully so I think I am entitled to some sort of recompense.'

'Such as?'

'How about if I kissed you there . . . and there . . . and maybe there?'

She looked at him, her eyes smiling. 'I think,' she said.
'Yes?'
'I think I'll think about it,' and they both laughed.

Twenty-six

Samuel and William leaned against the wooden five-bar gate with Bess sitting at their feet. From where they were standing, they had a good view of the moor stretching away in front of them, the high tors hidden in a grey mist.

Samuel sucked noisily on his unlit pipe. He wasn't in a good mood. He pulled the collar of his frayed jacket closer around his thin neck. He felt the cold a lot more these days.

William was also unhappy because when Samuel got in a bad mood, he took it out on him. Not only that, but William would end up doing all the chores because Samuel's old war wound would suddenly play up. It seemed to him that Samuel's bad temper spread out in all directions like a nasty stain, and he got most of it.

'Going to rain,' William said, weary of the oppressive angry silence that emanated from his scowling brother.

Samuel's bushy grey eyebrows moved slightly. It was the only answer he could muster.

'Perhaps we should be getting back?' he suggested, hopefully.

'You go if you want to, William.'

But William didn't move. He wouldn't go without his brother.

Samuel sighed; a deep mournful one.

'There's no point thinking about it, Samuel,' said William. ''E's gone and no doubt taken the lot with 'im. I knew we shouldn't have trusted 'im.'

Samuel turned slowly to face his brother, his eyebrows one thick overhanging line across his wrinkled forehead as he frowned. 'Then why the 'ell didn't you say so at the time?'

William shrugged. 'Well . . . didn't like to . . . really.'

'"Didn't like to really,"' mocked Samuel in a high-pitched voice. 'Do you know what you are?'

William looked at him with wide guileless eyes. 'What?'

'A prat. And what's more, you've always been a prat. It were exactly the same when we were lads. You'd go along with something 'cos you 'adn't got more than three dried peas inside that dumb 'ead of yours and then, when it all went wrong, you'd say, "I knew we shouldn't 'ave done it."' Samuel removed his pipe from his downcast mouth, reached into his pocket for his tobacco tin and refilled it. When he was quite happy that the tobacco was pushed down the way he liked it, he lit it, sending out angry plumes of blue aromatic smoke into the soft autumn air.

'Wasn't my fault,' said William defensively. 'You believed 'im too!'

'I might 'ave done, true, but not all of it the way you did. God, you're as soppy as that stupid dog of yours,' he said, pointing to Bess. 'She'll go to anyone if they offer her something to eat and so will you. Daft bloody bugger! You're no damn good for anything.'

'Not true, Samuel. We both fell for it. 'E said 'e would 'elp us and 'e didn't. Wasn't no fault of anyone, excepting 'im, of course.'

'Maybe 'e found it and did a bunk,' mused Samuel, staring at the grass on the other side of the gate. 'Maybe that were it. 'Cos now they found that dead body o' Killington, I don't suppose we'll ever find out what really 'appened up there.' He cleared his throat and spat noisily. 'Damned townies! You know what they'm like. Don't 'ave no sense of loyalty like what we do.'

'Exactly. I bet that's what 'e did,' said William. 'I bet that Patrick took the jewels after 'im an' that Killington 'ad a fight. 'Cos they 'aven't found 'im yet, 'ave they? Nor Killington's sister. Funny goings on, I say.'

'Yep. Certainly was.'

William relaxed. Samuel's dark mood was lifting and if that was the case, he might offer to cook tea tonight. William hated cooking. He had never been any good at it, but ever since their beloved sister had died, he'd been lumbered with it, except when Samuel offered. On those rare occasions, William had the chance to enjoy life just a little bit more.

'I suppose they'd be long gone by now,' said William.

'Yes, I suppose so. Taken the loot and run for it. I 'ear that there Interpol is looking for 'em. 'Cos,' he added after a pause, ' 'tis wrong really, 'cos we ought to 'ave 'ad our share of that gold. 'Tis only right. We're not wealthy. We'm pensioners.'

'Yes, and after all the help we gave 'im, an' all.'

They started to move off home.

'By the way, Samuel, what were that letter from the bank manager about?'

' 'E wants to see us to discuss buying some more shares. Seems we made a tidy profit last year.'

'Does that mean I can 'ave a new jacket, 'cos this one's got an 'ole in it?'

Samuel looked horrified, his deep-set eyes like two brown marbles. 'Of course not, William! 'Ow am I supposed to keep our 'eads above water if you're going to waste money on new clothes?'

'But I only thought –'

'Well, think again, my lad. The answer's no. Honestly, William, I don't know where you gets your fancy ideas from sometimes. A new jacket indeed!'

They sauntered back down the moorland track, two old men, hunchbacked and bandy-legged, leaning on their walking sticks.

'I suppose we couldn't 'ave a nice piece o' steak for tea then, Samuel?'

Samuel stopped mid-step and gave his brother a withering look. He didn't have to say anything.

'But why, Samuel!' asked his brother plaintively. 'We can afford it! I don't see why we can't enjoy ourselves sometimes.'

''Cos we're too old for all that sort of thing, that's why! Good grief, William, our father would turn in 'is grave if 'e were to 'ear you say that sort o' thing. Live frugally, 'e said, and the Lord will reward you, and that's what we shall do.'

They walked on in silence.

'Just think,' said William, as they neared the village, 'what we could 'ave done with the money from the Warrener Hoard. We could 'ave 'ad a fine time then.'

'Huh! Not if I 'ad anything to do with it. You and me, William, we're past all that sort of thing. Wine, women and such like ain't for upstanding members of the Church like you and me. No, I would keep it so that we could 'ave a proper funeral and a good monument. I don't want our neighbours to think we're too poor for that.'

William didn't reply. There was a group of teenage girls walking ahead of them, wearing very tight jeans. William stared and fervently wished again that he was young and didn't have to put up with his brother's ranting. He would have a good time, by God he would, whatever Samuel said.

Epilogue

Patrick pushed his sunglasses back up his nose. In this heat, he sweated so much that his glasses were always sliding down. He glanced over to Camilla. She still didn't look relaxed, even though they had been in Brazil for a year now.

'There is no extradition treaty, Camilla,' he'd explained as they'd flown out here. 'No one is going to come and get us. Anyway, there's nothing to get us for. We didn't kill your brother.'

'He wasn't my brother,' she'd replied. She was getting very tanned in the sun and was looking much better than when she'd first come out here when she was so tensed up he was afraid that she might break down altogether. He patted her comfortingly on the thigh, lightly kneading her perfect flesh. She responded by clutching his hand and smiling. She leant back on her sun lounger.

'Say it again, Patrick. Just one more time and I promise that I won't ask you again,' and she smiled coquettishly.

He kissed her hand, brushing the skin over his lips. He still couldn't believe it sometimes – this beautiful, beautiful woman, and she was all his.

'I love you, Camilla, so very much.'

She smiled and he knew that no matter how many times she promised, she would still ask him to say it again before the day was out. She always did.

He lay back in the sun and thought again about their finances. They had opened a night club with the money they made from selling the Warrener Hoard but they still had plenty left over. Such fabulous jewels could always find eager buyers, and so far their luck had held. They had managed very well and he had Camilla, of course. She made all the difference.

Rowena sat at her desk in her office at the Stoneygates Hotel. The new owners, a Swiss couple, had been impressed enough with her experience of management and catering to give her the manager's job. It had not been a foregone conclusion, but somehow, through all the publicity of Killington's death and Eddy's trial, Rowena had emerged relatively unscathed. She had made sure of it. She had testified against Eddy and on all occasions had protested her innocence to the police.

She smiled to herself; all hers, the whole place was all hers.

'Coffee?' asked her new secretary, an attractive young man with a bright toothpaste-commercial smile.

'Yes, please,' she replied. The telephone rang. She picked it up. 'Hello?'

'Reception here, Rowena. Phil Charles is here to see you.'

'What does he want?'

'A private matter, I gather.'

Rowena considered the prospect. Phil Charles was a renowned womanizer and had long had his eye on her. With him in tow, she could have anything she wanted. His wife was currently driving around in a Ferrari. He had so much money, he couldn't give it away.

'Tell him,' she began, 'tell him I'm busy and will be for the next year or two. Okay?'

The receptionist laughed. Rowena looked at the receiver and put it down. Her past was over and done with. From now on she had a business to run and married men weren't part of it.

'Oh yes, and what's all this then? I thought she was supposed to be having her morning nap?' Sian smiled, crossed

422

her arms over her chest and leant against the lounge doorframe.

Andrew smiled sheepishly and smiled at the gurgling infant. 'She wasn't sleeping so I thought —'

'You thought you'd pick her up and play games instead?'

'Something like that?'

'Honestly, I don't know. What am I to do with you both?'

'Give us a kiss and I'll tell you.'

'Not now. The painter has just finished. Come and see what he's done, and give me Lucy. You've got dog hairs all over you.'

He handed the pink and white baby, her fat cheeks beaming toothlessly, to her mother.

Outside in the yard, the painter was waiting for them.

'There you are, folks. Just what you wanted,' and they all looked up. On the gateway that now met visitors read a sign, 'High Tor Stables' and underneath in small writing it said, 'Proprietors: Andrew and Sian Mann'.

'A bit premature?' asked Sian, Lucy sitting on her hip and grabbing her hair with her chubby fists. 'We're not married yet.'

'Well, there's no point in writing one name when in a couple of months it's going to be another, is there?'

'True.'

He put his arm around her. 'You know, I never thought a man could be this happy, at least not twice in his life,' and he kissed her on the cheek.

'It goes to show, I suppose, that out of all the mess of last year, some good came but I wish . . .'

'What?'

'I wish Eck could see this. He would have been so happy.'

'I know, but if he's somewhere up there, he'll be smiling.'

'Yes, he would.'

'Oh by the way, I got a letter from a woman called Hildegard Mannheim this morning while you were out seeing to the horses. It seems I might have a long lost cousin coming to see me.'

'That's marvellous, Andrew! I wonder if there will be any family resemblance?'

'Oh bound to be. With looks as striking as mine – tall, blond, handsome – need I go on?'

'That's what we like about you, isn't it, Lucy? Such modesty,' and they laughed. It was the sound of people truly happy at last.